Romance in Paradise

JOSS WOOD
SARAH MAYBERRY
AVRIL TREMAYNE

MILLS & BOON

First Published in Great Britain 2017
By Mills & Boon, an imprint of HarperCollins*Publishers*
1 London Bridge Street, London, SE1 9GF

ROMANCE IN PARADISE © 2017 Harlequin Books S. A.

Flirting With The Forbidden, Hot Island Nights and *From Fling To Forever* were first published in Great Britain by Harlequin (UK) Limited.

Flirting With The Forbidden © 2014 Joss Wood
Hot Island Nights © Small Cow Productions Pty Ltd. 2010
From Fling To Forever © 2014 Belinda de Rome

ISBN: 978-0-263-92986-7

05-1117

FLIRTING WITH THE FORBIDDEN

BY
JOSS WOOD

Joss Wood wrote her first book at the age of eight and has never really stopped. Her passion for putting letters on a blank screen is matched only by her love of books and travelling—especially to the wild places of Southern Africa—and possibly by her hatred of ironing and making school lunches.

Fuelled by coffee, when she's not writing or being a hands-on mum Joss, with her background in business and marketing, works for a non-profit organisation to promote the local economic development and collective business interests of the area where she resides. Happily and chaotically surrounded by books, family and friends, she lives in Kwa-Zulu Natal, South Africa, with her husband, children and their many pets.

DEDICATION

Vaughan and I have been married for twenty years this year and he's my biggest fan, my best friend and my favourite travelling companion.
He's also pretty hot…

This book is dedicated to him to say thanks for making me coffee every morning, for being a brilliant dad, for loving me so much and for the fun that is our life.

PROLOGUE

Eight years earlier...

NOAH FRASER LOOKED at the crown moulded ceilings above his head and tried not to think about the action in his pants—hmmm, at least he wasn't wearing a kilt. Truthfully, he could understand what was happening in his pants far more easily than he understood the mess in his head. Lust was easy, and there was a straightforward and time-honoured process for getting shot of it. But since the obvious was out of the question—it required a great deal more privacy than he currently had—he knew he had to distract himself.

He'd spent a lot of the past five years feeling horny—thanks to several tours of duty in dusty countries with little to no female interaction—and he'd learned a couple of techniques to relieve the frustration. Running through the process of dismantling his favourite weapon, the MP5 submachine gun, in the field usually did the trick.

Safety check. Check.

Noah banged his head back against the arm of the couch and cursed softly. What he really wanted was to get naked with that annoyingly sexy bundle of energy beyond the bedroom door. He was head-over-heels in *lust* with her...and a whole bunch of *like*. He could handle the lust...sorta, kinda...but the like had him tied up in knots.

It was a time of firsts for both of them. He was her first

bodyguard and hers was the first body—and what a body it was too!—he'd guarded. His mission was to keep her safe, and apparently hers was to crack the inscrutable façade he'd been told to present. It wasn't easy keeping his demeanour deadpan, because she was funny and smart and had a dry sense of humour that he deeply appreciated. He'd soon realised that she was winding him up by practising her flirting skills on him and it had started a battle of wills between them: she tried to get a reaction out of him and he refused to give her one. He still wasn't sure what the score was, but if they had to judge the competition by his frustration levels then she was streaks ahead.

Release bolt by vigorously slapping the cocking lever out of the indent. Check.

Okay, slight improvement…not much, but some. Noah, curled up on her too-small couch, glared at the closed door and cursed himself for being a fool…and for being unable to concentrate. Concentration, focus, control—control was his thing.

Pull out the locking pin…

His mind drifted again. She had the most amazing smile… and a 'shoot-all-the-blood-to-his-groin' body! Firm, toned, luscious, sweet…young.

Noah pulled the pillow over his head and silently screamed into the fabric. *Nineteen*, for crying out loud! He couldn't believe he was losing his mind over a teenager. He was a flippin' moron. Morgan Moreau was too young and she was his principal. His principal! Six months out of the unit, he was new to bodyguarding and the CFT Corporation, but he was pretty sure that sleeping with his principal was high up on the list of bodyguarding no-no's.

Since he had no intention of getting his ass fired over a piece of ass, no matter how sexy and tempting it was, he pulled the pillow away from his face, heaved in a deep breath and opened his eyes.

'Crap!' he yelled, scuttling up into the corner of the couch.

'Some bodyguard you are. I could've stabbed you in the heart,' Morgan drawled.

'You're naked,' Noah croaked, dimly aware that the saliva in his mouth had dried up. It had probably joined his blood as it sprinted south.

Naked, naked, naked, his body panted. *Yeah, baby!*

Noah was unable to stop his eyes from scanning her body. Perky breasts, a flat stomach, a Brazilian... Oh, he was a dead man...a Brazilian.

What was he thinking?

'You have amazing powers of observation,' Morgan said, her sexy mouth curving upwards. Her voice was perfect for the bedroom: gravelly, low, sexy.

'Why...? What...? How...?'

Morgan perched on the edge of the couch and placed her elbow on her knee, immensely at ease in her nakedness—which ratcheted up his level of panic. 'I thought you were brighter than that, Noah. I'm here, you're here—let's have some fun.'

Noah, his last two brain cells working overtime, narrowed his eyes at her. 'Subtle.'

'Straightforward,' Morgan countered. 'So, what do you say?'

They could... Who would know? They could have a couple of nights of uncomplicated sex, and when they'd hunted down the group of fanatics threatening her famous and wealthy family he'd return to the field and they could both move on with their lives. He'd move on to another job and she'd pull the same thing on another guy...

Noah frowned at the thought. While he believed in equality, the thought of Morgan getting naked with someone else left a sour taste in his mouth. It was on the tip of his tongue to warn her not to do this with anyone else, but he bit the words back.

Which was weird. He didn't like being controlled, hated people telling him what to do, so why did he want to do that to her? This was all too confusing; he'd had his fair share of sexual encounters but this was out of his ken. Way, *way* out. Outer Hebrides out.

He dropped his eyes to her chest and realised that she had the most amazing nipples—pink and succulent. All he had to do was reach for her arm and tumble her onto his lap. One little tug...

Nineteen. His job. Nineteen.

She was entrancing. Look at those eyes...the colour of bold green glass...

Nineteen. Job. Principal! He'd get his ass fired. Noah craned his neck and, yes, *her* ass was more gorgeous than he'd imagined.

Noah, as hard as stone, rolled to his feet and yanked his shirt up and over his head, thinking he'd get her to cover up, but instead he just stared at what she offered. Who would know? Truly, who would ever know?

His brain was back-pedalling, but he was facing a gorgeous naked girl who was offering herself on a plate, and the fact that he actually liked her as well was a nice bonus. When had he last genuinely *liked* a girl?

Walk away, Fraser, just walk away...

Then he remembered that he'd never had a halo that needed polishing.

Morgan felt his hand encircle her wrist, and as he launched her up into his hard body she closed her eyes in sheer, pure relief. For one moment she'd thought that this strong, quiet, sexy Scotsman was about to say no, that he was genuinely thinking about walking away. But suddenly he was hard under her hands, and his mouth on hers was an absolute revelation.

He kissed her as if he owned her, as if she was—just for this moment in time—his and only his. His mouth was hot, silky, sexy. Morgan felt his fingers digging into the skin on her hips and she wished that he would do something with them… Instead he just kissed her: long, liquid slides that tasted like heaven-coated sin.

Then Noah placed his hands under her butt and lifted her up and—oh, oh, *oh!*—onto his jeans-clad erection. The muscles in his arms bunched and she slid her hand up and down that tanned skin, briefly tracing the Celtic cross tattoo on his shoulder. Dropping her head, she kissed that smooth skin while he carried her back to her bedroom with an ease that astounded her.

A strong, sexy Scotsman… She couldn't believe that this was happening. Finally!

Noah lowered her down to the cool white sheets of her bed and loomed over her, his mouth going to her breast and pulling it into his mouth. Then he slid a hand between her legs and she arched off the bed as hot, sexual power pulsed through her. He slid a finger inside her and lifted his head to look into her face.

'So hot, so wet,' he muttered. 'You are a soldier's dream, lass.'

Morgan lifted her head and then smacked it against the bed as he built up a fire inside her that threatened to consume her.

'Can't believe I waited so long,' she growled to herself. 'Man, you're good at this.'

His finger stopped, his mouth pulled away from her breast and cool air drifted over her wet flesh. It was hot and muggy outside, but she knew that she'd crashed into an emotional iceberg.

'Sorry. I didn't mean to say that,' she muttered as he withdrew from her and rolled himself away.

'Were you hoping I wouldn't notice?'

'Kind of,' Morgan admitted.

He was trying to control himself; she could see that. He opened his mouth to say something and snapped his words back, his eyes sparking dangerously.

'So, how does this work? Did you decide that your virginity was something you no longer needed and I was handy?'

No! Yes! Kind of… How did she explain that she felt comfortable with him? Safe? From the moment she'd met him she'd known that he was authentic, solid. In her world, she didn't encounter those characteristics that often. He made her feel grounded, real…special.

And it didn't hurt that he had a hard, droolworthy body.

'I just thought…you…me…it would be fun.'

'Fun, huh?' Noah ran his hand through his hair and shook his head in disgust. 'Morgan, just what the hell do you think you're doing?'

'Why are you so angry?' Morgan demanded, pulling a sheet up and around her. Every inch of her skin was now blushing and she felt humiliated and confused. Why was this a problem? She was offering her body, not asking him to do her laundry.

'You don't just give it away—especially to someone like…' Noah trailed off. 'Damn it! Don't you have a boyfriend? Surely you've had offers? I see how those guys you hang out with look at you!'

Her blood cooled at the thought. 'None of them can keep their mouths shut and, trust me, my hooking up with someone would be huge news. And a very big feather in someone's cap.'

Since she hadn't slept with any of the society boys—sons of her mother's friends, acquaintances and connections—she knew that she was a fish to be hooked, a prize to be won. She wouldn't give any of those poncey, wishy-washy pseudo-men the satisfaction.

Noah looked ill—green—and Morgan's heart dropped like a brick. Only *she* could make a guy nauseous with an offer of sex.

'So you went trawling, huh?'

Trawling? Morgan frowned. Was he nuts? He was a far

better choice on any weekday and twice on Sundays. 'No, I— What's your problem anyway?'

'Just trying to figure out where I am in the pecking order. Above the pool boy but below the riding instructor? What comes next? Are you going to offer to pay me?'

Okay, now he was way off course. 'Stop being a jerk, Noah! Look, I like you, and I thought that you might like me...just a little. I thought that we were almost friends, and I'd rather do it with an almost-friend than someone who sees me as a prize.'

But Noah wasn't listening. He swore, his Scottish accent becoming rapidly more pronounced.. 'I knew this was a bad idea. What is *wrong* with me? I cannot believe that I let my libido override my common sense, my professionalism. Acting with integrity, my ass. She'd knock me into next year if she knew.'

Who? What on earth was he talking about?'

Noah shook his head as if to clear it and glowered at her. 'Put some clothes on. This isn't going to happen. Not now, not ever.'

Noah took one last look at her, then swore softly again as he turned and walked out of the room, slamming her bedroom door behind him.

Morgan winced and cursed the tears that stung her eyes. 'Guess that's a big old Scottish no, then.'

Curling into a ball, she lay on her bed and stared out through the open sash window. Sleep refused to come, and when she did manage to drift off she woke up to a stranger in her flat.

Noah had left and in his place was a female bodyguard— just in case, Morgan thought grimly, she was so desperate to get laid that she seduced the next male bodyguard who was assigned to her.

If losing her virginity had been the goal, then half the

population in the world could have sorted her out. But she didn't want half the population...

Stupid man; she wanted *him*.

CHAPTER ONE

NOAH FRASER DODGED past a couple kissing and ran his hand across his prickly jaw. His eyes flicked over the waiting crowds, mentally processing faces against his internal data bank, and nobody blipped on his radar until he saw a tall, thin man with his hands in the pockets of his expensive trousers.

He frowned and wondered what was so important that Chris had to meet him here.

Twenty hours ago he'd boarded a plane at the Ministro Pistarini International Airport just south of Buenos Aires, after a week spent doing a full-spectrum security analysis for a museum. He'd identified threats and risks and then provided them with solutions to plug the holes. It was a part of the business they were trying to grow and it was lucrative.

Because he was a frugal Scot, he still felt guilty that he'd upgraded his seat to business class, but he just hadn't been able to face the thought of wedging his six-foot-three frame into a minuscule economy class seat to spend thirteen hours in cramped misery. As Chris kept reminding him, business class also allowed him to review his files in privacy, to catch a couple of twenty-minute power naps, to drink good whisky. He'd worked hard for a long time, he told himself, and he— the business—could afford it.

Noah rolled his shoulders as he made his way through

Customs, looking forward to a decent shower, a beer and to sleeping for a week.

Of course sleeping for a week was a pipedream; he was working all hours of the day to build his company, and sleep was a luxury he just couldn't afford. Self-sufficiency and financial independence were a lot higher up on Noah's list of priorities than sleep.

Who knew why he was being met by Chris, his oldest friend, partner and second-in-command at Auterlochie Consulting? Something must be up. He swallowed as dread settled over him. The last time Chris had met him at the airport it had been because Kade, one of their best employees, had committed suicide. God, he didn't want to deal with something like *that* again…

'No one has died,' Chris said quickly and Noah wasn't surprised that he'd read his mind.

They'd learnt to read each other's faces—sometimes their thoughts—in dusty, unfriendly situations and it was a trait they'd never lost.

Noah did a minor eye-roll as Chris shook his hand and pulled him into that one-armed hug he did so well. Only Chris could get away with that kind of PDA; when you'd saved a guy's life you had to overlook his occasional sappiness.

Noah adjusted the rucksack on his shoulder as they made their way across the terminal. 'What's up?'

Chris jammed his hands in his pockets and gestured towards the nearest coffee shop. 'I'll explain. You look like hell.'

Noah grinned wryly. 'Nice to see you too.'

Ten minutes later Noah was slumped into a plastic seat at one of the many generic restaurants scattered throughout the hall. He sent his friend a sour look and took another sip of his strong black coffee. By his estimation he'd been awake for more than thirty hours and he was feeling punchy.

'How did the assessment go?' Chris asked.

'Brilliant. They took all my suggestions on board and paid the account via bank transfer before I left the office. The money should be through already.'

'It is. I checked. It's easy money, Noah.'

'And we can do it with our eyes closed. If we start getting a reputation for providing solid advice at a good price, I think we could double our turnover—and soon too.'

'We've already exceeded our initial projections for the business. In fact, we're doing really well.'

'We can do better. I want to build us into being the premier provider of VIP protection and risk assessment in the UK.'

'Not the world?' Chris quipped, gently mocking his ambition as he always did.

Chris was less driven than he was, and had his feet firmly placed on the ground. It wasn't a bad thing. Noah had enough ambition for both of them. They were great partners. Chris was better with people: he had an easy way about him that drew people in. Their clients and staff talked to Chris; he was their best friend, the elder brother, a mate. Chris was the touchy-feely half of their partnership.

Noah was tough, decisive and goal-orientated; the partner who kicked butt. He called it being disciplined, reasonable, responsible and dedicated in everything he did. Chris called it being a control freak perfectionist. And emotionally stunted. Yeah, yeah...

Well, that was what happened when you grew up far too fast... Noah ran a hand over his face as if to wipe away the memories of his childhood, of picking up the pieces when his mother died, the wrench of losing his brothers. He pulled in a breath and along with it control.

He *was* in control, he reminded himself. It was a long time ago that he was sixteen and had felt the earth shaking under his feet.

He saw Chris's insightful look and summoned up a smile. 'I've scheduled world domination for next year,' he quipped.

'What was the response when you told our employees that we wanted them to do a mandatory session with a psychologist every six months?'

'They grumbled, but they understood. Kade's death has rocked them all. You *do* know that we'll have to do it too.'

Noah blanched. 'Hell, no.'

'Hell, yes. Kade was our responsibility and we didn't pick up the signs. What if we're working too hard, trying to keep too many balls in the air, and we miss the signs in someone else? We have to be as mentally healthy as—*more* mentally healthy than—any of our employees, Noah. That's non-negotiable.'

Since Chris was the healthiest, most balanced person he knew, Noah didn't have to be a rocket scientist to know that Chris was talking about him. Chris thought he was too stressed—working like a demon, juggling far too many balls. He knew that Chris was worried about him burning out, but he also knew that that he was nowhere near the edge...

Working hard never killed anyone—and besides, he'd been to the edge before and he knew what it looked like. He was still miles away.

Chris slapped the folder he'd been holding onto the table and pushed it towards him. Flipping open the cover, Noah looked down into the laughing face of a green-eyed blonde. She was standing between her famous mother and father, her brother behind them. The most successful family on planet earth, he thought. Rich, successful, close. A unit.

He felt a pang of jealousy and told himself that despite the fact that he had not been part of his brothers' lives for most of their formative years he was now, and they weren't doing so badly.

Noah concentrated on the photo below him. Morgan... she'd grown up. She was wearing a tight, slinky cream dress that stopped inches below her butt and revealed her giraffe-long legs. Her blonde hair was pulled back into a smooth ponytail and her naturally made-up face was alight with joy. She looked fantastic. Happy, charismatic.

Hot.

Doing a stint as her bodyguard had nearly killed him. Apart from that one incident he'd never before or since needed the same amount of control and determination as he'd summoned the night he'd walked away from the gloriously naked Morgan Claire Morrisey Moreau.

Noah flipped through the papers in the file. 'Floor plans of the Forrester-Grantham hotel in New York. Photos of the Moreau jewellery collection… I thought the Moreaus were Amanda's clients—have always been CFT's clients?'

Amanda. Their ex-boss and his ex-lover. As petite and as dangerous as a black widow spider, she looked like every other ball-breaker businesswoman in the city.

Except that Amanda *actually* broke balls. She'd certainly tried to go for his when she'd found out that he was leaving the CFT Corporation to start a company that was in direct competition with hers.

That hadn't been a day full of fun and giggles.

'Well, as you know, James Moreau and I went to school together,' Chris said.

Noah shrugged off his tiredness to connect the dots. James Moreau: CEO of Moreau International, brother to Morgan and son to Hannah 'Queen of Diamonds' Moreau and Jedd Moreau, one of the world's best known geologists.

Moreau International owned diamond and gemstone mines, dealt in the trading of said gems—especially diamonds—and had exclusive jewellery stores in all the major cities around the world. Hannah, as the face of the company, had always been a target, and CFT routinely provided her and Jedd with additional bodyguards when they needed more protection than their long-term driver/guards. That protection was only extended to James and Morgan and other high-ranking executives within MI when MI's security division or CFT received a particular threat, or were monitoring a situation where extra protection was needed.

Eight years ago, just after he'd left the SAS, Noah had been unlucky enough to end up guarding the nineteen-year-old Morgan for a week because a well-funded but stupid militant environmental group had been protesting MI's involvement with mines in a nature reserve in Uganda. Huge threats had been issued until it had been pointed out that it was an oil company mining for natural gas and not MI looking for gems.

Morgan had never been in any real danger, but no one had been prepared to take the chance. As the rookie, he'd got the so-called 'creampuff' assignment to guard the teenager. He'd never told anyone that it had probably been one of the best weeks of his life. Sure, he'd vacillated between wanting to wring her neck and fantasising about her, which had been off-the-scale inappropriate since she'd been his principal and he'd been six years older than her—and a million years in experience. But he'd laughed—internally—been relaxed in her company and had enjoyed her scalpel-sharp mind.

Noah felt heat creep up his neck and he stared at the fingers that gripped his coffee cup. He'd lost his mind that night...well, almost. He'd nearly risked everything he had—his sole source of income at that time—to make love to her. The consequences of his actions still made his blood run cold. If CFT had found out he would have been canned and would never have been able to get another job in security again. And security was what he did—what he'd trained for—the only skill he'd had at that time.

He'd left the army, his first and only love, to find a better-paying job so that he could put his two younger brothers through college. CFT had offered him a fantastic salary which he'd nearly thrown away to sleep with Morgan Moreau.

Who'd just wanted him to break her duck!

Chris's voice pulled him back to the here and now. 'I've

been working on James to send some business our way, told him we've expanded into security analysis, and he's thrown us a bone.'

'Oh, yay,' Noah deadpanned.

'If we pull it off it gives us an in at Moreau and we want them as clients.' Chris reminded him. 'World domination, remember? Moreau's is a good place to start.'

'I know, I know… Okay, what is it?' He tapped Morgan's picture. 'Does she need a bodyguard again? Who has her family upset this time?'

'She doesn't need protection.'

'Good.' Noah lifted an eyebrow at Chris. 'What's the job?'

'Every five years the Moreaus host a grand ball for charity, and they combine the ball with an exhibition of the family collection of jewels—which is practically priceless. Some of the biggest and the best diamonds and jewels collected over generations of wealthy Moreaus,' Chris explained. 'There has been a massive increase in armed robberies at such jewellery exhibitions, and James wants a complete, intensive threat analysis. I know it's a puffball assignment, but you just need to head to New York for a meeting, have a look at their current security arrangements, check out the hotel—do what you do best. With luck we'll get the contract to oversee the security, based on your report. But for now, it's just a couple of days in New York and we have an in with Moreau.'

'When is this meeting?'

'In the morning. I have you booked on a flight leaving in an hour.'

'Why can't you go? You're James's mate, not me.' Noah groaned. 'I'm beat.'

'I've got a meeting scheduled with another client, and you are far better at security assessments than I am. You're brilliant at planning operations, getting in and out of places and situations you shouldn't be, and you can see stuff from a criminal perspective.'

'Thanks,' Noah said dryly.

Noah pushed his chair out and stretched his long legs. He linked his hands behind his head in his favourite thinking posture, his eyes on Morgan's photograph which lay between them on the grubby table. Gorgeous eyes and slanting cheekbones, and she had a wide, mobile mouth with a smile that could power the national electrical grid.

Noah licked his lips and forced his thoughts away from that dangerously sexy mouth. Slowly he raised his eyes to Chris's face. He leaned forward and rested his arms on the table. 'Why don't you just shoot me now?'

'It's an option, but then I'd be out of a partner. It's a few days, Noah, in an exciting city that you love.'

'Clothes?'

'Bag in the car. I went to your flat and picked out some threads.'

Noah swore and flipped the cover of the folder closed. 'Guess I'm going to New York.'

'Atta boy.'

Noah narrowed his eyes at his partner. 'You're a manipulative git.'

Chris just grinned.

Sapphires, rubies, pearls. Diamonds. The usual suspects. And then there were the less common gems that sparked her imagination. Alexandrite that changed from green in daylight to red under incandescent light. Maw Sit-Sit, the same green as her eyes. Almandine Garnet, purplish red and the neon blue of Paraiba tourmaline.

Having access to the gemstone vaults of Moreau International was a very big perk as a jewellery designer, and it allowed Morgan the chance to offer her very high-end clients one-of-a-kind pieces containing gemstones of exceptional quality.

Morgan looked up at Derek, their Head of Inventory, and the security guard who'd accompanied the jewels to her airy, light-filled design studio on the top floor of the

Moreau Building on Fifth Avenue from the super-secure fourth floor that housed the jewellery vaults. Morgan knew that there was another vault somewhere in the city, and others in other places of the world, which housed more gemstones. Her mother didn't believe in keeping all their precious eggs in one basket.

'I'll take the Alexandrite, the tourmaline and both garnets.' Morgan scanned the cloth holding the jewels again. 'The fifteen-carat F marquise-cut yellow diamond and I'll let you know about the emeralds. Thanks, Derek.'

Derek nodded and stepped forward to help Morgan replace the jewels in their separate bags. She signed an order form as Derek spoke.

'I have some apparently amazing Clinohumite coming in from a new mine in Siberia. Interested?'

Interested in the rare burnt orange gems that she could never get enough of? *Duh.* 'Of course! I'll owe you if you can sneak a couple of the nicer ones to me before you offer them to Carl.'

Carl was Head Craftsman for MI's flagship jewellery store which was on the ground floor of the building. A rival to Tiffany and Cartier, Moreau's made up the third of the 'big three' jewellery stores in New York City. Carl had his clients and so did Morgan, and they shared one or two others. They happily waged a silent war, competing for the best of the Moreau gems that were on offer. And for the clients with the deepest pockets.

'I'll offer you two per cent above whatever Carl offers for the Clinohumites. Don't let me down, Derek, I want those stones.' She might be a Moreau, but her business was separate to the jewellery store and the gemstones. She had to buy her stones at the going rate and sell at a profit...and that was the way she liked it.

'Of course. I owe you for designing Gail's engagement ring. She still thinks I'm a god.'

Morgan laughed. 'I'm glad she loves it.'

Even though he had a hugely responsible job at Moreau's, he would never have been able to afford the usual prices Morgan commanded. Sometimes she thought that the money she charged for her designs was insane but, as her mother kept insisting, exclusivity had its price, and the Moreau price was stratospheric.

Morgan heard the door to her studio click closed behind Derek and his guard and sat down on a stool, next to her workbench. She twisted a tanzanite and diamond ring on her finger before resting her chin in the palm of her hand.

Morgan Moreau Designs. She couldn't deny that being a Moreau had opened doors that would have been a lot harder to break down if she hadn't possessed a charmed name associated with gemstones. But having a name wasn't enough; no socialite worth her salt was going to drop squillions on a piece of jewellery that wasn't out of the very top drawer. Morgan understood that they wanted statement pieces that would stand out from the exceptional, and she provided that time and time again.

It was the one thing—probably the only thing—she'd ever truly excelled at. She adored her job; it made her heart sing. So why, then, exactly, wasn't she happy? Morgan twisted her lips, thinking that she wasn't precisely unhappy either. She was just…feeling 'blah' about her life.

Which was utterly ridiculous and she wanted to slap herself at the thought. She was a Moreau—wealthy, reasonably attractive, popular. She ran her own business and had, if she said so herself, a great body which didn't need high maintenance. Okay, she was still single, and had been for a while—her soul mate was taking a long time to make an appearance—but she dated. Had the occasional very discreet affair if she thought the man nice enough and attractive enough to bother with.

She had a life that millions of girls would sell their souls for and she was feeling sorry for herself? *Yuck*.

'Earth to Morgan?'

Morgan looked up and saw her best friend standing in the doorway of her studio, her pixie face alight with laughter. Friends since they were children, they'd lived together, travelled together and now they worked together...sort of. Riley was contracted to design and maintain the window displays of the jewellery store downstairs. She was simply another member of the Moreau family.

'Hey. I'm about to have coffee—want some?'

Riley shook her head. 'No time. Your mother sent me up here to drag you out of your nest. She wants you to come down and join the charity ball planning meeting.'

'Why? She's never included me before.'

'You know that's not true. Every year she asks if you want to be involved, and every year you wrinkle your pretty nose and say no.'

'You'd think she would've got the message by now,' Morgan grumbled. Organising an event on such a scale was a mammoth undertaking and *so* not up her alley. She'd just make an idiot of herself and that wasn't an option. Ever.

She'd felt enough of an idiot far too many times before.

'Well, she said that I have to bring you down even if I have to drag you by your hair.'

'Good grief.'

Morgan stood up and stretched. She took stock of her outfit: a white T-shirt with a slate jacket, skinny stone-coloured pants tucked into black, knee-high laceup boots. It wasn't the Moreau corporate look, but she'd do.

Morgan walked towards the door and allowed it to close behind her; like all of the other rooms in the building, entrance was by finger-scan. Keys weren't needed at Moreau's.

'Did you get your dress for Merri's wedding?' Riley asked as they headed for the stairs.

'Mmm. I can't wait. We're hitching a lift with James on the company jet, by the way. He's flying out on the Thursday evening.'

'Perfect.'

And it was… Their friend Merri was getting married in her and Riley's hometown of Stellenbosch, South Africa, and Morgan couldn't wait to go home. She desperately missed her home country; she'd love to return to the vineyards and the mountains, the crisp Cape air and the friendly people. But if she wanted to cement her reputation for being one of the best jewellery designers in the world—like her grandfather before her—then she needed to be in fast-paced NYC. She needed clients with big money who weren't afraid to spend it…

And talking of exceptional, she thought as they stepped out of the lift onto the fifth floor, where Hannah and the New York-based directors of MI had their offices, she had to start work on the piece Moreau International had commissioned her to design and manufacture that would be sold as part of the silent auction at the charity ball. Maybe that was why Hannah wanted her at the meeting…

CHAPTER TWO

MORGAN WATCHED AS her glamorous, sophisticated mother stepped out of her office in a lemon suit, nude heels and with a perfectly straight platinum chin-length bob.

'I need a decision about the jewellery for the auction,' Morgan announced as Hannah approached them. 'Do you have any gemstones in stock that you want me to use? What do you want me to design? Diamonds? Emeralds? Rubies? Classic or contemporary? Is that why you want me at this meeting?'

'Hello to you too, darling,' Hannah said in her driest tone. 'How are you?'

Morgan waved an elegant hand in the air. 'Mum, we had coffee together this morning; you didn't say anything then about me having to come downstairs.'

'It's a conference room, not a torture chamber, Morgan,' Hannah replied, her tone as dry as the martinis she loved to drink. 'Nice photo of you in the *Post*, by the way.'

Since she hadn't been out recently, Morgan wasn't sure where she'd been photographed. 'Uh…where was I?'

'At the opening night of that new gallery in Soho.'

Her friend Kendall's new gallery; she'd popped in for five minutes, literally, and it couldn't go undocumented? *Sheez!* But she was, very reluctantly, a part of the NYC social scene, and because she was a Moreau whenever she made an appearance she was photographed extensively. Many of those photographs ended up in the social columns and online.

Hannah folded her arms and tapped her foot. Good grief, she recognised that look.

'Morgan, it's time we talked about you joining Moreau International in an official position.'

Morgan sighed. 'Has six months passed so quickly?'

They had an agreement: Hannah was allowed to nag her about joining the company every six months. For the last twelve years they'd had the same conversation over and over again.

'I've decided that I want you to be MI's Public Relations and Brand Director.'

Run me over with a bus, Morgan thought. PR and Brand Director? That was a new title. 'Mum, I'm happy doing what I'm doing—designing jewellery. You and James are doing a fabulous job with MI. You don't need me.'

And she was damned if she was going to take a job away from a loyal MI employee who was way more qualified for the position than she'd ever be. And—funny, this—she actually wanted to get paid for what she *did,* not who she was.

But she had to give Hannah points for being persistent. She'd been trying to get her to work for MI since she was sixteen—shortly after they'd received the happy news that Morgan was just chronically dyslexic and not selectively stupid.

It had only taken her mother and a slew of medics, educational psychologists and shrinks to work that out. Everyone had been so pleased that they'd found the root cause of her failing marks at school, her frustration and her anger.

The years of sheer hell she'd lived through between the time she'd started school and her diagnosis had been conveniently forgotten by everybody except herself.

Water under the bridge, Morgan reminded herself. And she knew her mum felt guilty for the part she'd played in the disaster that had been her education.

Morgan knew that it hadn't been easy for her either. She'd

been thrust into running MI in her mid-thirties, when her adventure-seeking husband had decided that he didn't like the corporate life and wanted to be MI's chief geologist, discovering new mines. Hannah, with her MBA in business and economics, had taken over the role of MI's CEO, juggling its huge responsibilities with two children, one of whom had made her life a great deal more difficult by her inability to meet her mother's and teachers' expectations.

How often had she heard variations on the theme of, 'She's such a bright child; if only she would try harder.'

Nobody had ever realised how hard she'd always been trying, how incredibly frustrating it had been not to meet her goals and everybody else's. Had they honestly believed that she didn't want to learn to read and write properly? That she'd enjoyed being the class freak?

Ages eight to sixteen had been a suck-fest of epic proportions. Finally being diagnosed as being chronically dyslexic had freed her, a little, from the shame and guilt she'd felt for years. She'd started to believe that her learning disabilities weren't her fault and her relationship with her family—well, mostly with her mother—had rapidly improved. Her mum was still a controlling corporate queen, and she still marched to the beat of her own drum, but they'd found a way back to each other—even if they did have to have this conversation every six months.

Morgan knew that she wasn't stupid, but she also knew that working for MI would require computers and reading and writing reports. While she *could* do all of that, she just took longer than most—okay, a lot longer—and the corporate world couldn't and wouldn't wait that long. And shouldn't…

Until she was the best person for a job, she wouldn't take it. Not to mention that her dyslexia would become an open secret; she wouldn't be able to keep it under wraps. Wouldn't that be fun? She could just see the headlines: *The ultimate dumb blonde… Gorgeous but thick… With her looks and money, who needs brains anyway?*

She'd heard them all before—even from someone she'd loved...

Morgan shuddered. *No, thank you.* Call her stubborn, call her proud, but she wasn't going to expose herself to that much ridicule again.

Besides, designing jewellery was her solace and her joy—her dream job. If only Hannah would see that and get off her back about working for MI her relationship with her mum would be pretty much perfect.

Morgan took her mum's hand and squeezed. 'I love you for the fact that you believe I should play a bigger part in MI, but I am neither qualified nor suited for the corporate world, Mum. I don't *want* to be part of that world. I'm happy being on the fringes of MI.'

'I will wear you down someday.' Hannah sighed loudly. 'On another subject, I want you to haul out your designer dresses and start creating hype around the ball at social events.'

Morgan gagged. '*Ugh.* Don't I do enough already?'

'Hardly.' Hannah sniffed. 'One function every two weeks and cutting out early isn't good enough to promote your business, and not nearly good enough to promote the ball. You need to charm more people than you're currently doing. Darling, you are a social disgrace. How many invitations did you turn down this week alone?'

Morgan shrugged. 'Ten...twelve?'

'Helen, my personal publicist, said that you were invited to at least twenty-five, maybe more. Soirées, charity dinners, afternoon teas, breakfasts...'

Morgan tipped her head and counted to ten, then thirty, before attempting to speak rationally. 'Mum, I have a business to run, designs to get out the door. I work, just like you do. Okay, I don't oversee a multinational company but I work. Hard.'

'You're a Moreau; you should be out more. Can you start going to some more formal parties? The benefits, the political fundraisers, the balls? That is where the money is, dar-ling—the people who can actually afford the price of the ball tickets. We need to target the people who have the *real* money, and they are at the more sedate functions.'

Sedate meaning deadly dull. 'Don't nag me, Mother. You know I hate those stuffy functions where the conversation is so…intense. The situation in Syria, the economy, the plight of the rainforests.'

'Because, you know, those issues *aren't* important…' Riley said, her tongue in her cheek.

Morgan glared at her. 'I feel…' She wanted to say *stupid* but instead said, 'I feel out of place there.'

Like all the other issues related to her dyslexia, it had taken her many years to conquer her social awkwardness and to decode social cues. She still battled with new situations, and she knew that many people took her occasional lapses of concentration and her social shyness as self-absorption and disinterest. Nothing could have been further from the truth. She generally loved people, but she could never tell if they loved her back.

When she added that to her 'I wonder if he sees me or just the family money' concerns, dating was a bit of a night-mare…

And, really, she would rather have a beer in a pub in jeans and a T-shirt than be in a ballroom in shoes that hurt her feet.

Riley smiled at her and Morgan recognised the mischie-vous glint in her eyes.

'You poor child…being forced to dress up, drink the best champagne in the world and eat the finest food at functions that are by invitation only. It's almost abuse—really, it is.'

Morgan's searing look promised retribution for Riley's teasing and her encouragement of her mother's campaign to get her to be the reigning young socialite of New York City.

Morgan wrinkled her nose at her mother. 'You and James just do it so much better than me. You're suave and sophisti-cated and far more charming than I'll ever be—with or without the big D. Look, we've discussed my contribution to the ball so can I go now?' Morgan asked hopefully.

'No, I'd still like you to attend this first planning meeting with Riley, Jack—our PR director—and the new consultant James has appointed to assess security,' Hannah said as they walked down the carpeted passage to the boardroom.

On the walls either side were framed photographs of the Moreau collection of jewels.

'Why can't Moreau's own Chief of Security handle it? He always has,' Morgan said, because she felt she should show *some* interest.

'Since the last Moreau ball there have been a number of armed robberies on jewellery exhibitions.' Hannah rapped her fist against the frame that held a picture of the Moreau Diamond—a gem Morgan's three times great-grandfather Moreau had bought from a broke Russian aristocrat and which had once been owned by Elizabeth of Russia. 'Fifty-three carats, D-colour, flawless. Worth more than five million dollars. You want to risk it getting stolen?'

When she put it like that…

'Our jewellery collection is priceless, Morgan, so James has contracted Auterlochie Consulting to look at every security hole we have and to plug it. Their best operative will be in charge…'

Auterlochie…Auterlochie… Why did she know that name?

'In you go, darling, and smile!'

Hannah placed a hand on her back and she bared her teeth at her mother as she stepped into the conference centre. Her hand still on the doorknob, she looked around—and her head jerked back as dazzling blue eyes connected with hers.

Deep brown hair… Auterlochie… A deep Sean Connery voice explaining that it was a town in the Scottish Highlands, situated on a loch, and he'd once visited it with a friend. Two young boys had fished and explored the icy banks there, and he'd told her when he opened his business it would be called Auterlochie something.

It was the one of the longest sentences he'd strung together, and Morgan had been enthralled by his Scottish accent and the light of determination in those fantastic cobalt eyes... Noah Fraser.

Morgan's heart splattered as it hit the floor. *Bats on a broomstick.*

She stepped back behind the door and squeezed her eyes shut. Eight years and she still wished she could acid-wash the memory out of her brain.

'Excuse me. I really need to go to the bathroom.'

'Oh, Morgan? Right now? The meeting...'

Hannah's voice followed her down the hall.

In the upscale visitors' bathroom where she'd fled after Hannah had dropped her verbal meteor strike, Morgan sat on the lid of a toilet and stared at her hands. She knew she had to get moving, get to the meeting, or her mum would hunt her down like a rabid fox but she didn't know if she could face Noah Fraser again.

She'd rather flush herself down the toilet bowl.

'Morgs?' A fist rapped on the door. 'You in there? Your mum is *not* a happy camper.'

Morgan leaned forward and flipped the lock to open. Riley pulled the door open and frowned. She sent her a pointed look. 'Why are you hiding out in the bathroom?'

Morgan bit the inside of her cheek. 'Did you meet Noah Fraser?'

'The security guy? Yes. Very intense, very hot.'

Morgan swore and dropped her face to her hands.

'And the problem is...?'

Morgan briefly explained her history with Noah and Riley lifted her hands in confusion. 'So you made a move on the guy and he said no? It was a long time ago, Morgan.'

Morgan knew that if there was anyone who would understand what she was about to say Riley was it. They'd been friends forever and she had witnessed Morgan's constant struggles with the system. Shortly after the incident with Noah she'd moved in as Morgan's flatmate. Riley had watched her struggle through college to get her diploma in Gemology and Jewellery Design—it had taken her double the time to get as anyone else, even with a scribe—and she knew the challenges she faced on a daily basis and had supported her through the hard times.

'Okay, I need more details. So tell me about Mr Melt-My-Panties. And hurry up—your mother is going to have both our hides soon.'

'When I was nineteen the parents had some kidnapping threats made against them by some weird group and Noah was assigned as my bodyguard.'

'Uh-huh…'

'After a week of hanging with him I threw myself at him—actually, I threw my *naked* self at him.' Morgan nodded at Riley's wince. 'He kissed me, discovered I was a virgin, and then he declined the offer. I was so humiliated. I liked him—felt so at ease with him despite the fact that he hardly spoke—and his rejection felt like—'

'Like what, hon?'

'I can't explain it, and I don't know why, but his rejection made me feel swamped with shame. Every emotion I'd ever experienced with my dyslexia—the lack of self-belief, the fear of judgement—dropped on me like a ton of bricks. It was horrible. He made me feel worthless again. And now is not the time to tell me that nobody can make me *feel* worthless!'

'Okay. No lectures. Did he know that you were dyslexic?'

'No, I was very careful to keep it from him. For that summer I was Morgan without the big D. That's what made it even harder, I think… He rejected me anyway. Around him I was the most normal I had ever been and it still wasn't enough. I still can't think of that night without feeling cold and clammy.'

'Oh, honey… Well, you know you're not worthless. You've worked hard to climb out of that pit of feeling *less than* and not valued. Why are you letting those feelings, and that man, chase you into a bathroom stall? You're better than that.'

She *was*, dammit. 'I know that...' she muttered.

'Then get your butt out of there and pick up your chin. You'll be fine. Me, I'm not so sure.' Riley wiggled her butt.

Morgan lifted her hands in query. 'What's the matter with you?'

'I think my panties are starting to melt...can I hit on him?'

'Sheez, Ri!' Morgan snapped. 'No, you can't hit on him! I mean, yes, you can... *Aarrgh!*'

Riley's chuckles followed her out of the bathroom.

This time he'd sent *her* running.

Judging from her hasty retreat and her *oh, crap!* look, nobody had told her he would be at the meeting. While he hadn't expected Morgan to attend this meeting, at least he'd been prepared to run into her. And he'd had a six hour flight to practise his *oh-it's-you* face.

He understood her belting out of the room; he'd fought the same impulse himself. That and the inclination to grab her and pick up where they'd left off years ago. She'd be naked, of course...

Noah looked down at the table he was sitting at and concentrated hard. Thirty-three years old and he was grateful that his crotch was hidden from view by a sleek boardroom table.

Get a grip, Fraser. Distraction... Years ago he'd used firearm drills; now he just flipped open his iPad and checked his emails. Ten minutes later he glanced at his watch and stifled a frustrated sigh. The meeting still hadn't started.

He'd made Morgan run off screaming into the... Well, not the night, but he still couldn't blame her. It wasn't his finest memory and *he* hadn't been naked...with a Brazilian... *Do not go there, Fraser.*

He glanced over to the corner, where Hannah Moreau and her son James, who'd just entered the conference room, were standing. He'd met James once before, and despite the fact that he was one of the richest men in the world he rather liked the guy. He was smart, decisive, and didn't give off an air of being precious.

He also knew, from Chris, that he played a cracking game of touch rugby, didn't play polo, and could talk to miners and millionaires with equal ease. He couldn't help hoping that Morgan had turned out equally well.

Not that he cared—much—one way or the other.

Noah saw the conference door open and didn't realise that he'd sucked in his breath. The arty-looking redhead stepped through the door first, and exchanged a look with James that was part defiance, part attraction—something cooking there—and then Noah focused his attention on the figure in the doorway.

'Sorry I kept you waiting, everybody. Hi, James.'

James Moreau whirled around and immediately crossed the room, pulling Morgan into his embrace. Morgan's butterscotch-coloured head rested on his chest and she closed her eyes as she returned the hug. When she opened them again she looked straight at him—now utterly composed—with those clear, deep green eyes, and it was his turn to feel something akin to exposed and vulnerable…as if she'd cracked him open and his every thought, emotion, fear was there for her to read.

In another reality—the one where he wasn't losing his mind—Noah remembered his manners and forced himself to his feet, taking a moment to pull his thoughts together and to display his usual expression. He called it inscrutable; Chris called it bored indifference. He pulled in a shallow breath and made himself relax while Morgan shook hands with the others in the room. He watched her interact and knew that her smile wasn't as wide as it could be, that the muscles in her slim shoulders were taut with tension, that she was trying to delay the moment of having to acknowledge his presence.

Well, he wasn't entranced with the idea either. Entranced with *her*, yes. With the reality of being entranced by her…no.

He didn't do entranced.

'Noah,' James said, placing a hand on Morgan's stiff back and urging her towards him, 'I don't know if you remember my sister Morgan?'

Since the memory of her naked is forever printed on my retina, I should think so.

Noah's mouth twitched, and when Morgan glared at him he thought that she'd worked out what he was thinking. 'Of course. Nice to see you again, Morgan,' he said, in his smoothest, blandest voice.

Wish you were naked, by the way.

'Noah,' Morgan said. Her eyes flicked over him, narrowed, and then she gave him a 'you're a bug and I'm desperate to squash you' look.

What was her problem? He hadn't asked her to proposition him… Was she still annoyed because he'd said no? *Come on, it was eight years ago—get over it, already.*

Noah held her defiant stare. He'd perfected his own implacable, don't-mess-with-me stare in the forces, and it had had more than a couple of recruits and higher-ranking officers buckling under. When Morgan started to flush he knew had he won their silent battle of wills. This time.

'Take a seat everyone.'

Noah turned back to the table and pulled out the chair next to him for Morgan, gestured her into it. She narrowed her eyes at him, yanked it back another couple of inches in a flouncy display of defiance and dropped into it. Noah could smell her scent, something light and fresh, and felt a rush of blood heading south, making him feel almost light-headed. She still wore the same perfume and it transported him back to that night so long ago, when he'd tangled with temptation and by the skin of his teeth escaped.

'Right, the first item of business…' Hannah said, in a crisp, no-nonsense voice when they were all seated and looking at her expectantly. 'I'm handing over the responsibility of the ball to you, Morgan, and it's not under discussion. Make me proud.'

CHAPTER THREE

WHEN SHE WAS very tired, stressed or emotional Morgan saw dots in front of her eyes and the letters on a page danced and shuffled about. However, this was the first time the room had ever moved, that faces had bopped and objects jiggled.

Morgan closed her eyes and wondered if she had imagined the last thirty seconds. She'd thought she'd heard her mother say that she wanted her to take over the organising the Moreau Charity Ball—the most anticipated ball on the international social scene, held once every five years, displaying the full collection of gemstones and jewellery the Moreau family had acquired over many generations.

There were only three thousand guests attending, five hundred of whom were invited by Hannah herself from among their loyal customers, long-time business associates and preferred suppliers. For the rest, whether they were royalty or the average Joe, they had to place a bid for a double ticket and the highest bids won the highly sought after tickets.

It was outrageous how much people were prepared to pay for a double ticket. Simply inconceivable... And that was why, along with the auction, the Moreau Charity Ball raised tens of millions for the various causes they supported around the world.

But for their money their guests expected the best entertainers, visually stunning dress sets, Michelin star quality food—the whole gilt-plated bang-shoot.

It was rich, it was exclusive, it was the social highlight of the half-decade. And if you wanted to be part of the experience then you paid, stratospherically, for the privilege of being there.

And Hannah wanted *her* to run it? Morgan felt her throat constrict. She lifted her left hand and didn't realise that she was groping for Noah's hand until his strong fingers encircled her palm and squeezed.

'Breathe,' he told her, his voice authoritative even though it was pitched at a volume only she could hear. 'Again; in and out. There you go.'

Morgan felt the room settle as oxygen reached her brain and lungs. When she thought she could speak she licked her lips and considered removing her hand from Noah's strong grasp. But since it seemed to be her only tenuous link to reality, she left it exactly where it was.

Morgan made herself look at her mother, who had the slightest smile on her face. 'Is this a joke?'

'Not at all,' Hannah replied. 'I'd like you to plan, organise and execute the ball.'

'But—'

'Riley will help you with the creative side—help you pick the theme, do the design. You both have an amazing streak of creativity and I know that it will look visually spectacular.'

Morgan shook her head, wishing she could speak freely and say exactly what was on her mind. *I don't do well with reading reports, writing reports, analysing spreadsheets. You know this! I've worked really hard to conquer my dyslexia, but it's still there and it becomes a lot worse when I'm stressed. This ball will stress me out to the max! I don't want to mess this up; it's too important for me to be in charge of.*

Hannah's eyes softened but determination radiated from her face. 'Honey, I know that you will be fine. I know that you also have your own commissions, your own business to run, so the full resources that are available to me are available to you too. We'll hire you a PA for this project; she'll type your reports and be your general gopher. James will keep an eye on the finances and you'll liaise with Jack regarding the promotion and advertising of the ball. Noah will draw up plans to keep the jewels safe, and I'll be on the other end of a mobile. You just have to co-ordinate, make decisions, boss people about.'

'You're good at that,' James inserted with an easy grin.

And in a couple of sentences her mother, without announcing to the room that she had a problem reading and writing, waved away her biggest concerns.

Morgan reluctantly pulled her hand out from Noah's and flushed, because she could sense those deep blue eyes on her face. What must he think of her? she wondered. That she was a candidate for an upmarket loony bin?

'Why are you bowing out, Hannah?' Riley asked, as forthright as ever.

Hannah picked up her pen and tapped the point on the stack of papers in front of her. Morgan saw a quick, secret smile on her face and frowned. It was a good question, and one she was sure she knew the answer to... Three, two, one...

'I need a break—to step away from the business for a while.'

There it is and here we go again... Morgan thought. Now they were getting to the bottom of things. Every ten years or so her parents decided that they should try and live together again. They loved each other, but they loved each other more when they had continents between them. They refused to accept that while they adored each other they just couldn't live together. How many times had her father moved in and out of the Stellenbosch farmhouse and, later, the Englewood mansion?

Morgan sent James a quick eye-roll and he responded with a faint smile.

'Jedd and I have realised that we've been married nearly forty years and we want to spend more time with each other. He's going to try to be a little less of a mad geologist and I'm going to accompany him on his travels. So I need you, Morgan, to organise the ball for me.'

Morgan expelled her pent-up tension in a long stream of air. If this was about her parents' marriage then she gave her mum a week and she'd be on the company jet back home. Hannah couldn't go five minutes without checking her email or applying her lipstick. Her father spent weeks in jungles without making contact, sleeping in tents and hammocks and, she suspected, not washing much.

A week, maybe two, and Hannah would be back and yanking the ball's organisation into her beautifully manicured hands. Fine by her. She just had to ride it out.

What a morning, Morgan thought. Noah, the ball, her parents; she felt as if she was in sensory and information overload.

'Right, down to business,' Hannah said sharply.

Morgan frowned and held up her hand. 'Whoa! Hold on, there, Mum.' Morgan narrowed her eyes at her beautiful, wilful mother. If she gave her mother an inch, she'd gobble her up. 'I will sit in on this first planning meeting and then I will decide how involved I want to become—because I know that you will whirl back in here in two weeks' time and take over again.'

Blue eyes held green and Hannah's mouth eventually twitched with a smile. She nodded, looked around the table and pulled on her cloak of business. 'Okay. Now, we've wasted enough time on our family drama. Back to work, everyone.'

By the end of the two-hour meeting Morgan felt as if her head was buzzing. She desperately needed a cup of coffee and some quiet. Just some time to think, to process, to deal with the events of the morning.

She wanted to run up to her studio, lie down on her plush raspberry love seat and just breathe. But instead, because Hannah had asked her super-nicely, she was accompanying Noah to the Forrester-Grantham Hotel—the oldest, biggest and most beautiful of Manhattan's hotels. It had the only ballroom in New York City big enough to accommodate the ball's many guests, and the fact that it was lush, opulent and a six-star venue made it their instinctive hotel of choice.

Morgan had been delegated, by her mother, to introduce Noah to the hotel's Head of Security and discuss the current security arrangements for the ball.

Yippee.

Riley, the last to leave, closed the door behind her and Morgan was left alone with Noah. She watched as he unfurled his long body and headed for the refreshment table in the corner. He placed a small cup beneath the spout of the coffee machine and hit the button marked 'espresso'. He was different, Morgan thought. His body, under that nice grey suit, still seemed to be as hard as it had been eight years ago, but his hair was longer, his face thinner. Okay, he was older, but what felt so different? Maybe it was because now he radiated determination, a sense of power...leaving no one in doubt that he was a smart, ambitious man in his prime.

Noah snagged two bottles of sparkling water from the ice bucket, held them loosely in one hand as he picked up the small cup and brought it back to the table. To her surprise, he slid the cup and a bottle towards her.

'You look like you need both,' Noah said, pushing away the chair next to her with his foot and resting his bottom on the conference table so that he faced her. He picked up a bottle of water, twisted the cap off and took a long sip.

Morgan lifted the cup to her lips, swallowed and tipped her head so that it rested against the high back of the leather chair. Her mind skittered over all the questions she wanted to ask him: where did he live? He wasn't wearing a ring but was he married? Involved? Why had he said no to her all those years ago?

She opened her mouth to say…*what?*…and abruptly closed it again.

The right corner of Noah's mouth lifted and Morgan felt her irritation levels climb. 'What are you smirking at?' she demanded.

'You, of course.'

Of course.

'Well, stop it! Why?'

Noah lifted one shoulder and looked at her as he put the water bottle to his lips. Lucky water bottle… *Really, Morgan! Do try to be less pathetic, please.*

'You're sitting there thinking that politeness demands that you have to talk to me and the only thing you want to talk about is why I walked away so long ago.'

The ego of the man! The arrogant, condescending, annoying son-of-a… He was *so* right, damn him.

'I haven't thought of you once since you left,' she said, with a credible amount of ice in her voice.

'Liar,' Noah said softly, his eyes sparking with heat. 'You've *also* wondered what it would've been like…'

Also wondered? Did that mean that he had too? And why was she even having this conversation with him? In fact, why was he talking at all? The Noah she knew needed pliers and novocaine to pull words out of him.

'Well, I see that you've grown some social skills. Have you found that talking is, actually, quite helpful to get your point across?'

See—she could do sarcastic. And quite well. *Hah!*

'My partner nagged me to improve.'

His partner? Who was she? How long had they been together? Did they have children?

Noah laughed softly. 'You have the most expressive face in the world. Why don't you just ask?'

'Ask you what?' Morgan feigned supreme indifference. 'I have no idea what you mean.'

'Again...*liar*. When I say partner I mean Chris—my business partner.'

Single! Yay! Her girl-parts did a stupid happy dance and she mentally slapped them into submission because he hadn't really answered the question.

'And you?'

Morgan lifted her perfectly arched dark brown eyebrows at him. She knew that they were the perfect contrast to her blonde hair. And they made her eyes look greener than they actually were. 'That has nothing to do with you.'

Noah grinned and disturbed the million bats squatting in her stomach.

'You are such a duchess.'

Morgan bared her teeth at him. 'And don't you forget it. And, just to make it clear, I do not—*ever*!—want to discuss Cape Town.'

'It's a nice city.'

Morgan growled. 'What we *did* in Cape Town.' She pushed out the clarification between clenched teeth.

'*We* did? All *I* did was kiss you—you were the one who was naked and hoping to get lucky.'

She was going to kill him...slowly, with much pleasure.

Morgan ground her teeth together. How was this *not* discussing the issue? Did he not understand the concept of letting sleeping dogs lie? Obviously not.

Noah pushed his hair away from his face and rubbed his hand across his jaw. 'As much fun as it is, exchanging barbs with you, I do need to say something about Cape Town.'

Please don't. I've been humiliated enough.

Noah looked at her with serious eyes. 'I should've handled it—you—the situation—better, Morgan.' He held up a hand as her mouth opened and she abruptly shut it again. 'It took guts to do what you did and I was cruel. I'm sorry.'

Morgan realised that she was wearing her fish-face and snapped her teeth together. He was apologising? Seriously?

'So, that's all I have to say.'

Ah… It was more than enough and, quite frankly, she'd still prefer to pretend it had never happened. But she had to respect him for apologising, although she had played her own part in the train wreck that had been that night.

She rubbed her suddenly sweaty palms against her thighs. 'Okay, then. Wow. Um…thanks. I suppose I should apologise for hitting on you naked. I was rather…in your face.'

'A woman who looks like you should never apologise for being naked,' Noah said, humour sparking in his eyes.

It made her want to smile at him and she wasn't quite ready to do that. Nearly, but not quite yet.

'Can we…*ahem*…put it to bed?' he asked.

Morgan rolled her eyes at the very unsubtle pun.

Way past time to change the subject, Morgan thought. 'Mum said something about you being on your own? That you're not with CFT any more?'

Noah nodded. 'I have my own company doing pretty much the same thing CFT are doing. Except that we're branching out into security analysis; this is our first job for MI. I'm here to make recommendations about what systems should be put in place to secure the collection. That's the first step. Hopefully it'll lead to us installing those systems.'

'Are you good at it?'

'Very.'

'Okay, then.' Morgan twisted her ring around her finger and half shrugged. 'Today aside, I don't have much to do with the ball, but I would hate to see anything happen to the collection. It's fabulous; the gems are magnificent and the craftsmanship is superb.'

'Nothing to do with the ball? I think your mum has other ideas.' Noah finished his bottle of water, carefully replaced the cap and placed it on the table. 'If we get the job to install the systems then I will make damn sure that nothing happens to the collection. My business would be ruined if a diamond chip went missing, and that's not a risk I'm prepared to take.'

Morgan went cold at the thought of losing the collection. The value of the pieces meant nothing to her, but the fact that her family was the custodian of Elizabeth of Russia's diamond ring, a pearl won by an eighteenth-century Maharani wife, and the first diamond to come out of the first Moreau mine, meant a great deal. They were valuable, sure, but they were also historically important.

But if Noah was in charge of securing them then she knew that they would be fine. He exuded an air of capability and competence and, like all those years ago, when she'd felt secure enough to hand herself over to him, she felt confident about the collection's safety.

Noah was reliable and proficient.

Everything she wasn't—outside of her design studio. He was a living, breathing reminder of why she could never organise the ball. She would be stepping so far out of her comfort zone... A million things could go wrong and probably would and she'd be left holding the can. Nope, this was her mum's baby and would remain so.

Besides, she so didn't need the stress, the responsibility or the hassle of dealing with the sexy and not-so-silent-anymore Noah Fraser, with his sexy Scottish burr and sarcastic smile.

'Come on—time to go,' Noah said, standing up.

He watched as she uncrossed her legs and stood up. He looked her up and down and his eyes crinkled in amusement.

'Looking good, Duchess. Of course not as good as you looked back then—'

'I was nineteen,' Morgan protested, conscious that she'd picked up more than a pound since she'd been a perfect size four. 'Anyway, I'm that not much bigger.'

'You're not big at all, Duchess; you know you look great. My point was back then you were naked.' Noah placed a hand on her back and pushed her towards the door. 'Naked is always hard to beat.'

'Taxi, Miss Moreau?'

Morgan sent Noah a look in response to the doorman's question.

He shook his head slightly and jammed his hands in the pockets of his pants. 'No, thank you. It's a beautiful afternoon; we'll walk.'

'Enjoy the rest of your day, Miss Moreau. Sir…'

Noah fell into step with Morgan as she turned right and headed to the traffic lights to cross Park Avenue. It was moments like this when he was reminded just how famous the people he protected actually were. When the doormen and staff of one of the most famous hotels in the world recognised you and greeted you by name, as numerous people had Morgan inside the hotel, you had pull, clout—a presence.

Morgan, surprisingly, took it all in her stride. She'd greeted some of the staff by name, introduced herself to others. She didn't act like the snob he'd expected her to be.

'Amazing hotel. I've never been inside before,' he commented as they waited for the light to change so that they could cross the road.

A taxi driver directly in front of them leaned out of his window and gestured to the driver of a limousine to move and a transit van dodged in front of another cab, which resulted in a flurry of horns and shouted insults out of open windows.

New York traffic…crazy. And they drove on the wrong side of the road.

Morgan, adjusted the shoulder strap of her leather bag, looked back at the imposing entrance to the hotel and smiled. 'Isn't it amazing? I love it.'

'A couple of the staff nearly fell over to greet you. Must be crazy, being so well known.'

'Oh, I've been going there since I was a little girl; for tea, for dinner, for drinks—and of course we host the ball here every five years. It's a great place.'

'Great, yes. Safe? I'll be the judge of that.'

Morgan grinned. 'Oh, you and my Mum are going to get along just fine.'

It was a stunning spring afternoon for a walk back to the MI offices.

'Hey, Morgan. Over here!'

Noah turned around and a camera flash went off in his face. He cursed.

'Who's the dude, Morgan?'

A paparazzo, wearing an awful ball cap and a fifty-thousand-dollar camera, popped up. Seeing Morgan's thundercloud face, he lifted an eyebrow in her direction.

'This is why I hate going anywhere with you in New York,' Noah complained in his best petulant tone. 'Nobody ever pays any attention to *me*!'

Morgan looked startled for about two seconds before her poker face slid into place. 'Are you whining?' she demanded, not totally faking her surprise.

'I've been nominated for three BAFTAs *and* I've won a BSA but do I get the attention? No!'

Both Morgan and the pap looked puzzled. 'A BSA?' the pap asked, confused.

'British Soap Awards. And you call yourself a pap? Your UK counterparts would kick your ass!'

'Who are you again?'

It went against every cell in his body, but Noah forced himself to toss his head like a prima donna. 'Oh, that's just wonderful!' He looked at Morgan. 'I've wasted enough time—can we please go now?'

Morgan's lips twitched. 'Sure.'

Noah gripped Morgan's elbow and turned her away.

She sent him an assessing look from under her absurdly long lashes. 'Who *are* you again?'

Noah grinned. 'He's going to spend the next couple of hours combing through photos of Brit celebrities before he realises that he's been hosed.'

Morgan grinned. 'Excellent. Quick thinking, soldier. It won't stop him from printing the picture, but it did stop him from hassling me further.'

'Cretin.'

'Um...is there anyone back home that might get upset by seeing us together? If there is, you should give them a heads-up.'

Who would care if his photo appeared in a society column? It took a moment to board her train of thought. Ah...a wife, partner, girlfriend or significant other. He thought he saw curiosity in her eyes about whether he was involved with someone or not.

'I'll bear that in mind.'

Frustration flicked across her face at his reply. Yep, definitely interested—which was, in itself, interesting.

'Does that happen often? The cameras in your face?'

Morgan jabbed the 'walk' button to cross the road. 'All the time. It's deeply annoying and I wish they'd leave me alone.'

'Well, you *are* one of the world's wealthiest heiresses.'

Morgan's pulled a face as they crossed the famous street. 'Moreau International is wealthy—me, not so much. And I'm not that much of a social butterfly. Much to my mother's despair,' Morgan said quietly as she pulled oversized Audrey Hepburn sunglasses out of her black bag and slipped them on. 'Would you believe me if I told you that I'd rather pound a stake into my ear than attend a soirée or a cocktail evening?'

He wouldn't, actually. Look at her—she radiated confidence, class and poise. She was Morgan Moreau and her blood ran very blue. Unlike his, which was of the cheap Scottish whisky variety.

You're a long way from home, lad. Remember that.

'Then why do you do it?'

Morgan sent him a surprised look, opened her mouth to

reply and shut it again. She dodged around a group of teen-agers looking in a storefront window and looked resigned. 'So, what did you think of Sylvester Cadigan?' she asked a few moments later.

Change of subject, but he'd circle back round to her later. 'He seems competent. He wasn't happy that I demanded a complete and detailed dossier of the security arrangements they put in place for the last ball. He thought that I was questioning his professionalism.'

'Weren't you?' Morgan sent him a direct look with those bottle-green eyes.

'Sure I was. I don't trust anyone.' Especially when it was *his* rep on the line. 'I'll have a lot more questions for him tomorrow, after I've reviewed the dossier he's emailing me.'

'Do you need someone from Moreau to attend that meeting?' Morgan asked as they approached the gold and white façade of Moreau's Gems.

'No. We're going to investigate entrances and exits, look at the surveillance system. I think I can manage without someone holding my hand.'

'Good,' Morgan said, and gestured to the building in front of them. 'MI's flagship store, established in 1925.'

Noah looked at the façade of the jewellery store and swallowed down his impressed whistle. The very wide floor-to-ceiling window was lavishly decorated in a 1920s theme, Noah guessed. There were feather boas, deckchairs with tipped-over champagne bottles, strings of pearls hanging from or wrapped around silver ice buckets. Brooches pinned to berets left in sand, discarded chiffon dresses under a spectacular emerald and diamond necklace. Rings scattered in beach sand.

He hadn't passed the window when he'd arrived that morning, going directly to the separate doors that led up to the MI corporate offices. The window was fantastic and made him want to explore the store and see what other treasures were hidden within. And that, he supposed, was exactly the point.

'Amazing.'

'Riley's work,' Morgan replied proudly. 'She's utterly marvellous at what she does. She changes the display every month and she keeps it top secret. On the first of every month we all traipse down here, along with a horde of shoppers, to see what she's done. It's like Christmas every month.'

'She's very talented.'

'All the big stores keep trying to steal her away but she's loyal to us. Although she and James knock heads continuously. She demands carte blanche to do what she wants with the windows; James demands that she runs her designs past him first.' Morgan waved at a store employee through the glass. 'Having Riley and James in the same room is fabulous entertainment. They argue like mad. I can't wait to hear her ideas on themes for the ball.'

Oh, God, here comes the girly stuff. 'Themes? What's wrong with putting on some fancy duds and showing up?'

'*Pffft!* You sound just like my father. How would that be different from the other sixty balls happening in the city alone? We organise the *Moreau Ball,* not just *a ball.*'

Morgan turned away and headed to the MI entrance further down the street.

'How long will you be in New York for?' she asked, super-casually.

It was the first vaguely personal question she'd asked him and he wondered if he had imagined the flicker of attraction cross her face.

He was pretty sure *his* attraction had flashing neon bulbs and a loud hailer.

'If I get all the information I need I'll try and fly out tomorrow evening. I'll draw up my report, with recommendations and time-frames, then email it to you, James and your mother,' he said as they stepped up to the entrance of MI and the automatic doors swished open.

A guard gestured him to move away from Morgan; he stepped up to sign in at the security desk and to be patted down for the second time that day. Then he followed Morgan through the metal detectors and on to the bank of elevators.

'I'll arrange security clearance for you so you can swipe your way through,' Morgan said as they waited for a lift. 'Where are you staying tonight?'

The lift doors opened and they stepped inside. He could smell her scent, feel her heat, and their eyes collided in the floor-to-ceiling mirrors as he answered her question. 'In the MI company flat in the Lisbon Building, on West and Fifty-Seventh Street.'

'I know where it is. I live in the apartment above it. James, when he stays in town, is above me in the penthouse. My parents are in the family house in Englewood Cliffs.'

Noah shook his head. 'Never heard of it. Where is that?'

'Northern New Jersey, Long Island. About…hmm…ten miles from downtown Manhattan.' The tip of her pink tongue peeked out from between her luscious lips. It made him wonder what that mouth would feel like, how that tongue would taste. Still the same? Better?

'So, I'm single.'

Morgan looked confused. 'Okay. Thanks for sharing that.'

'You?'

Where was this going? 'Um…me too.'

Noah placed his shoulder against the mirror and couldn't believe what he was about to say next. His accent deepened as he spoke softly. 'Do you know something?'

'What?'

'MI have not, officially, signed any contract, so I'm technically not affiliated or contracted to MI yet. I don't think we're going to be working together, because you don't seem to have much inclination or willingness to organise this event…'

'Try *none*—and can you tell my mother that?' said Morgan, then frowned. 'And your point is…?'

'My point is that, technically, I can do this...' Noah stepped closer to her, placed his hands on her hips and dropped his head so that his mouth lined up with hers. 'I want to see if you taste the same.'

Morgan's eyes widened as her hands came up to rest on the lapels of his suit jacket. 'Uh...what are you doing?'

'Kissing you. Because we're both single, we're not linked by business, and because I want to,' Noah whispered against her lips.

They were as soft as they looked, as piquant as he remembered. They softened under his and he lifted his hand to push it under the weight of her hair, encircling her slender neck with his large, hard hand. Morgan whimpered and arched towards him, her hands snaking up his chest to link behind his neck. She stood up on her tiptoes and his tongue darted out to touch hers.

All sense of propriety and sensibility left him as he spun her around and pushed her up against the wall. His hand roamed the backs of her legs and under her butt cheeks as he lifted her hips into his erection, felt her breasts flatten against his chest. She was so hot, so feminine, and she was as into this kiss as he was.

All he could think was, where had he found the strength to walk away all those years ago? He wanted her—now—and considered pulling her to the floor...except that they were in a lift and the doors could open at any second...any freakin' second.

Noah pulled his hands off her butt and yanked his mouth off hers. He backed away—two steps, big deal—and tried to control his heaving breath. Morgan looked no better: shell shocked, kiss-bruised lips, strips of colour across her cheekbones. Anybody who saw them now would know exactly what they had been up to.

Morgan kept her eyes on his face and when the lift opened onto the executive floor, where they'd been earlier, she watched him get out. When Noah realised she wasn't fol-

lowing him he placed his hand on the door to keep it open
and looked back at her.

   'You aren't getting out here?'

   'I'm going up to my studio. Top floor. Bye. And, Noah?'

   'Yeah?'

   'That was one helluva kiss.'

CHAPTER FOUR

MORGAN HAD DELIBERATELY not thought about his kiss all day. Well, she'd tried not to think of his kiss... Okay, truth: she hadn't thought of much besides his kiss!

To put it another way, she'd done little more than stare out of the window for the whole afternoon.

She was glad to be home, glad to be in her apartment where she could drop all manner of pretence and admit that Noah's lips on hers had rocked her to her core. She staggered over to her plump red and white striped couch, dropped her bag to the floor and sank down into its welcoming softness.

She'd kissed Noah Fraser.

Inside her body, every single cell she possessed was in revolt. A picture of the little molecules on a protest march flashed in her head...grumpy little cells each carrying placards with various sayings like: *Do Him!*, *We Want Orgasm Reform!*, or simply, *Sex! Now!*

She couldn't argue.

Her body craved Noah, and she wished she could use the excuse that she'd had none for a while...but she had, surprisingly, not so long ago. It hadn't been 'rock my world' sex, but it had been nice, pleasant, fulfilling and, best of all, very, very discreet.

With her high profile she valued discretion. She just hadn't realised that in that case *discreet* had been a synonym for married. She'd been surprised and shocked when—at the last minute, admittedly—she'd decided to attend a cocktail party she'd said she wouldn't be at. He'd been there with his very beautiful, very thin Venezuelan wife and they'd both known that her tipping a glass of red wine into his lap, accidentally on purpose, had been a poor substitute for her slapping him into next year.

Morgan placed her thumb on one eye and her index finger on the other and pushed.

She had kissed Noah Fraser. Again.

Actually, kissed was totally the wrong word... She'd inhaled him, Frenched him...devoured him. She could still feel his long fingers searing through her pants, the rasp of his two-day beard, the silkiness of his hair as she pulled it through her fingers.

He kissed liked a dream, like a man should kiss: with authority, skill, strength and tenderness. If he made love like he kissed... Morgan whimpered as she felt the pool of heat and lust drop to her womb. She was minutes off an orgasm and that was from just the memories of his kiss!

What if he touched her breasts, slid his fingers...? She didn't know if she was strong enough to survive the experience.

It took her a moment to realise that someone was pounding on her door and she wrinkled her nose. James frequently came by when he was in town and hung out, mostly to avoid their mother nagging him into attending an event. James was as allergic to the social swirl as she was... Was she a bad sister if she pretended not to be here?

She didn't want to talk to anybody. She just wanted to relive Noah's lips on hers, his scent in her nose, the hard muscles she'd felt in his shoulders.

Bang! Bang! Bang!

Bats...

'Who is it?' she demanded in a croaky voice as she pushed herself to her feet.

'Noah.'

The only person she wanted to see and the last person she'd expected. Morgan yanked the door open and there he stood, jacket and tieless, his fist about to connect with the door again.

Morgan put out one finger and pushed his clenched fist down. 'You pounded?'

Noah placed his hands on her hips and without a word pushed her backwards and kicked the door shut behind him.

'Oh, well, just come on in,' Morgan said, trying for sarcastic and hitting breathless.

Noah dropped his hands from her hips and slapped them on his. 'I've been thinking…'

'Did you hurt yourself?' Morgan asked sweetly.

He ignored her. 'On a scale of one to ten, what are the chances of you being in charge of this ball?'

'About…hmm…minus one thousand and fifty-two.'

'Thank God.'

'Why?'

'Because I don't sleep with my clients. Or my colleagues. Ever.'

'You nearly beat down my door to tell me that?'

'Try and keep up, Moreau. I don't sleep with clients.'

Morgan, starting to catch a clue, felt her heart-rate accelerate. 'And since I'm not going to be organising the ball I won't be your client,' she said slowly as she wrapped her head around the implications of those words.

'There you go.' Noah nodded 'I walked away years ago…'

'I know. I was there.'

That was a conversation for another day, and right now she didn't give a foo-foo. She wanted to know if he was here for the same reason she wanted him here. So that they could take that hot kiss they'd shared in the lift to its logical conclusion. And if he was toying with her again she'd have MI Security toss his gorgeous body off the roof.

Noah's eyes glinted blue fire. 'I don't want to spend the next eight years wondering…'

Morgan forced the lust away in order to think. It was hard, but she had to do it. 'You're leaving tomorrow to go back to London?'

'More than likely. There's nothing more I need to do here workwise…at this time.'

'So you are here for one night…one incredible, exceptional, crazy night.' she said, enunciating each word. 'Are we on the same page, here?'

Noah pushed a hand through his messy hair. She could tell it wasn't the first time he'd done that this evening. 'Yeah. Deal?'

Phew! She was going to get lucky! All her little cell protestors threw down their placards, lay down and assumed the 'do me' position. Morgan considered doing the same.

'What do you say, Morgan?'

Yes! Stop talking and take me now, yes! 'Okay, yes, that's a deal.' Morgan started to lift her shirt. She wanted to get naked—*now.*

'Stop. Don't,' Noah said, his voice low and urgent.

Morgan looked at him, fear and fury flashing in her eyes.

Noah took two steps to reach her and clasped her face in his hands. 'Relax, Morgan, I just want to undress you myself. Inch by gorgeous inch.'

'Oh.' Morgan's hands fell to her sides. 'Okay.' She tipped her head back and up, so that she could look into his eyes. 'You think I'm gorgeous?'

'Very—and stop fishing for compliments, Duchess. Try kissing me instead.'

The warmth in his eyes was at odds with his teasing words and Morgan felt her lips tip up in response.

Noah dropped a kiss on her nose before swooping down and covering her mouth with his, his tongue sliding against hers, long and smooth. 'You sure you want to do this, Morgan?' he muttered as his hand palmed her butt.

'Still sure.' Morgan angled her head away so that he could taste her neck, that sensitive spot just under her ear. His broad hand covered her breast and shivers skittered over her skin. Her fingers went to his shirt buttons and soon her hands were on warm male flesh, hot muscle and sexy skin. Her fingers danced over a very impressive six-pack and over the V of hip muscle that descended into his pants.

Noah groaned in the back of his throat as he slowly pulled her T-shirt up her torso, his eyes darkening at the white scraps of lace that covered her full breasts. He pulled her shirt up and over her head and dropped it to the floor, before running a finger along the edge of the lace. 'Pretty.'

Morgan sucked in her breath as his finger touched her hard nipple.

He hooked his hand under the lace and revealed her breast to his sizzling gaze. 'Very pretty indeed.'

His hot mouth covered her as he flipped open her bra and pulled it down her arms. Groaning, he banded his arms around her and, kissing her mouth, walked her backwards to the plump couch, lowering her to the striped fabric when the seat hit the back of her knees. Noah knelt down in front of her and picked up her booted foot, glowering at the knee-high laced boots.

Noah cursed. 'This is going to take far too long.'

'Not so much.' Morgan grinned, reached around to the back of her calf and pulled a zip down the boots. 'Hidden zip.'

'Brilliant.' Noah pulled her boots off impatiently, yanked her pants down her legs, and Morgan giggled when he tossed them over his shoulder. He sat back on his haunches, still dressed only in his suit pants, and looked at her, naked but for a little scrap of lace at the juncture of her thighs. She'd thought she would feel self-conscious, shy, uncomfortable, but how could she feel anything other than sexy and powerful when such a hard-bodied, lusciously masculine man looked at her with pure approval on his rugged face?

Then Morgan saw momentary hesitation in his face, knew that his big brain was trying to crash their party. She was *not*

going to be denied this again… If she had to tie him down—
ooh, that sounded like fun—she was going to have this man
on top of her, around her, inside her.

She leaned forward and placed her hands on his bare
shoulders. 'Stop thinking. I want this. So do you. Tomorrow is another day with another set of rules. Tonight there
is just us…no work, no history, no flaws. Just two people
who want each other. Okay?'

'Yeah.'

Noah nodded and Morgan released her tension in a long
sigh as one hand came up to cover her breast, his thumb idly
brushing her peaked nipple.

'I have a question,' Noah said reverentially, his eyes on
her panties.

Morgan wished he'd shut up and get on with what was
important—i.e. giving her a mind-blowing orgasm—but she
made herself speak. 'Okay…what?'

'Do you still have a Brazilian?'

'Well, soldier, why don't you take a peek?'

Bang! Bang! Bang!

Their heads flew up and turned in unison. Both looked
at the door in utter disbelief.

Noah, his hand in her panties, lifted his eyebrows. 'Expecting someone?'

'Uh—no.' And she wanted them to go away, while she
and Noah got back to what they were doing…which was
him doing her.

And doing her rather well.

Bang! Bang! Bang!

'Morgs, you've got thirty seconds, then I'm using my key.'

'James!' Morgan looked horrified as she pushed Noah
away. 'Clothes—where are my clothes?'

'Scattered,' Noah said as he stood up. 'Get dressed and
I'll delay him.'

'Open the door, Morgan!' James yelled. 'And who is
with you?'

'We're coming!' Morgan yelled back.

'Not in the way we'd hoped,' Noah stated as he reached for his shirt.

'Shut up!' Morgan growled, wiggling into her pants. 'Pass me my bra.'

Noah scooped up her bra, threw it towards her and tucked his shirt into his pants. When she was dressed, he gestured towards the kitchen.

'Got anything alcoholic?' he asked.

Morgan nodded towards an antique drinks cabinet in the corner and flipped open the bolt to her front door.

'James,' she drawled, 'have you ever heard of the concept of calling before you arrive? It's called etiquette. I'm sure Mum tried to teach us some.'

Morgan turned away and walked towards Noah who, being a good Scot, had found her expensive bottle of whisky and was pouring a healthy amount into three glasses.

'Morgan.'

Something in her brother's voice had all the hairs lifting on the back of her neck and arms. She turned around slowly and really looked at her brother. His face was bone-white and there were deep grooves in the lines running down next to his mouth. His eyes, green like hers, were flat and hard in his face.

'What's wrong?' she demanded. 'Is it Mum?'

James lifted up his hands. 'She's okay...really she is, Morgs, but something's happened.'

Morgan sensed Noah's approach and instinctively turned to look at him. He was rolling up the sleeves of his shirt and paused briefly, lifting an eyebrow in James's direction.

'What are you doing here anyway, Fraser?' James scowled.

Morgan figured that James really wouldn't want the answer to that question. Besides, he was a big boy—he could figure it out himself. Instead she gripped the back of one of the kitchen stools and tried to find her voice. 'Mum? What's happened, Jay?'

James gave Noah another tough look before running his hands over his face. 'Mum had an…incident earlier tonight.'

'Define "incident",' Noah said, and all traces of her earlier lover dissipated with those two words. He was in work mode, professional to the core. Serious, smart, and very, very dangerous.

'Jackson was walking Mum through the parking lot of Luigi's—she was meeting Dad for supper—when they were jumped by three guys.'

'Who is Jackson?' Noah grabbed a glass and handed it to Morgan. 'Drink.'

'My mum's long-time bodyguard and driver,' Morgan answered, grateful for something to do with her shaking hand.

Noah passed a whisky to James and gestured for him to carry on.

'Luckily Dad and Henry—Dad's bodyguard—were in the parking lot at the same time and saw what happened. Jackson and Henry reacted quickly—' James released a huff of frustration and sipped his whisky. 'The bodyguards got into it with the kidnappers while Dad picked Mum up— she'd been tossed to the ground in the fight—and bundled her into the car.'

'But not hurt, right?'

'Grazed chin and knees, sprained wrist,' James replied, the muscle in his jaw ticking.

'It's okay, Morgan.' Noah reached over and squeezed her shoulder. 'She's fine. What then?'

'Our guys—especially Henry—are pretty tough, and they managed to subdue two of them. The other got away.' James banged his glass onto the granite counter and splashed whisky. 'Before the police arrived they told them that they were part of a group who were looking to exact retribution for the fact that MI are in the process of reopening an emerald mine in a remote area of north-east Colombia.'

'Why don't they want it reopened?' Morgan asked.

'The mining, trucks and security will interfere with the local drug cartel's transport routes, and with increased population will make the inhabitants less...*reliant* on the generosity of the drug lords. I also suspect they are mining illegally as well,' James replied. 'They said that there are orders out to get MI out of the region.'

'Really blethered on, didn't they?' Noah said, his voice bland.

'Sang like canaries,' James replied. 'Probably because they had a knee in a kidney or a wrist about to be broken.' James folded his arms and rested his bottom against the counter in front of the coffee machine. 'The bottom line is that they want MI out of Colombia and they will do it by...'

Morgan saw his hesitation, the way he looked at her. 'By...?'

'By trying to kidnap someone else. You, me, other executives. I have told the executives in Colombia to be on high alert, and we're doubling their security—and the mine's. But you and I are definite targets. I want protection for you.'

Not again, Morgan thought. She hated having someone follow her around, monitoring her movements...constantly hovering.

'I've called CFT. They will have someone here in two hours. So if you could just stay put until they get here?'

'And Mum? How are we going protect her?' Morgan asked.

'Dad is taking her to the house in the Cayman Islands. You know how secure it is out there.'

'Good. That's good.'

James sent her a direct look. 'Any chance of you joining her there?'

Was he insane? She had jewellery commissions to complete and deliver and—damn it!—with her mother gone someone had to organise the ball. Her mum couldn't do that from the Cayman Islands or anywhere else. She needed to be here—in the city. So who was left to do it? *Me... Damn!*

'I'll take the protection, if you think I must, but I'm staying put.'

James blew air into his cheeks. 'CFT personal protection agents will be here soon. Will you accommodate them?'

What choice did she have? It was at times like these when the reality of how different her life was from that of a normal woman her age became very clear. This was when the fact that she was a Moreau—part of a prominent, hugely wealthy family whose business interests could upset people even a continent away—really smacked her in the face.

That wasn't normal. None of this was normal.

'That's not going to happen.'

Noah made sure that his voice was low, cool and utterly non-negotiable. In unison, James and Morgan turned to him, both pairs of bottle-green eyes surprised and suspicious.

James's eyes hardened a fraction of a second before Morgan's did. He could see that neither of them appreciated him jumping into the conversation but he didn't care. He just folded his arms across his chest and narrowed his own eyes.

'I'm not remotely interested in your opinion,' James told him. 'I'm making arrangements for my sister's protection.'

'So unmake them,' Noah suggested calmly. 'I will act as her personal protection detail.'

'What?'

The siblings' faces registered surprised confusion—and, really, could he blame them? They'd both forgotten that close body protection was what he did, was his business. And wasn't he here for the express purpose of getting his company more MI business? That whole world domination thing?

That was a good reason why he wanted to be the one to protect Morgan, but there were others. Since leaving the unit he'd done lots of close protection before moving into training the new officers. He knew how up close and personal bodyguards had to get to their principals, and there was no way that he was going to allow any CFT hound-dogs that close to Morgan. Fact: the only person that was getting into her personal space in the near future was him.

And, lastly, he wanted the best for Morgan. And he was it. There was a reason why Amanda had offered to double his already stratospheric salary if he stayed with CFT. He was that valuable, that good. Morgan deserved the best, and that was him.

Fact.

'I'm here. I'm already working for you.'

'I didn't realise that sleeping with my sister was part of your duties,' James said, in a very cool, very dangerous voice.

Noah didn't react. Mostly because he felt like punching James on his perfect nose... He didn't like being caught on the back foot, but he had to respect James for calling him on it. If he had a sister he'd do the same. 'Technically, I'm not employed by MI yet—'

'And the chances of you ever getting on the payroll are decreasing rapidly,' James stated.

Damage control, Noah thought, and fast. 'I'm good at what I do, Moreau, and what happened or didn't happen here earlier has nothing to do with that. Morgan and I are both consenting adults and we have an understanding.'

James looked at Morgan. 'Which is...?'

Noah remained silent. Hey, this was *her* brother—if she wanted to explain, she could.

'Well?'

'This has nothing to do with you, big bro,' Morgan stated, lifting her chin.

'You're my baby sister!'

'But I'm not a baby! I can have sex if I want!'

Both James and Noah winced. Noah scratched his forehead and was grateful that *his* brothers didn't require him to monitor *their* social life, because this was the social equivalent of a kick to the groin.

Time to end this conversation, he thought.

'Moving on,' he said briskly, 'and back to the subject at hand. Call Amanda Cope from CFT and ask her who her best bodyguard was—*ever*. I guarantee she'll say me. She hates me, but she's inherently honest. You want and need the best person out there guarding your sister. I'm it and I'm already in place.' It wouldn't hurt to sweeten the pot. 'I'll also give you a fifteen per cent discount on my personal protection fees because I'm doing an analysis on the security for your ball.'

'I don't want you as my bodyguard,' Morgan said.

'Tough,' Noah shot back.

James ignored her and held Noah's stare for thirty seconds before pulling his mobile out of his pocket and scrolling through his contacts. He was actually going to call Amanda! *This could go badly wrong,* Noah thought as James greeted her.

Morgan gripped his wrist and her nails dug into his skin. Even though they were sharp, he still felt heat and lust and attraction rocket up his arm. If he got this right, then acting as her bodyguard was going to be a casual stroll through hell….with a hard-on.

'Noah! Listen to me. I don't want this…*you*!' Morgan hissed.

Noah gently pulled her fingers off him and held her hand in his. 'Shh, I'm trying to listen.'

'I'm going to kill you,' Morgan threatened.

'Later…'

James was speaking. 'I don't need to know why he left, or what you think Auterlochie are doing wrong in the market place, Amanda; this has nothing to do with the rest of your guards or my personal security detail. It's one guy, looking after my sister. I just need to know whether he's good or not.'

When James's frown lifted from a trench to a furrow Noah knew that she had been her customary honest self.

'The best agent you ever had? Well, then…' James disconnected and slapped his mobile into the palm of his hand.

He glared at Noah. 'Fifteen per cent discount on both jobs because you started off by annoying me.'

Ouch.

'Deal,' Noah agreed.

'And keep your hands off my sister,' James growled.

'Basic bodyguarding,' Noah agreed, and he knew that James wasn't sure whether he was messing with him or not. James still looked like a thundercloud so he looked him in the eye. 'I will be completely professional when it comes to Morgan, James. You have my word.'

Besides, her safety depended on it... He couldn't look out for danger if he was eyeing her rack. Or her butt. Or imagining those legs around his hips...

And, although it was a lot less easy to admit, he was grateful for the order to keep his hands off Morgan. She was the type of woman he normally avoided. One of the few women who had caught his interest on more than a physical level. She intrigued him—mentally, emotionally. There was more to her than being the Moreau heiress, the reluctant NYC socialite. And that scared the hell out of him. Besides, he was consumed by his business. He didn't have the time or the energy to give to a woman.

James's shoulders dropped as the tension seeped out of him. Noah knew that James considered his and Morgan's relationship now to be defined, bound by the two contracts he would sign with MI. But to Noah it was written in blood—because he'd given James his word. No agreement written on paper trumped that.

Noah held out his hand and James reluctantly took it. 'Anything happens to Morgan you're a dead man,' James told him.

'Anything happens to Morgan I *will* be a dead man—because that's the only way they'll get to her.'

James's face lightened with appreciation and Noah thought that he might, *maybe*, be back on relatively solid ground with the brother and boss.

'Do either of you care what *I* want or think?' Morgan demanded, her hands on her hips.

Noah shook his head and looked at James. 'Uh…no.'

Noah ducked the glass that she sent flying towards his head and winced when the crystal shattered on the expensive tiles. Maybe he should curb the off-the-cuff honest answers. Good thing she had the aim of a one-eyed toddler or that might have hurt.

And, more importantly, it was a waste of a very fine dram.

CHAPTER FIVE

WASN'T THERE A song about yesterday and troubles seeming so far away? Morgan wondered as she stomped back into her bedroom, kicking her door closed behind her. Yesterday's biggest problems had been how to re-set Mrs Killain's fabulous teardrop diamond earrings into a more contemporary, cleaner setting, whether or not to attend the opening night of the Ballet Belle's new production, and who to take to Merri's wedding.

In one day she'd been slapped with an additional job, an old almost-lover, the attempted kidnapping of her mother, and a new bodyguard whom she wanted to jump.

Bats! On a freaking broomstick!

Right. First things first. Think it through... Her mum's almost-kidnapping. *No, don't think of the 'what ifs'. Push the emotion away...*

Her mum was only superficially hurt, and by now both her parents were in the family jet on their way to a safe place. The house in the Cayman Islands was a well-kept secret and James would have arranged for additional guards for them. Her parents were out of harm's way. That was good news.

Right: problem two. With her mum out of town, someone had to get cracking on organising the Moreau Charity Ball, and it looked as if she was now that someone. How was she going to manage to do that and keep her dyslexia under wraps? The last thing she wanted was to see pitying looks on the faces of Moreau staff…or from anyone else. Unfortunately a lot of people still equated dyslexia with stupidity, and she couldn't just go around announcing, *I'm dyslexic, but my IQ is one hundred and forty-eight.*

No, her dyslexia was *her* issue to deal with, and she didn't require sympathy, pity, or for anyone to make allowances for her. She'd just insist on short reports and plough through them at night…she'd make lists and check and double-check them.

Yay! What joy.

As for her almost-lover and new bodyguard…

She was intensely irritated with Noah on so many different levels that she wasn't sure which one she ranked highest. How dared he and James talk over her head and make arrangements for her safety as if she was a child? Okay, there was a crazy Colombian gang who wanted to use her as a bargaining chip, but Noah could have asked how she felt about him guarding her. She wasn't sure what her answer would have been if he had asked her… *No, I'd rather shag you instead*?

James would have had a coronary on the spot.

Noah irritation number two. How could he switch gears so easily and smoothly? Oh, she was royally ticked that one moment his hand had been tipping her into orgasm and the next he'd been all work—Mr I'll-Protect-Her-and-Give-You-a-Discount!

And on top of that there wasn't any chance of her getting lucky now; she knew that Noah took his duties seriously, and if he wouldn't sleep with her while she'd simply been organising the ball then there was an ice chip's chance in a fat-fryer that—having taken on the role as her bodyguard—he'd even consider picking up where they'd left off earlier.

And, really, did she want to get it on with a man who could flip it on and off with such ease? He had too much control and she too little…where he was concerned.

Well, no more. She was going to stop acting like a tart around him; she'd be cool and calm and collected.

Cool. Calm. Collected. Yep, she could do the three Cs!

'Sulking?' Noah asked from the doorway and she whirled around, her heart slamming against her ribcage. She had shut the door behind her, hadn't she? She was sure she had...

'Heard of knocking?' she demanded, hands on her hips.

Noah crossed one ankle over the other as his shoulder pressed into the doorframe. 'There's broken glass and whisky all over the floor and it's not in my job description to clean up because you lost your temper. Or are you too precious to use a dustpan and broom?'

'Bite me.'

Noah smiled. 'Can't. I promised your brother I wouldn't lay a hand—or lip—on you.'

Morgan felt the bubbles in her blood start to pop.

'You don't have to sound so pleased about it!' Morgan stormed to the doorway and brushed past him, the red mist of temper clouding her vision. What was it about this man that made her long for more? They didn't know each other really, but the fact that he could brush their heat off so easily made her want to throw more than a glass.

Maybe him. Off the twenty-first-floor balcony!

Noah reached out, snagged the waistband of her pants and pulled her to a stop. 'Cool your jets, Morgan, and take a breath.'

'Let. Me. Go,' Morgan muttered through clenched teeth.

'No,' Noah's said.

His fingers were warm against the bare skin of her lower back. She cursed the tremors of attraction that radiated up her spine.

Noah kept his fingers bunched in her pants and moved round so that he was standing, far too close, in front of her. 'Talk.'

More orders? 'Bite me,' she said again

'Stop being a duchess and talk to me. Why are you so annoyed that I am guarding you?'

Morgan folded her arms across her chest to form a barrier between their bodies and glared up at him. 'You didn't want to listen to me when I spoke earlier—why should I bother talking to you now?'

Noah winced. 'Okay, maybe we were a bit heavy-handed.'

'Maybe?'

'Don't push it,' Noah snapped back. 'I wanted to be the one to guard you and I was damned if you were going to talk James out of it.'

Morgan glared at him. 'Because I'm a way to get in with James for you to get more MI business.'

Noah's eyes darkened with fury. 'Stuff the MI business. I did it because no one will protect you as well as I will. Being kidnapped is not a walk down Madison Avenue, Duchess!'

'Uh…'

Noah shoved his hand into his hair and tugged. 'God, you live in this protected little world, kidnapping threats or not. You have no idea what happens to rich people who are 'napped. You want me to go into details?'

Morgan, her temper rapidly subsiding, shook her head.

'So sue me for wanting to keep you safe above wanting to have sex with you!' Noah roared, twin flags of temper staining his cheeks.

He stepped back from her and she could see that he was trying to control his temper. So he had one? Why did that reassure her rather than scare her?

Morgan tipped her head. 'You don't like losing control, do you?'

He lifted a finger and pointed it at her. 'You…you…nobody spikes my temper like you!'

'Ditto,' Morgan replied quietly as green eyes clashed with blue. After a tense, drawn-out silence, Morgan raised her shoulders and spoke again. 'Are you finished yelling at me?'

Noah released a long breath and slapped his hands across his chest. 'Maybe.'

'Okay, then.' Morgan pushed her hair back behind her ears. 'So, I'll go and clean up the broken glass.'

Noah nodded. 'I need to go downstairs for five minutes to pick up my bag and laptop.'

'Well, at least I have a spare bedroom this time.'

Noah rubbed his forehead. 'Does it have an inter-leading door that can stay open?'

Morgan shook her head. 'No.'

'Then we sleep with the doors open.'

'That's not necessary. We have two doormen, and this is one of the most secure buildings in the city.'

'The doors stay open.' Noah walked to the door and when he reached it turned to face her. 'I can't allow myself to be distracted by you, Morgan. Your safety depends on it. So help me out, okay? No propositions, no flirting, no walking around naked.'

There was that arrogance again, and she hated the fact that it turned her on. Determined to show him that he didn't affect her, in any way, she lifted her nose in the air. 'I'll try and restrain myself.'

'You do that, Duchess.'

Noah stood on the balcony in the bright sunshine and looked down into the leafy greenness of Central Park, idly noticing that the park was full of early-morning joggers, cyclists, walkers. Whoever would have thought that Noah Fraser, that angry boy from Glasgow, would be standing here looking at one of the best views in the city. Certainly not him. If he ignored the fact that Morgan was a kidnapping target and he couldn't touch her now, it was one of those stunning spring days.

Spoilt, unfortunately, by his father's voice whining in his ear...on and on and on.

Noah had been sixteen when he'd lost his mother and

taken over the care of his paralysed and violently angry father and his two brothers, six and four years old. And if Michael had been a mean bastard on two legs then he'd become even worse on none.

Noah had cooked, cleaned and cared for his siblings while Michael had cursed God and cursed them. By keeping Michael's attention directed on him, he'd managed to shield the kids from the worst of his verbal and—when he had the opportunity—physical abuse.

Noah had adored those little monsters, and it had nearly killed him when Social Services had moved them into the care of his aunt—his mother's sister. It had been the right thing for them—Michael could have scarred a psychopath—but he'd felt as if his heart had been torn out of his ribcage. Aunt Mary had offered to take him in too, but someone had had to look after Michael; his mam would have turned in her grave if he'd been left on his own.

'You might be poor, Noah, but poor men can act with honour too.'

'What is honour exactly, Mam?'

'It's taking responsibility and keeping your word. Seeking the truth and acting with integrity. Doing the right thing whether people are looking or not. Being better than your circumstances.'

Those words, part of a discussion they'd had a couple of months before her death, had defined the rest of his life.

It was because of those words that he'd endured three years of being belittled, insulted, punched when he was within range, before he'd cracked. It had been the most terrifying moment of his life when he'd come back to himself and realised he was holding...

Don't think about it. Don't remember. Put it back into the cage you keep it in.

He seldom relived the full memory of that horrible day, but every day he recalled how close he'd come to the edge after losing control. The consequences of which would have been far-reaching and…dismal. Catastrophic.

The very next day he'd joined the army—the best decision of his life. Yeah, it had been tough at first, but he'd got three square meals every day and, while he'd been shouted at all the time, he'd realised that it wasn't personal. He'd tolerated it at first and then he'd loved it; it had become, in a way, an inadequate substitution for the family he'd lost.

He'd moved around in the Forces, eventually ending up in the SAS.

Before leaving for Catterick, for his initial training, he'd arranged for a local care-giver to provide Michael with the help he needed: cooking, cleaning and, he'd hoped, occasional bathing. The cost of his care had come out of his meagre army salary, but it had been a small price to pay for his freedom.

He was still paying.

'Your brothers haven't called or visited for over six months.' Michael moaned.

He didn't blame them.

'Useless, both of them. Living with those Robinsons has made them soft… Mike is working as a nancy photographer and Hamish is no better. A bloody chef… Jaysus…and you paid for their education. Waste of money, I tell you. They'll never amount to anything.'

The fact that Mike was working on a respected national newspaper and Hamish was working in a Michelin-starred restaurant as a sous-chef had passed Michael by. With their crazy schedules the brothers didn't spend nearly enough time together, Noah thought. While they emailed and called regularly, they didn't meet often and he missed them.

He had to make more time for them…

'I said I wouldn't take your calls any more if you slag off Hamish and Mike, Michael. Don't do it again,' Noah warned.

He wished he could break the ties with this old man but he was his father. *Family.* Warped, possibly nuts…but you didn't just walk away from your responsibilities. You took what was tossed at you and you dealt with it. But, hell, hadn't he paid enough, done enough, sacrificed enough?

Michael did have one use, though: he was a reminder of how dangerous Noah could be if he lost control. Apart from Michael, the only person who'd managed to push his buttons, to get past the steel lid he kept on his emotions, was that blonde bombshell next door.

And that scared the bejesus out of him. Why her? He'd met a lot of women over the past fifteen years. He'd had successful girls, poor girls, crazy girls and, after he'd finished guarding them, a couple of famous girls.

None of them had made him think of *what ifs* or *maybes*, of moving below the surface stuff of good sex and a couple of laughs. No one except Morgan had ever tempted him to walk into the minefield that was a committed relationship. He'd grown up watching his mother trying to keep her head above water with his crazy, cruel father and he had no intention of being swept away by love and spending the rest of his life trying to get back to shore.

But the fact remained that nobody made him crazy like Morgan Moreau.

Morgan looked up as Noah entered the kitchen via the balcony door. He looked decisive, authoritative, commanding: a natural leader that others looked up to. Dark suit, a white shirt over that broad chest, sombre grey tie hanging loose down his shirt to be tied later.

He also looked freakin' hot!

A shoulder holster held what looked like a very nasty gun...*whoa!*

'When did you get a gun? And from whom?' Morgan demanded, wide eyes on its black matte handle-butt-thingy poking out from the holster.

'It was dropped off early this morning,' Noah replied, heading for the coffee machine and reaching for a cup from the shelf above it. 'Don't worry, I'm licensed to carry a concealed weapon.'

Morgan gripped the back of one of the kitchen counter stools. 'You didn't have one in Cape Town.'

Noah flipped her a look over his shoulder as he tossed sugar into his black coffee. 'Yeah, I did. You just never saw it. Ankle holster when I was wearing jeans. Tucked into the back of my shorts or in my rucksack when we were on the beach. You weren't considered too much of a target so we took the decision not to scare you.'

'Huh.' Morgan wrapped her hands around her now cold coffee cup. Had she been that oblivious? Sure, she'd been nineteen, and blinded by the mammoth crush she'd had on Noah. He could have had a third leg and she would have ignored that too...

So, had anything changed? Morgan wondered. Actually, yes. There was a difference between crushing on him and crushing on his body. This thing between them was purely, utterly, comprehensively physical. *That's my story and I'm sticking to it,* she thought.

'Have they heard anything else about the other kidnappers yet?' she asked. If she knew anything about Noah then she knew that he would be on top of the situation, demanding updates as any came in.

'It's only been twelve hours, Morgan. And they've probably gone underground. New York is a city of eight million people; it's easy to disappear. It'll take time, hard looking and luck to flush them out.'

Morgan sighed and rested her chin in the palm of her hand. 'So, I'm stuck with you for the foreseeable future?'

'Seems like it,' Noah replied equably.

Morgan fiddled with the flat gold chain that rested against her emerald silk top. She'd teamed the shirt with white skinny jeans and black wedges. A black fitted jacket and a scarf would take the outfit from casual to smart. She tapped her finger against her coffee cup and eyed him over the rim. Should she ask this? Hmm, probably not…

What the hey? she thought. *Let's see what he says.*

'So, who's Michael?'

Noah's blue eyes hardened. 'Where did you hear that name?'

'My bedroom window was open; you can hear pretty much everything anyone says out there.'

'I must remember that.' Noah sipped his coffee, leaning against the kitchen counter as he did so. Morgan twisted her lips in annoyance; Noah was an expert in ducking questions he didn't want to answer.

Except that her curiosity was revving in the red zone. There had been something in Noah's voice earlier that she'd never heard before. It had been a combination of resignation, weariness and resentment. A little younger and a lot sad. For a couple of minutes he hadn't been the hard-eyed, hard-assed man who radiated confidence and determination. He'd just sounded like a man with some baggage who desperately wanted to put it in storage.

'And who are Hamish and Mike? Come on—you can tell me…'

'So, what's your schedule like for today?' Noah asked, his expression warning her to back off. Way off.

She wanted to push, to dig a little deeper, a little harder, but it wasn't his grim mouth or ferocious expression that had her hesitating.

It was the misery she saw under the tough-guy expression in his eyes. He didn't intimidate her in the least, didn't scare her one iota, but that flash of desolation had her stopping in her tracks.

'Off-limits subject?'

'Very.'

'Okay.'

His jaw relaxed; his fingers loosened on his coffee cup. 'What are your plans for the day, the week?' he asked again.

'I still have to meet with Cadigan about the security for the hotel, but if you promise to stay in the Moreau building then I won't have to drag you to that.'

'Like you could drag me anywhere,' Morgan scoffed.

A smile touched Noah's lips. 'Want to test that theory?'

He didn't wait for her answer, obviously super-confident that he could and would. Well, he might be stronger than her but he had no idea exactly how stubborn she could be. She'd match her stubbornness against his strength any time.

'Where's your schedule?' he demanded again. 'Diary? Calendar? Or do you have an assistant to keep track of your social life?'

'None of the above. It's all in my head.' She had a diary which she never used, and she didn't need an assistant.

'Publicist? Stylist?'

'Now you're just mocking me.' Morgan sighed and placed her forearms on the table. 'Once a week I call Mum's publicist and find out what functions are on for the next week that I absolutely *have* to attend.'

'How do you know that you've been invited?' Noah asked, pulling out a chair from the table and sitting down. He reached for an apple and crunched into it.

'It sounds ridiculous, I know, but we—the Moreaus— are invited to everything. It's a big social coup to get us to a function...well, maybe not so much my mother; she's a lot more socially active than my dad, James and me.'

Noah looked at his apple, took another bite, chewed and swallowed. 'You guys seem really happy, close...together. A golden family.'

Morgan leaned back and crossed her legs. 'Every family has its own problems, whether they are rich or poor. James spends far too much time alone because he's one of the world's most eligible bachelors. He can't trust a thing that comes out of any girl's mouth because he's convinced that they look at him and see an unlimited credit card, entry into a high social circle and houses all over the world.'

'What should they see?'

A smart, successful man who was lonelier than he needed to be? She wished he'd find someone. She wanted him to be happy. He'd been fabulous growing up...had spent hours—days—years!—helping her to read and write. Holding her when she cried, picking a fight when she needed to work off her frustration. Her older brother, her protector, the best person in her life.

Morgan swallowed and shrugged.

'And you? What's so wrong in your life? You're rich, gorgeous, successful.'

Lonely, isolated, scared that someone will find out that I'm chronically dyslexic and will judge me for it. Terrified to step out of my comfort zone; scared to try and fail... So frightened of disappointing myself and others that I'd rather not try something than run the risk of failing...

Yeah, she was a poster child for a healthy and happy It Girl.

'I have...issues... Don't we all?' See—she could duck the very personal questions too! She twisted the oversized Rolex on her arm and carried on. 'As for my parents—my dad and my mum love each other to death but can't live together long term...'

'But they're trying to revitalise their marriage,' Noah protested. 'She's handing over control to James!'

'James, for all intents and purposes, has been running MI for the past two years. They both pretend that Mum still has her hand in, but in reality James calls the shots and she likes it that way.'

Morgan let out a sound that was half a snort and half a laugh.

'Scenes like yesterday's happen every so often—normally when my mum wants something and doesn't know how else to get it. She wants me involved in MI and she's determined to get me into the fold. Organising the ball is the first step. I guarantee that if I'd refused to do it—as I had intended to—

she would've been back in the city within a week, organising the ball, poking her nose into MI business and driving James crazy. She'd also have been telling me that my dad drove her nuts and there was a reason why they lived apart.'

Morgan scowled at her coffee cup. 'I love my mother dearly, but she's a force of nature and determined to get her own way. If she could find the kidnappers she'd probably say thank you to them for forcing her to leave the country, because now I *have* to organise this damn ball.'

'Harsh,' Noah said, but humour glinted in his eyes. 'Paranoid too. So what's the big deal about this ball? Suck it up and do it.'

Morgan glared at him. 'Easy for you to say. Anyway, back to the original subject…'

'Your social life…or lack of it.'

'Which is about to change because I'm expected to go out and about, promote the ball and get a buzz going. Got a tux?' Morgan demanded.

'Not here.'

'You're going to need one if you intend to accompany me to these functions.'

'And I do.'

'The biggest danger I face there is being bored to death, closely followed by the effects of a rogue margarita or a cheeky cosmopolitan.' Morgan pushed her cup away.

'Listen—and don't shoot the messenger—I need to go as your date,' Noah stated. He lifted a shoulder at the annoyed look on her face. 'Yes, I know what I said…we now have a completely professional relationship. But somehow, miraculously, the kidnapping attempt hasn't hit the papers and the MI PR person and the police want to keep it that way. James has a bodyguard occasionally but you don't. You having one now is going to raise questions that they'd prefer not to answer. So they want us to…*pretend*. James called me this morning and issued the directive.'

Morgan looked at him, caught completely off guard. 'What? You've got to be joking.'

'Trust me, I'd rather just be the bodyguard,' Noah muttered.

Morgan held up her hand. 'So, let me see if I've got this right. We were about to make love, because you weren't—quite—working for MI and I wasn't going to have anything to do with the ball. A one-night deal that worked for both of us which didn't happen because *you* volunteered your close protection services and told me that I am categorically off-limits. And now we have to pretend that we are lovers? Is this a sick joke?'

'Either that or someone has concocted a great way to torture us,' Noah agreed.

Morgan held her head between her hands and closed her eyes. 'This is going to drive me crazy.'

'We can share the padded cell,' Noah agreed.

'Any chance of you resigning?' Morgan lifted her head and looked at him, hope on her face.

'Sorry, Duchess. Not a chance. I'd rather go mad with you than go out of my mind worrying about you if I were off the job. Burying you would also suck.'

Ah, nuts… That was a hard point to argue.

CHAPTER SIX

IN HER STUDIO Morgan squinted at her computer screen and groaned audibly. She was stuck on the first page of the computerised file that detailed all the steps for organising the Moreau Charity Ball and she was already frustrated. Irritated. And, worse, shaking with fear in her designer shoes.

Date of event determined?
Liaise with banqueting manager at F-G.
Determine specific target audience for personal invites.
Objectives set in accordance to mission statement and vision of MI Foundation.
Complete risk assessment; not only to security of gemstone collection but also to brand and customer perception.

Dear Lord, she thought fifteen minutes later, couldn't they use plain English—and why was it so vague? Where was the 'how to do' part of the list? She hadn't even been aware that the MI Foundation *had* a mission statement, and she'd thought the vision was simple: raise and donate money.

Dammit, *this* was why she shouldn't be in charge of anything more complicated than *See Jane Run*.

Her mother had to be taking a new hormone pill to think

that she could organise the ball—never mind her crazy idea of joining MI as Brand and Image Director.

Morgan swallowed the tears that had gathered in the back of her throat. 'I am not stupid,' she whispered under her breath, glaring at the screen. 'I am not stupid. I am *not* stupid.'

Okay, then, why do I feel so stupid?

Morgan heard the rap on her door and looked up to see Noah through the glass window. She tapped the tip of one index finger with the other, indicating that he should use the finger scanner to enter. Two seconds later the door was opening and Noah, *sans* jacket and tie, entered her studio. She hastily slammed the lid of her laptop closed and inwardly cringed. What could be more mortifying than Noah finding out the scope of her learning problems? There wasn't a lot, she decided as he held the door open and looked at the finger scanner.

'Nifty. A retina scanner would be better, but the fingerprint scanner isn't bad.'

Morgan leaned back in her chair and crossed her legs. 'If the scanner worked then I presume that Security gave you everything you needed to negotiate your way through this super-secure building?'

'Yep.' Noah looked around her studio and she winced at the mess.

On the wooden benches across one wall sat her presses and pliers, mandrels and blocks. Hammers, files, more presses. The wall above it was covered in sketches, some finished, of ring and necklace designs, all of which held the name of the client scribbled across it and the price quoted.

She bit her lip and wondered what he'd think of her studio, with its plants and cosy seating, battered bench and industrial lighting. Yeah, it was eclectic and messy, colourful, but it worked for her. She could sit down at the bench and fall into a creative space that exhilarated her and made time fly. Sometimes the designs changed from the original sketch she'd been working to, but she'd yet to have a client complain of the changes made since they were all, invariably, better for it.

She sighed. Designing jewellery was probably the only aspect of her life that she felt completely confident about.

Noah walked over to the bench and squinted at her sketches. She saw his head pull back and presumed that he was reacting to the prices.

'Can I ask you something jewellery-related?'

Morgan's head shot up—not so much at the question but at the note of tension in his voice.

'Sure.' Oh, yeah, his body was coiled tight, and she narrowed her eyes as he pulled his wallet out from the back pocket of his black pants. He flipped it open, dug in a tight fold and pulled out a silver ring with a red stone. He tossed it to her and she snatched it out of the air.

'What's the stone?'

Before looking at the gem, Morgan looked at the setting. The band was old silver, a delicate swirl of filigree, feminine but with strong lines. Lovely, she thought. Really lovely. Whoever had made the ring was a superb craftsman, she decided as she picked up her loupe and walked over to the window. Holding the ring between two fingers, she lifted the loupe to her eye, angled the ring to the light and the breath caught in her throat. Red beryl, one of her favourite stones; very gorgeous and very rare.

'Bixbite or red beryl. Very rare. Very valuable.'

Noah walked over to her, stared down at the ring and frowned. 'Nah, can't be.'

Morgan arched an eyebrow at him. 'You a gemmologist now, soldier? Trust me on this: it's red beryl, my favourite stone…probably set around nineteen-twenty. It would've been mined from the Wah Wah mountain range in Utah.'

'Huh.'

Morgan frowned when Noah reached out, plucked the ring out of her grip with possessive fingers and put it back into his wallet. 'Where did you get it? And why can't it be valuable?' she asked.

Noah just shrugged and Morgan put her hand on his arm to keep him from turning away. 'Answering my question is my price for the valuation.'

'It was my mother's—passed down from my grandmother. I was given it shortly after she died and I've kept it with me ever since. It would be my lucky charm if I believed in lucky charms,' Noah said, with the reluctance of a child facing a dentist's appointment. 'Her family wasn't...wealthy, so I'm surprised that they possessed something this valuable.'

Forget reluctance. Now he sounded as if he was having root canal without pain relief. Noah did *not* like talking about himself or his family. She wanted to ask how his mother had died—and when—but his expression was forbidding. She wasn't brave enough to go there.

'It's very lovely. And it either belongs on a finger or in a safe, soldier,' Morgan said. His expression begged her to change the subject so she relented. 'How did the meeting go with the Head of Security at the Forrester?'

Noah turned away and walked over to the window, looking down on the busy road beneath them. 'I have some concerns that he needs to address. I'll put them in a report and email it to you.'

Morgan wrinkled her nose. 'Can't you tell me instead?'

'What is it with you and your hatred of reading reports?' Noah asked, resting his butt on the window sill. Sunlight picked up deep golden-brown streaks in his hair and created a bit of an aura around his head. He looked like a rough, tough, gun-toting bad-ass angel.

Morgan clenched her thighs together and ignored the pulsing down below. She really had to get her hormones under control. This was beyond ridiculous.

'Uh...reports. They are just a hassle to read.'

Noah's eyebrows pulled together. 'You don't like reading?'

'Not particularly.'

Noah crossed his legs at the ankles and folded his arms. 'So, what *do* you read? *Tatler* and *Heat*?'

And there he went, making assumptions. 'If I don't like going out in society why would I want to read about it? Actually, *snob*, my favourite authors are Jane Austen and Ernest Hemingway. Harper Lee, John Steinbeck—all the classics.'

'But you just said that you don't like to read.'

Yeah, but not that I don't love books. She did love books—devoured them by the bucket load. Except that along with the paperback she bought the audio book, so that she could read along. Truthfully, she frequently just opted to listen and not read.

Morgan flipped Noah a look and saw that he was looking very confused. Right, time to change the subject before he probed a little deeper. She wasn't ready—probably would never be—to tell him about her dyslexia. It wasn't something she believed he needed to know— now or ever.

'I have a list of this month's events that I need to attend,' Morgan said, picking up the piece of paper she'd printed earlier from the email she'd received from Helen. She walked over to Noah and watched as he speed-read the document. Lucky man.

'Ballet? *Uck*. A ball? Save me... But I can handle the art exhibition; I really like Davie's work.'

'You know Johnno's art?' Morgan asked, surprised.

Noah folded his arms and tipped his head. 'Now who's being a snob? I went to his exhibition in London. Fantastic.'

'Do you have any of his pieces?'

'Duchess, I could only afford to look—not buy.' Noah drawled. 'Maybe one day. Anyway, my partner can't find my tux in my flat. I think it's at the cleaners and has been for the last six months.'

'You left your tux at the cleaners for six months?'

'I've been in and out of the country and I forgot, okay? My tux wasn't high up on my list of priorities. So when do

I need a tux by…?' He looked at the piece of paper she'd handed him. 'Crap! Tonight?'

'Yep.' Morgan laughed at his look of horror.

'Jeez, give me some warning next time.' Noah grumbled.

'Hey, *I'm* the one who has to decide what to wear, do my hair, shoes, jewellery. Make-up. You just have to put on a tux. Big deal,' Morgan shot back. It took work to look like the Moreau heiress people expected to see. A designer dress, stunning salon hair, perfect make-up. The right jewels for the right dress.

'Yeah, but I have to get a tux and get into character…you know…work out how I'm going to pretend to have the hots for you. It's a difficult job, but someone has to do it.'

She was so distracted by the humour dancing in his eyes that it took a while for his words to make sense. When they did she blushed from head to toe and her fist rocketed into his bicep. It made all the impact of a single drop of rain falling in the desert.

'Jerk!'

'Was that supposed to be a punch?' Noah asked, and grinned as she shook her fingers out. '*Wuss*. So, are you going to stay here for the rest of the afternoon while I go and buy myself a tux? Can I trust you to do that?'

Morgan shoved out her lower lip. 'Maybe.'

Noah's face hardened and his mouth flattened. 'You leave this building without me and there will be hell to pay, *Duchess*.'

Morgan pulled in a huge breath. She didn't mind him calling her Duchess, but not in that cold, bossy voice. 'I'm not an idiot, *soldier*. I won't leave until you get back. And if you weren't being such a jerk I'd tell you that if you went across the road to that very famous store over there—' she looked past him and pointed her finger towards the renowned corner shop '—in the men's department there is a salesperson named Norman. In his sixties, bald. Tell him I sent you and he'll sort you out with what you need.'

Morgan was surprised when Noah leaned over and placed his cool lips, very briefly, on her temple. 'Thanks.'

Morgan watched him walk away, and he was at the door before she realised that kissing her was out of bounds too. 'Hey, no kissing!'

Noah tossed her a grin that had her blood pumping. 'Just practising for later. Do some work, Duchess, you have a ball to organise.'

Morgan wrinkled her nose. Sad, but true.

Being a bodyguard pretending to be her latest conquest sucked, Noah thought a couple of hours later in the ball-room of the Park Hyatt, half listening to Morgan as she talked 'ball' to a society matron with a pigeon-egg-sized diamond in her wrinkly cleavage. Doing it with a twitching groin made the situation a thousand times worse.

It was her dress, Noah decided, taking the smallest sip of the glass of whisky he'd been nursing for hours. Moss-green and strapless, it fell from her breasts and skimmed her hips. At first glance it almost seemed demure, slightly bohemian, off-beat. Then she moved and the long slit to one side ex-posed most of a slim thigh and his blood belted south. That thigh was smooth and silky, and even sexier because noth-ing covered it except perfect, perfect skin.

Funny and interesting... She was a killer combination. Bright as anything too. She picked up sarcasm, nuances, innuendo and irony, and he could read humour, annoyance and interest as the emotions flickered into her eyes. She'd been fêted all evening and he now realised what she'd meant when she'd said that the Moreaus were welcome everywhere. Conversation stopped when she joined a group, male tongues fell to the floor, women smiled and tried not to look jealous, and she was constantly and persistently asked about the ball.

'How do we get personally invited to the ball?'

'How much do you think we have to bid to secure a ticket?'

'Do you have a theme yet?'

'Do remind your mother that we served together on the blah-blah-blah committee and worked together on the meh-meh-meh project.'

Didn't these people have any pride?

But Morgan just smiled, changed the subject and moved on to another group if the person was too persistent.

'Don't you think so, Noah?' Morgan asked, and Noah sent her a blank look.

Morgan's lips lifted, and he knew by the gleam in her eye that she knew his thoughts were miles away.

'That this year's ball is going to be utterly amazing?' she clarified.

'Uh...yes...'

Wrinkly cleavage leaned across Morgan and showed him far more of what he didn't need to see. 'So, how long have you two been dating?' she demanded.

Oh... Noah looked at Morgan and waited for her to answer.

'We've known each other a long time, Vi,' Morgan said softly, her eyes on his mouth.

The twitch turned to an ache.

'Well, he's a lot better that a lot of those other creatures you've dated, Morgan.'

Morgan's lips lifted with amusement and she tipped her head. 'You don't think he looks too bodyguardish? All "don't mess with me or I'll wipe the floor with your face"?'

'Sitting right here,' Noah reminded them.

'Is that a bad thing?' Vi demanded. 'He *does* have very nice shoulders.'

'Mmm...and a nice butt.'

Noah glared at Morgan and lowered his voice. 'Morgan... enough.' As in *Behave yourself or I'm going to retaliate*.

He knew that she'd got the message because her eyes narrowed at his challenge. Noah looked up at the waiter who had placed the next course in front of her and saw the other plate he held—*his* plate!—wobble as his young knees buck-led under the force of that smile. He couldn't blame him, so he snatched at his plate before the mini-cheese platter ended up in his lap.

Morgan smiled at him before turning to another man on the table. Noah sneaked a look at his watch…it was after eleven already, and people were table-hopping or getting up to dance.

Maybe they could leave soon…

'Morgan, my honey, it's so nice to see you. We don't see enough of your pretty face at these events.'

Noah lifted his eyebrows at the plummy tones and looked at Morgan. The man had his eyes fixed on Morgan's chest and his manicured fingers rested on her shoulder. Noah, re-acting instinctively, slid his arm around the back of Morgan's chair, knocked his hand away and cupped her slim shoulder in his hand. Soft, silky…

Morgan turned slightly, leaned back towards him, and he caught a whiff of her hair: citrus and spice. Lust rock-eted to his groin.

'Morgan…' It was another voice demanding her attention.

Give the girl a break, Noah thought, turning to look up into the face of an elderly gentlemen who looked as if he could do with more than a couple of sessions in the gym and a year on a low-carb diet. Manners pulled them both to their feet and Noah watched as Morgan's knuckles were kissed in an old-fashioned gesture.

'It's so wonderful to have you here at the benefit, Mor-gan, and the room is abuzz with the news that you are taking over the reins of the charity ball from Hannah,' he gushed.

'Well, not quite, Alexander,' Morgan hedged. 'Mum is still in charge.'

'As you know, this ball aims to raise money for scholar-ships for deprived students in the poorer areas of our great city.'

Noah did an inner eye-roll at his pompous words, but Alexander wasn't quite done with the speechmaking.

'Our foundation was a recipient of a portion of the money raised from your ball five years ago, so I thought that you could do a short speech about the ball. In a couple of minutes? Wonderful.'

Smooth, Noah thought, he hadn't given her much chance to refuse.

'And who is your escort, Morgan?' Alexander held out a hand to Noah, which Noah shook. 'Alexander Morton—of Morton's International…banking, dear boy.'

Even when he'd *been* a boy he'd never been anyone's 'dear boy', Noah thought as he shook the soft, fishy hand and resisted the urge to wipe his own on his pants leg.

Morgan made a couple of standard responses to Alexander's queries after her family, but he could hear the tension in her voice, could see it in her suddenly tense jaw.

She was seriously and completely rattled. He wondered why.

Pretend they are naked, Morgan told herself as she gripped the podium and looked out over the expectant faces below. *No, don't think they are naked, you're feeling traumatised enough. They are cabbages…they are dolls…*

They were people waiting for her to fall flat on her face. She wasn't going to disappoint them…

Dear God, she thought, sucking in air, this was her worst nightmare. The room whirled and swirled. She couldn't find the words, didn't know what to say…what was she doing up here? She didn't—couldn't—do speeches, especially unprepared ones.

Her knuckles whitened and she gnawed on her lip as the murmurs from the restless crowd drifted up towards her.

Help. She pulled her tongue down from the top of her mouth and managed to find a few words. 'Um…good evening, ladies and gentlemen.'

Bats! What now? She couldn't think, couldn't find the words...*frozen, there* was the word. She was utterly iced up.

Then Morgan felt movement next to her and a large, familiar hand rested on hers and gently lifted her stiff fingers from the podium.

'Good evening, ladies and gentlemen, my name is James Moreau. Thank you for allowing Morgan and I a few minutes to tell you about the Moreau Charity Ball.'

James... She hadn't even known that he was at the ball tonight. Rescued again. Morgan briefly closed her eyes and felt the panic recede. *Thank you, my darling big brother.*

Morgan squeezed James's hand in gratitude and linked her fingers in his as she listened to his fluid off-the-cuff speech. He soon had his audience laughing and eating out of his hand...the smooth-talking devil.

'I owe you,' she said under cover of the applause. 'I was bulldozed up here.'

'Then bulldoze back, Morgs,' James retorted. 'What would you have done if I wasn't here?'

'I don't have a clue,' Morgan admitted as he led her back into the clapping fray. She tugged her hand out of James's and wiped her glistening forehead with the tips of her fingers. 'I need to visit the ladies' room.'

James gave her a critical look. 'You're as white as a sheet. You need lipstick and a shot of brandy.'

Morgan placed her hand on her sternum as her stomach churned. 'At the very, very least,' she agreed.

On the edge of the dance floor Morgan took the hand that Noah held out and stepped into his arms. He felt solid and strong...and best of all *real*. Just for a moment she wished she could place her head on his shoulder and rest awhile. This was why she hated the social swirl so much; the party-girl cloak she pulled on to get her through evenings like this weighed her down. She felt exhausted and such a fraud.

'So, what was that about?' Noah asked, his voice some-where above her temple.

'What?' It was a stupid question because she immediately knew what he was referring to.

'James rushing to your rescue? I never imagined that you would be at a loss for words. You looked like your knees were knocking together.'

Why did he have to be so perceptive? James had assured her that they'd pulled it off, that most people had thought she was just waiting for him to join her at the podium, but if that was so then why had Noah noticed her nerves? And if he had noticed how scared she was, who else had? Oh, bats, did that mean that everyone was laughing behind her back? Sniggering?

She stepped back, lifted her hands and tossed her head. 'I want to go home now,' she told him, pleased that her voice sounded reasonably steady.

'Why?' Noah demanded.

Because I feel like a fool... 'I have a headache.'

'Not buying it, Duchess.'

Noah placed his hand on her hip, picked up her hand again and pushed her back into the dance. She followed his lead automatically and wished that the floor could swallow her whole. She felt hot with humiliation and cold when she thought about what was being said behind her back.

Morgan made herself meet his far too discerning eyes and didn't realise that her pulse was beating a hard rhythm in the base of her throat.

'Noah, I simply don't care whether you think I am talking rubbish or not. I'm done with this evening, I'm done talk-ing and, frankly, I'm done with you too. I need some space and some time alone.' She shoved a hand into her hair. 'Can you, for once, just act like a bodyguard? Can you stop talk-ing, keep your opinions to yourself and just leave me the hell alone?'

Noah's head jerked back and his implacable remote mask dropped into place. 'Certainly.'

He gestured to the edge of the floor and kept a respectful distance as they walked back to the table. His voice was devoid of emotion when he spoke again. 'If you'll give me a minute, I'll just organise the car.'

Morgan felt a wave of shame as she watched his broad back move away. She'd taken a hunk of his hide because she was feeling vulnerable and mortified. But mostly because she knew that he was strong enough, secure enough, to take it.

It was the perfect end to a long and terrible evening.

'Where's Noah?' Riley asked, dumping her files on the coffee table in Morgan's lounge. Sinking to the silk carpet, Riley took a grateful sip from the glass of white wine Morgan handed her.

After nearly a week of living together, in the non-biblical sense, Noah had finally realised that she was safe alone in the apartment by herself, and every day after work he left her to make use of the state-of-the-art gym and indoor swimming pool within the apartment block, Morgan explained.

'So, how does it feel to be living with a man?' Riley asked, kicking off her heels and crossing her legs.

Morgan sat down on the edge of the couch opposite her and half shrugged. 'Weird, actually.'

'And are you still in separate beds?'

Morgan glared at her. 'What do you think?'

'Judging by that killer look, I'd say your hormones are on a constant low simmer.'

'You should know,' Morgan replied.

As Riley was the only person outside of her family who knew about her dyslexia, Morgan was the only person who knew that Riley had fallen in love with James at first sight and had never quite managed to tumble out of it. She covered her feelings towards him by acting like a diva artist whenever he was around.

'He wants me to do an underwater theme for the windows next month,' Riley grumbled, reading her thoughts.

'Why?'

'Because he's just been scuba diving in Belize and was "blown away" by the coral reefs. I told him that I needed personal experience to do a theme like that.'

Knowing that would never have been the end of their conversation, Morgan tipped her head. 'And he said what in reply?'

'He used that super-sarcastic tone of his and said...' Riley tossed her bright red hair and lowered her voice. '"Then why don't I just take you with me next time?"'

'Jeez, I just wish you and James would get your stuff together, find a room, get it on and then get on with living happily ever after.'

'Like he's ever going to see me as anything other than your best friend.' Riley tapped her nail against her glass. 'Oh, wait—are you talking about us or about you and Noah?'

'Both of us. Although that won't happen to Noah and I.'

'Why not?'

'This thing between us is purely physical, Ri. We don't discuss anything personal.'

'Why not?' Riley repeated.

Morgan shrugged.

'Don't want to venture further down the rabbit hole?' Riley asked.

Morgan looked up at the ceiling.

'I think he might be the one guy who'd understand the dyslexia, Morgs.'

'I doubt it,' Morgan replied, leaning back and putting her feet up on the coffee table. 'He's a perfectionist: highly driven and ambitious. Besides, Noah and I...it would be just about sex—about this crazy chemical reaction we have to each other.'

'You like each other.'

'We don't *know* each other.' Morgan took a huge sip of

wine and rested the glass against her cheek. 'Anyway, I'm not looking for a relationship with Noah. Sex—yes...have you seen that body?'

'Shallow as a puddle.' Riley grinned before leaning back on her hands. 'To be honest, I think you don't tell the guys you date about the dyslexia because you hope they'll bail.'

'Oh, come on!'

'Oh, you *so* do. How many times have you met a nice guy? You date and then you sleep together. Things go really well until he starts picking up that things are a bit off. That you don't write down a message properly or you get the directions to a restaurant wrong. You don't explain and you retreat.'

'I don't do that,' she protested, even though she knew she did.

Riley gave her a hard look. 'Noah isn't like that, Morgan. He wouldn't hold the dyslexia against you.'

'Back away, Ri,' Morgan warned. 'Nobody understands until they have to live with me. You know what I'm like. Sometimes the reading is easy; other days I can barely read my own name. I would drive him crazy in six months. I'm inconsistent, and that's annoying and confusing. Some days I can take on the world; sometimes I can't even read simple instructions. I hate those black holes, and if *I* find them difficult to deal with how would my lover feel?'

'You should at least respect them enough to give them a chance to try.'

'I respect myself too much to be constantly putting my heart out there to possibly be broken,' Morgan retorted.

'Are you feeling comfortable in your little self-protected world?' Riley asked sweetly.

'Yes, thank you very much! The world expects something from "the Moreau heiress" and being chronically dyslexic isn't part of the package.'

Riley mimed playing the violin and Morgan threw a cushion at her head. Riley groaned as it hit her wine glass and wine splashed all over the table.

Noah walked in through the front door as the wine glass fractured and broke. He looked from Riley to the broken glass and back to the spilt wine before finally looking at Morgan. 'Duchess; are you throwing a temper tantrum because another of your subjects has disagreed with you?'

CHAPTER SEVEN

AFTER ORDERING PIZZA from their favourite pizzeria Morgan called James, checked that he was home and told him to come down and share their meal. He arrived with two bottles of her favourite wine: a Merlot from their winery in Stellenbosch.

'One for you and one for Riley, my two favourite wine-o-holics,' he said, depositing them on the kitchen counter. 'Hey, Ri.'

'James.'

James yanked open a drawer and pulled out a corkscrew. 'Started on the designs for my underwater window yet?'

'Yeah, I've scheduled it in for...*never*. Does that work for you?' Riley replied as she opened a cupboard door and took out four glasses.

'You *do* remember that I sign your paycheque, don't you?' James retorted.

'Then fire me; I'll pick up a job with Saks or Bergdorfs with one phone call. And they'll double my salary,' Riley replied in the same genial tone. 'Actually, why don't *you* double my salary and I'll consider staying?'

'Okay, I'll schedule that in for...*never*. Does that work for you?' James dumped some wine into her glass and handed it over. 'Cheers.'

'Bite me.' Riley took the glass and stomped over to the lounge, resuming her seat on the floor next to the coffee table.

Morgan rolled her eyes at Noah, who was sitting at the dining room table, his laptop in front of him, a glass of whisky at his elbow. He was dressed in battered faded jeans and a casual cotton shirt and his feet were bare. Sure, he was a sexy man, but he was also a man who didn't hold a grudge. They'd had a rocky day or two following her outburst at the ball and now they were back to being friends.

But it would be so much more fun if he was hanging around because he wasn't being paid to do so.

'Is anyone doing anything about finding those kidnappers?' she demanded, putting her hands on her hips and glaring at James.

'Only the NYPD, our own security and another private investigation firm I hired to find them. That not enough for you, Your Majesty?' James pushed a glass across the granite counter in her direction.

'Your Majesty? That's even better than Duchess!' Noah smirked.

'Call me that and you're dead,' Morgan warned him. 'Riley and I need to talk about themes for the ball,' she said, hastily changing the subject. 'Would you like to be part of that conversation?'

James and Noah exchanged identical horrified looks. 'Sports channel?'

'Hell, yeah!' Noah agreed, and followed James to the smaller second lounge. It held a large-screen TV and two comfortable couches.

He spoke over his shoulder to Morgan. 'Call me when the pizza arrives. I'll go down and get it. Do *not* leave the apartment.'

'Blah-blah-blah,' Morgan muttered in reply, and pulled her tongue at his back.

'I saw that!' Noah called, without turning around.

Morgan pulled her tongue again at his reply.

'I saw that too.'

Grrr.

* * *

'Treasure ship, masked ball, burlesque, the Russian Court, Vegas,' Morgan listed through mouthfuls of pizza. They were surrounded by files of fabric samples and Riley's rough sketches. Morgan was curled up into the corner of the couch, Riley was still in place on the floor, and James sat in the chair behind her, his long legs on either side of her slim frame. Noah sat in the other chair, a glass of gorgeous red wine on the table next to him.

It could be a group of friends in any other lounge in any other city in the world, just hanging out and eating excellent pizza. It was so normal, and he was still coming to terms with how normal the Moreau siblings could be. Yes, James ran a multi-billion-dollar corporation, and Morgan had an unlimited trust fund, but nobody, seeing them now, would guess that.

'I like the burlesque theme. Bold, opulent, sexy.' Morgan said dreamily. 'We could have various stages scattered throughout the ballroom with different acts to the same singer. Burlesque routines, circus acts, acrobatics…'

'Strippers?' James asked hopefully, and Noah smiled.

Morgan sent him a cold look. 'Would you like me to get disinherited? Or to be dead because our mother has killed me? Anyway, we could have models dressed in corsets and thigh-high stockings and masquerade masks, all wearing Moreau jewellery.'

Noah's head whipped up as her words made sense in his head. 'Not a chance,' Noah told her. 'No live models wearing any jewellery.'

'Why not?' Morgan demanded. 'It would be brilliant…'

'It would be stupid,' Noah replied. 'You're adding a human element that can be exploited; nobody but me and your curator gets access to those jewels.'

'But…' Morgan started to protest.

Noah stared her down. 'My reputation, my rules. Remember?'

'*Arrgh*. We'll discuss it another time,' Morgan said.

She was like a dog with a bone, Noah thought. Stubborn and wilful. Why did that turn him on? Then again, everything about her turned him on.

Riley leaned her head on James's knee and yawned. Noah noticed that James lifted his hand to touch her hair, thought about it and dropped it again. Oh, yeah, there was definitely something brewing with those two. Some day the lid on their self-control would pop and they'd find themselves in a heap of trouble.

Just like he would…

Living with Morgan was killing him. Not sleeping with Morgan made every day a torture. And he knew that she felt exactly the same way. He saw it in the way she looked at him; her eyes would deepen with passion and her breath would catch in her throat and he'd know…just know…that she had them naked and up against the wall. When…*if*…they finally got to do this, New York would experience a quake of significant proportions.

Unfortunately his problems with Morgan went a lot deeper than he'd ever thought possible. Right down to the core of who he was.

He'd never had such a physical reaction to anyone, *ever*. Why it had to be Morgan he had no idea. She could send him from nought to sixty in a heartbeat and have him laughing while she did it. And that was the reason why he had to keep his distance from her—physically, emotionally. He would never give anyone control over him.

She had the ability to make him lose it; definitely in bed, possibly emotionally and, most terrifying of all, in anger. She really knew how to push his buttons. What if they had a fight and he was pushed too far? What would he do? Who would he become? Would he revert to that angry feral boy who'd stood in that grotty kitchen and held a knife to his father's throat? The kid who had watched as droplets of blood beaded on that stubbled neck, enjoyed the sour smell of fear that permeated the air? The Noah who had seriously considered ending it all…the insults, the abuse, the weight of responsibility that had landed on his shoulders?

That person scared him: the uncontrolled, wild, crazy person he could be when he allowed emotion to rule. He was currently locked in a cage and sensible; controlled Noah kept guard over him. And sensible Noah could only do that if he stayed away from emotional complications. Like Morgan.

He couldn't afford to let Morgan in, to allow his guard down, to be the person he could be…

It wasn't going to happen with her or with anyone else.

'What do you think, Noah?' James asked him.

Noah pulled himself back to the conversation. What had they been talking about? Were they still discussing the theme of the ball?

'Burlesque sounds good,' he said lamely.

Morgan laughed as she tossed the crust of her slice of pizza into the empty box. 'Where did you go? We're talking about going home for the wedding. We're leaving in a fortnight.'

Noah sat up, ran a hand over his lower jaw and slapped his brain into gear. 'Back up. Going home? Where? What wedding? Why didn't you tell me about this?'

Morgan pouted. 'I'd hoped this would be over by then.'

'I asked you for a detailed schedule of everything you were committed to in the foreseeable future. Why wasn't this wedding on it?' Noah demanded. How was he supposed to protect her if she didn't keep him informed? Honestly, it was like dealing with an octopus with twenty tentacles.

Riley looked at James. 'I think this is our cue to leave so that they can fight without an audience.'

'I do not fight,' Noah growled. 'I negotiate.'

'No, he orders. He just tells me what to do and expects me to stand there and take it,' Morgan agreed, unfurling her long legs. She stood up, kissed Riley and then James on their cheeks as she said goodnight.

James hugged her, stood back and brushed her hair from her forehead. 'You're my sister, and I know you can be a pain in the butt. Don't make this harder for him than it has to be. Don't forget to tell him about Johnno's exhibition tomorrow night, and the Moreau Polo Cup Challenge on Saturday at Liberty Park. Then we go to the wedding in Stellenbosch in two weeks' time.'

'Got it.' Morgan cut Noah a glance, and when she spoke again her attitude was pure factitiousness. 'Noah, we have an art exhibition tomorrow night, a polo cup on Saturday and a wedding in Stellenbosch in two weeks' time. Put them on the schedule.'

Noah's face promised retaliation. *Bring it on, soldier.*

Noah bade Riley and James goodnight and waited until the door had closed behind them before turning back to Morgan. 'Stellenbosch, South Africa?'

'Yep,' Morgan answered flippantly.

He didn't respond—just waited for a further explanation for why she hadn't thought it was important to fill him in.

Morgan tapped her foot in irritation. 'The kidnappers are in New York. I'm going on the private jet to my home town, where I know everyone, to a wedding that has more security than the Pentagon.'

'Why?'

'Merri, my friend, is marrying into a very influential, very connected political family. Security will be tight.'

'And where will you be staying?'

'At Bon Chance—our house on the family farm. Vineyard.' Morgan picked up the empty pizza boxes and the bottle of wine. 'Grab the glasses, will you?'

'Good plan, since you might throw something when I tell you that I'm coming too.'

Morgan's shoulders stiffened at his sarcasm. 'I told you— it's not necessary. James and Riley will be staying in the house, as well as James's protection people, and the wedding will be secure. The kidnappers are here in New York!'

Noah walked over to the dishwasher, yanked it open and dumped the glasses inside. 'I'm going, Morgan. Until the threat to you is neutralised I'm sticking to you like a shadow. Now, I can either go as your date-cum-bodyguard or just as your bodyguard. I'm equally comfortable with either. Your choice.'

'That might be a bit awkward.'

Awkward... He didn't see why. Morgan turned away and Noah frowned. Strangely it took him a minute to make the connection. 'You've asked someone else to be your date?'

Morgan nodded. 'Yes. '

Noah managed to keep his face implacable but inside he fought the urge to punch his fist into that shiny, fancy fridge. 'Who is he?' he said through gritted teeth.

'A friend. An old friend.'

'That's not all of it,' Noah pushed.

Morgan whirled around. 'Do you want the details? Okay, then! He's an ex-boyfriend who I'm still fond of. He's also a friend of Merri's and we keep in touch. Satisfied?'

'Not by a long shot,' Noah snapped, forcing down the green tide of jealousy swelling up his throat. He made himself stop thinking about Morgan in someone else's arms—dancing, laughing, flirting with another man. This was business... What would he do if it was only business?

He breathed deeply and forced himself to think the problem through. 'If the security at the wedding is as good as you say it is, then I'll deliver you to the wedding and pick you up when you're done.'

Morgan's eyes sparked with anger. 'What if I want to sleep over?'

Was she trying to kill him? Seriously? 'That's not going to happen, Duchess, unless it's with me.'

'Big words from a man who won't even let himself touch me unless he's pretending to be my date!' Morgan hissed.

Give me strength, Noah prayed. 'I gave your brother my word.' He pushed the words out through gritted teeth.

'Well, there's no law that says I have to wait for you, soldier. So if I want to sleep with someone then I will.'

'You bloody well won't!' Noah gripped her arms with his hands. His eyes glittered and he could feel his temper licking the edges of his tongue. 'What would be the point, anyway? You'd be imagining it was me the whole time.'

'You arrogant—' Morgan placed her hands on his chest and shoved.

Annoyed beyond reason, he gripped her shoulders with his big hands and fought the urge to shake her. Instead he slammed his mouth onto hers and yanked her up against his body. He placed one hand low on her back, fingers spread out over her backside, and his other hand held her head in place. Her made-for-sin mouth was hot below his.

Noah could feel her mentally fighting him, her mind cursing him, even though he knew that her body wanted this as much as he did. Pure orneryness kept her mouth clamped shut, and her slim body was rigid with shock. Dropping his hand from her head, he stroked her arm, urging her to relax, and eventually both their tempers ebbed away under the sensual heat they created.

He knew that Morgan was trying to fight the temptation to wind her arms around his neck and fall into his body. It seemed so long since he had touched her, and yet it was like yesterday. She was toned, yet fragile, hot and sexy.

Noah concentrated on applying exactly the right amount of pressure and kept his hands still. He kissed the corner of her mouth and slowly worked his way inwards, nibbling and caressing as he went along. His tongue flicked and retreated, coaxed hers out to play. He sighed in triumph as she groaned and opened her mouth to his. Instantly his tongue accepted her invitation and curled around hers while he pulled her close.

Unable to resist this a moment longer, Morgan threw her arms around his neck and moulded her body against his.

Plunging her fingers in his hair, she wound a calf around his and pressed herself up against his hard frame.

Long, luscious, passion-soaked minutes later Noah knew that he'd reached the point of no return—that if he carried on for another minute he would be lost, doing exactly what he wouldn't allow himself to do. It took every ounce of his legendary self-control to wrench his mouth from hers, to step back, to meet her eyes.

He moved his hand so that he held her jaw, brushed his thumb over her full bottom lip.

Morgan spoke, frustration in her passion-smoked voice. 'You're really stopping?'

He nodded and jammed his hands into the pockets of his jeans so that he didn't reach for her again. 'Really am.'

He watched as Morgan's smoky eyes cleared and confusion replaced heat. 'I don't know why, or how, you can even *start* it. Especially knowing that you're not going to take it further.'

All he knew for sure was that he was a masochist, a glutton for punishment. He could try to explain—temper, jealousy, they were all factors—but his biggest motivator was that at that moment he hadn't been able *not* to kiss her.

Noah watched as the last spark of fight went out of Morgan. She took a step towards him, dropped her head and curled her fingers into his shirt.

'I hate this,' she said in a small voice.

And he hated the thought that he—this crazy situation between them—could make her sound so small, defeated.

He resisted the urge to pull her into his embrace, to soothe her. He didn't do touchy-feely so he just stood there, trying to ignore the surge of protectiveness that threatened to knock his feet from under him.

'Hate what?' he asked quietly.

'This…all of this. The bodyguarding. Being so attracted to you, not being able to touch you, to get it…*you*…out of my system.' Morgan rested her forehead in the middle of his chest. 'It's horrible... I don't like feeling this out of control.'

'I know.'

He had to touch her, so Noah rubbed his hand up and down her spine. It was killing him too. His hand moved up between her shoulder blades onto her neck and under her head. He pulled the hair at the back of her neck and gently tipped her head back.

'I gave my word...it's important to me that I keep it,' he said, looking down into her mesmerising eyes.

'I know. Dammit...I *respect* that. I just don't *like* it!'

Tell him something he didn't know. He didn't consider it a lazy day on the beach either.

Morgan stepped back, wrapped her arms around her waist and tipped her head to one side. 'I wish I could yell at you—scream. I want to act like a diva and fire you and stomp away and throw things.'

'You can if it makes you feel better,' Noah offered on a small smile. He had to hand it to the lass: he never knew what she was going to say or do next—she was *never* predictable.

'Consider yourself yelled at and fired,' Morgan said on a long, tired sigh. She looked at him. 'Any chance of you saving me from the loony bin and actually staying fired?'

Uh, no. That wasn't happening. A cold shower would happen, but him leaving...? 'Nope.'

'Didn't think so,' Morgan grumbled as she left the kitchen.

'This is it.'

Morgan looked out of the window of the cab and frowned when she didn't see the swish art gallery she'd expected to see. She looked across the road but there was nothing in the immediate vicinity except a closed dry cleaners and a rather grubby-looking diner. The other side of the street held a pawn shop and a strip club.

Where were they?

'Are you sure this is three-six-two?' Morgan asked.

Dark eyes glared at her from the front seat of the cab. 'You said six-three-two, lady. Three-six-two is uptown.'

Morgan closed her eyes at his harsh voice.

'Take it easy, buddy,' Noah said in a calm voice.

'She said six-three-two,' the cabbie insisted.

'You'll still get paid, so relax.' Noah laid a hand on her knee. 'Where's the invite, Morgan? Let's check the address.'

Morgan felt heat infuse her cheeks and rise up her neck and was grateful for the early evening shadows in the cab. She flipped open her clutch bag and pulled out the invitation. She glanced at the numbers and thrust the invitation towards the taxi driver.

'Six-three-two,' she muttered.

The driver glanced down at the invitation and shook his head in disgust. 'Jeez, lady, whassa matter wi' you? This says two-three-six!'

'Back off, man, she made a mistake,' Noah said in a hard, cold voice, and with a final huff the driver whirled around in his seat, slammed the car into gear and abruptly pulled off into the traffic.

Morgan licked her lips and waited for Noah's probing questions as they retraced their route. How was she going to talk her way out of this?

'Sorry.'

Noah shrugged and leaned back in his seat. 'You're tired…we both are. Mistakes are easy to make. Ignore him.'

Noah looked out of the window and Morgan glanced at his masculine profile. That was it? Where were the questions, the demands for an explanation, the mockery for making such a basic silly mistake? Why didn't he follow up on the cab driver's question, probe a little deeper?

Did he know and not care? Did he suspect and was distancing himself from the problem? Was he just simply not curious or, even scarier, didn't he give a hoot?

At the gallery a little while later, Morgan was still thinking of his non-reaction in the taxi and how she'd managed to dodge the explanation bullet. She stepped away from the group of people who were talking around her, looking past Johnno Davie at Noah, who was standing in front of one of Johnno's massive paintings. It was one of the few non-abstract paintings on display: a nude on a bed in a symphony of gold and cream, with hints of blush. It didn't need the tag *Sophie—Naked and Relaxed*; anyone with half a brain could tell exactly what Sophie had been up to before Johnno had decided to capture her on canvas.

Morgan wondered if Sophie knew that her…*ahem*…satisfaction was part of Johnno's latest collection.

Morgan lifted her glass of wine to her lips and watched Noah as he stared at the canvas. He was perfectly dressed for an art exhibition in NYC: dark jeans, a white button-down shirt and a black jacket.

Noah's immense self-control scared her—she admitted it. He'd been as swept away by their kiss last night as she had and yet he'd managed to pull back, to step away. She thought that she could be naked and he could be inside her, a fraction off orgasm, and if he decided to jam on the brakes he would. Oh, Morgan knew that he was self-motivated and determined, and that he kept his own counsel—that his natural way of interacting with people was to be brief and succinct, focusing on practicality above emotion—but even so sometimes she thought that there was another Noah trying to escape. A Noah who was a little more relaxed, a little impulsive—someone who was desperate to have a good time—but every time that Noah stepped over the line he got slapped back into his cage.

It was almost as if Noah was scared to let himself feel…

What had happened to him that had made him wary of… of…*himself*, really?

Morgan stared at his broad back as she walked over to him. She playfully nudged his shoulder with hers. 'I'm sorry about the confusion with the address earlier. I got the numbers mixed up.'

'Mmm…as I said, it happens.'

Morgan folded her arms across her raspberry-coloured poncho dress. It was a favourite of hers, with a one-shoulder neckline with a batwing sleeve. The dress fell to mid-thigh and she wore it with nude spiked heels and long, dangly earrings made from garnets.

'Listen, I need to say something. I'm sorry…about that kiss last night.' Noah held his hands in the pockets of his jeans and straightened his arms. 'I shouldn't have…'

'Here we go again… Noah, for goodness' sake, we are adults! We shared a kiss, and if you didn't have the control of a Tibetan monk we would've done much more.'

Noah glanced around as her voice lifted in frustration. '*Inside* voice, dammit!'

'What *is* the problem? And don't give me that garbage about not being professional and the promise you made to my brother.'

'Why don't you talk louder? I don't think the people at the far end of the gallery heard you,' Noah muttered as he gripped her arm and pulled her closer to the painting. 'And I *did* make a promise to your brother…'

Morgan turned her back to the room and looked at the painting. 'The old promise-to-my-brother excuse.' Morgan lifted up her arms and then fisted her hands. 'You know what…? Forget it! I've never chased after a man in my life and I am *not* starting with you!'

Noah muttered an expletive and raked his hand through his hair. 'Morgan…no, don't walk away.' He waited a beat before talking again. 'I've worked really hard to establish my business and, no matter how stupid you think it is, people *will* look to see how I conduct myself with you and they *will* judge that. I need to be seen to be professional and competent.'

Anyone would think she was asking him to do her in Central Park as Saturday afternoon entertainment. She saw him fiddle with his collar… He did that, she realised with a flash of insight, when he was feeling uncomfortable or when he was hedging. Or flat-out lying.

'That might be part of it but it's not the whole truth. The important truth.' Morgan looked him in the eye. When his eyes slid right she knew she had him and he knew that she had him. So he did what all men did when they were caught out: he changed the subject.

'Okay, say we have this hot fling. And afterwards, Duchess, what then?'

Morgan frowned and lowered the glass she'd raised to her lips. 'What do you mean?'

'We scratch this itch and then what happens? What are you expecting?'

Morgan took a sip of wine and considered his question. What did she expect? What *could* she expect?

What could she give?

After a moment's thought she came to the only logical, practical conclusion she could. 'I don't expect anything, Noah. You don't seem to be the type who needs or, frankly, wants a relationship, so if we did find ourselves in bed I'd expect nothing, because I know that you have nothing to give me.'

Besides, I'm too scared to take the chance of loving someone, being found unworthy, getting my teeth kicked in.

'You make me sound like a robot,' Noah muttered.

Morgan suspected that if he opened those cage doors he'd be anything but robotic—he'd be fearless and passionate and unstoppable. But right now he did have elements of the mechanical about him. Except when he was kissing her...

Morgan reached out and tapped his chest with one French manicured finger. 'You need to have some fun, Fraser. Lighten up.' Maybe they both did. 'The world won't fall on your head, you know.'

'You sound just like Chris. And my brothers.'

Whoa...stop the presses! Noah Fraser had volunteered some personal information! 'You have brothers?'

'Well, despite what you think, I wasn't cloned in a Petri dish,' Noah said, his tone grumpy.

'Younger? Older? Where are they? What do they do? Are they married?'

'Jeez, mention one little thing and I get a million questions.' Noah stopped a waiter, asked for a mineral water and rolled his eyes at her obviously curious face. 'Two much younger brothers, twenty-three and twenty-one. A sous chef at a London Michelin-starred restaurant and a freelance photographer who sells to several national newspapers. Neither are married and they both live in London. Satisfied?'

'Not nearly. Are they also buttoned-down, controlled and restrained?'

Noah took his mineral water from the tray presented to him. He looked past her shoulder to a place that was somewhere in the past. 'No, I stood as a shield so that they didn't turn out like me.'

And what on earth did he mean by *that*? Morgan opened her mouth to ask but he gestured to the painting and forced a small smile onto his face. 'It looks like a multiple to me.'

It took Morgan a minute to catch up, and when she did she cocked her head. 'Maybe it was a really good piece of chocolate.'

'Dream on,' Noah scoffed, before he fell serious. 'I have to admit I love this painting. I'd buy it in a heartbeat if I had enough cash floating around.'

Morgan leaned forward and peered at the tiny, tiny price in the corner of the tag. Holy bats…that was a lot of money—even for her. Morgan stepped back and looked at the painting again…she agreed with Noah. It was a sensational piece of art: fluid, sexy, happy. She could see it on the wall above her bed…

Sophie had had a really fine time, Morgan thought on a smile. But maybe it was time to give her a bit of privacy and get her out of the gallery.

'Let's go home,' Morgan said impulsively.

Noah looked at her, surprised. 'It's not even eight-thirty yet. And we were going to that cocktail party at the Hyatt.'

'I just want to go home, have a long bath and an early night. I want to drop the cloak. I need to be me tonight.'

'Sorry?'

Morgan waved his questions away. 'Ignore me. So, what do you think?'

'Hell, no, I *want* to stick around and make small talk with people I don't know.'

Morgan laughed at his sarcasm, handed her glass over to a passing waiter and inclined her head towards Johnno. 'I just need a quick word with the artist.'

'I'll be waiting at the door. Make it quick, Duchess.'

CHAPTER EIGHT

BACK IN MORGAN'S apartment, Noah glanced to the other side of the couch and smiled when he saw that Morgan had shuffled down, her head on a cushion, eyes closed and her sock-covered feet touching his thigh. Noah placed his beer on the side table and glanced at his watch; it was just past nine-thirty.

Standing up, he walked over to her and gently removed the earphones she'd plugged into her ears earlier. Her hand still loosely clutched her iPad and he pulled that away too. She liked listening to music while she read, she'd told him earlier, and wasn't that keen on TV, so he was welcome to watch what he liked.

Noah heard sound coming from the earphones and lifted one bud up to his ear. Instead of music, a low, melodious voice filled his ear. Frowning, he tapped the tablet and quickly realised that Morgan was listening to an audiobook, Ken Follet's *Pillars of the Earth*—a book he'd read years ago and thoroughly loved.

Noah had barely any time to react as Morgan launched up and tried to whip the tablet from his grasp. Her fingers skimmed the tablet as he moved it out of her reach.

'What the hell are you doing?' she demanded. 'Give it back!'

'Calm down, Duchess. Anyone would think you're hiding something here.' He grinned. 'Erotica? How to be an It Girl manuals?'

Morgan just glared at him, reared up and tried to take the device again.

'Oooh, temper. Now, I definitely know you're hiding something!'

'Stop being an ass! Give. It. Back!' Morgan shouted.

'Nah...I want to see what you're hiding. Bad music? Sappy movies? Your addiction to Angry Birds? Badly written cowboy books?'

'Noah!'

Noah tapped the menu and scrolled through her books. Frowning, he looked at the books on the device—there were many, and they covered a wide range of genres and subjects. But they were all audiobooks. He scrolled up, backwards, checked her files, and eventually realised that there wasn't a single e-book anywhere on the device.

'Only audiobooks, Morgs? Are you too lazy to read?'

He saw the colour seep from her face and her eyes fill with hurt. He frowned, knowing that he had misstepped badly, but he wasn't sure why his comment had had such an effect on her.

'Just give it back, Fraser,' Morgan said in a small voice.

Pride and defiance now flashed in her eyes, but underneath he could still sense her embarrassment and her vulnerability.

'My reading habits have nothing to do with you.'

'Reports are a hassle to read.'

'Can you give me a verbal report instead?'

He rubbed his jaw. Could it be...was it possible...that Morgan couldn't read? No, come on...*everyone* could read in this day and age, right? And she was so smart. There had to be another explanation.

Morgan sat back down on the couch and stared at the floor. Instinctively he balanced himself on his haunches and pushed her hair behind her ears, gently stroking the tender skin behind her ear.

'Do you have a problem with reading?'

She didn't reply and wouldn't meet his eyes. He hated to ask but he needed to know. 'Can you read...at all?'

Morgan jolted up and looked at him, her eyes wide and horrified. 'Of course I can read! Not well or fast, but I can read!' She stumbled to her feet, walked across the carpet and turned to look at him, her expression belligerent. 'Go on—say it. I dare you.'

'What?' Noah asked, genuinely confused.

Morgan placed a hand on her cocked hip and lifted her chin. 'I've heard them all, Noah—all the wisecracks, all the jokes. *She's got the looks and she's got money—what does she need a brain for? She's so thick that she'd get trapped on an escalator if the power went out. Quickest way to drown her? Put a mirror on the bottom of the pool—*'

'That's enough. Stop.' Noah held up his hand and kept his voice even. Who had said such brutal things about her? Whoever it was deserved a kick up the ass. It would be his pleasure to do it. 'Come and sit down, lass,' he said eventually, his voice gentle.

Noah waited until Morgan had perched on the edge of the couch, her bottom lip between her teeth. He resumed his position on his haunches in front of her.

'I'm not going to make fun of you, Morgan, but I do need to understand.' Noah rested his hand on her knee. 'Dyslexia?'

Morgan sighed. 'Chronic.' She glared at him again. 'But know this: I am *not* stupid, Noah. I have an exceedingly high IQ. I am *not* a dumb blonde.'

'Anyone with half a brain can see that.' Of course she wasn't stupid. She had the vocabulary of a Scrabble master and a brain that could tie him up in knots. 'You're probably one of the smartest women I know.' He ran a finger down her chest, skimming over her T-shirt between her breasts. 'This body is a work of art, but this—' he lifted his hand

and gently tapped her temple with his finger '—what's in here scares the daylights out of me.'

Morgan's eyes lightened in pleasure and a whole lot of relief. He smiled as a peachy blush spread over her cheekbones.

'It's just another part of you and you have absolutely nothing to be ashamed of. So, who was the loser?'

'The loser?'

'The guy who threw those comments at you. Name? Address? Name of the cemetery you want his dead body dumped at...'

Morgan's small smile disappeared quickly. She stared at her hands. 'First lover—a couple of months after you. I convinced myself that I loved him. He told me that I couldn't take a joke. He was verbally abusive but I gave him the ammunition to hurt me. Since then I've kept the dyslexia to myself.'

Noah uttered an obscenity and rubbed his hand over his face. 'Seriously, Morgs. Give me his name and I can cause him a world of pain.'

Morgan placed the tips of her fingers on his cheek. 'I appreciate the offer, but he's not worth the jail sentence.'

'You're no fun,' he complained mildly. She thought he was joking yet he'd happily use some of his nastiest unarmed combat skills on any man who so much as looked at Morgan the wrong way.

Noah sighed, looked at the shelves and shelves of books lining the walls surrounding them. How hard it must be to look at them but not be able to use them. 'So tell me about the paperbacks, Morgan.'

'I have a print copy for every audiobook I have. I used to try and read along, but the narrators read too fast so the words swim and dance and I get a cracking headache by page five.'

Noah unfurled his long length and sat down on the couch next to her. 'You don't need to keep it a secret, Morgan.'

Morgan dipped her head so her forehead touched his collarbone. 'Yeah, I kind of do.' She snuggled closer to him and his arm went around her slim back as he leant back against the couch. 'I'm not just a little dyslexic, Noah, I'm really bad. And some days I'm terrible.'

'Is that why you were so reluctant to organise the ball?'

'Yeah. It's too important for me to fail at it...and I don't want to disappoint my mum. It's hard, trying to live up to the Moreau name. The family are all terribly well educated—they all have two degrees; my dad has three—and I scraped through college by the skin of my teeth, taking twice the amount of time anyone else did.'

'You just told me that you are not stupid,' Noah pointed out. 'Surely they know that too? And as educated people don't you think that they admire you for trying something outside of your comfort zone? I know I do, and I only have one degree.'

'They keep telling me that. Maybe I'm just scared of disappointing myself.' Morgan tipped her head back to look at him. 'What do you have a degree in?'

'Business and history,' he admitted reluctantly. 'Love history. It's still my favourite subject.'

Morgan sighed happily. 'Then I must show you some of the old diaries from the first Moreau prospectors—the brothers who discovered the mines. They were wacky and colourful and quite unethical.'

'I'd love to read them.' Noah gently pulled her ponytail. 'You look exhausted, Duchess. Why don't you go to bed?'

'I'm tired, but I probably won't sleep,' Morgan admitted. 'My brain is whirling.'

'You need something to de-stress you.'

He stood up, scanned the bookshelves and found what he was looking for. Yanking the book from the shelf, he sat down again, stretched out his legs and tucked Morgan back into his side.

'If I remember correctly, you were just about to start chapter six.'

Morgan's eyes were as big as saucers. 'You're going to read to me?'

Her eyes filled with emotion and Noah winced. Oh, jeez, maybe he'd insulted her by offering to read to her. Maybe she hadn't heard a thing he'd said earlier about how smart he thought she was...

'I'm sorry. Look, it's not because I don't think you're... Bad idea, huh?'

Morgan's fingers on his lips dried up his words. 'No, it's probably the sweetest thing any man has ever done for me.'

Noah grimaced. 'Sweet, huh?'

'Yeah—very, very sweet.'

Noah pulled another face. 'Yuck, that's not how any ex-Special Forces soldier would like to hear himself described. Now, will you please shut up? I'm trying to read here...'

Noah handed Morgan a glass of champagne and, from behind his dark sunglasses, cast a look down her long, long legs. Every other woman at the Moreau Polo Cup Challenge was dressed to the nines, but Morgan, in tailored white shorts that ended at mid-thigh, and a white and green gypsy top revealing her shoulders and messy hair, looked every cent of the millions of dollars she was supposed to be worth.

Earlier, just because he was curious, he'd timed her to see how long she took to get ready. Ten minutes. He'd known women who took ten minutes to put on mascara. He really, really liked the fact that she didn't fuss.

And that she still managed to look super-hot.

'Do you ride?' Morgan nodded to the field and the charging, sweaty thoroughbred horses.

Noah snorted. 'Not many stables where I grew up.'

'Where *did* you grow up, Noah?' Morgan asked.

Well, he'd cracked the door open... Noah sighed, thought about ducking her question, remembered that she'd shared her biggest secret with him and told himself not to be a jerk. 'I grew up in Glasgow, in a bad part of town.'

Morgan kept her eyes on the field. 'Did you have a tough childhood?'

'Yeah.'

And that was all he was prepared to say. Besides, it was all such a long time ago. He was with a gorgeous girl at a fancy event and he didn't want those memories to corrode his enjoyment of this stunning spring day.

'So, tell me about your date for the wedding,' he said casually.

Noah frowned as a tall, slim Spaniard in a white polo shirt and jodhpurs streaked with dirt leaned over the fence, placed his hands on Morgan's shoulders, kissed her on both cheeks and then lightly on the mouth. Morgan laughed, patted his cheek, and conversed with him in passable Spanish. Their conversation ended with another flurry of cheek-kisses and, *dammit*, another brush of her mouth.

Noah resisted the urge to reach for his gun.

'Friend of yours?' Noah asked, unaware of the bite in his voice.

'Juan Carlos. Playboy. Polo player. He taught me to tango,' Morgan said in a dreamy voice.

'That had better be all he taught you,' Noah said in a low mutter.

Morgan's mouth twitched. 'A *duchess* never tells. Andrew—how *are* you?'

Kiss, kiss…flirt, flirt…

Noah looked at his water and wished he could ask for a whisky as she dived into conversation with yet another polo player who'd ambled up to greet her. She would drive any sane man to drink, Noah decided as a bead of sweat ran down his spine.

He wanted to remove his navy linen jacket but he wouldn't. He didn't want to raise questions about why he was wearing a sidearm to one of the most elite social events in the city. He was on constant alert at functions like these;

there was no security, people came and went, and anything could happen.

Unfortunately no one was close to finding the kidnappers and the tensions at the mine remained unresolved; in fact they had just got worse, and they'd all been warned to be on high alert.

James had flown out to Colombia to try and resolve the dispute, and a posse of CFT personnel were guarding his back. That was why James wasn't at the Polo Challenge and why Morgan would be handing out the prizes to the polo players—and no doubt kissing eight or more fit, rich, polo-playing numbskulls.

Oh, joy of joys.

Polo Boy number two walked away and Morgan pushed her glasses up into her hair and fanned her programme close to her face. 'What were we talking about?'

'Your date for the wedding.'

He caught the tiny wince. 'Oh…him.'

'Yeah, *him*. Want to come clean, Morgs?' Noah asked, a smile hiking up the corner of his lips.

Morgan placed her champagne glass on a tall table and sighed. 'I lied. I was trying to wind you up—'

'You succeeded,' Noah mumbled, thinking that it was the thought of her sleeping with someone else that had ignited his temper and led to the urge to kiss her, brand her, possess her. 'So, he's fictional?'

Morgan scuffed the grass with the tip of one of her apple-green wedges. 'Mmm.'

Noah slowly pushed his shades up into his hair and looked down into her face, idly thinking that he loved the handful of freckles on her nose that make-up never quite seemed to cover. 'Do you lie often?'

'No. Only when I'm pushed beyond reason.'

'I'm very reasonable.' Noah protested.

'Pfft.' Morgan rolled her eyes.

Noah rested his forearms on the fence. 'I've been thinking about something you said the other night at the art exhibition.'

'What did I say?'

'You said something about the cloak you'd like to drop... what did you mean by that?'

Morgan took a little while to answer. When she did her voice was softer, vulnerable. 'Don't we all have cloaks or armour that we drag on to protect us from the circumstances we find ourselves in? Something we do, or say, a way that we act to get us through whatever it is making us feel uncomfortable? A cloak that covers all our insecurities, the real us that we don't want people to see?'

Noah gave her words some thought. 'Your flirty, charming party-girl persona...that's your cloak? The bright, bubbly, charming flirt? The real you is quieter, more introspective... dreamier.'

Morgan cocked her thumb and extended her index finger. 'There you go. And you only know that because we've been living in each other's pockets. And your implacable and remote face that discourages all conversation is yours. Your can't-touch-me mask is supposed to discourage anyone from wanting to dig deeper, to get to know you a bit better.'

Noah couldn't help wincing. He did do that—did keep everyone at an emotional distance.

He rubbed his hand across his face. 'You've come closer than anyone—ever.' He caught the flash of fear in her eyes, saw her take the tiniest step backwards. 'And that makes you uncomfortable,' he added.

'Wary.' Morgan looked out at the busy field. 'We can hurt each other... No, let me rephrase that. You can hurt me...if we ever change from friends to lovers.'

'*If* we change—and I'll try not to, Morgan—you have to know that I wouldn't be able to promise you for ever. All I can say is that I would be monogamous, that I'd treat you well as long as it lasted—be it a week or months. But at some point our paths would split and I'd be back in London, doing what I do.'

'I know.'

'If you want more from me than a fun time in bed then maybe we should just quit while we're ahead. Stay as *Duchess* and *Soldier*.' Noah folded his arms and hoped she couldn't see how much he hoped that she didn't choose option B. Because that would, well...*suck*. 'So, what's it to be?'

Morgan played with the emerald and diamond studs in her ears. 'I'm probably going to regret this, but we do have unfinished business between us.' She sent him a coy look and the humour was back in her eyes. 'By the way, are you into threesomes?'

If he'd had anything in his mouth he would have sprayed her, or choked. As it was, he felt he had to pick his jaw up from the floor. 'What the...? Who? What? Are you being serious?'

'Well, by the time this situation is resolved my friend Sophie from the gallery will be sharing my bedroom. I thought I should warn you.'

Noah felt his heart slow down to a gallop as her words started to make sense. 'Morgan, you nearly gave me a heart attack! You bought Johnno Davie's painting?'

'I did.' Morgan smiled. 'It'll be delivered when the exhibition is over.'

They turned as someone called her name.

'Ooh, I'm being summoned. I need to go and hand out the prizes and flirt with the players.'

Noah couldn't help the possessive hand he put on her back, the growl in his voice. 'Keep it to a minimum, sweetheart. Remember that I'm armed and dangerous. I'd hate to have to shoot one of them.'

Morgan touched her lips to his cheek and whispered in his ear. 'Just to be clear, soldier, Sophie is the closest you are ever going to get to a threesome that involves me.'

He could live with that. Heck, he was happy fantasising about a 'onesome' with her.

A few days later Noah heard the lobby phone chime and got up from the dining table where he had been working on staff scheduling—his normal Auterlochie work hadn't stopped, so he worked from Morgan's dining room table or the MI conference room. He picked up the phone.

'Hey, Patrick.'

He'd become good friends with the doormen—both ex-cops, with excellent service records—and Patrick's voice boomed in his ear.

'I have Miss Riley here, plus two guys carrying mannequins and stuff. Can I send them up?'

'What? Hold on, let me take a look.' Noah walked backed to his laptop and pulled up the live feed from the lobby. Patching into the apartment building's security feed had been his first task when he'd moved into the apartment weeks ago. True enough, there was Riley, chatting to two young guys holding two life-size mannequins.

Why was Riley bringing mannequins up to the apartment? He wasn't sure he wanted to know.

He went back to the phone and thought for a minute. The situation in Colombia had descended into near anarchy and threats were flying. Hannah and Jedd were still not allowed to leave their house in the Cayman Islands. He'd spent twenty minutes on the phone with James earlier that day and they'd agreed that Morgan should curtail her social obligations. So now he had to try and keep her in the apartment as much as possible...which would be a butt-pain, because resisting the urge to haul her off to bed was now on a par with him splitting the atom.

'Put Riley, the mannequins and the bags into the lifts and send the men home. I'll help her unload on this side,' Noah told Patrick, and went back to his laptop.

When the doors had closed on Riley and her plastic companions, he called to Morgan.

'Hey, Riley will be here in twenty seconds with some life-size dolls. Why?'

'Yay!' Morgan said, coming from the bedroom and towel-drying her wet hair. She draped her towel over the back of the couch and Noah fought the urge to ask her to put it back in the bathroom. He was obsessively neat, courtesy of the army, and she was a slob. Her untidiness drove him nuts.

Noah opened the front door, and walked over to the lift. As the doors opened he grabbed one mannequin and tucked it under his arm. 'Friends of yours, Ri?'

'Ha-ha.'

Riley handed him a duffel bag and he walked back to the apartment and dumped them in the hallway. He went back for the second dummy and Riley followed him, carrying the second smaller bag.

He watched, amused, as Morgan and Riley sat the mannequins—expensive ones, with arm and leg joints—on the colourful couches. Morgan squealed and immediately reached for the duffel bags. Thinking that they probably needed alcohol for whatever they were up to, he went into the kitchen and opened a bottle of wine. When he returned with two glasses in hand his eyes widened at the rainbow-hued lingerie now scattered over the coffee table. No, not lingerie…sexy-as-sin burlesque costumes. Beaded and decorated corsets with fluffy skirts and feathers. And there were some without skirts, skimpy, with oversized clips to attach to stockings.

His mind instinctively imagined Morgan in one of those outfits and he cursed when his pants stirred. High heels, stockings… He thought of the survival courses he'd taken in the SAS. Nothing sexy about those…

Thoughts of sex bolted away and his heart ran cold as Morgan picked up a duffel bag and a treasure trove of jewellery rained down on the table. Emeralds, rubies, diamonds, gold…so much gold. Pearls, sapphires… If Morgan had liberated the MI jewellery collection from the walk-in safe on the fourth floor—and he knew she had access to do that—he was going to freakin' kill her. Slowly, and with much pleasure.

'Oh, my, look at his face.' Morgan chuckled as she held Riley's arm and doubled over with mirth. 'Quick, grab your mobile and snap a pic. We'll call it *Nervous Noah*.'

'In a moment you are going to be *Mortuary Morgan*,' Noah replied as he approached them. He handed over the wine and picked up a necklace with a canary-egg-size diamond hanging off a gold clasp. He examined the stone, didn't see the deep sparkle and reflections a diamond that size should have and his blood pressure dropped. 'Paste. You nearly gave me a heart attack!'

Morgan grinned. 'They are all paste, and it's fantastic that we have them to play with.'

Noah held up his hand. 'I think *I* need wine for this…hold on.' He went back to the kitchen, brought another glass and the bottle back and perched on the arm of the chair. 'Now, what are you doing, exactly?'

Morgan crossed her legs Indian-style and with her wet hair and make-up-free face she looked a teenager. Like she had when she was nineteen, when she'd stolen his breath from his lungs. Nothing much had changed there, Noah thought.

'Okay, so you said that we can't have live models showing off the collection…'

'Categorically not,' Noah said.

'So, Riley and I want to place mannequins on round plinths throughout the ballroom, each of them in a gold burlesque birdcage *à la Moulin Rouge*. We'll put them in provocative poses—on swings, bending over, et cetera. The mannequins will all be dressed in burlesque costumes— sexy corsets and stockings, high heels and masks.' Morgan picked up a handful of lace and stockings. 'The great thing is that we have paste copies of all the jewellery collection and Riley has the mannequins, so we can experiment before we make a final decision.'

'Why?' Noah asked.

Morgan, who was examining a pearl necklace, frowned up at him. 'Why what?'

'Why do you have paste copies of the jewellery collection?' Noah asked patiently.

'Oh…a Great-Something Moreau needed to raise some cash to buy another mine and he handed over the collection as collateral. He didn't want it known that he was cash-strapped, so before he did that he had paste copies made of the jewellery. He got the jewels back but ever since, whenever the family acquired a new piece, a copy was made. Riley and I played with these as kids.'

'Huh. So they are exact replicas?'

'Absolutely.' Riley draped a long string of pearls around her neck. 'So what do you think of our birdcage idea, Noah? Can the real jewels be secured?'

Noah thought for a minute. 'I want an area between the guests and the cages, about a foot and a half, where we can put a pressure plate so that if anyone steps up to a mannequin it'll trigger a silent alarm.'

Morgan looked at Riley. 'We can do that.'

'I want in on the design of the birdcages. I want to put laser beams between the rods, so that if anyone breaks the beam it'll trigger an alarm.'

Morgan lifted a bustier of white silk embossed with silver beads and waved his security issues away in order to play with the colourful garments and the fake bling.

'Okay… Look at this one, Ri! Such a gorgeous red, with black inserts, and the feathers make a teeny-tiny skirt. If we teamed it with those striped thigh-highs…dynamite! Let's dress a mannequin in an outfit, choose the corresponding jewellery and mask, photograph it and do the next one. And where on earth did you find all these outfits?'

'A burlesque show that lasted six weeks on Broadway.

Apparently the costumes were fabby, the performers not so good.'

Noah put his wine down, stood up and picked up a mannequin, looking it over.

'What on earth are you doing, Noah?' Morgan asked.

'Seeing where we can place a motion sensor so if the jewels are moved once they've been put in place it will trigger—'

'A silent alarm.' Morgan and Riley chorused.

'Smartasses.' Noah dropped the mannequin and thought that he badly needed some testosterone before he started to grow breasts. 'I'm going to watch some manly sports on ESPN. Have fun playing with your grown-up Barbies, girls.'

Noah's hand drifted over Morgan's hair as he passed her. He wasn't sure if she noticed because she was frantically scrabbling through the piles of multi-coloured, beaded and luscious garments to look for…who knew what?

Concentrating on sport was a nightmare when he couldn't stop imagining Morgan in a tiny black and red corset sparkling with diamond-like beads, black striped thigh-high stockings, red 'screw me' heels and an elaborate Mardi Gras mask…straddling his hips, his hands on the smooth, warm, bare flesh above those heart attack-inducing stockings…

He dropped his head back against the arm of the couch and adjusted his jeans. Could a man die from lack of sex and frustration? He was convinced that it was a distinct possibility.

CHAPTER NINE

MORGAN KNOCKED ONCE on the conference door and popped her head in. Noah, on a video conference, flicked a glance at her, smiled, and looked back at his screen.

'I sent off the quote for that corporate security analysis in Hungary, Chris. I think we might—'

Morgan leaned her shoulder into the doorframe and waited for him to finish his conversation. Look at him—so sexy with his tousled hair and wire-rimmed reading glasses. Morgan felt the usual rush of lust, quickly followed by the warm and fuzzies. She suspected if they ever got to have sex he'd be an amazing lover: sweet and tender, hot and fast, slow but hot… She suspected that, like the many facets of his personality, the variations to his lovemaking would be endless. But right now she loved talking to him over the first cup of coffee in the morning, over a glass of wine at night, arguing about the fact that she was the untidiest person he'd ever met. She couldn't imagine him not being in her life and knew, with or without sex, that she could, if she wasn't very, very careful, fall chaotically, crazily in love with him.

She couldn't, shouldn't…wouldn't. Some day soon the situation with the Colombian mine would be sorted out and he'd go back to London, to his life and business there.

'Hey, what's up?' Noah asked, pulling his glasses off his face and resting his forearms on the table. A cup of cold coffee, his mobile and his wallet were placed in a neat row on the other side of his laptop and his sidearm was snug against his shoulder.

Morgan placed her hands behind her back. 'It must be really difficult, trying to run your business from here, Noah.'

Noah looked around. 'It's not so bad. I'm plugged into the server at work—it's practically the same as if I was working in my office and Chris in his. The only difference is arguing face to face instead of over Skype.'

'Well, I'm still sorry if guarding me is an inconvenience.'

'Better than the alternative of you being kidnapped. Or dead.' Noah placed his arms behind his head. 'How was your day? Still battling with the Barnado piece? Has she settled on a design yet?'

She was currently dealing with an ultra-picky client with the concentration span of a cricket. 'Nope. I've been wading through cost projections for the ball and my eyes are crossing.'

'Need some help?' Noah asked.

He asked it in the same voice he used when he wanted to know whether she wanted coffee. As if she was so very normal...and to Noah she was. Her dyslexia was just another part of her—like her untidiness or her freckles.

'Morgs, do you need help?'

Noah repeating his question pulled her back.

'I'll make time if you need me to.'

'No, I'm good. I heard from James; we'll be flying out at five tomorrow afternoon and we'll be in Cape Town mid Friday morning. I told Merri about you. She said that it's a garden wedding and one more person won't make a difference, so she's insisting that you attend with me.'

Noah raked his hand through his hair. 'If the security seems okay then I'm quite happy to leave you there, Morgan. I really don't feel like attending another stuffy function, talking to people I have nothing in common with.'

Morgan walked over to him, laid a hand on his arm and felt his warm skin beneath her fingers. He'd rolled up the sleeves on his casual duck egg blue button-down shirt and she could feel the raised veins in his arms. 'It won't be like that, I promise. Merri is a hoot—stunningly beautiful, but utterly laid back. And the rest of my good, solidly normal friends will be there… Ellie, Jess, Clem and their men. You'll like them.'

'Jeez, Morgan, I don't know.'

'Please, Noah?'

'Does anyone ever say no to you when you flutter your eyelashes and do your Puss-in-Boots look?'

Morgan's lips twitched at the corners. 'Not often, no.'

'Didn't think so. Do I have to wear the tux again?'

'It's a garden wedding. No tux needed.'

'Finally a sensible bride.' Noah glanced at his watch. 'Are you ready to go home?'

Morgan shook her head to clear it. 'Actually, I wanted to tell you that I need to go into Moreau's Gems to see a customer. He's demanding a second opinion on a valuation Carl has given him and insists on getting one from a Moreau. Idiot. He made a scene earlier, and Carl made an arrangement for me to meet him after-hours—which is now.'

Noah frowned. 'Is that normal? Meeting clients after-hours?'

Morgan shrugged. 'Yeah, we meet with clients at the time that suits them, not us. Anyway, he's there now and waiting for us.'

'Security?'

'They aren't allowed to leave until Carl does,' Morgan said, cocking her head at them. 'It's a client, Noah, and it happens all the time. Fifteen minutes, in and out, and then we can order Thai for supper.'

Morgan saw the look he sent to his screen and the frustration that flashed in his eyes. 'I can ask one of the security officers from the lobby to see me there and back if you're busy. Fifteen minutes, tops.'

Noah seemed to be considering the option for a minute,

but he eventually stood up and pulled on his jacket. 'Nope. Let me just send an email delaying my next conference call and I'll come down with you.'

He bent over the screen and his hands flew over the keyboard. He hit 'enter' and picked up his mobile and wallet. Then his eyes met hers and her heart spluttered, misfired and coughed to life again.

Morgan held her breath as his strong hands encircled her jaw and throat and watched wide-eyed as he tipped his head and his lips hovered just above hers. She saw something in his eyes that she hadn't noticed before: something soft, almost tender. Morgan gripped his wrists with her hands and kept her eyes locked on his, waiting for him to swoop down and claim her lips in a kiss that she knew would blow her socks off.

She wanted to sink slowly into the hot whirlpool of his mouth. He would be more delicious than she remembered, far tastier than her imagination suggested. Noah caressed the side of her neck and she inhaled the intoxicating scent of his skin. If she moved a fraction closer she would feel the thrust of her breasts against his chest...their skin would only be separated by his shirt and her silk T-shirt.

Worse than the thumping lust that pooled between her legs, the rapid beat of her heart, was the thought that she was one step closer to losing her heart. It was slipping further away from her and she knew that if she allowed it to fall out of her hand it would be his for ever.

Noah stepped back, but his big hand still grasped the side of her neck and his thumb touched her jaw and tipped her head up.

He muttered an obscenity and her eyes widened.

'One of these days—hours—minutes—I'm not going to be able to step away from you.' Noah moved back and gestured towards the door. 'Let's get this done. I've still got work to do tonight.'

So did she—really important work, Morgan thought, troubled.

Like figuring out how to ensure she didn't fall in love with him.

Morgan had gone somewhere in her head, Noah thought as they hit the pavement outside MI headquarters and moved into the busy end-of-day crowds, and he had no idea where. He'd almost kissed her and then she'd got this weird look on her face and wondered off to a place where he couldn't reach her.

Maybe she was thinking about the design she was battling with, or the ball; he knew how much she had on her plate at the moment and was surprised at how well she was coping. The dyslexia popped up now and again, but he knew that it was nothing that she couldn't handle. It got worse if she rushed or was stressed, and he'd worked out that if he distracted her she frequently relaxed and could then read whatever she'd been stuck on before. He was also beginning to believe that her dyslexia was directly related to her confidence and her happiness; if she was relaxed she had far fewer problems than she did if she was stressed.

He knew that sex would be a brilliant distraction… *Promise to James, promise to James.*

The Moreau's Gems door was locked so Noah knocked. Morgan shook her head at him and pressed a discreet button on the side of the door. He heard a click and frowned when the door popped open.

'There are cameras inside Carl's office; they can see who is at the door,' Morgan said, grinning at his obvious paranoia.

'Where's the guard?' Noah asked as he pushed Morgan inside.

'Probably making coffee. I don't know, Noah! Jeez!' Morgan said. 'Come on, Carl will be in his office.'

Noah made sure the door was locked behind him and looked around. His Spidey Sense was going nutso. It was

the same feeling he'd had numerous times in the army, when
he'd known things were going to go to hell in a handbasket.

Cold shivers ran down his spine and he instinctively *knew*
that he'd just walked them into a heap of trouble. He placed
a protective arm around Morgan's waist and pretended to
nuzzle her ear.

'If I call you Duchess, you drop like a stone to the floor,'
he said, in a low voice that only she could hear.

Morgan—funny girl—rolled her eyes at him as they approached the main counter holding a precious display of
some of the world's best gems set in amazing designs. He
withdrew his gun and Morgan's eyes widened.

'What the heck are you doing? Put that away. It'll go off
and you'll hurt someone!'

Seriously? He was a highly trained operative and if he
made it 'go off' then he'd damn well be intending to hurt
someone. *Honestly—civilians!*

He made the mistake of sending her a pointed look and
out of the corner of his eye saw movement. The next minute a boot connected with his wrist and his gun went flying.
Where had he come from? he thought as he dodged a knife-
swipe at his belly. He heard Morgan's whimper, ignored it,
saw an opening and ploughed his fist into a throat. His attacker crumpled.

Then all hell broke loose.

Noah yelled at Morgan to move and shoved her out of
the way as he bulleted over a counter and slammed into the
space behind—where a suited thug waited for the opportunity to gut him like a fish. Noah waited for the attack,
grabbed the arm attached to the knife, broke his ulna and
launched his elbow into a temple. Out of the corner of his
eye he saw another shadow and his foot flew out and connected with the chin of another knife-wielding lout who'd
come to his friend's aid. It just glanced off a granite face and
he came at him again.

The fight was a blur of motion…kick, punch, kick from

both of them. Noah knew that he couldn't worry or even think about Morgan just yet—not while he had to contend with this better-trained and skilled attacker. Noah bounced on his toes, waited for his opening and hooked a fist into his sternum, following up with a well-placed kick to his groin. Just because he was angry, he picked the guy up and tossed him into a counter. Glass and jewellery flew out of the case.

Whoops!

'Stop.'

The voice came from behind him and every muscle in Noah's body contracted. He wiped his bleeding mouth with his hand before slowly turning around. Fear turned to terror as he let his eyes drift down and saw the thick forearm crushing Morgan's windpipe and the knife at her throat. This man was tall, better-dressed, and had a scar that went from the corner of his mouth to his temple. His eyes would have been better suited to a snake. This was someone to be feared, he realised. No conscience, no empathy, just sheer evil intention.

Kidnapper number four. Noah swore as he walked around the annihilated counter and into the centre of the room.

'I'm going to walk her out of here and neither of you will get hurt.'

Moron, Noah thought. 'Do I look like I mind getting hurt? Let her go and *you* won't get hurt.'

A reptile smile to go with the reptile eyes. Noah expected to see a forked tongue at any moment. He flicked his glance to Morgan, who was looking at him, her gaze steady. Good girl—she wasn't panicking. He was close to it, he thought, as a drop of blood rolled down her neck and soaked into her T-shirt.

He'd cut her...

He was going to kill him for that.

'What do you want?' Noah demanded.

'Her, of course. Negotiations will be so much easier in Colombia if we have a bargaining chip.'

Noah shook his head. 'That's not going to happen. Where are the store employees?'

Snake-eyes shrugged. 'In the back. They might need medical care; we had to *persuade* them to call Miss Moreau down.'

Persuade as in beat the crap out of them to make them obey.

'We've been watching you for weeks—waiting for an opportunity. We couldn't afford to wait any more so we set a trap and you walked straight into it.'

Tell me about it. If one of his employees had done the same they'd be fired. He'd been distracted...by Morgan. *Maybe you shouldn't guard someone you want to sleep with...do you think, soldier?*

'I'm going to rip you apart,' Noah said.

And he would. That was a promise. Nobody threatened Morgan...ever.

'You okay there, Duchess?'

On cue she dropped like a stone, pulling Snake-eyes off-balance. Noah became a blur of speed, motion and deadly intent as he kicked the knife out of his hand and followed up with a lightning-fast punch to his stomach. Air whooshed out of his opponent as he sank to his knees.

Just to make sure that he had the upper hand, Noah wound his forearm around his neck and considered doing the specialised jerk that would send him into the ever after.

'You think you can put your grubby hands on my woman? Put a knife to her throat? Cut her?' he demanded, his voice rough.

He heard a faint gurgling and Morgan's desperate pleas from the other end of the long tunnel he was in. He continued to threaten his captor, tightening his grip with every word he spoke.

Morgan's hand smacking his head jerked him toward reality.

'The guy is turning blue! Let him go! You're going to kill him!'

Noah looked up at her, ignored her tear-filled eyes and shrugged. 'He hurt you. No one hurts you and gets away with it. You're bleeding.'

'It's a scratch, Noah. Look—the police are here. Let them take care of him.' Morgan slapped his head again. 'Let him go! *Now!* Please, Noah. Don't do this.'

Noah released the pressure and heard a couple of deep, rattling and relieved gurgles from his captor.

Noah felt sanity flowing back into him and withdrew his arm. He flipped the sleazoid over and smacked his head into the floor. *Oops...*

'Open the door, Duchess. And please tell them that I am one of the good guys and not to shoot me.'

Noah opened the door to Morgan's apartment and his hand on her back urged her into her home. She headed straight for her squishy couch and sank down onto the edge, staring at the multi-coloured Persian rug below her feet.

He was coming off the adrenalin high and was starting to feel every punch and kick he'd taken. He yanked his tie up and over his head and dropped it, very unusually for him, on the back of the couch. His lip was still bleeding and under the butterfly bandage the cut on his cheek was telling him—loudly—that it was there. His knuckles were bruised and bloody.

But Morgan was fine...mostly. Her neck was bruised from having that muscled arm applied to it, and there was a small nick on her neck from the knife. He kept looking at her to check that she hadn't developed another injury the EMTs might have overlooked.

'Sore?' Noah demanded when she touched her fingers to her throat.

'Mmm.' Morgan looked up at Noah's ravaged face and managed a smile. 'I'm fine, I promise.'

Noah crouched on his heels in front of her and rested his forehead on her knee. 'I thought I'd lost you, Morgan.'

Morgan lifted her hand to touch his cheek, letting her fingertips flutter just beneath the cut on his cheekbone. 'You're too good to lose anyone.'

'I was going to kill him,' Noah said. 'I lost control... *again.*'

'What do you mean?' She touched the deep frown between his brows. 'Noah? What's wrong?'

'Apart from the fact that you were nearly kidnapped and killed? That my heart stopped when I saw that knife to your neck?'

Morgan's eyes widened as his voice became louder with every word.

'That I nearly lost you and I can't lose anyone—ever again?'

'Okay, Noah, calm down.'

'I nearly got you killed in there because I wasn't concentrating!'

'Stop shouting! I'm pretty sure that people can hear you in the lobby.'

'You! Nearly! Died!'

Morgan shook her head. 'Yet here I still sit—alive, but starting to think that you're one crazy man. You were there. You saved me,' Morgan said, her eyes on his mouth. 'My real-life hero.'

'Don't call me that! It should never have happened,' Noah stated, his voice full of disgust. 'I walked you into an ambush...what was I thinking?'

'Stop beating yourself up... Oh, wait—someone already did that today.' Morgan's eyes and twitching mouth invited him to find his sense of humour.

'Ha-ha.'

Noah looked up into her beautiful eyes. His gaze travelled over her face and he winced at the small cut on her neck, the faint bruises on her throat. He'd already forgotten that his cheekbone was cut, that his bottom lip was split and puffy, that his body was battered and bruised.

She was okay. That was all that mattered. Life was too short and he knew that he could not go a minute more without making love to her. He needed her, craved her…emotions he found difficult to admit to. But he'd come so close to losing his life. And—far more scarily—her life.

Life, he decided, was too sweet to waste another minute denying himself the pleasure of making her his.

Noah's eyes darkened with passion and he couldn't resist any longer. When his lips met hers his tongue delved and danced and she responded, and he felt awed by the pent-up longing in her kiss. Unaware that his kisses were just as demanding, as urgent, he sucked in his breath when Morgan's hands moved to the bottom of his shirt, tugging it out of his jeans. Desperate to feel his flesh on hers, he moaned his frustration and resented the brief separation from her body as he stepped away from her to pull his shirt over his head.

Morgan leaned forward and ran her lips across his chest, stopping to flick her tongue over his nipple, to rub her cheek on his chest hair. Noah flipped open her shirt buttons and pulled the fabric apart, revealing her lacy pink bra and luscious chest to his gaze. She was so feminine, he thought. From her sense of humour to her resilience, her long legs and bold eyes, the texture and smell of her skin, she embodied all the traits that he'd spent his adult life looking for.

He finally—*finally!*—had his hands on her, and his imagination had fallen far short of the reality of how life-affirming touching her was. This time there would be no stopping him—stopping them. He needed her, had to have her, to be in her, around her, sharing this experience with her.

Noah felt Morgan's body soften, surrendering to the moment and to him. He bumbled through removing her clothes—suave he was *not!*—but eventually she lay back on the cushions, gloriously, stunningly naked except for the tiny scrap of flimsy lace that covered her crotch. He kept his eyes on her, planning which part of her luscious skin he'd suck on first—hard pink nipple, soft inner thigh?—as he quickly shed the rest of his clothing while Morgan watched him through heavy, half-closed eyes.

On a muttered curse, he reached for his discarded pants and pulled his wallet out of his back pocket. Scattering cards and cash, he found the condom he had taken to carrying around with him and ripped the top open with his teeth. He dropped the condom onto the table and he saw that Morgan was neither surprised nor shocked when he grabbed the flimsy material of her panties and snapped the thin bands that held the triangle in place. Her hand reached out to encircle his erection and he immediately rubbed himself against her most secret places, asking for her permission to enter. He wanted to take his time, to adore every inch of her body, but he'd waited for so long—weeks, years!

His fingers and his mouth followed where his erection had been, and under his touch Morgan surrendered, dissolved, just as he'd known she would. He knew the exact moment to pull back, when she could tolerate no more, so he lifted his head to adore her breasts with his mouth, tongue and lips.

Morgan patted the table, found the condom and stretched down to close her fingers around him. He relished the sound of her breathing, heavy in the quietness of the evening. The latex whispered over him, her fingers making the prosaic action the most erotic sexual play. Green eyes clashed with blue as she tugged him towards her, and he felt as if he'd come home when her softness wrapped around his solidity and enclosed him in her wet warmth. Noah slid one hand under her hip and the other cradled her head into his neck as he both encouraged her to ride with him and promised protection from the storm to follow. They were together.

Noah moved within her and Morgan followed. He demanded and Morgan responded. Deeper, longer, higher, faster. She met him stroke for stroke, matching his passion, glorying in her power. Then she shuddered, splintered. and through the swells of her climax Noah fractured with her.

It was heaven. It was home.

Emotionally, physically depleted, Noah pushed his face into Morgan's neck, breathed, sighed, and for the first time in far too long relaxed completely.

She was safe and she was his. Finally.

CHAPTER TEN

STELLENBOSCH, WESTERN CAPE. Home, Morgan thought as she flopped back onto the mattress of the canopied bed and groaned in delight. This was her favourite place in the entire world; the Bon Chance Wine Estate nestled into the mountains that embraced the family wine farm. This was where, as a child, she'd run wild with Riley and the children of the workers, all of them barefoot and dirty, their faces smeared with the juice of the mulberries they'd picked off the trees in the orchards, their pockets filled with the biscuits or mini-cakes Mariah, the cook, had tucked into their pockets.

On arrival, the kitchen had been the first place she'd headed to and there she'd been, her hair grey and her caramel face wrinkled, but her eyes shining with love.

After Mariah had met Noah and hugged James and Riley, and they'd all had a cup of her thick and strong stove-percolated coffee, she'd ushered them off to their rooms to freshen up—but not before tucking a large biscuit into Morgan's hand.

Morgan sat up, sat cross-legged on the bed under the antique wooden canopy and reached for the biscuit she'd placed on the side table.

'Are you going to share that?' Noah asked from where he stood in her open doorway.

Morgan waved him in as she bit down. 'No,' she said as the taste of vanilla and warm butter exploded on her tongue.

Noah walked in, took the biscuit from her hand and snapped it in half. He ignored her vociferous protests and popped it into his mouth. 'Damn it, that's good,' he said, after swallowing.

'Wait until you taste her pan-fried trout with almonds. That's on the menu for tonight.'

Noah walked over to the wooden sash window, placed his hands on the windowsill and looked out. 'It's so beautiful here, Morgan,' he stated quietly. 'The vines, the mountains...'

Morgan climbed off the bed and joined him at the window. 'Isn't it? This, more than any other place on earth, is my home. It's where we mostly grew up. A Moreau forefather bought this place in the late eighteen-hundreds, with the profits out of the first diamond mine they worked, but the house and winery date back to the beginning of the century.'

'The house is fantastic. From the moment you drive through those gates and up the oak-lined driveway you know that you are entering a place that's imbued with history. The white gables, the exposed wooden beams, the wooden floors. And, God, the furniture.'

Morgan looked amused. 'You've been around wealth before, soldier, why are you sounding so impressed?'

Noah gave her cheek the gentlest of flicks. 'I'm not impressed by wealth and you know it. It's the...*history*—the idea that your great-great-grandmother ate at that same table in the dining room that we will eat at tonight. It's the continuity of family...'

'Tell me about yours, Noah. Your family.'

Noah shook his head and his eyes hardened. 'The only thing to tell is that they are nothing like yours. Socially, economically, mentally...the other end of the spectrum' Noah looked around and raised his eye at the very luscious wooden canopy bed. 'And that is one heck of a bed. One might say that it is fit for a duchess.'

'If you play your cards right I might invite you into it.' Morgan batted her eyelashes at him.

'If you play your cards right I might say yes.' Noah batted his eyelashes back.

Morgan laughed and he grinned.

Noah stepped up to her, rested his temple against hers, his hands loose on her hips. 'James said that we're having a wine-tasting in the cellar in fifteen minutes, and as much as I want you I also want to take my time with you. Every waking moment during that interminable flight I spent planning what I intend to do with you...to you.'

Morgan licked her bottom lip as her hands drifted down over his stomach. 'Bet I could make a case for quick and fast now.'

Noah looked tempted, then swatted her on the backside before he walked away to the door. He gestured her through it 'Stop leading me into temptation and show me Bon Chance.'

Morgan grinned as she drifted past him in a cloud of mischief and expensive perfume. 'So you're admitting that I *can* lead you into temptation?'

'You know that you can,' Noah muttered, and placed his hand on her lower back to push her away from the bedrooms and towards the magnificent yellow wood staircase. 'Behave, Duchess.'

'But I'd so much rather *mis*behave...'

Noah hooked his arm around her neck and placed his hand over her mouth. 'Man, you're a pain in the ass.'

Morgan giggled as she placed her butt on the banister and slid down the stairs, landing on her feet in the hall. It was good to be home. And it was fabulous to be home with Noah.

Noah pushed open the massive oak door to Bon Chance and ushered Morgan through it, his hand on the centre of her back. She inhaled his sexy aftershave and held his arm as she slipped her sky-high open heels off her feet.

'I love this dress,' Noah stated, pulling the fabric of the

top layer of blush-pink silk organza between his finger and thumb and rubbing. The mini under-dress was a patchwork of different pinks...V neckline, black trim. She liked it, but judging by the gleam in Noah's eyes he couldn't wait to get her out of it.

Morgan tossed her clutch bag on the hall table, placed her hands on her back and stretched, pushing out her chest. She grinned when his eyes dropped and stayed on her chest.

Sometimes being a girl was the best fun ever—especially when you had a super-starry, sexy soldier looking at you with lust in his eyes.

'So, my friends weren't so bad, were they? You spent a lot of time talking to Jack and Luke,' Morgan commented.

Noah pulled his eyes up to her face. 'Uh...Jack knows my brother Mike. Journalist and photographer.'

'Small world.' Morgan glanced into the formal lounge. 'Do you want a nightcap? My dad likes a drop of Macallan every night.'

'My favourite whisky. Sounds good.'

Morgan walked in her bare feet into the lounge, shut the French doors behind her and opened a cabinet, revealing tumblers and a couple of bottles of whisky. 'There's an iPod on the shelf over there—do you want to choose some music?'

Morgan sighed when Sarah McLachlan's voice filled the room. Taking a glass over to Noah, she pressed the drink into his hand. She was about to step back when Noah's arms snaked around her waist and pulled her to him.

'No, stay here. Dance with me again.'

Morgan swayed on the spot with him and then took the glass out of his hand and took a sip. Anyone would think that she had never danced with a man before, yet never had she been so aroused this quickly. Standing up on her toes, she grazed his chin with her lips and slowly kissed his mouth. The music vibrated with desire, with love lost and found.

She heard the bang of crystal hitting wood and felt one of Noah's hands on her bottom, the other on the side of her face. Tongues tangled and hands rubbed at the restrictive barrier of clothing as the plaintive music faded into white noise. She groaned in the back of her throat as hearts clashed and tongues collided, stroked, duelled. One song drifted into another and Morgan murmured her dismay as Noah lifted his head and rested his forehead on hers. He tangled his fist in her hair and tipped her head up so that he could look into her sparkling eyes.

'I need you, Morgan. I know we shouldn't keep doing this…I promised your brother…'

'You saved my life. Trust me, you are James's new best friend—'

'But I still need you. Want you.'

'Then take me,' she whispered.

Her eyes drifted closed and her lips parted as she tipped her head to allow him access to her neck, to the very sensitive spot in the hollow of her throat. He pushed his hand up under her dress and lifted it. Easily, quickly, he found her nipple with his thumb. Morgan groaned, desperately wanting his lips and mouth to continue the exquisite torture. She slid her hand over his hip and stretched her hand so that she barely brushed his erection. It was a faint touch, but Morgan felt the electricity power through him. She felt strong and powerful, and she increased the pressure of her touch and had Noah moaning aloud.

Fumbling with the buttons on his shirt, Morgan eventually pulled the fabric apart and spread her hands over his chest, exploring his defined pecs and his washboard stomach. Pushing the shirt off his shoulders, she touched his collarbone with her tongue and inhaled the scent of his masculine skin.

'You're killing me here, lass. If you carry on like that it's not going to be slow and it's not going to be pretty.' Noah muttered.

'I never asked for either.'

Noah's hand skimmed her thigh and moved across her pelvis. His thumb rested on her mound and she groaned when it drifted lower, yelped when he hit the spot.

'It would be easier if we just got naked,' Noah replied, spinning her around and looking for the zip that held her dress together. Morgan felt cool air on her back and sighed when Noah's hot mouth touched her spine as her dress dropped. His big hands reached around to clasp her breasts and his fingers pulled her nipples into rock-hard points.

This was better than she could have imagined. Noah unclasped her bra and it fell to the floor in a pretty puddle of pink froth, and then her panties were pushed down her legs and she stood naked, her back to his chest, his lips on her neck.

'You're so beautiful.'

Noah turned her around and watched her with lowered lust-filled eyes as he dropped his hands to undo his belt. Morgan gripped the back of the antique couch and licked her lips as he pushed his pants down his legs, standing in front of her in a pair of plain black tight trunks, strained by his very impressive erection.

Two seconds later his trunks were on the floor, his hands were under her thighs and he was lifting her up, his penis probing her slick, wet folds. He held her eyes as he surged into her. He was hard and wonderful and her body shuddered.

'So wet...so warm.'

Morgan moaned as she linked her arms around his strong neck. Her clitoris brushed against his groin as he pulled her even closer and she moaned and tipped her head back. She ground herself into him as Noah looked for and found her mouth. His tongue swirled and slid as he pumped his hips. Morgan groaned as she felt the fierce upward swing of concentrated pleasure...reaching out for that dizzying release... She lifted her hips and mashed herself against him.

'Take it, baby. Use it,' Noah said, his voice low and intense in her ear. 'Use me! Take it all.'

She was all feeling, all concentrated pleasure, as she did

what he said. She bucked and pumped, sinking into him and then using her hands against the couch to push up and away from him so that she could crash down on him again. Power and release built as her body became a vessel of shimmying, sensational pleasure.

Reaching, reaching, and then bursting, flying, Morgan flung her arms around Noah's neck and held on as she split into a thousand pieces and was tacked back together with fairy dust. Somewhere, somehow, she knew that Noah had followed her over the edge; she could hear him panting in her ear, could feel the aftershocks rippling through his muscles, the slight softening of his erection inside her.

Morgan lost track of time; she wasn't sure how long she sat there, half supported by the couch, half by Noah's bulging-with-muscles arms. But eventually Noah slid out of her and held her as her feet touched the floor, holding her arm to make sure that she was steady.

Noah brushed her hair back from her face. 'You okay?'

'Good. Really, really good,' Morgan said on a yawn. 'Boneless.'

Noah picked up his pants, stepped into them and tucked himself away as he did up the fly. 'Let's get you dressed and into bed.'

Noah picked up her dress and she shimmied it over her head. Picking up their underwear, he shoved it into his pockets and picked up his shoes. Taking Morgan's hand, he pulled her towards the French doors.

'Upstairs.'

'I don't think I have the energy to climb those stairs.' Morgan looked at the stairs doubtfully. 'I'm utterly exhausted.'

Noah bent his knees, grabbed her around the thighs and tossed her over his shoulder. Morgan squealed and laughed and slapped his back. 'I was joking, Noah! Put me down.'

'I live to serve, Duchess. Stop wriggling or I will drop you on your imperial ass.'

* * *

Morgan woke up late and rolled over in her massive bed, looking for Noah. Not finding any part of his masculine bod in her bed, she sat up and scowled. He'd sneaked out, the rat, after a night spent exploring her in the most intimate ways possible. He'd reached for her time and time again and they had only drifted off to sleep when the sun had started to yawn, allowing its weak early-morning rays to drift over the mountain.

Being with him had been—bar none and by far—the best sex of her life. The sexy, slightly stand-offish soldier was an amazing lover: demanding, adoring, creative. He hadn't allowed her to feel any modesty and had encouraged her to be forthright and honest. She'd felt comfortable telling him what she liked and didn't like him doing.

There hadn't been any 'getting to know you' or 'wanting to impress you' sex. It had been down and dirty—more like 'I want to know how far I can push you' sex.

More like the type of sex people had when they had known each other a while and were really comfortable in bed together. Weird and astonishing for their first few times together.

Morgan glanced at the clock. It was just past nine and, while she could easily roll over and go back to sleep, she wanted to be with Noah, here in her most favourite spot in the world.

Morgan pushed back the covers and padded over to the en-suite bathroom. Hearing muted voices in the passage-way, she cocked her head. Riley and…her brother? What was James doing on this side of the passage? His room and study were on the other wing of the house—to the right of the staircase and not to the left.

Curious, she padded on tiptoe to the door and cracked it open. Her eyes widened as she saw James, still dressed in the pants he'd worn to the wedding and with his smart grey shirt bunched in his hand.

'If you say it was a mistake, I swear I'll stab you with...
something,' Riley hissed.

'Dammit, Riley, you are like my—'

Morgan put her hand against her mouth to stifle her laughter as Riley, obviously naked beneath a silky short robe, plastered her mouth against James's and slapped her hands on his butt. She kissed him thoroughly and with some skill, Morgan noticed, and when they came up for air James looked shell-shocked.

'You didn't say that when you were moaning my name in the throes of passion last night.'

'Ri—okay. But—'

'I am not your sister or your friend. And I'm done pining away for you. You have ten seconds to decide if you want to explore this heat we have always had or whether you are walking away for good. But you should know that if you walk that's it. You don't get a second chance.'

'Riley, I—'

'Ten seconds, nine, eight, seven—'

'It's not that easy.'

Yes, it is, you ass! Morgan wanted to shout. *She's the best thing that ever happened to you!*

'Six, five, four, three...'

Morgan bit her lip as her best friend counted down and her stupid brother just stared at her with miserable eyes. Morgan closed her own eyes at the immense pain she saw in Riley's before the door closed in James's face.

Morgan fought the urge to step into the passage and slap some sense into James. She knew it wouldn't help. James was as stubborn as she was—maybe more. She couldn't help him see what was right in front of his face; couldn't force him to feel love when he didn't.

Morgan watched him walk down the passage and then glanced to Riley's closed door. To knock or not to knock? Normally she would just barge in there and offer comfort, curse her brother just to make Riley smile. But she suspected that this went too deep, meant too much, and her gut instinct was to leave Riley alone. She would reach out when she could and when she was ready to.

In the meantime she had her own six-foot-three man to find.

Morgan, dressed in a very brief pair of faded denim shorts, flip-flops and a tank top—early autumn in South Africa still spiked the temperatures to boiling—took the cup of coffee Mariah poured her and with a muffin in her hand walked out through the back door of the house. Mariah had said that she'd seen Noah walk in the direction of the southside vines and the dam, and that was nearly an hour ago.

Morgan, munching on her cheese and spinach muffin and sipping her coffee, tipped her face to the sun and pulled in deep breaths of fresh mountain air. She wished that they weren't flying out later tonight, that she and Noah could hang out here a bit longer. There was no security threat, no pollution, no crazy traffic, no boring functions to attend, no ball to organise. It was impossible, but it was a lovely dream to indulge in as she looked for her lover-slash-bodyguard.

Morgan dusted her hands against the seat of her pants to get rid of the crumbs and waved to some labourers working the vines.

And there he was, Morgan thought, sitting on the edge of the dam, his arms loosely linked around his knees, his dark hair glinting in the sun. He hadn't shaved and his stubble gave him a rugged look that had her mouth watering. Warmth pooled between her legs as she remembered the feel of those back muscles that red T-shirt covered, the hard butt underneath his cotton shorts. He was beautiful: masculine grace wrapping a fantastically loyal spirit and a sharp brain.

Morgan approached him quietly, covered his eyes with her hands and whispered in his ear. 'Guess who?'

Noah didn't say anything. He just pulled her hands down

and held her arms so that she was plastered against his back, her head next to his, her breasts mashed into his chest.

'You okay, Noah?' she asked quietly. 'What's going on in that head of yours, soldier?'

A part of him—a big part of him—wished he could open up, just release all this churned-up emotion inside him. He wanted to tell her that he couldn't decide whether he regretted sleeping with her or not...that being with her had been everything he'd dreamt of and more and also, on the other hand, his biggest nightmare. He'd lost himself in her body, had adored every minute of her, and he mourned his lack of self-control as he'd lost himself in her. He wanted to tell her that when she'd drifted off in the early hours of this morning he'd just lain next to her and watched her breathe.

She'd decimated him with her soft lips, her whispered moans, her delicate hands on his not-so-delicate body. She'd touched his heart with her murmurs of delight, her whispers of gratitude at the way he made her feel, and his heart had swelled when he'd heard his name on her lips as he tipped her over into orgasm time and time again.

But on the flipside of the coin he hadn't even started to think what effect sleeping with her would have on his job, on his ability to keep her safe. They'd caught four more kidnappers but another gang could be contracted tomorrow. Until the situation in Colombia was definitively resolved she wouldn't be completely safe, so he would remain in place as her bodyguard. Would thoughts of what they did to and with each other distract him if something else happened? Would he be less sharp, less aware, less able to say no to her when she wanted to do something or be somewhere that could place her in danger?

Morgan pulled her hands out of his grasp and sat down beside him on the grassy bank, staring at the water. Now and again the water rippled as a trout broke the surface to look for food. In another life he could imagine being here with Morgan, casting a fly while she lazed on the bank, a glass of wine in her hand.

Noah leaned back on his hands and looked past the dam to the vines in their perfect rows, and from there to the purple-blue mountain looming over the farm. 'It's such a stunning place, Morgs. I can't understand why you're in New York when you can be here.'

'Clients, mostly. But I should take more time to come back here.' Morgan pushed her hair behind her ears. Then she placed her palm on Noah's thigh, gently squeezed and lifted it again. 'Please don't regret what happened between us, Noah. It was too good for regrets.'

'It's so complicated, Morgan,' he said in a gruff voice.

'I think you make it a great deal more complicated than it is,' Morgan replied. 'We're friends who have shared our bodies. We had a great deal of fun, and if we do it again we'll have fun again.'

Noah frowned. 'So, you're not looking forward? Expecting anything from me?'

Morgan crossed her legs, picked a blade of grass and ran it through her fingers. 'I was talking to Riley about this a little while ago, and spending more time with you has just reinforced my opinion that I'm not cut out to be with someone long-term.'

Noah frowned, utterly confused. 'Why not?'

'I've shielded you from my dyslexia—shielded you from what I go through on a daily basis. I shield everyone. I never read the news; I watch it. I try to avoid writing anything down because my handwriting looks like a chicken's scrawl and I can't spell. At all. I don't drive unless I know exactly where I am and the route I'm travelling, and I never drive in New York or any other city.'

'Okay.'

'On the few occasions I do write something on the computer I call Riley to check the spelling.'

'Um...spellcheck?' Noah volunteered.

'It doesn't help if you don't recognise the word, Noah.'

Oh, flip. He hadn't thought of that.

'Look, I've done tons of research on dyslexia and there are a couple of things I can't wrap my head around. Both of them involve a steady relationship. One is that if I get involved then I can't do it halfway. I'd want the whole bang-shoot. Marriage, kids…everything. Having kids is a risk, because dyslexia is hereditary and I couldn't bear it if my husband blamed me for his child struggling at school. The other is that one day, as hard as I will try to prevent it, my partner will feel frustrated with me and then disappointed. Quickly followed by him thinking that, despite how hard we've tried, something is lacking. In me.'

Noah stared at her profile for a long, long time before pulling in a deep breath. He looked for the right words but only two hovered on his tongue. 'Horse crap, Morgan.'

'Excuse me?' she gasped, shocked.

'That is the biggest load of self-indulgent horse crap I've ever heard—' Noah cursed as his mobile disturbed the country silence of the morning. He pulled out his mobile, checked the display and frowned. 'Sorry, it's my father's carer. I need to take this.'

As the feminine Scottish lilt travelled across the miles, giving him news he didn't want to hear, Noah felt the world shift under his feet. He dropped the phone to the grass and bent his head as he struggled to make sense of her words.

Fell out of his wheelchair. Hit his head. Bleeding on the brain. Dead…

'Noah?'

He felt Morgan's cool hand on his cheek.

'Hon, what's happened?'

'He's dead. He's finally dead.' Noah heard the words but his brain had no connection to the words his tongue was speaking. 'I thought I'd be happier.'

'Who's dead, Noah?'

'My father.' He ran his hand over his face. 'I have to go

to Scotland. I have to tell my brothers. Man, can't we just go back to our conversation? I want to tell you why I thought you were talking rubbish. It doesn't have to be like that...'

The trees were dancing and the water in the dam was rising and falling. What was happening to him?

Morgan gripped his hands. 'Just breathe, Noah. In and out.'

'So many times I wished he was dead, and now he is and I don't know what to feel.' Noah stared at the sky. 'I need to go, Morgan. I need to tell my brothers.'

He heard his irrational gabbling and felt embarrassed. He never gabbled...wasn't irrational.

'You will tell them, Noah. Just breathe for now, take in the news, stop thinking and let yourself feel.'

Noah shook his head and jumped to his feet. *Hell, no!* The last thing he wanted or needed to do was feel.

Morgan followed him up, placed her hands on his chest and looked up into his ravaged face. 'Noah, stop. Listen to me—no, don't push past me! You're as white as a sheet. *Listen* to me!'

Noah forced himself to concentrate on her words.

'I'm going to walk away and you are going to sit down and take it in. Take a deep breath and look around. You've just heard that your father is dead. Take a moment. Feel. Cry. Do what you need to do. There's going to be a time when you need to be strong, and the next fifteen minutes, half an hour—the rest of the day if that's what you need—isn't that time.' Morgan touched his cheek with her fingers. 'Take the time, Noah. Please.'

Noah saw the sympathy in her eyes and bit his lip, fighting the emotion that was threatening to crash over him. If she had let him walk, do what he needed to do, he could have pushed it away, but if he had to stay here then he didn't want her seeing the mess he would probably dissolve into. The anger, the regret, the swamping, swamping guilt.

'Go.' Noah muttered the word, shoving his hand into his hair. 'Go now.'

Morgan nodded once, then bent down, quickly scooped up his mobile and tucked it into her pocket. He watched her walk away and it was only when she was out of sight that he allowed the first hot, angry, guilty wave of emotion to crash over him.

CHAPTER ELEVEN

MORGAN WALKED FROM the galley area of the jet and sat down next to Noah, who was staring out at the solid black expanse that was the African continent below them. She pressed a whisky into his hand and put her temple on his shoulder. 'How are you doing, soldier?'

Noah took a sip, shuddered, and gestured to the window. 'I never realised how dark Africa really is. You hardly ever see lights.'

So, not ready to talk, then.

'Just miles and miles of nothingness,' Morgan agreed, tucking her feet up under her. She'd shed her shoes earlier and she reached for the soft blanket that she'd put on the chairs opposite them and pulled it over her knees.

'Cold?' Noah asked, slipping his arm around her and pulling her closer.

'A little.'

Noah kissed her hair before taking another sip of his whisky. 'I never expected you to commandeer the family jet to take me to London, Morgan.'

'It was James's suggestion, Noah. I'm sorry we couldn't leave earlier, but they were doing some maintenance on it.' Morgan replied.

James had been quick to offer the use of the plane, saying that the jet could turn around in London and come back to pick them up. So they'd return to New York a day later? The world wouldn't stop. Morgan knew that there was a reason why she adored her brother. It made it hard to remain annoyed with him over the hurting-Riley issue.

'It's an expensive exercise, Morgan. I could've just caught a normal flight. And I didn't expect you to come with me. I was going to send another operative to guard you while I was away.'

'I don't want to train someone else,' Morgan joked, and then sighed at his worried eyes and his serious face. 'Noah, relax. We're hugely rich and we can afford to send the jet anywhere we want, whenever we want. We wanted to get you to London in the quickest, most comfortable way possible. I wanted to be with you because I don't think that anybody should be alone at a time like this.'

Noah kissed her head again. 'I'm not used to people doing stuff for me.'

'Yeah, I realised that. Talking of which, James contacted Chris and gave him a heads-up. He'll meet you at the airport with another guard for me and I'll let you do what you need to do. I'd like to stay with you, but that might not be what you want.'

Noah was silent for a long time and Morgan subdued her pang of disappointment. Of course he didn't want to have to worry about her at a time like this... Yeah, they had slept together, but that didn't mean he wanted her to invade his emotional space.

'When you're done—when the funeral is over—the jet will take us back to New York. That's if you're coming back with me.'

Noah rubbed his eyes. 'It's so difficult to think. To decide what to do next.'

Morgan placed her hand on his thigh and left it there. 'I know... Well, I don't know, but I can imagine.'

'My brothers—'

Morgan remembered the comment he'd made at the art

exhibition. 'As much as you want to, you can't shield them from this, Noah.'

'Yeah.' Noah turned his head to look out of the window again into the black nothingness.

She'd never known anyone who needed someone to release what was obviously years of pent-up emotion more than he did. She knew that there was a huge and possibly tragic story here—that Noah was dealing with far more than just—*just!*—the death of his dad. Morgan wished she could shake it out of him, but she also suspected that she was the last person he'd allow to peek into his soul.

He saw himself as the protector, the guardian, but he didn't realise that in order to give you had to be able to receive. That you had to be strong enough—physically, mentally, *emotionally*—to do that. She worried about him… worried that as soon as the plane landed he would be all business in a 'let's-get-this-done-and-sorted' mode. She didn't know much about death but she knew that he had to grieve, had to mourn. He couldn't keep tamping down his emotion because one day he would erupt and splatter.

But this wasn't her party and she couldn't make him cry if she wanted to. All she could do was to be here, offering her unconditional support.

'We were raised in a bad area of Glasgow,' Noah said, his accent broad and his voice low.

He was still staring out of the window and Morgan didn't move a muscle, scared that he'd stop talking if she reacted at all. 'My father was frequently out of work. He had few skills and no desire to get any more. He lived off the dole and drank most of it away. My mum took whatever work she could find and kept him under control—mostly. He was an angry man and liked being that way.'

Morgan pushed her shoulder into his, pushed her fingers into his hand and kept her silence.

'My mum wanted to move out; she could get a job in her brother's inn in Kelso. He didn't want to move but she finally persuaded him to visit with her. They borrowed a car and my brothers and I stayed behind—I can't remember why. My father wasn't an experienced driver and it was wet and they spun off the road. Mum was killed instantly. Michael was paralysed from the waist down.'

Michael, he called his father Michael. Not Dad—just Michael.

'Long story short: he became our worst nightmare. Anger turned to rage, rage to violence, and if you think a man can't be physically violent confined to a wheelchair then you should've seen him. I watched my brothers become walking robots, scared to move—to breathe—and I called Social Services, They arranged for them to go and live with my aunt—my mum's sister.'

'And you?'

'Somebody had to stay and look after him. I lasted three years,' Noah said. 'I was nineteen when I joined up.'

'What happened that made you leave?' Morgan asked, because she knew that something major had happened. Noah, being Noah, with his unquestionable loyalty, would have had to have an excellent reason to walk away.

Still looking out of the window, he said, 'I said he was abusive and he was. Verbally, physically... But that day had been a quiet day—no drama from him. He'd actually been behaving himself. I walked past him and saw this cold look in his eye, and then his fist flew out and he punched me in my...you know...'

Morgan's eyes widened but she kept her voice even. 'Groin?'

'Yeah. I just reacted. We were in the kitchen and...I don't know what happened but I lost time. When I came back I was holding a knife to his throat and he was begging me not to kill him. I wanted to; it would've been so easy.'

'But you didn't.'

'No, I walked away, made arrangements for his care and joined the army. I left him alone.'

Morgan turned to face him, lifted up her hand and touched his chin, forcing him to look at her. 'You spent three years in a horrid situation with an abusive father. You earned the right to walk away, Noah. Knowing you, you've probably supported him financially all this time.'

'Yes, I have—but you don't understand!' Noah sounded agitated. 'I nearly *killed* him, Morgan!'

Morgan raised her eyebrows. 'But you *didn't*, Noah! He was an abusive father who inflicted violence on you. He sucker-punched you—in a man's most vulnerable place!—and it was the straw that broke your back. I'm surprised that you *didn't* kill him, Noah.'

'You don't understand! I lost control! Like I nearly did the other day.'

'Oh, Noah, millions of men would think that you showed immense control by *not* killing him! And you were nowhere near losing control last week.'

Noah looked at her with wide shocked eyes and she could see him trying to process her words. 'Have you ever spoken to anyone about this? Chris? Your brothers? A psychologist?'

Noah shook his head.

She was the only person that knew his secret? How could that be? 'Maybe you should. Maybe they can convince you that you were just a boy, trying to survive and doing the best you could in a dreadful situation.'

Noah closed his eyes and rested his head on hers. 'I'm so tired, Morgs.'

Morgan pushed his hair off his forehead. 'Then why don't you rest awhile? Push the seat back and try and sleep, okay?' Morgan pulled the lever on his seat and watched as he stretched out. She passed him a pillow, pulled another blanket over him, before flipping her seat back and lying so that she faced him. Holding his hand, she watched as he drifted off to sleep.

'Morgs?'

'Yes?'

He yawned and his voice was thick with sleep when he spoke again. 'Stay with me, okay? I'd like you there…at the funeral and when I tell my brothers.'

'I'll be there,' Morgan whispered, and watched him while he slept.

Noah was as jittery as a crack addict desperate for a fix. He stood in front of one of the many houses in the grimy brick block and placed his hand on the incongruous red railing—and quickly lifted it when he felt the sticky gunge on his skin. Wiping his palm on his jeans, he played with the keys in his hand.

He hadn't been back to the house he'd been raised in in nearly fifteen years and he didn't want to go inside now. He just wanted to put this entire nightmare behind him. But before he could he had to bury his father tomorrow and clean out his house today. Postponing wasn't an option, because his brothers were flying in later and would insist on helping him. Their aunt's house was their real home, and he didn't want them to see the reality of how their parents had lived.

He didn't want Morgan seeing it either, but she wouldn't be dissuaded from accompanying him. He'd pleaded for her to stay in the hotel room, had offered another bodyguard for the day so that she could spend the day sightseeing, but she'd refused.

She was coming with him and he'd have to deal with it, she'd stated, calmly and resolutely. Nobody should have to clear out their parents' house alone.

He wasn't sure whether to be grateful or to strangle her. He looked over to her, dressed as he was in old jeans and a casual sweater. But she still looked out of place in this place of dank and dark buildings covered in grime and graffiti.

Over the past day or so Morgan's presence had kept him centred, grounded, able to go through the steps of organising the funeral, notifying the few relatives they had left, and that hard conversation with his brothers, who'd taken the news rather prosaically. He couldn't judge them for their lack of grief; they'd had minimal contact with Michael for most of their lives and didn't have a personal relationship with him. He also knew that their offer to come to the funeral was more to support him than to say goodbye to their father.

Yesterday, after a long, cold, tough day, he'd lost himself in Morgan's body, stepping away from the memories of the past and the reality of his father's passing and losing himself in her smooth skin, her frantic gasps, her warm, wet heat. And when guilt had welled up and threatened to consume him whole, when he'd felt like punching a fist through a wall, her words, spoken quietly but with such truth, drifted through his head.

'Millions of men would think that you showed immense control by not killing him. You were just a boy, trying to survive and doing the best you could in a dreadful situation.'

Morgan. She was becoming as necessary to him as breathing and he either wanted to beg her never to leave him or he wanted to run as far and as fast away from her as possible.

Noah saw movement across the road and caught the eye of the obvious leader of a gang of teens across the road. He gave them a don't-mess-with-me stare. They ducked their heads and moved off and Noah sighed. *There but for the grace of God go I,* he'd thought, on more than one occasion.

'Let's go in, Noah, it's cold out here,' Morgan suggested, her hand on his back.

Noah shook himself out of his trance and walked up the cracked steps into the mouldy building. He shuddered as he breathed in the smell of decaying food and despair.

He automatically turned to the door on the left and his hand shook as he tried to place the key in the lock. He didn't know why they bothered with locking up; he knew that one solid kick would have the door flying open. When he couldn't make the connection between key and lock he considered it a viable option.

Morgan took the key from his hand, jabbed it in the lock

and pushed open the door. She stepped inside and Noah wanted to warn her not to…that his father was unstable, volatile, capricious.

No, his father was dead. Noah bit his bottom lip, looked around and swore. Nothing had changed; the old blue couch was just paler and grubbier, the furniture that much more battered. And, man, it was messy. His father had always been a slob but Noah had paid for a cleaner, for someone to look after him.

'How did he live like this?' Noah whispered. 'If the carer didn't clean, then did she feed him, look after him?'

Guilt threatened to buckle his knees, sink him to the floor.

Morgan tossed him a glance and immediately went to the old fridge, yanked it open. She pulled back at the smell but pointed out the milk, the cheese. Slamming the door shut, she pulled open the freezer section and nodded.

'There are quite a few homemade meals in here, Noah, and lots of dirty dishes in the sink. He was eating. And, look, there's a note on the fridge, saying that the carer was going on holiday. She got back the day he died. I think.'

'Thank you.' Noah looked down as he kicked a half-empty bottle of whisky at his feet. So the drinking hadn't stopped.

He couldn't do this with her here… Couldn't handle seeing his classy NYC girl in a smelly flat filled with dirty dishes and soiled clothes and windows covered with soot and grime. Couldn't handle the pity he thought he saw in her eyes. He wanted to cry but he couldn't do that with her— couldn't let her see him at his weakest.

'Morgan, please leave.'

Morgan looked at him with huge eyes. 'I don't want to. I don't want you to do this on your own. Let me stay, please.'

Noah dropped his head and felt the walls of the room closing in on him. He desperately wanted to be alone, wanted some time to himself, to sort through the emotion to find the truth of what he was feeling. He knew it was time to pull away from her now, to find some distance. He wanted to take back his life, his mind, his control. He wanted to stand alone, as he always had. He needed to know that he could, that he didn't need that gorgeous blonde in his life, standing in his corner.

Why had he even explained his past to Morgan? Where had that crazy impulse come from? Being side-winded after hearing that Michael was dead? Now he felt as if he was standing in front of her, his chest cracked open, and inviting her to wreak havoc. By allowing her inside he'd handed her his pistol and invited her to shoot him in the heart.

He was the closest he'd ever come to falling over that long cliff into love, and he couldn't help thinking whether he would be feeling the same way if his father hadn't died—if his feelings for her didn't seem deeper because there was so much emotion swirling around him.

He just wanted to step away from this freakin' soul-searching and get on an even keel again. He wanted to feel normal.

Morgan folded her arms across her chest. 'Talk to me, Noah. Please.'

'You're not going to like what I say,' he warned her.

'Talk to me anyway,' Morgan said, perching her butt on the side of the rickety dining room table. She stood in nearly the same place as he had when he'd taken a knife to his father's throat...

He stared at the old television screen. 'My parents are both dead and I should feel free. Except that I don't.'

'Why not?'

'Because you're here.'

'Do you want to explain that?'

Noah shoved his hand into his hair and tugged. 'I don't want you to think that just because you're here we have something serious happening. I don't want you thinking that we're in some sort of relationship...'

'We are. If nothing else, we are friends.'

'Friends?'

Noah snorted, thinking that by allowing her to come with him he'd tied himself to Morgan, bound himself into some sort of relationship. He was furious that she'd pricked through his self-sufficiency and made him rely on her.

He looked around the room and felt anger whirl and swirl. 'I left this place fifteen years ago and I swore that I would never feel vulnerable again. I vowed, after walking away from him, that I'd never feel weak again.'

Yet here he was, shortly before burying the person who'd taught him that lesson, putting himself in the same position. With her.

He was such a fool. He couldn't, *wouldn't* ever rely on someone else again…and this touchy-feely crap he had going on with Morgan stopped now.

'I don't want you here. I want you gone.'

Had he actually voiced those words? He must have because her head jerked back in shock and all colour drained from her face.

'Noah…'

'This—you and I—it stops. Right now.'

'You're tired and upset and not thinking straight,' Morgan said after a moment, and he could see that she was trying to keep calm, desperately looking to keep the conversation, the situation, rational.

In normal circumstances her words might have jerked him back to sanity, but nothing about standing in his father's filthy house, being bombarded with ugly memories and emotions, was normal. If he wasn't in such a turbulent mood he'd readily admit that when it came to him she generally knew exactly what to say. How to make him laugh, think, want her with every breath he took.

He didn't *want* to want her like this; didn't want to deal with the tender emotions only she could pull to the surface. Didn't want to deal with anything right now…

'Why don't I give you some space?' Morgan sucked in her cheeks. 'I'll wait for you outside.'

Morgan turned to walk to the door but his harsh voice had her stopping just before she reached it. 'No. I don't want you to wait. I don't want this—you—any more.'

He saw, maybe felt the shudder that rocketed through her, saw her head fall. He fought the urge to go to her, to soothe, to protect. The child in him protested that *he'd* never been soothed, protected.

'I never promised you anything and I always said that I would leave.'

Morgan finally turned around, lifted her head and gave him a withering look. 'Stop acting like an ass, Noah. I understand that this has been a rough time for you, but don't take your anger out on the people who love you.'

Noah leaned backed and stretched out his feet. 'So now you *love* me?'

Morgan's eyes froze. 'I'm not even going to dignify that with a reply. You're angry and hurt and acting like a jerk. You're just going through the stages of grief—albeit quicker than most. First shock, you skipped denial. and now you're feeling angry.'

'No, you're looking for an excuse because you don't want to hear what I'm saying.'

'Which is exactly what, Noah? Put your cards on the table, Fraser.'

Well, okay, then. 'I don't want you in my life any more.'

'That's not how you felt this morning, last night, twenty minutes ago.'

That was the truth.

'It's how I feel now. I don't like feeling this connected to someone—feeling like my heart wants to explode with joy just because you're in the room. I want to feel normal again—me again... Not a twisted-with-emotion sap.' Noah ground the words out, forcing them around his reluctant tongue. 'I don't want to love you! And I certainly don't need you. I was perfectly fine on my own.'

He hadn't been, his heart shouted, but he shut out its screams.

Morgan shook her head, blinked away the emotion in her eyes and bit her bottom lip. He felt lower than an amoeba infected with anthrax. What was wrong with him? He was tossing away the best thing in his life...*ever*.

'Well, that was very clear.'

Morgan lifted her chin and he had to admire her courage.

'Well, screw you and your lousy, spiteful, wimpy attitude.' She grabbed her bag off the table and yanked it over her shoulder. 'I'm going back to the hotel.'

Noah watched her take a couple of steps before remembering that she was still a target, Glasgow or not. 'You can't leave by yourself!' he shouted.

Morgan bared her teeth at him and he was quite sure that her eyes were glowing red. He couldn't blame her.

'Watch me. I'd rather be kidnapped by rabid Colombians than spend one more minute with you!'

Noah stood up, pulled out his mobile and nodded, his face grim. 'That's easy to make happen.' Pushing buttons, he held it up to his ear, and his voice was rough when he spoke. 'Amanda?' He waited a minute before speaking again. 'Listen, I know that we've had our problems but do you have any agents in Glasgow who can take over Morgan Moreau's protection detail?' He waited a beat and spoke again. 'No, I need him now. Like within the next half-hour...hour. You have? Great.'

Noah rattled off the address and bit his lip. 'Thanks. Amanda. I think the threat level to her has mostly been neutralised. but tell him that if anything happens to her—if she breaks even a fingernail—he's dead.'

Noah disconnected the call and slapped his mobile against the palm of his hand. He looked at Morgan, whose eyes were wide with shock, humiliation and hurt. He wanted to take her in his arms, apologise, but he knew that the smarter course of action would be to walk away from her while he still could. While his heart was still his and not walking around in her hands.

'Your wish is my command, Duchess,' he said with a mocking bow.

Now he just had to keep himself from hitting redial, cancelling the new bodyguard, gathering Morgan up and keeping her for ever.

It was the longest, quietest, hardest, most excruciating wait of his life, and when she walked out to the car with a kid who looked as if he should still be in school he stood in his old house, sank to the couch and, for the first time in fifteen years, cried.

CHAPTER TWELVE

A WEEK LATER Riley walked into Morgan's studio, two cups in her hand, and Morgan sighed at the green logo of the twin-tailed mermaid on the cup. It was a mega hazelnut-flavoured latte, her favourite, and she needed it—along with Prozac and probably a padded cell.

'Hey, I was just about to buzz you,' Morgan said. 'I need help.'

'Okay.' Riley took a seat on the stool next to her at the workbench. 'You look like hell. Still crying?'

Morgan took a deep breath and nodded. 'Yeah. You?'

'Mmm... What a pair we are. You've heard the news?'

'That James is on his way back from Colombia and a deal is imminent?'

'Yeah.'

Morgan sighed and pointed out a word on her computer screen. 'What's this word?'

Riley bent down and peered over her shoulder. 'Vichyssoise.'

'Jeez, I can't read in English and they throw French words in,' Morgan grumbled. 'Do you have some time? Can you go through this menu for the ball with me?'

'Sure.'

She and Riley spent the next fifteen minutes discussing the ball, finalising the menu and the entertainment, the decorations and the ticket sales—which were going through the roof.

'We also need to approve the design of the mannequin cages and we need Noah's input there.'

Morgan stared at her fingers. 'Feel free to call him. I won't.'

She felt the tears in the back of her throat. His words from a week ago still bounced around her skull.

'I don't want you here any more.'

He'd preferred to face his demons alone than have her around. What did that say about her? She could understand him dumping her when they got back to New York, when he got bored with the sex, but she'd seen how much pain he'd been in, how he'd been struggling to deal with the memories of his past, and she'd thought that he'd want her there—that he wouldn't want to go through that alone.

But, no, Noah hadn't wanted her around.

All her life she'd tried to be good enough—for her family, for herself. She knew that she didn't always reach the standard she'd set for herself, and mostly she was okay with that. But to be told, during such a sad time, that she wasn't wanted or needed had lashed her soul.

She simply wasn't good enough…

'Horse crap, Morgan.'

She heard Noah's words spoken at Bon Chance as clear as day and actually looked around for the source of that statement. When Riley didn't react she looked inside herself and heard the phrase again.

'The biggest, load of self-indulgent horse crap.'

Morgan almost laughed as emotion swelled inside her. She wasn't sure where it came from, what its source was, but she recognised the power of it, saw the pure truth for the first time in a week, months—her entire life.

'Bats on a freakin' broomstick,' she muttered.

'Pardon?' Riley looked up and frowned.

Morgan looked at her best friend and put her hand over

her mouth in surprised shock. 'What happened with Noah wasn't about me…it was about *him*.'

'Okay, I have no idea what you're talking about,' Riley complained.

'Him kicking me into touch wasn't about me—wasn't about me not being good enough. I just assumed it was because I always assume the worst about myself. I keep saying that it's hard for people to deal with my dyslexia. but in truth I've never come to terms with it. And because of that I assume that everything is about me. My habitual reaction is to think that I'm not good enough, to think the worst of myself.'

Riley leaned back and clapped a slow beat. 'Well, glory hallelujah, the child has seen the light.'

Morgan stood up and paced the area in front of Riley. 'He told me what the problem was but I didn't listen. He said that he didn't like feeling so connected to me—something about his heart and feeling joy when I was around. That around me emotion twisted him up.' Morgan pointed her finger at Riley. '*He's* the one who's scared, who doesn't know what to do with me. He felt insecure and emotional and… Damn it, I'm going to smack him into next year!'

Riley smiled. 'I'd like to see you try.'

'He was hurting and not knowing why he was grieving for his father—the man was a waste of oxygen by all accounts—he didn't know how to channel his emotion and he lashed out. He needed me, but he was scared to need me. Everyone else he needed had either left him or let him down. He had to push me away to protect himself.'

'Look at you—you're a female Dr Phil.' Riley crossed her legs. 'So, what are you going to do, Morgs?'

'Go to him, of course. I might understand better, but I'm still mad that he kicked me into touch.' Morgan smiled grimly. 'Oh, I'm *so* going to kick some gorgeous SAS ass.'

Riley nodded. 'That's my girl.'

* * *

Back in London, in his favourite pub, Noah took a listless sip of his beer and looked up as his brothers sat down on the bar stools on either side of him. It seemed that Chris, who was outside taking a call, felt he needed reinforcements for the lecture he intended to dole out. *Wuss.*

Noah sent a look to the door and thought that he could get by Chris if he wanted to. He'd taken on a room full of Colombian thugs—nearly killing one in the process—and won.

Yeah, run away from this conversation like a coward, Fraser—like you did from Morgan. Just to add to the long list of things he'd done lately that he wasn't proud of.

Hamish slapped him on the back and placed their orders for drinks. 'So, let me see if Chris has the story straight. You still haven't spoken to Morgan and apologised?'

No small talk, no lead-up just...*pow!* 'Essentially.'

'You really are a git, big bro',' said Mike, lifting his glass and toasting him. 'Though admittedly it *is* nice to see that you have clay feet. But dumping Morgan...' Mike leaned forward and frowned at him. 'Did you get punched in the head? In other words, *are you freaking insane*?'

Noah lifted his hand to protest and saw that Chris had joined his merry group. 'Thanks,' he said, sarcastically. 'Did they need to know?'

'Sure they need to see their control freak big brother unhinged,' Chris said on a smile.

'I am *not* unhinged,' Noah said through gritted teeth. Miserable and dejected, but still clear-thinking.

'Mmm, that's why you're the model of efficiency at work. *Not.*'

'You talk like a teenage girl,' Noah muttered.

'You're acting like one,' Chris countered.

'And I am not unhinged! Unhinged was what I felt like when I saw that knife to her neck. When I contemplated what life would be without her...' He hadn't meant to add that.

'You're living a life without her,' Mike pointed out. 'And how's *that* working out for you?'

'Shut up, Oprah.'

Bloody awful, but the point was… What was the point? All he knew was that he was scared to love her, scared to lose her, and scared to live this half-life without her in it. He just wanted to go back to his life as it had been before he met her, when he'd been heartless and independent and unemotional.

When life had been easy and uncomplicated. It hadn't quite worked out that way. Yet.

And he really didn't want to have this conversation with his brothers and Chris. There was nothing wrong, in his opinion, with those old-fashioned men-to-men conversations, where they didn't discuss emotions at all. But, no, he had to be saddled with three touchy-feely, new age guys who thought it was perfectly reasonable to discuss his broken heart.

'The least you can do is talk to her,' Hamish suggested.

'Back off,' he growled into his beer.

'Either that or go to my bothy in the Highlands and lick you wounds in private,' Chris suggested.

'Will any of you follow me there and carry on bleating in my ear?' Noah demanded.

They looked at each other, shook their heads. 'Not for a day or two at least.'

'Sold.' Noah slapped his hands on the bar. It was exactly what he needed: time and solitude to think, recover and re-live his time with Morgan.

No, that wasn't right. To *get over* Morgan. Because that was what he had to do, the sensible thing to do.

Ten days from that momentous day—the one that had ended with Noah kicking her out of her life—and she was back in Scotland, Morgan thought, her hands on the wheel of the rental car. She was driving in a country halfway across the world.

James had worked out an agreement at the mine that was complicated and confusing, and the details of which she cared absolutely nothing about. What was important was that everyone was thoroughly convinced that the threat to their well-being was neutralised and her mother and father had come out of hiding thoroughly sick of each other. Her father had disappeared on a trip to investigate a mine in Botswana and her mother had started poking her nose into MI business and, more annoyingly, ball business. Situation normal there.

James and Riley were either snipping at each other, ignoring each other or avoiding each other. Situation... She didn't even know how to categorise their situation...crazy?

The CFT guards—even more robotic than Noah—had gone back to being robotic with someone else and her apartment had become her own again.

Situation so very *not* normal there.

She hated it. She hated the silence and the fact that there was no one to drink wine with, chat with, curl up around at night, make sweet love to in the morning.

She missed him. With every breath she took. But more than anything else she was so steel-meltingly angry with him that he'd just walked away—because she couldn't concentrate on a thing and because her stress levels were stratospheric.

She couldn't design, couldn't make decisions on the ball, couldn't eat, couldn't sleep.

She had a business to run, an important social event to organise, and after she'd given him many, *many* pieces of her mind she'd put him aside and resume her life—go back to normal. She was not going to beg, to tell him she loved him, adored his body, loved his generous, protective spirit. She wouldn't tell him that she'd fallen in love with him eight years ago and never really stopped. *Dammit.*

Morgan felt the familiar cocktail of love and misery and anger churn in her stomach. How dared he throw comments mentioning joy and love at her head and then kick her out of his life? He was the most courageous man she knew except when it came to loving—*keeping!*—her. Well, she wasn't just going to lie down and accept it...

Telling him where to get off and that she was worth taking a chance on were the *only* reasons she was on this godforsaken road in the middle of the Scottish Highlands, probably lost. Again.

Okay, depending on how wretched he was, she might let it slip that she missed him and that she loved him—maybe. Probably.

Morgan yawned and shoved her exhaustion away. She'd landed at Heathrow yesterday, threatened Chris with dismemberment if he didn't tell her where he was and nearly bitten his head off when he'd offered to take her to the bothy close to Auterlochie. She could find it herself, she'd stated grandly, and now she wished she'd taken him up on his offer. Because this place was desolate, and it was getting dark, and there were scary cows with big horns that glared at her from the side of the road.

As night and the temperature fell Morgan saw the glimmer of a stone cottage off the road and wondered if this could possibly be the bothy Noah sometimes escaped to. There were no lights on in the house, and there wasn't any sign of the deep green Land Rover Chris said he used up here.

There was only one way to find out, she thought, bunching her much hated map in her hand and storming up to the front door. After knocking and getting no response she found the door opened to her touch, and she looked around a large room: kitchen at one end, lounge at the other. Through the closed door she presumed there was a bedroom and bathroom. There were battered couches, one that held a jersey draped over its arm. Morgan picked it up and sighed when she inhaled Noah's familiar scent.

The cabin was also ridiculously tidy, and she knew she was in the right place.

She loved him...but she was going to kill him when she

saw him. For making her fall in love with him, for making her chase after him, for being a totally stupid, pathetically scared of commitment, moron *man*.

'What? Not naked this time?' Noah said from the doorway.

Morgan dropped the shirt and whipped around. Her heart bounced and then settled as her eyes drifted over him in the half-light of the cottage.

Kill him...slowly...

'Can you put some lights on?' Morgan asked politely.

'Why?'

'So that I can see your face when I scream at you.'

Morgan blinked as he flicked the switch on the wall next to the door.

Noah walked into the room and shoved his hands into his jeans pockets. Morgan cocked her head at him and saw that there were blue shadows under his eyes and his mouth looked grim. Tense. Possibly scared.

Good. He should be.

'You don't seem very surprised to see me,' Morgan said.

'Chris gave me a heads-up that you were on your way but I expected you hours ago. I was out looking for you. What happened? Did you get lost?'

With that comment he lit the fuse to her temper. 'Of *course* I got lost, you idiot! Lots and lots of times! I forgot to check if there was a GPS when I hired the car! I have dyslexia and I can't read a damn map at the best of times. When I'm sad and stressed and heartbroken and miserable and depressed it's near impossible!'

She scrunched the map into a ball and launched it at his head.

'Tell me how you really feel, Morgs.' Noah struggled to keep his grin from forming.

Morgan looked at him, hurt and shocked. 'You think this is a joke? That the pain you've caused me is funny? I've been travelling for days so that you can *laugh* at me?'

Noah scrubbed his hands over his face. 'No—God, no! Sorry. I didn't mean that. I'm just amazed that you are here; you nearly missed me. I was going to leave in the morning. I'm really, really happy that you *are* here.'

Morgan gave him a stony look. 'Sure you are.. Look, this is stupid. I'm probably very stupid... I'll just go.'

Noah moved to stand in front of the door. 'You're not going anywhere, and you are definitely not driving anywhere in the dark. You might end up in a loch.'

Morgan tried to push him out of the way but she couldn't move his bulk. 'You lost the right to tell me what to do, to protect me, when you kicked me out of your life and sicced those CFT agents on me!'

'I intend to protect you for the rest of your life, if you'll let me.'

Everything in Morgan's body tensed as she looked up into his gorgeous face. The humour had fled and his eyes were deep and serious and radiating truth. And love. And hope. Her heart lurched.

'Come and sit down, Morgan. Please.'

Okay, maybe she could just hear him out...just a little. Morgan allowed Noah to take her hand and she perched on the edge of a couch. Noah pulled the battered coffee table closer to the couch and sat on it, facing her.

'I was—*am*—happy to see you, When I couldn't find you...I thought you'd plunged off the road or crashed somewhere. I was considering calling out a search party when I saw your car pull in here. I belted back here, just so relieved that you are okay.'

'Uh-huh.'

'Secondly, I was planning to leave tomorrow. I was going to go home.'

'Back to London.'

'Back to *you*. You are my home, Morgan. You're the place where I want to be.' Noah touched her hand with his fingers. 'I've spent the last week trying to convince myself that I'm better on my own, that I can live without you, that I'm independent and a hard-ass and I don't need anyone. And I don't need *anyone*, Morgs. I just need you. I love you. More than I can express and much more than you will ever know,' he added, his voice saturated with emotion.

'But you sent me away!' Morgan's fist rocketed into his shoulder. 'I loved you, but you sent me away like I was nothing!'

'I sent you away because you were *everything* and I was scared.' Noah gripped her fist and kissed her knuckles. 'I'm stupid when it comes to you—haven't you realised that yet? Do you want me to grovel?'

Morgan sniffed as her head and her heart started pounding with the warm fairy dust sparkles of happiness. 'I can't imagine you grovelling well.'

'True.' Noah kissed her knuckles again and held her eyes. 'I'm sorry that I acted like a jerk.'

'I've been miserable without you. I can't do anything without you,' Morgan grumbled, her fingers on his cheek.

'I know.'

'No, you don't understand. The dyslexia has been really bad—'

'Babe, it's not that. I've also been less than useless at the office…why do you think Chris sent me up here? I couldn't think, hold a reasonable conversation, I forgot meetings and stopped midway through my sentences. I couldn't function without you.' Noah's other hand clasped her face and his thumb drifted over her cheekbone. 'It has nothing to do with the dyslexia and everything to do with the fact that you and I are better together than we are apart.'

'So it seems.'

'Do you remember what you said at Bon Chance? Just before I heard about Michael?'

Morgan nodded.

'I want the whole bang-shoot too—with you. I don't care how many dyslexic kids we have because they will be *our* kids and they will be brilliant in their own ways—just as you are. I will never think anything is lacking in you, or them. Yeah, I'll get frustrated with you—as you will with me— but it will never be caused by your dyslexia. And I will love you, hard, often, passionately, for ever.'

'Oh, Noah. I love you too.' But Morgan thought she should issue one more threat before she allowed pure happiness to envelop her. 'I came here to kick your ass.'

'I'd much prefer to kiss yours.' Noah's curved lips drifted down to hers. Before they touched, he spoke again. 'I don't suppose you packed any of those burlesque corsets, did you? I've been having a few fantasies about them...'

Morgan smiled against his mouth. 'No, you're going to have to earn a corset. You can start by kissing me, soldier.'

'With all my pleasure, Duchess.'

EPILOGUE

Four months later...

IN A CROWD of three thousand people Morgan knew exactly whose hand touched her back—recognised the gentleness in his strong touch. Morgan lifted her solid black mask and smiled at Noah, who'd refused her entreaties to wear a costume as befitting a 1920s burlesque-themed ball or a mask. Then again, nobody could quite pull off a tuxedo like her soldier.

Well, a tuxedo jacket. The lower half of his tuxedo consisted of a kilt in the Fraser tartan, complete with furry sporran.

Noah could pull off a kilt too. Not that she would ever tell him that—she was having far too much fun teasing him about his 'Scottish skirt'.

And naked... Actually nobody could pull off naked as well as Noah could, and as soon as she was done with the ball they were headed for Stellenbosch, where she intended to devote her considerable energies to keeping him naked as much as possible.

Noah placed both his arms around her and held her as they stared down at the crowds below them. The ballroom glittered and heaved with colour, laughter rose and fell, and champagne and other fine spirits flowed. Couples whirled around the dance floor and other guests stood in front of the birdcages and looked at the beautiful pieces of jewellery art.

'Why are you hiding up here on this little balcony by yourself?' Noah asked.

'I just need a break,' Morgan answered. 'Isn't it spectacular, Noah?'

'It is, and you should be proud of yourself. You did this, Duchess. This is all yours and it's fabulous.'

'Well, mine and Ri's. We work well together.'

Morgan rested her head on his chest and stroked his hand with her fingertips. 'By the way, Mum has agreed to using some of the money raised tonight to make a hefty donation to that dyslexic foundation I visited the other day. They want me to sit on their board.'

'Are you going to tell them—tell people about your dyslexia?' Noah asked, turning her to face him.

'I thought...maybe. What do you think?'

'I think that you—apart from the fact that you are the untidiest person alive—are awe-inspiring.' Noah kissed her nose. 'I have something for you.'

'You do? Will I like it?'

Noah looked uncharacteristically serious. 'I hope so. Buying a gift for the Diamond Queen's daughter is a nightmare of epic proportions, and everyone I've spoken to has a different idea about what you like. Riley says one thing, James another—mostly just to take the opposite view to Riley, I think.'

'I have to do something about those two, and soon,' Morgan muttered, her eyes narrowing.

'Hey, concentrate! We're talking about your present. And the angst I've gone through to get it.'

Morgan grinned. 'Sorry. So, what did I do to deserve a present?'

Noah tipped his head in thought. 'Well, you do this little thing with your tongue...'

Morgan blushed. 'Noah! *Jeez!*'

Noah touched her cheek with the back of his knuckle. 'I love you with everything I have and the last months have been crazy exciting.'

'Do you miss London? Your brothers? You've uprooted your life...' Morgan said, a little worried. He'd made huge changes to his life to be with her and she needed to know that he had no regrets.

'We've expanded Auterlochie by opening another branch in the city, and I've moved into a gorgeous flat with a woman who says she loves me and gives me frequent sex. Such a hard thing to do...' Noah said, his eyes laughing at her fears.

Morgan rolled her eyes. *Okay, then.* 'So, about my present...what did you buy me?'

'Not so much buy as...' Noah pulled a box out of his pocket and handed it over. 'We talked about getting married at some point and I wanted to make it official. I know it's not the fanciest or the biggest or the—'

'Shut up, No,' Morgan said, flipping open the lid. Inside, cleaned and sparkling, sat his mother's red beryl ring—the one she hadn't seen since that day in the studio.

Morgan swallowed and put her hand on her chest as she stared at the box in her hand.

He could have had a ring designed by Carl, bought her the flashiest diamond and got down on one knee in front of all these people and proposed, but nothing, Morgan knew, would have had a greater emotional impact on her than receiving his beloved mother's ring.

Morgan pulled it out and handed it back to him.

'You don't want it?' he asked quietly, disappointment in his eyes and voice.

Morgan shook her head, her eyes welling. 'I want you to put it on me. And as you do it,' she added, as Noah picked up her hand and held her ring finger, 'I want to tell you that I'm honoured to wear this ring and that, like her, I will always love you.'

Noah kissed her lips and held her against him, and she felt warm and protected and so very, very loved in his arms.

After a long, emotion-soaked moment he whispered in her ear. 'I'm loving your dress, Duchess.'

She grinned and curtsied. 'Merci.'

She'd had a steam punk green and black corset designed for the evening and teamed it with a black tulle and organza skirt that rode low on her hips and exposed a strip of her belly. It had been worth every penny to see Noah's eyes bug when he'd first caught sight of it.

'I can't wait to get you alone,' Noah said, nuzzling her neck. 'I'm going to have so much fun taking it off you.'

Morgan bent her knees, dipped her hand under his kilt and touched his warm thigh. Her eyes sparkled as she looked up into his face. 'And I'm going to have lots of fun taking *your* skirt off you.'

'It's a kilt!' Noah howled for the umpteenth time that night. 'Respect the kilt!'

Morgan grinned, knowing that her happiness was echoed in his eyes. 'I deeply respect what's under the—'

'Don't say skirt.'

Noah captured her face in his hands and kissed her lips as her hand danced up his thigh.

'Duchess?'

'Yes, soldier?'

'Behave.'

Morgan's eyes laughed at him. 'Absolutely...*not.*'

* * * * *

HOT ISLAND NIGHTS

BY
SARAH MAYBERRY

Sarah Mayberry lives in Melbourne, Australia—at the moment! With something like eight moves in the past ten years under her belt, she always keeps the cardboard boxes and packing tape within easy reach. When she's not moving or planning to move, she's writing, reading, cooking or trying to get motivated to do some exercise. Oh, and she loves a good movie night. By the time you read this, she also hopes that she will have become a dog owner.

Huge thanks go to Pamela Torrance for giving up her time in the midst of her own upheaval to offer me pointers on what English people sound like. Thanks for the reality check, Pamela—consider the front end "your" part of the book!

As always, this book would not exist without the support of Chris, the heart, backbone and brain of my life. And, of course, Wanda, who never fails to knock me into shape and curb my excesses and cheer me towards the finishing line.
Bless you!

1

ELIZABETH MASON STARED at the wedding registry in her hand. Printed on expensive linen paper beneath the green and gold Harrods logo, it was a roll call of prestigious brand names: Villeroy & Boch, Royal Doulton, Lalique, Noritake, Le Creuset. There were two dinner sets listed—one for everyday use, one for entertaining—cookware, stemware, cutlery, a champagne bucket, various pieces of barware, vases, platters, table linens...

If their wedding guests bought even half the items listed, she and Martin would have a house full of finely crafted, beautiful things with which to start their married life. Their home would be a showpiece, perfect in every detail.

Elizabeth pressed a hand to her chest. The tight feeling was back. As though she couldn't get enough air. She lowered her head and concentrated on regulating her breathing.

In, out. In, out.

A delicate piano sonata trickled over the sound system. A salesman brushed past, directing a customer to the Royal Worcester display. A bead of perspiration ran down Elizabeth's side.

She had to get a grip on these panic attacks. This was supposed to be a happy time. In eight weeks she would be marrying the man she'd been dating for the past six years and starting a new life with him. She shouldn't be feeling panicky or anxious.

"These are lovely, Elizabeth."

Elizabeth looked up to see her grandmother holding a glass from the Waterford Crystal collection. Light fractured off the highly polished surface of a champagne flute that appeared to be an exact replica of the set her grandparents had at home.

"They're beautiful," Elizabeth said. "But I think Martin prefers a more modern look. He's very keen on the Riedel flutes."

She could feel heat creeping into her face. She'd always been a terrible liar. *She* was the one who preferred the more modern design—Martin didn't give a fig about glassware. But she could hardly come right out and state her preference.

"Have a closer look, see how they feel in your hand," her grandmother said, gesturing for Elizabeth to join her.

Elizabeth opened her mouth to reiterate her objection— then closed it without saying a word. She knew what would happen once her grandmother realized Elizabeth didn't share her taste. Grandmama wouldn't say anything, of course, because it wasn't her way to express displeasure so directly, but her mouth would turn down at the corners and she'd be withdrawn for the rest of the day. She might not come to dinner, or perhaps there would be some mention of her heart medication.

It was emotional blackmail, of course, something Grand-mama was a master at. Over the years she'd shaped Elizabeth's decisions and actions—major and minor—with the merest flutter of a hand or the mention of a headache or a doctor's visit. Even though Elizabeth understood the manipulation behind the behavior, she'd always given in. It was easier that way—and, really, at the end of the day, did it matter if she and Martin drank from the Waterford glasses instead of the Riedels if it made her grandmother happy?

So instead of standing her ground, she joined her grandmother and held the glass and agreed that it had a very pleasing weight in the hand, perfect for special occasions. Her grandmother collared a saleswoman and began asking questions about the manufacturing process and whether it would be possible to order replacement glasses in the future should any breakages occur.

Elizabeth stood to one side with a small, polite smile on her face. Around her, sales staff glided amongst the displays, talking in hushed, reverential tones. Everywhere she looked there were exquisite, fragile, priceless things, arranged to appeal to even the most fastidious eye.

Her gaze fell on a nearby table of cut-glass whiskey decanters. She had a vision of herself grabbing the table and upending the whole damn thing, sending the decanters smashing to the ground. It was so real her hands curled as though they were already gripping the table edge, and she could almost hear the crash of breaking glass and the shocked cries of the staff and customers.

She took a step backward and gripped her hands together.

Not because she thought there was any danger of her actually upending the display. There was no way she'd ever do such a thing.

She took another step away.

It's just prewedding jitters, she told herself. *Nothing to worry about. Every bride feels this way before her wedding.*

Except this wasn't the only reckless, anarchic impulse she'd had to quell recently. At last week's Friends of the Royal Academy luncheon she'd had to stifle the urge to throw back her head and scream at the top of her lungs when old Mr.

Lewisham had droned on about the quality of the napkins in the Academy's coffee shop and what it said about "society's declining standards." And yesterday she'd found her steps slowing outside a tattoo parlor near King's Cross station, admiring the tribal rose motif snaking up the arm of the girl behind the counter. She'd actually taken a step inside the store before common sense had reasserted itself and she'd remembered who she was.

"Elizabeth. Did you hear a word I just said?" her grandmother asked.

Elizabeth snapped into focus. Both the saleswoman and her grandmother were watching her, waiting for her response.

"Sorry, Grandmama, I was daydreaming," she said.

Her grandmother patted her arm fondly. "Come and have a look at the Wedgwood."

Smile fixed firmly in place, Elizabeth allowed herself to be led away.

IT WAS LATE AFTERNOON by the time she returned to her grandparents' Georgian town house in Mayfair. Her grandmother had come back after lunch for her afternoon rest, leaving Elizabeth to keep her appointment with the florist on her own. Elizabeth had dropped in to visit her friend Violet's boutique in Notting Hill on the way home and the hall clock was chiming six as she entered the house. She let her bag slide down her arm and started pulling off her scarf and gloves.

It was Tuesday, which meant Martin would be arriving any minute. He always ate here on Tuesday night. Just as he always played squash on Wednesdays and took her out for dinner on Fridays. If she hurried, she'd have time to freshen up before he arrived.

The housekeeper had stacked Elizabeth's mail neatly on the hall table and she flicked through it quickly as she turned toward the stairs. An official-looking envelope caught her eye and she paused. Martin had asked her to order a copy of her birth certificate so he could apply for their marriage license, since he was unable to request the certificate on her behalf. She tore the envelope open to confirm that it had finally arrived. One more thing to cross off her to-do list.

She unfolded the single sheet of paper, glancing over it quickly to check everything was in order. Elizabeth Jane Mason, born August 24, 1980, mother's name Eleanor Mary Whittaker, father's name—

Her scarf and gloves slipped from her fingers to the hall floor as she stared at the name beneath the box clearly marked Father's Given Name and Surname.

Sam Blackwell.

Who the hell is Sam Blackwell?

Her father was John Alexander Mason. Born January 16, 1942, killed in the same light-plane accident as her mother twenty-three years ago.

This had to be a mistake. It had to be.

Elizabeth focused on the closed door at the end of the long hallway. She started walking, certificate in hand, an uncomfortable tightness in her belly.

The sound of low, masculine laughter could be heard from behind the door of her grandfather's study as she drew closer, but for the first time in her life she didn't bother to knock.

"There's been some kind of mistake," she said as she barged into the room.

"Elizabeth. I was wondering when you'd get home," Martin said.

Her fiancé stood and approached to kiss her, his gray eyes crinkling at the corners as he smiled. As usual he was dressed immaculately in a tailored three-piece suit and conservatively striped silk tie, his dark hair parted neatly.

Instead of offering her mouth for his kiss, she thrust the certificate at him.

"Look. They've made a mistake. They've got my father's name wrong on my birth certificate."

For a split second Martin stilled. Then he shot her grandfather a quick, indecipherable look before turning his attention to the birth certificate.

"I thought you were going to have this delivered to the office so I could take care of the marriage license." Martin spoke mildly, but there was an undercurrent of tension in his voice.

Elizabeth looked at him, then at her grandfather's carefully blank face, and she knew.

It wasn't a mistake.

"What's going on?" Her voice sounded strange, wobbly and high.

"Why don't you have a seat, Elizabeth?" her grandfather suggested.

She allowed herself to be ushered into one of the button-back leather chairs facing the formidable mahogany desk. Her grandfather waited until Martin had taken the other seat before speaking.

"There is no mistake, I'm afraid. The man you know as your father, John Mason, was actually your stepfather. He married your mother when you were two years old."

For a moment there was nothing but the sound of the clock ticking. Elizabeth started to speak, then stopped because she had no idea what to say.

She'd been devastated by her parents' deaths when she was seven years old. For the first few months she'd lived with her grandparents she'd cried herself to sleep every night. She treasured the small mementos she had of her childhood—the vintage Steiff teddy bear her parents had given her when she was four, the rock fossils they'd found together on a family holiday, the empty perfume bottle that had once held her mother's favorite scent.

But now her grandfather was telling her that her parents weren't both dead, that it was her stepfather who'd died. That her real father—the stranger whose name was listed on her birth certificate—might still be alive and well somewhere in the world.

"Why has no one ever told me this before?"

"Because it wasn't necessary. I won't go into details, but Sam Blackwell is not someone we want involved in your life. John Mason was your father in every other way, so we didn't see the point in bringing up something that was best forgotten," her grandfather said.

There were so many assumptions in his speech, so many judgments. And all of them made on her behalf, with no consultation with her whatsoever.

Elizabeth's hands curled into fists. "Is he alive? My real father?"

"I believe so, yes."

She leaned forward. "Where does he live? What does he do? Is he in London? How can I contact him?"

"Elizabeth, I know this is a shock for you, but when you've had a chance to process I'm sure you'll agree that it really doesn't change your life in any substantial way," Martin said.

Elizabeth focussed on Martin for the first time. "You knew."

"Your grandfather told me after I proposed."

"You've known for *six months* and you didn't tell me?"

"Don't be angry with Martin. I requested that he respect my confidence. I didn't see the point in getting you upset over nothing," her grandfather said.

Nothing? *Nothing?*

"I'm thirty years old. I don't need to be protected. I deserve the truth. And my father being alive is not *nothing*. It is very decidedly *something*."

Martin shifted uncomfortably. Her grandfather placed his hands flat on the leather blotter on his desk and eyed her steadily.

"We did what we thought was best for you."

This was usually the point in any argument with her grandparents when she retreated. They'd taken her in when her parents died and bent over backward to ensure she had a happy childhood. They'd sent her to the best schools, attended every school play and recital and parent-teacher night, taken her on holidays to France and Italy—all despite her grandmother's heart condition and frail health. Elizabeth had grown up with a strong sense of obligation toward them and a determination that she would never be more of a burden than she had to be.

She'd excelled at school, then at university. She'd never stayed out late or come home drunk. She'd never had a one-night stand. Even her husband-to-be had come with their seal of approval, since he worked at her grandfather's law firm.

She owed them so much—everything, really. But she also owed herself. And what they'd done was wrong.

"This was my decision to make. You had no right to keep this from me."

Because she didn't trust herself to say more, because rage and a bunch of unwise, unruly words were pressing at the back of her throat, she stood and left the room. She'd barely made it halfway up the hall when she heard Martin coming after her.

"Elizabeth. Slow down."

He caught her elbow. She spun on him, pulling her arm free.

"Don't you dare tell me to calm down or that this doesn't matter, Martin. Don't you dare."

Her chest was heaving with the intensity of her emotions and he took a step away, clearly taken aback by her ferocity.

"If I could have told you without breaking your grandfather's confidence, I would have. Believe me." He was deeply sincere, his eyes worried.

"You're my fiancé, Martin. Don't you think you owe your loyalty to me before my grandfather?"

He ran a hand through his hair. "Under ordinary circumstances, yes, but your grandfather and I have a professional relationship as well as a personal one."

"I see." And she did. Martin was hoping to be made partner at the firm this year. The last thing he wanted was to rock the boat.

He reached out and took her hand, his thumb brushing reassuringly across her knuckles. "Elizabeth, if we could go somewhere private and talk this through, I'm sure you'll understand that everything was done with your best interests at heart."

Her incredulous laughter sounded loud in the hall.

"My best interests? How on earth would you know what my best interests are, Martin? You're so busy telling me what's good for me, you have no idea who I am or what I really want. It's like those bloody awful Waterford champagne flutes. No one cares what I think, and I'm such a pathetic coward I swallow it and swallow it and swallow it, even while I tell myself it's because I want to do the right thing and not upset the applecart."

Martin frowned. "Champagne flutes? I have no idea what you're talking about."

She knew he didn't, but it was all inextricably entwined in her head: her anger at her grandparents and Martin for this huge betrayal of her trust, her feelings of frustration and panic over the wedding, the suffocated feeling she got every time her grandparents made a decision for her or Martin spoke to her in that soothing tone and treated her as though she were made of fine porcelain.

"I can't do this," she said, more to herself than him. "This is a mistake."

It was suddenly very clear to her.

Martin slid his arm around her shoulders, trying to draw her into a hug. "Elizabeth, you're getting yourself upset."

The feeling of his arms closing so carefully around her was the last straw. She braced her hands against his chest and pushed free from his embrace.

"I want to call off the wedding."

Martin blinked, then reached for her again. "You don't mean that. You're upset."

She held him off. "Violet has been saying for months that I should stop and think about what I'm doing, and she's right. I don't want this, Martin. I feel like I'm suffocating."

"Violet. I might have known she'd have something to do with this. What rubbish has she been filling your head with now? The joys of being a free and easy slapper in West London? Or maybe how to get a head start on cirrhosis?"

He'd never liked Violet, which was only fair, since her best friend had taken a violent aversion to him from the moment they'd first met.

"No, actually. She pointed out that I was going to be thirty this year and that if I didn't wake up and smell the coffee I'd be fifty and still living the life my grandparents chose for me."

"What a load of rubbish."

She looked at him, standing there in his Savile Row suit, his bespoke shirt pristine-white. He didn't understand. Maybe he couldn't.

She knew about his childhood, about the poverty and the sacrifices his working-class single mom had made to send him to university. Elizabeth's life—the life they were supposed to have together once they were married—was the fulfillment of all his aspirations. The high-paying partnership with the long-established law firm, the well-bred wife to come home to, the holidays on the French or Italian Riviera, membership at all the right men's clubs.

"We can't get married, Martin. You don't know who I am," she said quietly. "How could you? *I* don't even know who I am."

She turned and walked up the hallway.

"Elizabeth. Can we at least talk about this?"

She kept walking. Her grandparents were going to be upset when they heard she'd called off the wedding. It wouldn't simply be a case of her grandmother having a headache—this would instigate full-scale damage control. They'd use every trick in the book to try to make her see sense. They'd make her feel guilty and stupid and wrong without actually accusing her of being any of those things. And she was so used to not rocking the boat, to toeing the line and doing the right thing that she was terribly afraid that she might listen to them and wind up married to Martin and unpacking all those expensive Harrods housewares in her marital home.

She needed some time to herself. To think. To work things out. Somewhere private and quiet. She thought of Violet's apartment above her shop and quickly discarded it. Even if it wasn't only a one bedroom, she wouldn't find much peace and quiet in Violet's hectic world. Plus it would be the first place her grandparents would look for her. Then she remembered what she'd said to Martin—*I don't even know who I am*—and the answer came to her.

She would go to her father. Wherever he might be. She would find him, and she would go to him, and she would start working out who Elizabeth Jane Mason really was, and what she really wanted.

FOUR DAYS LATER, ELIZABETH OPENED her rental car window and sucked in big lungfuls of fresh air. Her eyes were gritty with fatigue and she opened them wide, willing herself to wakefulness. She'd been traveling for nearly thirty hours to reach the other side of the world and now the foreign, somber-hued scrub of rural Australia was rushing past as she drove southwest from Melbourne toward Phillip Island, a small dot on the map nestled in the mouth of Westernport Bay.

She'd spent the past few days holed up in a hotel room in Soho while Violet leaned on her police-officer cousin to use his contacts to locate Elizabeth's father. The moment she'd learned that Sam Blackwell's last known place of residence was Phillip Island in Victoria, Australia, Elizabeth had booked a room at a local hotel and jumped on a plane.

She hadn't spoken to her grandparents beyond assuring them she was fine and perfectly sane and determined to stand by her decision to cancel the wedding. Her grandfather had tried to talk her out of it over the phone, of course, but she'd cut the conversation short.

Whatever happened next in her life was going to be her decision and no one else's.

The San Remo bridge appeared in front of her and she drove over a long stretch of water. Then she was on the island and the thought of meeting her father, actually looking into his face and perhaps seeing an echo of her own nose or eyes or cheekbones, chased the weariness away.

She had no idea what to expect from this meeting. She wasn't even sure what she wanted from it. A sense of connection? Information about where she came from? A replacement for the parents she'd lost when she was only seven years old?

The truth was, she could hardly remember her mother and father—or the man she knew as her father. There were snatches of memory—her mother laughing, the smell of her stepfather's pipe tobacco, moments from a family holiday—but precious little else. Her mother was always slightly sad in her few clear memories, her stepfather distant. Despite her lack of recall—or, perhaps, because of it—she'd always felt as though something profound was missing in her life. Her grandparents had been kind and loving in their own way, but their careful guardianship had not filled the gap the loss of her parents had left in her heart.

A gap she'd never fully acknowledged until right this minute. It was only now that she was on the verge of meeting her biological father for the first time that she understood how much she'd always craved the wordless, instinctive connection between parent and child, how she'd envied her friends their relationships with their parents.

Her hands tightened on the steering wheel and she gave herself a mental pep talk as she drove into the tree-lined main street of the township of Cowes, the most densely populated township on the island. It was highly likely that her father didn't even know she existed. Arriving on his doorstep full of expectations was the best way to start off on the wrong foot. She needed to be realistic and patient. They were strangers. There was no reason to think that they would feel any special connection with each other, despite the fact that they shared DNA.

And yet her stomach still lurched with nervousness as she turned the corner onto her father's street and stopped out the front of a cream and Brunswick-green house that had all the architectural appeal of a shoe box. Clad in vertical aluminum siding, it featured a flat roof, a deep overhang over a concrete porch, sliding metal windows and a patchy, brown front lawn.

A far cry from the elegant, historically listed homes of Mayfair. She wiped her suddenly sweaty hands on the thighs of her trousers.

She had no idea what kind of man her father was. What sort

of life he'd led. How he might react to his long-lost daughter appearing on his doorstep.

She'd had a lot of time to think about what might have happened between her mother and father all those years ago. In between dodging phone calls from Martin and reassuring her grandparents, she'd made some inquiries. She'd discovered that John Mason and her mother had married in January 1982 when Elizabeth was seventeen months old—further proof, if she'd been looking for it, that the birth certificate was accurate and John was not her father.

What the marriage record couldn't tell her was when her stepfather and mother had met or how long they'd dated before they got married or if there had been another man on the scene at the time. Her father, for example.

Her grandfather clearly didn't have a great opinion of Sam Blackwell. She wondered what her father had done to earn his condemnation. She'd been tempted to confront her grandfather again before she departed and insist he tell her everything he knew, but after a great deal of debating she'd decided not to. She was going to meet her father and talk to him and hear his story and form her own opinion about him.

But before she did any of that, she needed to get her backside out of the car and across the lawn to her father's front door.

She didn't move.

Come on, Elizabeth. You didn't fly all this way to sit in a hire car out the front of your father's house like some sort of deranged stalker.

And yet she still didn't reach for the door handle.

This meant so much to her. A chance to feel connected to someone. A chance to have a father.

Just do it, Elizabeth.

She curled her fingers around the cool metal of the door

handle just as her phone rang, the sound shrill in the confines of the car. She checked caller ID.

"Violet," she said as she took the call.

"E. How was your flight? What's happening? Have you spoken to him yet?"

"Long. Not much. And no," Elizabeth said, answering her friend's questions in order. "I'm sitting in front of his house right now, trying to get up the courage to knock on the door."

"You're nervous."

"Just a little."

"Don't be. Once he gets to know you, he'll be over the moon you've tracked him down."

Elizabeth pulled a face. Violet's vote of confidence was lovely, but if her father knew she existed—a big *if*—he'd clearly had his reasons for keeping his distance for the past thirty-odd years.

"I don't know. Maybe I'm doing this all wrong." Elizabeth studied the slightly shabby house doubtfully. "Maybe I should have made contact with a letter or e-mail first. Used a lawyer to break the ice…"

"No. You've done the right thing. And even if you haven't, you're there now. All you have to do is knock on his door."

"You make it sound so easy," Elizabeth joked.

"Come on, E. You're a woman on a mission, remember? You're reclaiming your life, striking out on your own. Shaking off old Droopy Drawers was just the first step."

Elizabeth frowned at her friend's less-than-flattering description of Martin. "I wish you wouldn't call him that. Just because I've decided not to marry him doesn't mean he's a bad person."

"True. It's not as though he's going around *literally* boring people to death. Although he took a fairly good stab at stifling the life out of you."

"Vi…"

"Sorry. I just think it should be a punishable offense for someone as young as he is to carry on like a crusty old bugger. How many thirty-two-year-olds do you know wear cardigans with leather elbow patches?"

"Just because he dresses conservatively doesn't mean he's crusty, Vi. He's just…conservative," Elizabeth finished lamely.

"*Conservative?* I'm sorry, E, but conservative is not the word for a man who refuses to have sex in anything other than the missionary position. The word you're looking for is *repressed.*"

Elizabeth kneaded her forehead with the tips of her fingers. "You have no idea how much I regret ever saying anything to you about that, Vi."

Martin would be mortified if he knew that she'd discussed their sex life with anyone. Especially Violet.

Elizabeth blamed her dentist. If it hadn't been for the stupid article in the stupid women's magazine in his waiting room, there was no way she would have tried to talk to Martin about her "sexual needs and desires" instead of "vainly waiting for him to intuit" them, and there was no way she would have felt the need to seek counsel from her best friend in the embarrassing aftermath.

"I'm not going to apologize for refusing to let you sweep that sterling little moment under the rug," Violet said. "*Normal* people—note I'm stressing the word *normal,* as opposed to *uptight repressives*—talk to each other about sex and explore their sexuality and have fun in bed. They don't pat you on the head and tell you they respect you too much to objectify you, or whatever rubbish excuse he came out with after you'd finally got up the gumption to talk to him. And I love that he tried to make it all about you, by the way, and not about his hang-ups."

"I really don't want to talk about this again."

But Violet was off and running on one of her favorite rants. "For God's sake, it wasn't as though you asked him to tie you up and go at you with a cheese grater or something. You wanted to do it doggy style, big bloody deal. There were no small animals involved, no leather or hot wax."

"I've called off the wedding, Vi. This is definitely filed under The Past. You need to let it go."

There was a small silence on the other end of the phone.

"You're right. Sorry. He just really gets on my wick."

"Well, you'll probably never have to see him again, since he's hardly going to want to know me once he's gotten over the fact that I've dumped him. That should make you feel better."

A dart of fear raced down Elizabeth's spine as she registered her own words. She'd changed the course of her life by walking away from the wedding and she had no idea what might happen next. A terrifying, knee-weakening thought. But she refused to regret her decision. The truth was she'd never really loved Martin the way a woman should love the man with whom she planned to spend the rest of her life. She was fond of him. She admired his many good qualities. He made her feel safe. But he also exasperated her and made her yearn for...*something* she didn't even have a name for.

"E. Someone's just come into the shop and I have to go. But you can do this, okay? Just get out of the car and go introduce yourself. Whatever comes after that, you'll handle it."

"Thanks, coach. And thanks for all the hand-holding and tissue-passing and intel-gathering over the past few days," Elizabeth said.

"Pshaw," her friend said before ending the call.

Elizabeth put her phone in her handbag and took a deep

breath. It was time to stop fannying about and get this over and done with.

Her heart in her mouth, she opened the car door and stepped into the hot Australian sun.

2

NATHAN JONES WOKE TO a single moment of pure nothingness. For a split second before the forgetfulness of sleep fell away, he felt nothing, knew nothing, remembered nothing.

It was the best part of his day, hands down.

And then he woke fully and it was all there: the memories, the anxiety, the guilt and shame and fear. Heavy and relentless and undeniable.

He stared at the ceiling for a long beat, wondering at the fact that he kept forcing himself to jump through the flaming hoop of this shit, day in, day out. There was precious little joy in it and plenty of pain.

Then he forced himself to sit up and swing his legs over the side of the bed. It wasn't like he had a choice, after all. He wasn't a quitter. Even though there were times when it seemed damned appealing.

His head started throbbing the moment he was upright. He breathed deeply. It would pass soon enough. God knew he'd chalked up enough experience dealing with hangovers over the past four months to know.

The important thing was that he hadn't woken once that he could remember. If the price he had to pay this morning for oblivion last night was a hangover, then so be it.

He stood and ran a hand over his hair, then grabbed the towel flung over the end of the bed and wrapped it around his waist. He worked his tongue around his mouth as he headed for the door. Water was called for. And maybe some food. Although he wasn't certain about the food part just yet.

The full glare of the midmorning sun hit him the moment he stepped out of the studio into the yard. He grunted and shielded his eyes with his forearm. Looked like it was going to be another stinker.

He crossed to the main house and entered the kitchen. The kitchen floor was gritty with sand beneath his feet and he smiled to himself. Sam would have a cow when he came home, no doubt. Nate had never met a guy more anal about keeping things shipshape and perfect. A regular Mr. Clean, was Sammy.

The fridge yielded a bottle of water and he closed his eyes, dropped his head back and tipped it down his throat. He swallowed and swallowed until his teeth ached from the cold, then put the nearly empty bottle onto the kitchen counter. He was about to head to the shower when a knock sounded at the front door.

Nate frowned. He wasn't expecting anyone. Didn't particularly want to see anyone, either. That was the whole point of being on the island—privacy. Peace and quiet. Space.

He walked through the living room to the front hallway. He could see a silhouette through the glass panel in the door. As he hovered, debating whether or not to answer, the silhouette lifted its hand and knocked again.

"Coming," he said, aware he sounded more than a little like a grumpy old man.

The door swung open and he found himself facing a tall, slim woman with delicately sculpted features and deep blue eyes, her pale blond hair swept up into the kind of hairstyle that made him think of Grace Kelly and other old-school movie stars.

"Yes?" he said, his tone even more brusque. Probably because he hadn't expected to find someone so beautiful on his front step.

She opened her mouth then closed it without saying anything as her startled gaze swept from his face to his chest, belly and south, then up to his bare chest again. There was a long, pregnant silence as she stared at his sternum. Then she pinned her gaze on a point just beyond his right shoulder and cleared her throat.

"I'm terribly sorry. I'm looking for Sam Blackwell. I was told this is his place of residence."

Her voice was clipped and cultured, the kind of cut-glass accent he associated with the royal family and people who maintained a string of polo ponies.

"You've got the right place, but Sam's not around right now," he said.

"I see. Could you tell me when he'll be back?" She darted a quick, nervous glance toward his chest before fixing her gaze over his shoulder again. If he didn't know better, he'd think she'd never seen a bare chest before, the way she couldn't bring herself to look him in the eye. Six months ago he would have been amused and intrigued by her flustered reaction—she was a beautiful woman, after all.

But that was six months ago.

"Sam won't be back until the new year," he said. "Try him again after the fifth or sixth."

He started to swing the door closed between them.

"The new year? But that's nearly a month away." Her eyes met his properly for the first time, wide with disbelief and maybe a little bit of dismay.

His gut told him to close the door, send her on her way.

He had enough on his plate without taking on someone else's worries.

"Not much I can do about that, sorry," he said instead.

She pushed a strand of hair off her forehead. The movement made her white linen shirt gape and he caught a glimpse of coffee-colored lace and silk.

"Do you have a number I can contact him at?"

"No offense, but I'm not about to hand Sam's number out to just anybody."

She blinked. "But I'm not just anybody, I assure you."

"If you want to leave your number and a message with me, I'll make sure he gets it."

She frowned. "This isn't the kind of thing you handle with a message."

Nate shrugged. He'd offered her a solution, but if she wasn't interested…

"Then maybe you need to wait till Sam's back in town."

"I've travelled thousands of miles to see him, Mr.…?" She paused, waiting for him to supply his name.

"Nate. Nathan Jones."

"My name's Elizabeth Mason."

She held out her hand. After a second's hesitation he shook it. Her fingers were cool and slender, her skin very soft.

"I really need to make contact with Sam Rockwell," she said, offering what he guessed was her best social smile.

"Like I said, leave your number with me, and I'll make sure he gets it."

Her finely arched eyebrows came together in a frown. "Perhaps you could tell me where he is, then, if you won't give me his number?"

"Look, Ms. Mason, whatever this is about, if Sam owes you money or something else, the best I can do for you is to pass your number on. That's it, end of story."

"I'm not a debt collector." She appeared shocked at the idea.

"Whatever. That's my best offer, take it or leave it."

When she simply stared at him, he shrugged. "Fine," he said, and he started closing the door again.

"He's my father. Sam Blackwell is my father," she blurted.

That got his attention.

Sam had never mentioned a daughter, or any other family for that matter. Not that the omission necessarily meant anything, given that Sam wasn't exactly the talkative type.

Nate frowned. Why would Sam invite his daughter to visit when he knew he was going to be interstate?

"Sam didn't know you were coming, did he?"

"No, he didn't." She gave a nervous little laugh. "In fact, I suspect he doesn't even know I exist. Which makes me incredibly stupid to have jumped on a plane to come find him like this, but I didn't even think about the fact that he might not even be here—"

Nate took an instinctive step backward as her voice broke and tears filled her eyes.

Should have shut the door when you had the chance, buddy.

She tilted her head back and blinked rapidly. Nate considered and discarded a number of responses before reluctantly pushing the door wide.

"You'd better come in," he said.

She gave him a grateful look as she walked past him and into the house. He led her to the kitchen.

"You want some water?"

"Yes, thank you."

He waved her toward one of the beat-up vinyl upholstered chairs around the kitchen table, then grabbed a glass from the cupboard and filled it at the tap.

"Thank you," she said as he handed her the glass. "I promise I'm not normally like this. It's just that it's been a long flight and things have been a little crazy lately. And I really should have thought this through some more—" She shook her head. The hand holding the glass was trembling with emotion. "Sorry. I'm babbling again. I'm not normally a babbler, either."

She offered him a tremulous smile. She looked so vulnerable sitting there, so lost and confused.

Everything in Nate screamed retreat. He didn't need this.

"Look, I don't want to get involved in some kind of family dispute or *This Is Your Life* situation," he said.

Her smile disappeared as a deep flush rose up her neck and into her cheeks.

"I don't believe I asked you to get involved, Mr. Jones. I was simply conveying the facts of my situation to you."

"Well, if it's all the same to you, I'd rather not know even that."

"By all means." Chair legs scraped across the linoleum floor as she stood abruptly. "If you'd simply give me my father's number, I won't bother you a moment longer."

Nate reached for the pad and pen beside the phone and pushed them across the counter toward her.

"Give me your number, I'll make sure Sam gets it," he repeated.

She might be beautiful, she might even have what he suspected was a great ass under the expensive tailoring of her crumpled linen trousers, but he wasn't about to sic her on his old friend without some kind of warning.

She stared at him incredulously. "You're still not going to give me his contact details? Even after everything I've just told you?"

"Sam's my friend."

Her chest rose and fell as though she was fighting to restrain herself from saying something. Then her mouth firmed and her chin came up.

"Fine. Thank you for the water."

She turned toward the door.

"Aren't you forgetting something?" he said. He tapped the pen against the pad.

Her nostrils flared. Then, holding herself very upright, she strode to the kitchen counter and snatched the pen from his hand, writing her phone number in the elegant, curling strokes of a bygone era. When she was finished she dropped the pen onto the counter and lifted her chin even higher.

"I can see myself out, thank you," she said with enormous dignity.

"Where are you staying in town?"

"I fail to see how that's any of your business."

"In case your phone doesn't work for some reason, so I can leave a message for you," he explained patiently. Although he was fast running out of that particular commodity. He hadn't asked for Ms. Mason and her troubles to walk in the door.

"I'm sure it will be fine."

The look she gave him was so snooty, the tilt of her head so imperious he decided he'd done his good deed for the day.

"Fair enough. Don't blame me if I can't contact you for some reason."

A small muscle worked in her jaw. He had the distinct impression she was grinding her teeth.

"I'm staying at the Isle of Wight," she finally said.

"Duly noted."

She hovered for a second as though she didn't quite know what to do next, then she strode to the front door. She paused on the verge of exiting, looking back at him across the width of the living room.

"And by the way, Mr. Jones, where I come from it's good manners to put clothes on before receiving visitors," she said.

She was so hoity-toity, so on her dignity that Nate couldn't help himself—he laughed, the sound bursting out of him and echoing loudly off the walls. By the time he'd pulled himself together enough to notice, she was gone.

The smile slowly faded from his lips. It had been a long time since he'd laughed like that. A long time.

For no reason that he was prepared to acknowledge, he walked into the living room and pushed the curtain to one side. Despite her touch-me-not, refined air she had a sexy sway to her walk and he watched her ass the whole way to her car.

She opened the car and slid into the driver's seat, but didn't take off immediately. Instead, she simply sat there, her head lowered, her expression unreadable from this distance.

Trying to work out what to do next, he figured.

He told himself that she was none of his business, that he had more than enough shit to shovel in his own life, but he couldn't take his eyes off her. And he couldn't stop thinking about the way her hand had trembled when she held the glass of water. And how lost and scared she'd sounded under all that well-educated, well-enunciated hauteur.

"Bloody hell."

He grabbed a pair of board shorts from the laundry, tugged them on, then exited the house and walked down the hot concrete path toward her car. She didn't notice him approaching and she started when he rapped on the passenger window. She hesitated a second, then pressed the button to lower the glass.

"Look, Sam's in Sydney until the start of the race and won't get into Hobart until New Year's Eve at the soonest," he said. "But once he knows you're here, I'm sure he'll come straight back."

"Race? What race?"

"The Sydney to Hobart yacht race."

She bit her lip. "I've heard of that. Isn't it very dangerous?"

"Sam's an experienced sailor. One of the best."

"Is that what he does? Sail, I mean?"

"He hires out as crew mostly, and sometimes he delivers yachts for owners."

He took a step backward to signal the question-and-answer session was over. It wasn't his place to fill in the blanks for her. That was between father and daughter. Nothing to do with him.

"I'll let you know as soon as I've spoken to Sam," he said.

She hesitated, then nodded. The glass slid up between them and she started the car then pulled away from the curb.

Nate watched until she'd turned the corner. Guilt ate at him. He should have helped her more. Reassured her. She'd come a long way looking for a man she knew nothing about. He could have called Sam on the spot, told him—

Nate caught himself before he let the thought go any further. Since when had he made himself Elizabeth Mason's knight in shining armor?

He smiled grimly, the action more a show of teeth than anything else. Rescuing damsels in distress was hardly his forte, after all. Look what had happened to the last damsel who'd put her faith in him.

Tension banded his shoulders and chest. Pressure pushed at the back of his eyes and nose. His heart started to race as sweat prickled beneath his arms.

Olivia. Bloody, bloody hell.

He stared at the dry lawn beneath his feet, battling with himself. Then he strode toward the house and took the steps to the porch in one long-legged leap. Usually he tried not to drink before four o'clock, but trial and error had taught him that there was only one way to hold the anxiety at bay. He went straight to the kitchen and grabbed a can of beer from the fridge. He downed it quickly, closing his eyes and waiting for the alcohol to warm his belly. Vodka would be faster, of course, as would any other hard spirit. He wasn't sure why he clung to beer as his therapy of choice. The illusion that it still meant he had some self-control, perhaps?

Whatever. The tight feeling banding his chest eased and he reached for his second beer with less urgency.

After this, maybe he'd phone around, see who was heading out to Summerlands or one of the other surf beaches so he could catch a few waves. Kill a few hours before he could hit the pub at a more socially acceptable time and start drinking himself toward oblivion again.

And then another day would be over. One less trial to be faced. Hip, hip, hooray.

ELIZABETH STARED AT THE peeling paint on her hotel room ceiling. The sound of laughter and the hum of conversation drifted in the open window. She'd been trying to sleep for the past three hours, but the room she'd been assigned at the Isle of Wight Hotel boasted only an old oscillating fan to combat the heat. Even though she was lying in her underwear on top of the sheets it was like being in a sauna. A really noisy, loud sauna, thanks to the fact that her window looked out over the hotel's beer garden.

She was so tired she should have been able to sleep through a hurricane, but her mind was racing, going over and over the same ground. She didn't know what to do. Stay and wait for her father to come home? Go to Sydney and try to track him down somehow? Or—God forbid—return to England with her tail between her legs.

She hated the idea of having come all this way for nothing, but the idea of waiting and putting her trust in Nathan Jones was enough to fill her with despair.

She made an impatient sound and flopped onto her back. Every time she thought about Nathan Jones she got annoyed all over again. The way he'd told her straight up that he didn't trust her and that he didn't want to get involved in whatever was going on between her and her father. The way he'd shrugged so negligently when she'd been practically throwing herself on his mercy.

"Stupid beach-bum git," she muttered.

Because that was exactly what he was—a beach bum. He'd very obviously just rolled out of bed when he opened the door, even though it was nearly midday. His short, dark hair had been rumpled, his pale blue eyes bloodshot, and she'd caught a whiff of stale beer when she passed him on the way to the kitchen. It wasn't hard to guess what he'd been up to last night.

As for the way he'd stood around with nothing but a frayed towel hanging low on his hips and his ridiculously overdeveloped body on display...

She stirred, uneasy about the way images of his big, hard body kept sliding into her mind. The deeply tanned firmness of his shoulders. The trail of gold-tinted hair that bisected his hard belly and disappeared beneath the towel. The way his biceps had bulged when he crossed his arms over his chest.

The way he'd laughed at her when she'd reminded him that anyone with half-decent manners would have thrown some clothes on before inviting someone into his home.

She sat up and swung her legs to the floor.

Clearly, she wasn't going to get any sleep.

She crossed the threadbare carpet to where she'd left the shopping bags from her brief foray along Main Street earlier in the day. By the time she'd checked into her room her linen shirt had been damp beneath her armpits and perspiration had been running down the backs of her knees. She'd packed for an English summer, not an Australian one, and she'd quickly realized she would need to get a few items of lighter clothing if she was going to survive the next few days with her sanity intact. She'd bought herself a yellow-and-red sundress and a couple of pastel-colored tank tops. None of it was in her usual style—tailored, elegant—but it was light and breezy and much more suitable for the weather.

Now she pulled on the sundress and checked herself in the tarnished mirror on the back of the bathroom door. The skirt was a little shorter than she'd like—just above her knee—and the halter neck meant she couldn't wear a bra, but there was no doubting that the cotton fabric was blessedly cool compared to her own clothes.

She spent a few minutes coiling her hair into a neat chignon, then she checked her watch. Six o'clock. The whole evening stretched ahead of her, long and empty.

Maybe she should explore Main Street more thoroughly while the light lasted. Or perhaps she could walk along the jetty, maybe even along the beach…?

She crossed to the window to close it before she left the room and her gaze fell on the life and color and movement in the beer garden downstairs. There were dozens of holidaymakers clustered around tables, dressed in shorts and swimsuits and bright summer clothes, downing beer and wine and laughing with each other.

Every time she'd ever holidayed someplace warm she'd always been traveling with her grandparents or Martin. The sort of restaurants and hotels they favored were discreet and refined—a far cry from the raucous chaos on display down below.

A peal of laughter floated up through the window and Elizabeth found herself smiling instinctively in response.

If Violet was here, she'd go down and join in the fun, a little voice whispered in her ear.

Elizabeth frowned and pulled the window closed, flicking the lock into place.

She wasn't Violet. She couldn't just go downstairs and buy herself a drink and become part of the noise and the laughter. That simply wasn't the kind of person she was.

Who says? I thought this was about finding out who you really are, what you really want? Wouldn't going downstairs be part of that? the voice piped up again. Perhaps not very surprisingly, it sounded exactly like her best friend.

"You're a damned interfering nag, you know that?" she told her empty room.

But she knew the voice was right. She'd run away from her old life because she was afraid of the person she'd nearly become. If she was going to find herself, she needed to go looking. She needed to push against her old notions of who she was.

She grabbed her purse and her room key and made herself walk out the door before she could think herself out of it. Nerves fluttered in her belly as she descended the stairs and walked into the din of the crowded main bar. She paused for a moment to get her bearings, a little overwhelmed by the noise and the press of people and all the bare flesh on display. The smell of beer and fried food and suntan lotion hung heavily in the air, and the carpet underfoot was both sticky from years' worth of spilled drinks and gritty with sand that had been tracked in from the beach.

It's just a pub, Elizabeth, she told herself, *and they're just people. Nothing to be afraid of.*

She took a deep breath and threw herself into the melee, slowly weaving her way toward the bar.

"What can I get you, love?" the barmaid asked.

"I'll have a Pimm's and lemonade, thank you."

The barmaid frowned. "Pimm's. God, I haven't served that

for years." She turned toward the man working the other end of the scarred wooden bar. "Trev, we got any Pimm's, do you reckon?"

"Pimm's? I don't know. Let me check out the back." The barman glanced at Elizabeth curiously.

"It's okay, don't bother," Elizabeth said, feeling foolish. Of course they didn't have Pimm's. She was a long way from home, after all. About as far away as she could get.

She gestured toward the frosted glass the barmaid had just handed over to the previous customer. "I'll just have one of those."

"A VB? Not a problem," the barmaid said.

A minute later, Elizabeth was handed a tall, frosted glass full of beer. She took her first sip and gasped, surprised by how icy cold it was. After the heat of the day, however, it was hugely welcome and she took another big gulp as she spotted an empty table in the corner. Good. A table would give her a refuge to hide behind and make her feel less conspicuously alone.

She dodged a couple of well-muscled backs as she made her way across the bar. She was just about to put her drink down when a dark-haired woman slid her glass onto the table at the same time. They stared at each other, startled, then the other woman laughed.

"I'd call that a draw, what do you think? Should we toss for it?" the other woman said good-naturedly and Elizabeth recognized the familiar vowels of an East London accent.

"It's fine. You got here first," Elizabeth said politely.

It had been a mistake coming downstairs on her own, she could see that now. It was too loud, too hectic and she was jet-lagged and very uncertain about what move to make next. The sooner she drank her beer and returned to her room, the better.

"Hey! English! Cheers!" the other woman said, her face

splitting into a welcoming smile. She lifted her glass to clink it against Elizabeth's. "How long have you been in Oz for, then? Me and my bloke have been here nearly six months, in case you couldn't tell by the tan." The other woman proudly showed off her nut-brown arms. "Bugger skin cancer, I say." She gave another laugh.

Her name, Elizabeth soon learned, was Lexie and she insisted that she and Elizabeth share the table since Lexie was waiting for her boyfriend to join her and had no idea when he was going to show up.

"You can help me fight off these randy Aussie blokes until he gets here," she said with another of her loud, unselfconscious laughs. "Horny bastards, and they don't mind having a go, let me tell you, even when you let them know you're taken."

Somehow Elizabeth's one beer turned into two when Lexie insisted on treating her, then three because Elizabeth had to return the favor. By the time it was full dark outside she was feeling more than a little squiffy. By that time Lexie's boyfriend, Ross, had arrived with the rest of their friends and Elizabeth was drawn into their circle. When music started up out in the beer garden she went along quite happily as the rest of them swept outside.

Hips swinging in time to the music, cold beer in hand, she glanced around the bar, a dreamy, happy smile on her face. Despite her initial nervousness, she'd held her own with Lexie and Ross's loud, friendly group. No, more than held her own—she was having a good time. A great time. For the first time in her life there wasn't someone watching, waiting to remind her of what she should say or do or how her actions might be perceived. She wasn't worried about what Martin might think or living up to her grandparents' expectations.

She was on her own. Free. For the moment, anyway.

Which was when she glanced across the garden and locked eyes with Nathan Jones, leaning against the far wall with a beer in his hand as he watched her with a small, speculative smile.

3

NATE STARED ACROSS the sea of people at the woman in the bright, breezy dress. It was amazing the difference a few hours and, he guessed, a few beers could make. Gone was the pale, tense society princess he'd met this afternoon and in her place was a flush-faced blonde with a swing in her hips and a smile on her lips. He almost hadn't recognized her, but nothing could disguise the way she held herself and the tilt of her chin.

His gaze ran over her body again. Her red-and-yellow dress ended just above the knees and tied around her neck. The neckline was modest by island standards—half the girls in the pub had come straight from the beach and there were dozens of bikini tops and skimpy tank tops on display—but it was tight and low enough to reveal that Elizabeth Mason had great breasts.

He lifted his beer and took a long swallow, not taking his eyes from her the whole time. The smile faded from her face as their gazes connected, but she didn't look away, either, even though he was pretty damn sure she wanted to.

He wasn't sure what was going on. He'd noticed her sexually this morning, there was no denying that—the shape of her ass, the flash of her bra, the long line of her neck. But she wasn't the kind of woman he'd been spending time with lately—"spending time" being shorthand for casual sex, which was all he was good for these days. Elizabeth Mason had hard work written all over her. And that was before he even got into the whole mess of her being here to find her father.

And yet for some reason that he couldn't explain, he couldn't take his eyes off her.

Across the room, she finally looked away, turning her shoulder.

Against his smarter instincts, he pushed away from the wall and made his way toward her. He told himself every step of the way to rethink, to turn around and find some other woman to dance and drink and maybe go home with, but he didn't stop until he was standing behind her. Elizabeth must have sensed his approach because she tensed, the exposed muscles of her back flexing as though she was bracing herself.

"I figured you had to be around somewhere when Tania told me someone had tried to order a Pimm's," he said.

She didn't turn around, didn't so much as twitch.

He smiled. He hadn't been given the silent treatment since third grade. It hadn't worked then, either. He never had been able to resist a challenge.

He leaned a little closer, whispering right into her ear. "Do you want me to go away, Betty?"

"What do you think?" she said without moving.

He was standing so close he could see the fine blond hairs on the nape of her neck.

"I think that that was a pretty long look you gave me just now."

She swung to face him, ready to object. Her eyes widened when she registered his proximity. She took a quick step backward and crossed her arms protectively over her chest.

"Scared of me, Betty?" he asked, amused by how skittish she was.

"Of course not. And my name is Elizabeth, if you don't mind."

He cocked his head to one side. Was it his imagination, or did her accent get even snootier?

"Elizabeth is kind of an uptight name, don't you think? Makes me think of old ladies with scepters in their hands and cast-iron underwear."

"It's a very old, very traditional name, and it happens to be the one my parents gave me."

"Like I said, uptight."

Her nostrils flared. His smile widened into a grin. She was so prim, so proper—and so damned easy to get a rise out of. He hadn't had this much fun in a long time.

"What exactly is it that you want, Mr. Jones?"

He took a mouthful of beer and let his gaze slide past her chin to the neckline of her dress. Her perfume drifted toward him, something light and crisp and citrusy.

"Just being friendly. Making sure you settled in okay," he said.

She gave him a cool look. "Perhaps you could clarify something for me. Am I supposed to be charmed by all this? The smiles and the suggestive comments and the standing too close?"

"What do you think?"

"You don't want to know what I think, let me assure you."

"I can handle it, Betty, I promise. Hit me with your best shot."

She peered down her nose at him—quite the accomplishment given their difference in height. "My grandmother taught me that if you can't say something nice about someone, you shouldn't say anything at all."

"Your grandmother. That explains a lot."

Her eyes narrowed. "All right, then, since you insist, here

is what I think—that you believe an overdeveloped beefcake body and passable good looks give you a free pass to get away with anything where women are concerned."

He laughed. Couldn't help himself. "Overdeveloped? Which parts of me are overdeveloped?"

He watched, fascinated, as she blushed again.

"You have the fairest skin I've ever seen," he murmured. Every other body in the bar was brown from the Australian sun, but she was as pure and cool as a lily. He reached out a hand and ran his thumb along the curve of her cheekbone. As he'd suspected, she was as soft and smooth as silk.

She swallowed audibly. "Do you mind?" Her eyes were very wide, the pupils dilated.

"You know, I think I might, Betty," he said, surprising himself.

He dropped his hand. He'd crossed the bar to tease her, to fill in some time, to amuse himself on the way to oblivion. But she wasn't amusing. She was…disturbing, with her crisp, standoffish accent and tilted chin and uncertain eyes. For a moment they were both silent as they stared at each other.

"I'm not going to sleep with you, Mr. Jones."

That made him smile again. "No one asked you to, Betty."

Then, because she was too complicated, too messy, too challenging, he lifted his glass.

"Cheers," he said. He turned and walked away before she could say another word.

HE WAS UNBELIEVABLE. Earlier today she'd thought he was surly and uncooperative and rude, but now she added insufferably conceited and arrogant to the list of Nathan Jones's crimes. She honestly didn't know where he got off, touching her like that, standing so close she could smell the detergent he'd washed his clothes in and the sun-warmed, salty scent of his skin.

As for how he'd laughed at her and looked at her as though he could see straight through her clothes...

She'd never dealt with a man like him before. Cocky and arrogant and so...*physical* it was impossible to look at him and not imagine him on top of her, his heavy weight pinning her to the—

Elizabeth took a huge swallow of her beer. Why was it that when she thought about Nathan Jones her mind automatically descended below the waist?

She peeked out of the corners of her eyes to make sure that he really had disappeared into the crowd. He had and she relaxed a notch. With a bit of luck he'd leave the bar altogether and she wouldn't have to deal with him again.

A vain hope. Half an hour later she glanced across to where a few people had cleared some tables to create an impromptu dance floor to see Nathan in the middle of the swaying crowd, his arms around a small redheaded woman. The other woman was wearing a skimpy sundress with lots of strategic rips and tears in it, her swimsuit clearly visible underneath.

In London she'd be arrested for indecent exposure. At least Elizabeth hoped she would.

She watched as the woman wriggled in Nathan's arms, laughing into his face, one hand pressed flat against his chest. Nathan said something, then lifted his head suddenly and stared directly across the room at Elizabeth. She tensed as she met his pale blue eyes. She should have looked away before he caught her watching him. She should look away *now*.

Right now, before he got the wrong idea.

He lifted an eyebrow. Then the corner of his mouth curled up.

Smug bastard.

She tore her gaze away.

She could imagine what he was thinking—that the *uptight* English woman had the hots for him.

As if she'd be foolish enough to take up with a man like him, a man who was interested in nothing but sex. A man who wanted nothing but to get her naked and take his pleasure. A man who probably knew every sexual trick in the book and then some.

A wave of heat rolled over her.

Be honest with yourself at least, Elizabeth Jane. He fascinates you. You look at him and see every fantasy you ever had, every dirty thought you never dared share with anyone, including Martin.

It was true. It made self-conscious, nervous sweat prickle under her arms to admit it to herself, but it was true. She found Nathan Jones sexually attractive. Extremely sexually attractive.

How galling.

She turned and grabbed the nearby jug of beer and poured herself another glass.

He'd been so cocksure when he'd swaggered over to talk to her earlier. So confident of his reception. And she'd been so firm in her rejection. And all along he'd known. The look they'd just shared told her so.

He knew she'd been struck speechless by her first sight of him in all his bare-chested glory. He knew how images of his big body had been slipping into her mind against her will all day. How hot and sticky she felt just thinking about touching his firm, brown skin.

"Bloody hell," she whispered under her breath.

She felt as though she was on fire, could feel the echo of her heartbeat in the warm heat between her legs. She pressed her beer glass against her cheek, trying to cool down.

Crazy. This was crazy. She'd never felt so overheated and

overwrought in all her life. It must be the beer. Had to be. Otherwise—

A hand curled around her forearm and tugged her toward the dance floor.

"Come on, Betty, let your hair down," a voice murmured. "Dance with me."

She looked up into Nathan's lazy, heavy-lidded eyes. God, he was gorgeous. All angled cheekbones and straight nose and firm, chiseled lips.

She dug her heels in and shook her head as he pulled her another step closer to the dance floor.

"I don't want to dance. Not with you."

It was a lie, but it was also the truth. He terrified her. He made her scared of herself.

She tugged on her arm. He didn't let her go.

"Are you married?" he asked.

"No." Almost, but not quite.

"In a relationship?"

"No." Not anymore.

"Then what's the problem?"

He made it sound so simple, as though there were no other considerations apart from what she wanted and what he wanted right now. No tomorrow. No responsibilities or obligations or expectations.

When she didn't say anything she felt the grip on her arm loosen.

"Your call, Betty."

It should have annoyed her, the way he kept using that stupid diminutive of her name and the way he gave her a small, regretful smile and walked away again.

It didn't. Instead she was gripped with a sort of panicky, pressed fear that she'd just let an amazing opportunity slip through her fingers. When would she ever meet a man like him again? A feckless, pointless, incredibly sexy Lothario with nothing but pleasure on his mind? When would she ever be so far from home, so anonymous and free?

Because she didn't know the answers to any of those questions she pretended to herself that she'd narrowly escaped making a reckless, foolish decision and tried to look as though she was having a great time.

She watched him laugh and dance with another girl. Then another. She drank more beer and let her gaze run over his big, strong body as he moved on the dance floor or leaned against the far wall or stood in a loose circle with a bunch of surfer types, talking and laughing. She thought about the look in his eyes, remembered the way he'd touched her cheek. She thought about home, and how her grandparents had lied to her—with the best of intentions, yes, but it had still been a lie—and the way Martin touched her as though she were made of spun sugar and all the times she'd bitten her tongue and done the right thing and been a good girl, over and over again.

She thought about that moment in Harrods when she'd fantasized about destroying all that polished, expensive perfection.

I want him, a little voice whispered in her mind. *Why can't I have him?*

There were reasons—of course there were reasons—but they weren't good enough. They were safe and conservative and controlled and she was *so sick* of all those things. She wanted the unknown. Just this once. No one would ever know about it. It would be her secret, her moment of madness. A moment just for her, about her, about what she wanted, with no one else's feelings or opinions or judgments coming into play.

She put down her glass. Then she lifted her hands and checked to see that her hair was neatly pinned. Although why that should matter when she was about to proposition a man for the first time in her life, she had no idea.

She took a deep breath, then started across the room. She'd barely taken two steps before Nathan turned away from his friends and started weaving his way through the crowd toward the exit.

A surge of dismay rushed through her. He was leaving! Surely not, not when she'd just mustered the courage to ask for what she wanted. She paused for a split second, then she started pushing her way through the crowd, her movements increasingly urgent.

If he left without her saying what she wanted to say, doing what she wanted to do, she might never find the courage of this moment again.

She kept her eyes glued to Nathan's dark head and when he disappeared into the hallway leading to the front entrance she darted urgently past the last few people and was almost running when she entered the hallway.

It was empty. He'd already left.

Again, she hesitated. She couldn't very well chase him up the street. Could she? He'd issued his invitation, she'd rejected it. It was over. She'd missed her chance.

The disappointment and frustration she felt was so great that she was pushing through the double doors and out into the warm night before she could really consider what she was doing. There was no sign of Nathan on the street in either direction. Then she looked across the road toward the beach and saw a dark figure walking down the path toward the sand.

She crossed the road and strode to the top of the path. The moon was covered by clouds and the beach was dark, the water a glinting inky blackness in the distance. She set one foot on the sandy path, then stopped.

What was she doing, racing after a virtual stranger because he'd looked at her a certain way and said certain things? He was obviously going home for the evening. Whatever fleeting notion he'd had where she was concerned was long gone. She needed to turn around and go back to her room before this became embarrassing.

She turned away.

"Betty?"

She glanced over her shoulder. She could see Nathan silhouetted at the bottom of the path, a tall, broad shape.

Her heart kicked against her chest. She wiped her damp palms down the sides of her skirt. Then she walked down the path, into the darkness.

She stopped when she was standing in front of him. They were both silent for a beat.

"Were you going home?" she asked when the silence became excruciating.

"Getting some fresh air. Pretty warm in there."

Which meant she'd chased him out here like some sort of teenage desperado for nothing.

"I just thought... You asked me to dance before," she said lamely. "Maybe when you come back in we could...?"

His eyes glinted in the dim light. "You want to dance, Betty?"

She felt incredibly foolish and transparent. This was too, too humiliating. There was a reason why her first instinct had been to shy away from having anything to do with this man and this situation. She'd never done anything like this in her life before and she had no idea how to handle herself or him. For all she knew, she'd misread everything entirely and he really had been simply asking her to dance before.

"It doesn't matter," she said.

She turned away but his warm hand slid down her forearm and circled her wrist, stopping her from leaving.

"Come here," he said, very softly.

He tugged her gently toward him. For a moment she

resisted, her last doubts digging their heels in. Then his other hand slid around to cup the nape of her neck and she lifted her face as his head lowered toward her.

His lips were very soft as they found hers. She was surprised by how gentle he was, how sweet he tasted. His tongue flicked along the closed seam of her mouth, demanding entrance, and she found herself opening to him. And then he was inside her mouth, stroking, tasting, teasing. Sensation swamped her—her breasts flattened against his chest, the hard muscles of his arms pulling her closer, the avid hunger of his mouth. She made a needy sound and he pushed her head back farther as he delved more deeply, more greedily.

His hand left her nape to slide down her neck, across her shoulder and onto her breast. Liquid heat surged between her legs. She was so turned on it almost hurt. She pressed her knees together and dug her hands into the strong muscles of his shoulders and matched him kiss for kiss.

His thumb grazed her nipple through the fabric of her dress, then his warm hand slid beneath the halter top, making her gasp as he pinched and rolled her nipple between his fingers.

She had never felt like this in her life. So hot. So wet. So damned desperate to have a man's weight on top of her, inside her.

Nathan pressed his hips against her and she felt his erection against her belly. She slid a hand between them and traced him through the soft fabric of his well-worn jeans. So big, so thick.

He muttered something against her lips, then he ducked his head and kissed and licked a trail down her chest into her cleavage. He turned his head and sucked her nipple into his mouth, fabric and all, as both his hands found her ass. He squeezed her, hauling her closer, rubbing himself against her. His fingers curved beneath her butt cheeks, delving into the dark warmth between her legs. Teasing. Taunting. She shuddered and groaned.

"Please," she groaned, her head dropping back. "Please."

He lifted his head from her breasts and she heard him pull in a ragged breath. "Come on, Betty," he said, taking her hand.

He led her down to the beach. Her feet sank into the sand, and grit slipped between her feet and her sandals. She struggled to keep up with his long, urgent stride as he drew her away from the bright lights of Main Street and into darkness.

When the lights were a distant glow, he stopped and pulled her close again.

"Betty." He kissed her, and she could feel the smile on his lips.

Probably she should correct him—her name was Elizabeth, after all, and it looked as though they were about to have sex. But she didn't care. All her thoughts, all her focus were on one thing—the needy, desperate throb between her legs.

She slid her hands down the muscles of his belly to the waistband of his jeans. He wasn't wearing a belt and the denim gave easily as she tugged at one stud, then another, then another. She slid her hand inside his jeans and found the heat and hardness of him. She wrapped her fingers around him and stroked.

He started kissing her neck and she felt a tug behind her neck, closely followed by the coolness of the night air on her bare breasts as the untied halter of her dress dropped to her waist. He made an approving sound and cupped her breasts in both hands, his thumbs grazing her nipples over and over.

She started pulling at the waistband of his jeans, peeling them down over his hips.

"Easy, Betty," he whispered against her skin. "Easy."

"I want you," she said, the boldest words she'd ever spoken. "Inside me. Now."

He squeezed her breasts tightly in response. "What the lady wants."

As one they sank onto the sand, she on her back, him on top. Elizabeth opened her thighs and welcomed his weight as he pressed over her. He lowered his head and sucked first one nipple, then the other into his mouth. She arched her back and cried out. She was so close, so close. He hadn't even taken her panties off yet and already this was the most fulfilling, exciting sex of her life.

His hand skimmed up the inside of one of her widespread thighs and she gave an excited little gasp as his fingers found the damp silk of her underwear.

"Mmm," he said against her breast, clearly savoring her arousal. He stroked her through the damp silk before slipping his fingers beneath it to slide into her slick heat.

She closed her eyes and started to pant. His erection pulsed in her hand and she stroked her hand up and down more urgently, feeling the gentle velvet of the head, the silky steel of the shaft, the soft springiness of his hair.

He thrust a finger inside her. She bit her lip and lifted her hips, wanting more. A second finger slid inside her. She started to circle her hips.

So good. So good.

He pulled away from her for a moment and she felt him tugging at his jeans. She lifted her hips and pulled her panties down her legs, tossing them heedlessly to one side. She heard the faint crinkle of a foil packet and barely had time to register that he was using a condom before his weight was on her again and she was rising up to meet his penetration.

He slid inside her in one slick, powerful thrust, stretching her to the point of almost-pain. She sucked in a breath, her fingers clenching into his shoulders. She sucked in another as he started to move, pumping in and out of her, hot and hard and so good she couldn't believe it. His mouth was on her breasts, biting and licking and sucking her nipples. She slid her hands down onto the round, firm muscles of his backside and held on for dear life.

This was what she'd wanted. Mindless need. Heat. Slick wetness. This pressure building inside her. This wildness.

She could feel her orgasm approaching. She both craved it and feared it. She didn't want this to end. This was all her fantasies rolled into one, everything she'd ever dreamed about in the dark quiet of her bedroom while she pleasured herself with her own hands—no gentle words and respectful, considerate, careful caresses, just his hard body slamming into hers, the suck of his mouth on her breasts, the rasp of his hairy, hard body against hers, the rise of her hips to meet his, her hands, urgent and demanding on his body. This was almost everything she'd ever wanted, except—

"Could we… Could you… Do you think we could do it on our knees. With you behind me?" she asked.

He stilled. For a moment she thought she'd ruined everything. Martin had been appalled when she'd asked him to take her from behind. As sexual fantasies went, she hadn't thought it was too outrageous, but maybe nice girls didn't ask to do it doggy style. There were so many things she didn't know, after all. So many things she hadn't done.

Then Nathan withdrew from her and his hands found her hips. Excitement throbbed deep inside her as she followed his urging to roll over, rising up onto her knees almost immediately. He flipped her skirt up and out of the way and instinctively she arched her back, offering herself flagrantly. He muttered something under his breath. She felt the probe of his cock at her entrance, then he was sliding inside her, deeper than ever, filling her utterly.

"Oh. Yes! *Yes!*" she breathed.

It was better than she'd ever imagined. So deep. So full.

He started to move, stroking in and out of her. She heard

the slap of his thighs against her own, felt the rasp of his skin against hers. Heat rolled through her in waves, pushing her higher and higher. He reached a hand around her torso to tease her nipples. She started to gasp, pressing back against him urgently, tilting her hips and clenching her inner muscles.

So close, so close.

His hand slid down her belly and into the wet curls at the apex of her thighs. Then his fingers were teasing her in divine counterpoint to his thrusts, and she was done for.

Her orgasm hit her like a wall, rolling through her body, tensing her muscles, arching her back. She hissed between her teeth, groaned his name. And still it kept coming, pulsing, wet, mind-blowing. She felt him shudder, felt him push himself inside her with a new urgency, and then he was buried inside her, his body hard as granite against hers as he shuddered through his own climax.

There was a small silence afterward, a moment of absolute stillness, then he withdrew from her. She let her head drop forward, resting it on her fisted hands.

Her belly muscles were still trembling with the aftermath of her orgasm. Her legs felt weak. She even felt a little dizzy, as though all her blood had rushed south to the party and left precious little to spare for her brain.

"I thought Englishwomen were supposed to be uptight," Nathan said, his voice deep and amused.

"So did I."

She started to laugh. She felt amazing. Released. Relaxed. Revealed.

Right at that moment, nothing else mattered. Not the fact that they hardly knew each other, or that she was thousands of miles from home, or that she had no idea what to do next. There was only right here and right now. And it was damned good.

4

NATHAN WOKE IN A TANGLE of sandy limbs. He pushed a strand of pale blond hair off his face and blinked in the early morning light. For the first time in a long time his first thoughts weren't of Olivia. The reason for that was curled up against him on his bed, her backside snugged into the cradle of his hips, one of his arms draped around her body, his hand resting possessively on her breast.

Elizabeth Mason. Sam's daughter. The not-so-uptight English princess.

He was already half-hard, but he grew to full hardness as memories from last night came flooding back. Her hands down his jeans on the beach. The first slide of his fingers into her slick, ready heat. The way she'd begged him to take her from behind and then offered herself to him so eagerly. Her fervent, needy, lusty response to his every lick, suck, stroke or caress. They'd had sex again when they got back to his place, her on top this time, her cries ringing out into the night.

Not-so-uptight, indeed.

She stirred, her backside nudging against his stiff cock. He pressed a kiss to the nape of her neck, then nipped her skin gently. She tensed in his arms, fully awake.

Good.

He found her nipple with his thumb while he teased the sensitive skin of her nape with his tongue. Her nipples grew hard and she stirred again in his arms.

He eased her knee forward with his and reached behind himself to the bedside stand. Fifteen seconds later, he had a condom on and was pressing into her hot folds. She made an approving sound in the back of her throat as he slid inside her, the tight clench of her muscles closing around him.

She was incredible, so smooth and sweet-smelling and tight and wet. He rocked his hips, nudging just the head of his cock in and out, in and out. She moaned and he felt her inner muscles clutching around him. He'd meant to take it nice and slow—lazy, half-asleep morning sex—but she started to push against him and things quickly got urgent and sweaty and greedy. He grasped her hips and she rolled fully onto her belly, then up onto her knees.

He could feel how much she loved it like this, how much it excited her, which only made him harder and hotter. Then she arched her back and clenched her hands into the sheets as she came. He could feel her pulsing around him. Her inarticulate little sounds pushed him over the edge. He bent over her, panting his climax into her shoulder as he lost himself for a few precious seconds.

The ultimate forgetting. If only it lasted longer.

She collapsed on her belly afterward. He rolled to one side and took care of the condom. Then he flopped onto his back and for a moment they were both silent, the only sound their heavy breathing and the faint sound of the wind in the old liquid amber tree outside. The studio smelled of sex and clean sweat and her perfume and he let his gaze play over the perfect, fair skin of her back and her rounded, sweet-shaped behind.

That ass… That ass made him want to do a million bad, dirty things all at once.

"What time is it?" Her voice sounded husky and a little uncertain.

"Nearly seven."

She braced her elbows on the bed and propped her forehead on her hands. After a long moment she shifted her head slightly so she could see him out of the corners of her eyes. He raised an eyebrow when their gazes met.

She looked deeply uncertain and more than a little embarrassed. Maybe his first assessment hadn't been that far off. Maybe she was a little uptight, after all.

"Good morning," she said. She sounded very stiff, as though she'd rehearsed those two words several times in her mind before uttering them.

"Pretty good way to start it, anyway."

She rolled onto her back, carefully keeping the sheet over her breasts. Which struck him as being pretty amusing, considering he'd been inside her only a few minutes ago.

Her gaze slid toward the door and she frowned. He followed her eye line—her dress was crumpled on the floor just inside the doorway, a pool of red and yellow, her sandals kicked to one side.

He had a fair idea what she was frowning over, and his suspicions were confirmed when she reached for the T-shirt trailing off the end of the bed. He watched as she shrugged into it under the covers before sliding out of bed and collecting her dress. Her back turned, she stepped into the dress and didn't abandon his T-shirt until she was decently covered. He didn't have the heart to tell her that her skirt was caught up at the back, exposing the back of one lovely thigh and half a rounded butt cheek. She'd feel the breeze once she stepped outside, he figured.

She pulled her hair into a ponytail, plaiting it and then tucking it in on itself until it formed a loose knot on the back of her head. She had slender, graceful arms and hands, like a dancer's. He liked watching her move, even if her misplaced modesty was pretty damn funny.

He'd been so busy being entertained, it wasn't until she started to toe on her sandals that he realized she was about to race out the door.

While he hadn't exactly been a hound dog over the past few months, he hadn't lived like a monk, either, and he'd dealt with more than his fair share of morning-after coy looks and questions hinting at one night becoming more.

Clearly, there would be no such issues with his cool English lover.

"Is there a shoe sale on in town I don't know about?" he asked.

He ought to be grateful she was making it so clean and easy, but for some reason her eagerness to bail offended him. Not that he wanted her clinging to his chest and begging for a lifelong commitment, God forbid. But a little show of reluctance to draw a line under some of the best sex of his adult life might not go astray.

"I beg your pardon?"

He shrugged, not about to explain. If she wanted to go, she should go. He wasn't about to beg her to hang around.

He pushed back the covers and stood. She made a small, breathless sound as her gaze slid over his body. The hot, sticky look in her eyes went a long way to assuaging his ego. If he wanted to, he could have her in bed again within seconds.

The thought had barely registered before she reached for the door handle.

"I really have to go," she said.

Then, before he could open his mouth to respond, she was gone.

He blinked. Bloody hell. Talk about wham, bam, thank you, Nate. He'd never seen a woman so keen to get the hell out of Dodge before.

He shook off his irritation as he reached for a pair of cargo pants. So what? They'd had sex, it had been good, she'd bailed. Big deal. He probably wouldn't remember her name by the end of the week. Which was just the way he wanted it. No strings, no obligations, no guilt.

No possible way he could ever let anyone down ever again.

Pushing her from his mind, he went to make himself breakfast for one.

ELIZABETH REMEMBERED ENOUGH about the walk to Nate's place the previous evening to find her way back to the beach. From there it was a simple matter of turning her left shoulder to the water and walking until she hit the pier and the point where Main Street met the beach—except for the fact that with every step she was painfully aware of the fact that she was wearing no underwear. And that parts of her were feeling more than a little tender after three bouts of very active, very hot, very urgent sex with a man who gave absolutely no quarter in the bedroom.

She was such a hussy!

The way she'd chased after him. The way she'd propositioned him. The way—she pressed her hands over her face as the memory rushed up at her—the way she'd begged him to do her from behind.

She was shameless. Utterly shameless.

And the worst thing was, she didn't have it in her to regret any of it. It had been wonderful. She'd felt so free, so alive. And he'd been so amazing—generous and passionate and intuitive. He hadn't questioned anything, or made her feel silly or dirty or wrong, he'd simply thrown himself wholeheartedly into the moment. Just thinking about it made her want to—

She gave a shriek as an offshore breeze danced around her legs and her skirt kicked upward. She clamped her hands down on either side of her skirt. There was an older woman walking her dog down by the tide line and two joggers pounding the sand. She was sure they had all taken one look at her smudged makeup and mussed hair and understood that she'd just crawled out of bed. She didn't need to expose her naked nether regions to them to confirm the fact.

Which brought her to an important point she could no longer avoid: she had no idea where her panties were. The last time she could remember wearing them had been when Nathan had led her along the beach to find some privacy. She couldn't remember if she'd put them back on again for the walk to his place or not. She'd been so blown away after what had happened, so enamored of him, it was impossible to remember clearly.

A horrible thought hit her. What if she'd left them on the beach? The thought of her abandoned knickers being discovered by someone was enough to make her feel distinctly queasy. So very, very refined. If Grandmama could see her now...

Elizabeth pushed the thought away. She refused to feel guilty about last night. Yes, she'd had sex with an almost-stranger. The first one-night stand of her life. But it had been wild and sexy and sensual and she *would not regret it*. It was her private business and no one need ever know about it. What happened on Phillip Island stayed on Phillip Island.

Still, she kept an eye out for her knickers all the way back to the pub. She even backtracked a little, exploring the dry sand past the high-tide mark. She found nothing. She told herself that most likely they'd been swept out to sea and very badly wanted to believe it.

No one was stirring inside and she slunk up to her room gratefully. It was one thing to be determined not to feel regret and another thing entirely to do the walk of shame.

She showered and fell into bed for another couple of hours,

waking when the temperature began to climb again and the room became too stuffy for comfort. Sitting up in bed, she crossed her legs and pushed her hair back from her face and made some decisions.

Nate had offered to put her in contact with her father, even if it wasn't exactly in the manner of her choosing. She would wait until he heard something, then she would make her decision. There was nothing for her to rush home to, after all. She'd been working as a substitute teacher all year and the term was already over for her. Workwise, she could extend her stay in Australia until at least mid-January if she had to.

And—coward though it made her—maybe it would be better for herself and her grandparents to have a little breathing room before they came face-to-face again. Give tempers and ruffled feathers a chance to calm down.

And in the meantime, she would stretch her wings a little. Explore Cowes and the nearby beaches, get to know the locals a little. Find out what it was that Elizabeth Mason wanted in life if it wasn't marriage to a perfectly nice, perfectly perfect Englishman.

That ought to be enough to fill up her days. As for the nights…

A dozen hot and sweaty memories flitted across her mind. She pushed them away. Best not to think about the nights. She might be woefully naive in the world of casual sex, but she knew that looking for anything more than one night from a man like Nate was the emotional equivalent of playing Russian roulette.

She might have had a reckless moment, but she wasn't a reckless person.

NATE ARRIVED AT THE PUB shortly after six. The surf had been going off out at Kitty Miller Bay in the morning and he'd caught a lift out there with Tommy, then mowed the yard in the early afternoon. When he'd finished, he'd strung the old hammock between the studio and the liquid amber tree and sucked down a few beers in the drowsy afternoon heat.

Not a bad way to spend a day. If only he could stop his brain from thinking. Five minutes on his own without distraction and Olivia was there, filling his mind, tightening his gut, making him want to tear the world apart.

When beer alone didn't work its usual magic, he'd showered and pulled on a pair of jeans and a clean T-shirt and walked to the pub. There was more beer to be had there, of course—but the real lure was Elizabeth Mason. She of the sweet behind and soft, lily-white skin. In all the weeks he'd been holed up on the island, she was the first person or thing that had successfully distracted him from the mess in his own head long enough to offer any relief. He wasn't sure what it was that fascinated him so much. The apparent contradiction between her prim, conservative demeanor and the way she'd moaned in his arms? Her clipped British accent? The flashes of vulnerability and uncertainty he saw in her eyes?

She was a mystery. Perhaps that was all it was. An unknown quantity, an exotic, pale, well-spoken stranger in a world of nut-brown bodies, flat vowels, and sun and surf. Whatever. The important thing was that when he was with her he wasn't thinking about anything or anyone else.

She was sitting in the far corner with her English friends from the previous night when he entered the bar. She had her hair up again, neatly bound as though she was about to take dictation or chair a charity meeting. She was sitting straight, her posture perfect, with not even an elbow resting on the table. He smiled to himself as he ordered a beer. He bet she never slouched. Probably never swore, either, or jaywalked, or ate dessert before finishing her vegetables or cheated on her taxes.

Her head came up and her gaze searched the bar as if she

could feel him watching her. Their eyes met and locked. He reached into the front pocket of his jeans and tugged out a couple of inches of the scrap of pale blue silk and lace she'd left behind this morning. He raised his eyebrows in question.

"Yours?" he mouthed.

He had to bite back a laugh at her response. She jerked in her seat, then a rich tide of red rose up her chest and into her face. Her hands gripped the edge of the table, then she shot to her feet as though she was rocket propelled. He watched the bounce of her breasts as she marched toward him.

"You are disgusting," she said as she snatched her panties from his pocket and screwed them into a tight ball in her hand. "How dare you?"

He'd meant to tease her, but he could see that she was genuinely upset.

"Hey, Betty. Steady on," he said. He reached out to touch her arm but she jerked away from him.

Her hand was white-knuckle tight as she clenched it around her panties.

"I trusted you. Which makes me a fool, I see now. I thought last night was something private, between the two of us. How very naive and stupid of me."

"I'm sorry, okay? Don't get so hot under the collar. It was a joke."

"To you, perhaps. But now all the people in the bar know I slept with you last night. God only knows what they think of me."

Nate frowned. It had been a joke. A tease. No way had he expected her to react so strongly. Then he thought about her modesty this morning and realized that perhaps he should have. Clearly, she was a woman who worried about things like appearances and reputation. He bet himself a thousand bucks that she'd messed up her sheets this morning so that the hotel staff wouldn't guess she hadn't slept in her own bed. She'd probably been agonizing over where her panties were all day—then he'd walked in and teased her with his little show-and-tell routine.

"Relax, okay? Nobody saw, and nobody's thinking anything about you. They're all too busy getting pissed and trying to find someone of their own to shag to give two hoots about us."

She stared at him, her face stiff with tension. "What was I thinking? I must have been mad."

She said it so quietly he almost didn't hear her. Then she turned on her heel and pushed her way through the crowd until she reached the stairs. He watched her take them two at a time, her back stiff with tension.

"Shit." He took a mouthful of beer. Not in a million years had he meant to hurt her. He'd wanted to make her laugh, get that martial light in her eye, provoke her into insulting him some more in that hoity-toity way of hers.

He turned to face the bar, resting his elbow on the scarred wood. Next time he saw her, he'd apologize. Once she'd had a chance to calm down, she'd understand.

He tried to push the incident from his mind, but ten minutes later he glanced over and saw a waitress deliver a round of meals to the table where Elizabeth had been sitting. Her English friends looked confused and he could see them searching for Elizabeth as the waitress stood with an unclaimed burger and fries.

Great. She'd abandoned her dinner because of him.

Damn it.

He pushed his beer away and crossed the bar.

"Elizabeth wasn't feeling so great," he explained to her worried friends. He took the plate from the waitress. "Thanks, Sall. I'll take this up to her room for her."

"Sure. Thanks, Nate." Sally gave him a quick smile before heading back to the kitchen.

He left the table before Elizabeth's friends could ask any more questions, stopping by the bar for a quick detour before heading upstairs.

The barman had given him Elizabeth's room number and he balanced the plate on his raised knee as he knocked on her door.

There was a short pause before a voice answered.

"Who is it?"

"Room service."

Another pause. Then the door opened.

"I didn't— Oh. You."

Her face was still flushed and a few strands of hair had escaped from her neat hairdo.

"You forgot your burger." He lifted his other hand. "And I thought you might be thirsty."

Her gaze fell on the Pimm's and lemonade in his outstretched hand.

"I'm not hungry. Or thirsty."

He shouldered his way past her and put down the plate on the bedside table, placing the glass beside it.

"Better eat it quickly before it goes cold."

"I'm not hungry," she repeated. "And I'd very much appreciate it if you'd leave my room."

He studied her a moment, wondering how to get past her to-the-manor-born outrage. "Elizabeth. I'm sorry, okay? It was dumb. Really dumb. I was trying to be funny, not humiliate you. Okay?"

"Funny? Clearly your sense of humor and mine are vastly different, because making a public display of something that should be a very private matter is not my idea of amusing."

"Look, if I could take it back, I would. But I can't. And your burger is getting cold, and I don't want that on my conscience, as well."

She crossed her arms over her chest. "I'm not going to choke down food I don't want simply because you've suddenly developed a conscience."

She started to say more, but he reached down and grabbed a couple of fries and put them in her mouth.

She spluttered, but she was far too polite to spit them back out. He watched as she chewed furiously.

"You really are an absolute pig, aren't you?" she said once she'd swallowed.

"Maybe. Want some more?"

"No!" she said. Then her tongue darted out to lick a salt crystal from the corner of her mouth.

He laughed and she looked hugely chagrined. "Busted," he said. He offered her the plate again. "Going hungry isn't going to punish anyone except yourself."

"You think you're so clever and charming, don't you?" She snatched the plate from him.

She sat on the bed and rested the plate on her knees.

"Actually, no. I don't." He straddled the battered wooden chair by the window and rested his forearms on the back.

"Yes, you do. You think you're irresistible, but you're not. You didn't charm me just now, and you didn't charm me last night. I slept with you for my own reasons, not because of anything you did or said. And I'm eating my dinner because I paid for it and I'm hungry."

She picked up her burger and took a big, screw-you bite out of it.

"Whatever floats your boat, Betty."

She frowned at him ferociously until she'd swallowed and could speak again.

"Please stop calling me that. My name is Elizabeth."

"You're right. You're not really a Betty."

"Thank you."

"More of a Lizzy."

She sighed heavily, rolled her eyes and took another bite of her burger.

"Mind if I have one of your fries?" He didn't wait for her to respond, simply grabbed a handful.

"Have you ever seen the movie *Greystoke?*" she asked.

"I think so. That's the fancy Tarzan one, yeah? With Christopher Lambert? Why?"

"You put me in mind of a certain man who was raised by wild apes."

She looked pretty pleased with herself for getting a shot in, and he rewarded her with a laugh before helping himself to more fries.

"Nice one, Lizzy."

She tried not to smile, but her lips kept curling up at the corners.

"How's that burger?"

"Very nice. Thank you," she said grudgingly.

"I meant to tell you—I left a message with Sam today. Hopefully he'll get back to me soon."

"Oh. Can I ask what message you left?" She looked worried.

"If you're asking if I left a voice-mail message telling him about his long-lost, possibly unknown daughter, the answer is no. I simply told him he needed to call, stat."

"Well. Thank you."

"You're welcome. Are you going to eat the rest of that burger?"

"I suppose I should be grateful you didn't grab it from my hand," she said as she offered the plate to him.

She drank her Pimm's while he polished off the burger.

"I suppose you'd like me to leave you some of this, too?" she asked, arching an eyebrow in inquiry.

"Lizzy, I'm happy to say it's all yours. Foul stuff."

"Have you even tried it?"

"Yes. Once. Which was more than enough."

"It's very refreshing."

"Sure it is." He stood and dusted his hands down the front of his jeans.

She swallowed the last of her Pimm's, then stood, as well.

"We okay?" he asked.

She nodded briefly. Ever so gracious, as always. As always where she was concerned, he couldn't help smiling.

"At least wait until you've left before you laugh at me," she said primly.

"I wasn't laughing at you, Lizzy."

She walked past him and opened the door.

"Thank you for my dinner. And the apology."

He walked toward the door but stopped when he was in front of her.

"Don't I get a goodbye kiss?" he asked, his eyes on her full lower lip.

"I don't think that would be a very good idea, for a lot of reasons."

"So? It'd be fun, at the very least." He leaned toward her.

She put her hands on his chest. "Is fun all that you ever think about?"

An image of Olivia flashed across his mind. The blood on her face. Her fear-filled eyes.

"No," he said, then he closed the last, small distance between them and kissed her.

She tasted sweet and tangy from the Pimm's. He slid his hands over her shoulders and down her back to cup her ass. Her peachy, round ass. She made a low sound in the back of her throat. He stroked her tongue with his and pressed forward with his hips, instinctively seeking the heat and softness of her body. He was hard—had been half-hard the whole time he'd been in her room, simply from smelling her perfume and being close to her—and a small shudder of anticipation rolled through his body.

He slid one hand from her backside to smooth it up her ribcage to her breasts. Her nipples were already stiff, poking through the soft fabric of her sundress. He flicked one shoulder strap down, then the other, and her breasts were bare and he was filling his palm with warm, resilient flesh.

He plucked at her nipples, teased them, but he wanted to taste her, the way he had last night. He broke away from her mouth, kissing his way across her cheekbone, lingering at the soft skin below her ear, and continuing to her breasts. Her nipples were a pale shell-pink, small and pretty. He tongued first one, then the other. Elizabeth's hands slid into his hair, holding him against her breasts.

As if he wanted to be anywhere else.

He slid a hand down her thigh to the hem of her dress, sweeping beneath it. She spread her legs eagerly as his hand slid up her thigh and into wet heat. His cock ached as he remembered how tight she'd been last night, the fierce pull of her body on his.

He stroked her through the silk of her underwear and suddenly he couldn't wait a moment longer. One hand still on her mound, he lifted his head from her breasts and pushed her two steps backward until she was flattened against the wall. She watched him through heavy-lidded, smoky eyes as he fumbled at his waistband, dragging his fly down. He found a condom and slid it on with urgent hands. He was too impatient to wait for her to pull off her panties; he simply pushed them to one side, then he lifted her knee so it hooked over his hip and slid inside her.

She closed her eyes and moaned. Man, he loved the sounds she made, the little gasps and sighs.

He grasped her hips and started to move inside her. So tight. So hot. So damned good. He hitched her other leg up and she hooked her ankles together behind his back and thrust her hips forward to meet his strokes.

He could feel her excitement rising, the tension ratcheting tighter and tighter inside her. He lowered his head and licked her breasts, left, then right, pulling on her nipples until she gasped his name. Her fingers dug into his back and she held her breath, straining, almost there…then she pulsed around him, arching away from the wall.

He kissed her, swallowing her cry of release. He closed his eyes and concentrated on the slick heat encasing him, the warm brush of her breasts against his chest, the flex of her hips beneath his hands as she kept his rhythm.

There was nothing in the world except for her and him and the slide of their bodies and the sound of their breathing. Perfect peace. Absolute oblivion.

Too quickly his climax found him, tightening to a point of white heat and need until he pressed his face into her neck and thrust inside her one last time to shudder out his release.

He kept his face pressed into the soft skin of her neck for long moments afterward, regretting the loss of mindlessness, begrudging the return to reality.

Without releasing his grip on her hips, he pushed away from the wall and carried her to the bed. He stayed inside her as he lowered her onto the bed.

Then he started kissing her again, seeking that moment of peace once more.

5

Elizabeth woke to the soft snick of the door closing. She opened her eyes and propped herself up on one elbow, disoriented in the dark of the room. For a moment she didn't know where she was—her bedroom in Mayfair, Martin's apartment, the hotel room in Soho. Then the languid heat between her legs and the slight soreness of her breasts brought it all rushing back: Nathan, his visit to her room, sex against the wall.

She was in Australia. And she'd just spent her second night in the arms of the sexiest man she'd ever met.

She thought about all the times she'd lain beneath Martin, yearning for something other than his gentle, careful lovemaking. She hadn't known what that something was until she'd found it on the beach and against the wall in her hotel room. She'd wanted passion. Desire. Animal lust. She'd wanted sweat and grabby hands and panting and undeniable need.

She rolled onto her side and stared at the crack of light seeping beneath the blind on the window.

A few days ago, she'd never had sex anywhere except in a bedroom. She'd never experienced any other position except missionary. She'd certainly never been slammed against a wall and had her lover so desperate to be inside her that he hadn't even bothered to remove her underwear.

It was just sex, of course. Bodies rubbing against each other because it stimulated nerve endings and satisfied some primal urge. But if she hadn't seen her birth certificate, if she hadn't confronted her grandfather, if she hadn't acknowledged almost too late that there were fundamental problems in her relationship with Martin and that she was shoehorning herself into a future that suited everyone except herself, she might have married him. She might have made her vows and settled into a life half-lived. She might have gone on denying herself and her needs and never known the joy, the freedom of being able to express her desires. Better yet, to pursue them.

So, yes, it was just sex, but at the same time it felt like much, much more than that. As though she was on an archeological dig, searching for herself, and her sexuality was the first truth that she'd uncovered.

Memories from the night washed over her as she lay drowsing. Nathan's body, so hard and strong beneath her hands. The firm, deeply satisfying thrust of him inside her. The way he'd barely let her catch her breath and come down to earth before he started kissing and touching and torturing her all over again. He was an insatiable lover. Driven. Intense. Almost desperate, it had seemed to her more than once during the night, like a drowning man clutching at passion and desire to keep him afloat. The look in his eyes, the fervor in his caresses…

Elizabeth let out a huff of laughter at her own melodrama. Nathan Jones was a surf bum with a fabulous body and a talent for sex. There was no need to read anything else into his admittedly intense lovemaking. In fact, there was no need to overanalyze it at all. It was meaningless and pleasurable and wonderful, and she was content to leave it that way.

A knock sounded at the door, drawing her out of her thoughts. Since she knew only a handful of people in all of

Australia and only one of them knew where she was staying, she thought it was safe to assume it was Nate.

A slow smile curled her mouth. She'd thought he'd gone home, but perhaps he'd simply ducked out to buy a bottle of water or make a call or buy a newspaper or something and now he was back to put in an encore performance.

Remembering the morning sex they'd enjoyed yesterday, she hoped so. She got out of bed and wrapped a towel around her torso and opened the door.

And promptly gaped.

Because standing there in a very wrinkled three-piece suit, overnight bag in one hand, briefcase in the other, was Martin.

"My God. What on earth are you doing here?" she said.

Not the most welcoming of greetings, but he was supposed to be in London.

"I came to talk to you. Since you didn't seem to want to talk over the phone."

"But…this is *Australia!*" she said, still not quite able to comprehend his presence.

"Yes, after nearly twenty-four hours in the air, I'm well aware of that. Might I come in?"

It was a perfectly reasonable request—if they were still engaged. But they weren't. And she'd spent the night having sex with another man in the rumpled sheets just over her shoulder. It felt hugely, hugely wrong to invite Martin into the same space that she'd recently shared with Nathan. Especially when she was only wearing a towel.

"Could you give me a moment to dress?"

She closed the door before he could answer, feeling both guilty and ungenerous as well as angry and ambushed.

There was only one person who could have told him where she was: Violet. For a moment she was seized with the urge to call her friend and blast her for first blabbing, then not making contact to warn Elizabeth that she'd blabbed. She sat on the room's one and only chair and closed her eyes.

Who was she kidding? She could work up a righteous head of anger at Violet for blabbing and Martin for ambushing her but the truth was that she was swamped with guilt. A week ago, the man on the other side of the door had had every reason to believe that he would be spending the rest of his life with her. She'd given him her virginity at the ripe old age of twenty-three after dating him for four months. Six months ago, he'd asked her to marry him and she'd said yes. They'd had an engagement party and booked the Savoy for their reception and St. Stephen's for the ceremony and Paris for the honeymoon. And then she'd pulled the rug out from under his feet and run away to the other side of the world before the dust had even settled.

She owed him a conversation. An explanation. The fact that he'd chosen loyalty to her grandfather over loyalty to her didn't change that or excuse her actions. Yes, she had been shocked. Resentful, too, although she wasn't sure that Martin was the right target for her resentment. But she'd had time to calm down now and they needed to talk.

She dressed quickly in one of her new sundresses and brushed out her hair before tying it back in a simple ponytail. She would have killed for a shower, but it was not to be, not when Martin was standing out in the hall like Paddington Bear, abandoned at the train station.

She straightened the bed, then let him into the room.

"It's a long flight. Would you like a shower?" she asked, gesturing toward the ensuite.

"Yes. That's probably a good idea. I suspect my personal hygiene leaves pretty much everything to be desired right now." He offered her the ghost of a smile. "I won't be long."

She handed him a fresh towel and sat on the bed to wait as he disappeared into the bathroom.

This was going to be difficult. There was no getting around it. Martin had not flown halfway around the world to find closure. He'd come to talk her into coming home and getting married. And she was going to say no, and he was going to be hurt all over again.

She stared at her lap. It wasn't as though she had a choice. She couldn't marry him simply to avoid hurting him. That would only hurt him far more in the long term, even if she was prepared to sacrifice her own happiness in the name of doing the right thing. And she wasn't. She'd put a lid on her own feelings, wants and needs for too long, first bowing dutifully to her grandparents' idea of who she should be, then to Martin's.

No longer.

The water shut off abruptly and she crossed to the corner counter and turned the kettle on. By the time Martin emerged from the bathroom in a fresh white shirt and a pair of slightly wrinkled, tailored trousers the tea was ready to pour.

She made him a cup the way he liked it and passed it over wordlessly. He took the lone chair and she returned to her spot on the edge of the bed.

Martin glanced around the room, taking in the dingy carpet and basic furnishings before focusing on her. She held his eye and took a deep breath.

"Martin, I don't want to hurt your feelings, but I'm not coming back to London with you."

"I understand that you're keen to meet your biological father—"

"It's not that. That's why I'm here, yes. But that's not why I can't go back with you. I'm incredibly sorry that it's taken all this to open my eyes, but I can't marry you."

Martin looked down at the mug of tea in his hands. "Can I ask…is there someone else?"

"No." Which was true. Her decision to call off the wedding

had come long before she even knew Nathan Jones even existed.

Martin drew breath to ask another question and she rushed into speech.

"I know you're confused. I know this must seem like it's come out of nowhere, but it hasn't. It's been building for years. Ever since I dropped out of field hockey when I was fifteen."

Martin shook his head. "Hockey. I'm afraid I must be incredibly dense, Elizabeth, but I'm struggling to see how your hockey team has anything to do with our relationship."

"My grandmother hated the idea of me playing. She thought it was rough and dangerous, but I adored it. Then Grandmama came to the semifinal and I got checked and fell over and she was so upset after the game that I promised to quit on the spot. And I've been doing it ever since, Martin. I dropped English Literature and took up Fine Arts as an elective and didn't accept a full-time teaching position when I graduated because she wanted me to take over her seat on the Friends of the Royal Academy Committee and the other charities she sits on. I didn't get my hair cut because my grandfather prefers it long. I didn't go backpacking through Europe with Violet because they were worried about my safety—"

"You're saying you feel an obligation to please them."

"That's it, exactly. I love them enormously, but the truth is I've let them dictate too many of my decisions. To the point where I don't even know what I want anymore."

"I understand what you're saying, but it won't be like that once we're married. You'll be in your own home, your choices will be your own to make. I certainly have no plans to impose my will on you."

"Martin—" She broke off, feeling incredibly sad as she looked at him. "Don't you see? You were their choice, too, in a way. Don't you remember how they sat us together at the firm Christmas party, and how my grandmother encouraged you to ask me to dance? And how my grandfather kept asking you to drop his papers by at the house when he 'forgot' to bring them home from the office so we'd keep running into each other?"

"Elizabeth, I can assure you that the only reason I have ever been interested in you is for yourself."

She could see the devotion in his eyes, the adoration—and she knew she was utterly unworthy of it. Not because she was a bad person, but because he had an idea in his head of who she was, and it had nothing to do with the real Elizabeth.

She searched her mind for a way to explain the fundamental disconnect between them.

"Remember that time I wanted to talk about our sex life?" she asked. "Remember how I asked you to, you know, do it differently, and you refused?"

"I remember Violet putting ideas in your head."

"Those were my ideas, Martin. I wanted you to do those things to me. But you said you respected me too much."

"You'd prefer for me to throw you over my shoulder or do you in the backseat of my car rather than taking the time to ensure your needs are met, would you?"

"Well, honestly, yes. Sometimes I would. Haven't *you* ever wanted to do any of those things?"

He broke eye contact and slid his mug onto the bedside table before smoothing his hands down his thighs. The very picture of discomfort.

"Of course I've wanted to do those things. There are lots of things I'd like to do, but that doesn't mean I'm going to cast all other considerations aside and jump in, boots and all. Life isn't only about what you want, Elizabeth."

Elizabeth put down her own mug of tea. "I'm going to take a guess that when it comes to me the 'other considerations' that come into play are my grandparents. Am I right or am I wrong?"

Martin threw his hands in the air. "Again with your grandparents. Could you please stop trying to equate their values with mine? I respect them enormously, especially your grandfather. He's a brilliant lawyer and he's been an incredibly generous mentor to me. I owe him everything. But I'd like to think I have enough native wit and intelligence to make my own decisions."

She stared at him, frustrated. How to get through to him?

"Look me in the eye and tell me that when I asked you to do me from behind like a dog you didn't once think of my grandfather and what he might think and how much you respect him," Elizabeth challenged boldly.

"For God's sake, Elizabeth. What a question." His color was high as he shifted in his chair.

"Okay, fine, answer me this, then—have you ever done it that way with one of your other girlfriends?"

She saw the truth in his eyes before he glanced away. She leaned forward to capture his hands, forcing him to return his focus to her.

"Let's call a spade a spade here. For better or for worse, I'm fixed in your mind as the granddaughter of the man you respect more than any other person in the world. You said it yourself—you owe him everything. When you look at me, you see the granddaughter of Edward Whittaker first and me second."

Martin reversed their grips so that he was the one holding her hands. "Elizabeth, I love you."

"Martin, the woman you think you want to marry doesn't exist. She's a construct, cobbled together by my overdeveloped sense of duty and your desire to be connected to a man who, in many respects, has filled the role of father in your life. I would make a terrible, terrible wife for you."

"I don't believe that. Not for a minute."

"It's true. You might not see it now, but you will one day."

He stared at her and she could see realization dawn on him as he at last understood that he would be going home alone.

"I'm so sorry. I really am. You're a good, good man. And one day you are going to make some woman an amazing, wonderful, loving husband. But that woman is not going to be me."

His eyes were suspiciously shiny. He stood, pulling his phone from his pocket.

At first she thought he was calling her grandparents, but then she realized he was talking to the airline, booking the next available flight to London. She put her hand on his arm to get his attention.

"Why don't you stay for a few days? You don't have to go straight back, do you?"

He covered the mouthpiece on his phone. "I didn't come here for a holiday. I came here for you."

So she sat with guilt gnawing at her while he booked a flight home for late that evening, reminding herself over and over that she'd done the right thing for both of them, that whatever hurt she inflicted now was better than a divorce down the road when things would be even more messy and complicated and painful.

It didn't make her feel much better.

Martin ended his call and reached for his overnight bag.

"Now what are you doing?" she asked.

"I need to get back to Melbourne."

"It's only an hour and a half away. You can at least stay for breakfast, can't you?"

He considered her invitation for a long moment. "I don't particularly relish being the object of your pity, Elizabeth."

"I don't pity you, Martin. How could I? You're one of the smartest, most honorable men I know. I feel bad about the way things have turned out. I wish I'd found the courage to stand up for myself before the business with the birth certificate. But I don't feel sorry for you. Somewhere out there is a woman you're going to want to throw over your shoulder, and nothing in the world is going to stop you from doing it. I look forward to hearing about her when it happens."

He stared hard at the floor for a few beats, then he put down his overnight bag.

"Where do you recommend for breakfast, then?"

NATE HITCHED A LIFT out to Woolamai in the morning. The swell was high and the water crowded with fellow surfers keen to take advantage. He spent an hour in the water, got sandbagged twice and relentlessly drilled when a wave shut down with him in the curl. His brain felt washed clean and he was starving by the time he hit the beach.

A couple of New Zealand surfers were heading into town and he caught a ride with them. He thought about Elizabeth as he sat in the back of their pickup. The silk of her skin. The taste of her. The smell of her hair.

He'd had her three times last night, and still he wanted her again. He wasn't sure what was up with that, but he wasn't going to question it. Far better to have his head filled with visions of soft white skin and pretty pink nipples and pale blond hair than what he'd been living with for the past few months.

He wondered if he'd see her again tonight. Then he smiled to himself. He'd make sure he did. Why leave it to chance, after all?

He spotted the thick white envelope sticking out of his

mailbox as he lifted his board off the New Zealanders' roof rack. His mood soured. Just what he needed—a reminder of everything he'd turned his back on.

He tugged the envelope free on his way past, not even glancing at the red-and-black logo in the top left corner. He dumped his board by the back door and threw the envelope into the corner of the kitchen as he entered. It slapped against the stack of other envelopes piled there, all of them unopened. One day soon he'd get around to dumping the lot of them in the recycle bin.

He took a quick shower, threw on fresh clothes, then did a lap of the house, trying to decide what to do next, feeling off-kilter thanks to that damn envelope. Pathetic that that was all it took these days.

Thoughts of Elizabeth flashed across his mind again, but he could hardly go looking for her so soon after leaving her bed. He needed to watch himself where she was concerned as it was.

He did another lap of the house, anxiety nipping at his ankles. He didn't do alone time without a beer in his hands and it was definitely too early to drink. Making a quick decision, he grabbed his wallet and walked out the door. He'd head into town, get something to eat, maybe grab some groceries for the next few days. That ought to kill an hour or two.

The first person he saw when he hit main street was Elizabeth, sitting at one of the tables on the sidewalk outside the Euphoria Cafe. All his self-strictures about being careful where she was concerned went out the window. She looked so soft and cool and he could practically feel her skin beneath his hands. He was about to cross to her table when a tall, dark-haired man exited the café and sat with her. There was something about the way the guy looked at her that got Nate's back up. The feeling only intensified when the guy picked up her hand and held it. And she let him. She even laughed at something he said and squeezed his fingers.

Elizabeth had told him she was single. She'd lain down on the beach with him and tangled his sheets and a few hours ago had taken him in her mouth and made him a little bit crazy. So who the hell was this guy? This pale, overdressed stiff with his ridiculous pants and business shirt and banker's haircut?

He was already striding toward their table when it hit him that his reaction was way over the top. Elizabeth owed him nothing. They'd slept with each other twice. They'd made no commitments to each other, tacit or overt.

So why the hell was he standing at her table, glaring down at her?

"Lizzy. Long time no see," he said.

Her eyes widened with shock. "Nathan. Hello. Um. Yes."

Nate could feel the other guy checking him out and he straightened to his full height. Hard to tell with the other man sitting down, but Nate figured he had a couple of inches on him. He met the other guy's eye and offered his hand.

"Nathan Jones."

"Martin St. Clair," the guy said, his accent a perfect match for Elizabeth's clipped tones.

"Nathan shares a house with my father. He's helping me make contact with him," Elizabeth explained. She flipped her teaspoon over and over nervously.

"I see. It's nice to know Elizabeth has friends to help her out when she's so far from home," St. Clair said.

It was such a pompous, stiff little speech that Nate couldn't help smirking. St. Clair didn't look much older than him— early thirties—so what was with the big stick up his ass?

"I'm more than happy to help Elizabeth out. In fact, it's been my pleasure," he said.

Elizabeth's eyes narrowed, even as her cheeks turned pink.

That was the problem with that creamy English complexion of hers—it was a dead giveaway every time.

St. Clair was looking back and forth between the two of them, a frown on his face.

"Have you known Blackwell long?" he asked.

"About ten years or so." Nate could elaborate, but he chose not to. Knowledge was power, after all.

He switched his attention to Elizabeth, who was positively glowering at him now.

"I'm free to talk about that thing again tonight, by the way," he said. "What time suits you?"

"I'll have to get back to you." Her accent even more cut-glass than usual.

He shrugged. Then, because he was far too aware of her English lover or whoever St. Clair was, Nate slid his hand onto the nape of her neck and ducked his head to kiss her goodbye. She tasted like coffee and she jerked her head backward when he slipped his tongue inside her mouth.

"Nice meeting you, Martin," Nathan said as he straightened.

He gave them both a finger wave before turning and sauntering up the street toward the bakery.

So much for his perfect distraction.

ELIZABETH FOUGHT THE URGE to squirm in her seat. There was no way that Martin had not picked up on the not-very-subtle signals Nathan had been sending. The man had practically cocked his leg, he'd marked his territory so obviously.

She could only imagine what Martin must be thinking. She snuck a look at him from beneath her lashes. He was studying a sugar sachet, smoothing his thumb back and forth over the small square.

She felt a strong urge to apologize, even though that would

only confirm that she'd slept with another man mere days after ending their engagement. She opened her mouth, but something stopped her from saying the words on the tip of her tongue. She remembered the strange, almost scary euphoria she'd felt after that first night with Nathan. The feeling of freedom.

And suddenly it hit her that she didn't owe Martin anything. Their relationship was over. Had been since the moment she'd called off the wedding in London. She hoped that they would remain friends, but she wasn't going to pretend to be something she wasn't to achieve that. If Martin chose to judge her, that was his decision, not hers. At the end of the day, the only person whose opinion she needed to worry about was her own.

It was a strange realization. A revolutionary concept. She'd lived for the good opinion of others for so long, it felt like shedding a huge weight. Just last night she'd been mortified because Nathan had teased her by displaying an inch of her underwear in the bar. She'd retreated to her room and imagined what judgments people must be making about her, what they must be whispering to each other. She was so used to living in the fishbowl of her grandparents' elite, discreet social circle that it simply hadn't occurred to her to not care what anyone else thought.

Because, really, it didn't matter that a few people she'd probably never see again might suspect she'd had sex with Nathan Jones. In the big scheme of things, it was neither here nor there. It was none of their business. Pure and simple. And if they chose to judge her, then so be it. She couldn't control how other people saw her. Which, essentially, was what she'd been trying to do all her adult life.

She met Martin's gaze across the table.

"Thank you for breakfast. I know you want to get back to

Melbourne, but you should at least come for a walk along the beach before you go."

He put the sugar sachet down and placed his palms flat on the table.

"Thank you, but no. I think I need to go home."

She nodded. She understood. And she regretted his pain. But she was not going to apologize. For perhaps the first time in her life. She owed herself—her new self—that, at least.

They both stood and walked to the pub to collect Martin's bags. Then she walked him to his rental car and watched as he stowed his luggage. When he was done, he turned to her and eyed her for a long, silent moment, his gaze roaming over her face.

"Look after yourself, Elizabeth."

"I will. You do the same, okay?"

She hesitated, then she stood on tiptoes and pressed a kiss to his cheek. His lashes swept down as he closed his eyes, then, as she was about to withdraw, his arms closed around her and he pulled her close in a fierce bear hug.

She hugged him back, thinking about the many hours they'd spent with each other, the many kindnesses he'd shown her. She loved him very much—as a friend. He was a lovely man. He simply wasn't the man for her.

His arms loosened and she took a step backward. He cleared his throat.

"Goodbye, Elizabeth."

She waited until his car had driven out of sight before marching down to the beach. What on earth had led Nathan to put on such an obvious display? Was it some kind of chest-beating alpha-male thing? Or was it yet another example of his warped sense of humor, more teasing in line with his stunt with her underwear?

Whatever it was, it was unacceptable. The sun was at its zenith, the sand hazy with heat as she walked along the high-tide mark and then up the short track to her father's street. She spotted Nathan the moment she rounded the corner of the house; he was lounging in a hammock strung between his studio and one of the lower branches of the big tree that shaded much of the backyard. His eyes were closed and he was nursing a bottle of beer against his bare chest.

As angry as she was with him, it was impossible not to appreciate the sheer physical beauty of the man. Shaking her head at herself, she strode up to the hammock and gave it a hard yank.

The hammock tilted dramatically, dumping Nathan unceremoniously facedown onto the grass.

He swore, his words muffled. Then he rolled onto his back and stared up at her, his chest glistening with spilled beer. "What was that for?"

"Take a wild guess."

He braced his arms on the ground and pushed himself to his feet. She tried not to notice the way his abdominal muscles flexed invitingly.

"What you did was incredibly inappropriate. Not to mention embarrassing," she said.

"I kissed a friend goodbye. Where's the harm in that?"

"That wasn't a kiss. That was a brand. You were marking your territory."

"Don't flatter yourself, sweetheart."

She crossed her arms over her chest. "What was it, then? Why did you kiss me like that in front of Martin?"

He shrugged a shoulder before bending down to collect his beer bottle.

"I don't know. It was just an impulse. A bit of fun. Unlike certain people, I don't spend half my life staring at my own navel, analyzing every thought and body function."

"Well, maybe you should. It might stop you from behaving like a fifteen-year-old boy half the time."

To her enormous chagrin, he laughed. "Lizzy, we really have to do something about your insults. That one couldn't fight its way out of a soggy paper bag."

She pointed a finger at him. "Don't attempt to disarm me with your cheap charmer's tricks. You wanted to embarrass me this morning. You might not want to admit it, but I know it and so do you."

"You're way too uptight, you know that?" He reached for her, trying to pull her close.

She slipped out of his grasp. "No. No more. Good sex is not an excuse for bad behavior. You might not respect me, but I do. Goodbye, Nathan."

She turned on her heel and started walking.

"Lizzy."

She turned the corner into the driveway. She told herself it was probably a good thing to draw a line under whatever it was that had been going on between her and Nathan. She wasn't in the market for a holiday fling. She wasn't in the market for anything. She was here seeking contact with her father, nothing more.

"Elizabeth."

His hand caught her shoulder as she was about to step onto the road. They faced each other under the bright midday sun.

"I'm sorry, okay? I saw you with that guy, the way he was looking at you, and you'd told me there was no one else, and…I don't know. It just pissed me off."

She stared at him. Was it her imagination, or was Nathan telling her that he'd been *jealous* of Martin? She wasn't an expert on casual sex by any means, but she was pretty sure that possessiveness and jealousy were not supposed to be part of the equation. Especially with a guy like Nathan, a man who lived in a single room at the back of someone else's property and who surfed and drank all day then hung out in bars chatting up women at night.

"I think you might be the most confusing man I've ever met."

He reached out and tucked a strand of hair behind her ear. "You're no walk in the park, either, your highness."

He leaned close and she didn't resist as he pulled her into his arms and kissed her, long and slow. He tasted of beer and salt and his skin felt very hot when she slid her arms around him. He spread his hands on her back and widened his stance and they stood there kissing like fervent teenagers, their hips and bellies and chests pressed together.

Finally he broke the kiss, sliding his hand down her arm to take her hand.

"Come shower with me," he said.

But she dug her heels in, resisting. He raised his eyebrows and she shook her head, feeling suddenly hugely out of her depth. She'd had a grand total of two lovers in her life, including him. She wasn't stupid, but she was very definitely inexperienced when it came to matters of sex and men and dating. She had no idea what was happening between them, what he wanted from her, what she could expect from him. Nothing? Hot sex for as long as it stayed fun? One more night? A week? A month?

"What is this?" she asked quietly. Probably that was breaking some mysterious rule of the dating world she didn't know about, but she had to know. She needed parameters, some kind of guidance, because she sensed that it would be very easy to let herself get swept away by Nathan's sexy body and boyish charm and incredible intensity.

"It is what it is, Lizzy. Fun in the sun, for as long as it lasts."

It was on the tip of her tongue to ask him about his jealousy, where that fit in to his easy-breezy view of things. But then

he tugged on her hand again and she allowed him to lead
her inside. She told herself it was because she was hot and a
shower sounded wonderful and she wasn't ready to give up
the sex yet.

It was almost the whole truth, too.

6

THEY WASHED EACH OTHER in the shower, then they crossed the yard to his studio and spent the afternoon naked in his bed.

Elizabeth had never felt so depraved, self-indulgent and decadent all at once. When she was with him, skin to skin, the outside world ceased to exist. There was only the suck and lick and pull of his mouth on her body, the glide of his fingers on her skin, the hard planes of his chest and back and belly, the fierce power of his thighs, the thick, satisfying length of him inside her.

After the sun had gone down they showered again. He pulled on a pair of jeans and laid a fire in the brick barbecue on the back lawn. She rummaged in the fridge and managed to cobble together a salad while he cooked steaks over the coals. They sat on a picnic blanket to eat, then stretched out in the twilight afterward, their plates pushed to one side, each of them nursing a cold bottle of beer.

They talked about books and movies and travel as the heat of the day slowly faded, and when she mentioned her teaching he peppered her with questions and seemed genuinely interested in her replies. She was surprised by how well-read he was, how well thought out his opinions were. It dawned on her that he was much more than a beautiful face and a hard body. She'd known he was smart—he was too quick on his feet to be anything but. She simply hadn't appreciated how sharp he was beneath the tan and the sand and the worn denim.

He asked why she'd chosen to teach in the public rather than the private system and listened as she told him about the special literacy course she'd run last year, and somehow the subject shifted to travel and she learned he'd surfed the coast of South America as well as Africa and spent nearly two months in Rome as a young man.

As the evening wore on she became more and more confused. On one hand, Nathan presented as a lazy layabout, a man who spent his days lolling in hammocks or riding waves. And yet he had clearly lived another life, a life outside of this small island and this very modest, slightly down-at-the-heel house.

Then there was the dark intensity he brought to the bedroom. This morning she'd scoffed at herself for reading things into the almost desperate way he held her and made love to her. Lying next to him under the stars, listening to him, she couldn't help wondering all over again. Because there was definitely more to this man than met the eye. Definitely.

She turned her head to look at him, besieged by questions— none of which she felt remotely entitled to ask. He hadn't asked her anything, after all. He hadn't even asked about Martin, and when she'd mentioned her parents' deaths during dinner he hadn't even offered the usual "sorry" before changing the subject. He hadn't volunteered anything about himself, either. In fact, she knew nothing about him except for his name and where he lived.

"You've got that look on your face again, Lizzy. I don't like it," Nathan said.

She'd thought he was stargazing, which was why she'd

been studying him so blatantly. But apparently he had twenty-twenty peripheral vision.

"What look is that?" she asked, matching his casual tone.

"That thinking look. I'm right, aren't I? You were thinking, weren't you?"

"It's rather difficult to stop, actually."

"Now that's where you're wrong. You just need something to distract you."

She watched as he put his beer down then rolled toward her and plucked her bottle from her hand.

"A distraction," she said. "Any suggestions?"

Warmth pooled low in her belly as Nathan's gaze slid over her body.

"Mmm. Let me see if I can think of anything," he murmured.

He leaned over her, one long leg sliding over hers as his hand found her breast and his mouth found her lips. They kissed deeply as his fingers teased at her nipple through the fabric of her dress, pinching, flicking, rubbing. She shifted restlessly, already anticipating the weight of his body on hers, the push of him inside her.

His hand left her breast and smoothed down her ribs, then her belly. He stopped when he reached her mound, simply resting his palm over it for long torturous seconds. She felt the heat from his hand flow into her body and she lifted her hips in silent invitation. He smiled against her mouth and began to pleat the fabric of her dress between his fingers, slowly gathering it up. When he had the bulk of it bunched around her hips he broke their kiss and began to lick and suck his way down her body, laving her neck, suckling her breasts, pushing her skirt higher still and dipping his tongue into the tiny well of her belly button.

She started to tremble with anticipation as his mouth moved

lower and lower. If he was going where she thought he was going, this was yet another area where she was woefully inexperienced. She'd thought about it—a lot—wondered what the heat of a mouth might feel like against the delicate, sensitive skin between her legs. But she'd never been bold enough to ask Martin to go down on her, and he'd never offered.

She gave a small gasp as Nathan's tongue slipped under the elastic on the waistband of her panties. He looked up at her, a smile on his face. She knew he could feel her trembling. He knew exactly how excited she was.

"You like this, Lizzy? If I'd known, I would have come visiting sooner."

"I don't know," she said before she could stop herself. "I've never done it before."

His hand tensed on her hip. "You're kidding."

She stared at him, determined not to say another betraying word. He already had too much power over her, she wasn't about to give him more.

He laid his cheek flat on her belly and hugged her hips to him. "Poor Lizzy. We'll have to make up for lost time, then."

He pressed a kiss to her mound through the silk of her underwear, then proceeded to torture her with his hands and fingers as he traced the edges of her panties, dropping kisses on her inner thighs, licking here, tasting there, but always avoiding the throbbing, hot place where she craved him the most.

She clenched and unclenched her hands, fighting the urge to simply lift her hips and thrust herself into his face. He was determined to tease her, and she was determined to withstand his teasing. If it killed her.

"How you doing up there?" he asked after a while, laughter in his voice.

"Just fine. You bastard," she panted.

He laughed outright and hooked a finger into her waistband. She lifted her hips as he pulled her panties off, the muscles of her belly and thighs tensing as he pushed her legs wide and settled between them. Here again he took his sweet time, looking his fill in the light of the almost-full moon. She desperately wanted to cover herself with her hand but she knew that would only amuse him even more.

"You're so pretty, Lizzy. I bet you taste good, too," he said.

She held on to the blanket for grim life as he lowered his face toward her. She felt his breath against her skin, then she gave a low, deep moan as his tongue lapped against her sex for the first time.

He laughed against her most tender flesh and licked her again.

It was incredible. Indescribable. Hot and wet and soft and hard all at once. He settled in, sucking, teasing, using his hands, driving her crazy with each stroke of his tongue.

She moaned and lifted her hips and drove her fingers into his hair and trembled with her approaching climax. Then he slid a finger inside her and she fell apart, pulsing and crying out and bucking her hips.

It seemed to last forever, and when it was over, he pressed a kiss to her thigh and undid his jeans and slid inside her while she was still trembling with aftershocks. Incredibly, she felt the excitement begin to build again as he stroked into her, his big body tense above her. As if her pleasure had fed his, he came quickly, his fingers digging into her hips as he shuddered out his release.

It was only after he'd withdrawn and she was lying boneless and spent on the blanket staring up at the stars that she thought about the fact that they were in his backyard, in the open, where anyone could see them if they cared to look over the fence or walk down the driveway.

"Bloody Nora," she said, flipping her skirt down and sitting up to look around in alarm.

Nathan took one look at her face and started laughing again.

"It's not funny. Anyone could have seen us. My God. What if the neighbors have children? We could have scarred them for life!"

"They're weekenders, Lizzy. They won't be down for another few weeks when school holidays start."

She shook her head at her own abandon. When she was with Nathan, every other consideration went out the window. It was more than a little scary.

He rolled close to her, nuzzling her neck.

"Anyway, I'd be more worried about them hearing us than seeing us. You make a lot of noise, Lizzy."

She gasped and hit his shoulder, trying to push him away.

"I do not!" she said, even though she was well aware she'd practically been howling at the moon not five minutes ago.

He didn't let her go. He kept pressing kisses against the soft skin beneath her ear, his tongue darting out occasionally to taste her.

"I like it. I like it a lot," he whispered against her skin.

And that quickly it was back, the irresistible, undeniable heat. She turned her mouth toward him, kissing him hungrily. Giving herself up yet again to the moment and letting everything else—her future, her father, her curiosity about Nathan—fall by the wayside.

NATE WOKE GASPING FOR air, his body drenched in sweat. The remnants of his dream still filled his head—the blood, Olivia pleading for him to help her, the dark pressing in on him, the sensation of being trapped. His heart was pounding against his breastbone and his thoughts kept slipping and sliding out of his control as his body tried to cope with an adrenaline-fueled flight-or-fight response that had nothing to do with the reality of the here and now.

Elizabeth stirred beside him. He rolled away from her. The last thing he wanted was to have to deal with her questions right now. She murmured in her sleep, then quieted.

He moved to the edge of the bed. At least he hadn't woken screaming. He should be grateful for small mercies. He'd be wired all day with the aftereffects of the adrenaline overload, of course. Edgy and tense. And tonight the odds were good that when he slipped into sleep the memories would be waiting for him again. Fear was great like that—the way it fed on itself until fear of fear itself became the biggest bogeyman of all.

He stood. He needed a shower.

He was halfway to the door when his phone started ringing. He fumbled beside the bed, finding his cell in the pocket of yesterday's jeans. Elizabeth's eyes flickered open as he checked the caller ID.

"Sam," he said into the phone.

Elizabeth tensed as she heard her father's name.

"Nate. I can't talk long. We're about to head out for off-coast drills. What's up?"

"I needed to talk to you," Nate said.

"Fire away."

Elizabeth sat up, pulling the sheet over her breasts. Her eyes were anxious as she watched him and Nate felt the enormous responsibility of what he was doing—brokering the first contact between father and long-lost child.

"Mate, there's someone here to see you. Her name is Elizabeth Mason—"

He broke off as Elizabeth touched his arm.

"My mother's name was Eleanor Whittaker. He won't recognize Mason."

"Her mother was Eleanor Whittaker," Nate said into the phone.

He paused, giving Sam the opportunity to jump in. He had no idea whether his friend even knew he had a child or if Elizabeth's facts were straight or—

"How did she find me?"

Sam didn't sound very surprised. Which probably meant he was well aware of Elizabeth's existence.

And yet he'd never contacted her. Nate frowned.

"I'm not sure. Maybe you should ask her yourself. She's here right now."

"No. Don't put her on." Sam's protest came so quickly it couldn't be anything but a knee-jerk response.

Aware of Elizabeth hanging on his every word, Nate stood and grabbed a towel off the end of the bed, wedging the phone between shoulder and ear while he wrapped the towel around his hips. He made brief eye contact with Elizabeth as he headed for the door.

"Give me a minute," he said, then he strode outside.

He waited until he was in the far corner of the yard and out of earshot before speaking again.

"What's going on, Sam?"

"Listen, I can't do this right now. The race kicks off in a couple of weeks. I need to have my head in the game." Sam sounded panicky.

"She's flown halfway around the world to find you."

"I didn't ask her to come."

"Sam, she's your *daughter.*"

He'd known Sam for nearly ten years, ever since they'd crewed together on a mutual friend's boat. They'd sailed together, gotten drunk together, and for the past four months they'd been living together. If anyone had asked, Nate would have said Sam was an honorable guy—completely obsessed with the sea, sure, but a decent guy. Nate couldn't believe that the man he knew was prepared to simply blow his daughter off without even talking to her.

"I don't need the distraction right now, Nate. This is a big one. We've got a real chance of winning this year, which means we'll contest the Transpac and maybe even the Fastnet."

"Jesus, Sam, can you hear yourself? You're talking about a bunch of races and I'm telling you your daughter is here, wanting to meet you for the first time in her freaking life."

There was a short silence on the other end of the phone. Then Sam swore.

"All right. Put her on. I'll talk to her."

"Bloody generous of you."

"Give me a break, will you? You caught me on the hop."

"Right."

Nate stared at the open door to the studio. He was of two minds about handing the phone over. He'd seen the hope in Elizabeth's eyes when she heard who was calling. There was no way she wasn't going to be disappointed by her father's lackluster response. Hell, Nate was disappointed, and he had no vested interest in their relationship whatsoever. Sam had always been a difficult bugger, a loner with precious few social skills. But Elizabeth was his daughter.

Nate shrugged impatiently. None of this was any of his business—there was no reason whatsoever for him to feel protective and indignant on Elizabeth's behalf. Just because he'd slept with her a few times didn't make her his responsibility. He could barely get through the night without waking in a sweat and shaking like a baby. He had enough on his own plate without taking on someone else's problems.

He lifted the phone to his ear again.

"Give me a second. I'll go find her."

"How come she's hanging around at your place at eight in the morning, anyway?" Sam asked suspiciously.

Nate didn't bother answering. A man who could barely

muster the interest to talk to his own daughter had no right to ask those kinds of questions.

Elizabeth was pulling on her clothes when he entered. He offered her the phone.

"He wants to talk to you," he said.

She hesitated a moment, her gaze searching his face. Then she took a deep breath, squared her shoulders and reached for the phone.

"Elizabeth speaking."

Good manners dictated that Nate make himself scarce, but he wanted to make sure Sam was behaving himself first. He watched her face carefully as she listened to Sam on the other end of the phone.

"Nathan told me you were crewing for the big race. I'm more than happy to fly up to Sydney—"

She frowned as Sam said something on the other end to cut her off. Nate could guess what it was. Elizabeth lifted a hand and rubbed her forehead with her fingertips.

"I see."

There was a world of disappointment in those two words. Nate watched the expectation and anticipation slowly drain out of her. They hadn't spoken about it—he deliberately hadn't asked, and she hadn't offered—but he knew she'd had high hopes of her long-lost father. What person wouldn't? She'd probably imagined getting to know him, perhaps finding out they had things in common, slowly forging a bond....

"Of course. I understand," she said.

Nate headed for the door. He didn't want to play witness to her disappointment. He didn't want to feel for her. He didn't want to feel anything—had spent the past few months working damned hard, in fact, to achieve a state of numb indifference.

He went into the house and made coffee, telling himself

all the while that Elizabeth was an adult. She could look after herself.

He was dressed and pouring milk into his coffee when the bead curtain on the rear door rattled. He turned to find Elizabeth standing there. She'd pulled her hair into a ponytail low on the back of her head and her face looked very pale.

"Thanks for that. I appreciate it." She handed over his phone.

"You want some coffee?" he asked. Because no way was he asking if she was okay, or what Sam had said. He wasn't getting involved. He refused to.

"No. I'm fine. I might head back to the hotel, actually. Thanks for dinner and…everything."

She turned toward the door.

"You know your way back okay?" he asked, even though he knew she did, since she'd found him yesterday.

"Yes, thank you."

She offered him a small, polite smile before exiting. Nate listened to the beads rattle against one another. Then he took his coffee to the kitchen table and sat.

She was upset. God only knew what Sam had said to her. Some bullshit about how important the race was, or some other piss-poor justification for his lack of interest.

He pulled the morning paper toward himself and flicked to the cartoon page. He read all his favorites, then folded the page in half to tackle the crossword puzzle.

And through it all, he couldn't get Elizabeth out of his mind.

She deserved better. She'd come here looking for her father, for Pete's sake.

Before he could think twice, Nate pushed away from the kitchen table. There was no sign of her in the street. He lengthened his stride as he reached the track to the beach. He spotted her straightaway once he hit the sand, a lone figure trudging toward town with her sandals in her hand.

"Elizabeth," he called.

She paused and looked over her shoulder. He slowed to an easy lope as he crossed the final distance between them.

"You got plans for the day?" he asked when he reached her side.

She frowned as though she didn't understand what he was asking. "Plans?"

"Are you doing anything?"

"Oh." She blinked. "I was thinking of finding an Internet café so I could check my e-mail. But other than that…"

She shrugged. He hated the closed-down look behind her eyes. Bloody Sam. When Nate saw him next he was going to kick his ass.

"There's a good northeasterly coming through. Great day to take the cat out, if you're game."

"You have a cat?"

"A catamaran, the *Rubber Ducky*. A Hobie 16. You ever sailed before, Lizzy?"

"No."

He slung his arm around her shoulders. "Another first, then. What do you say?"

She looked confused for a moment, then she made an embarrassed sound and tried to wriggle out from under his arm.

"Trust you to bring that up. I knew I shouldn't have said anything."

"Your secrets are safe with me, Lizzy. I promise."

She stopped struggling. He tugged on her ponytail.

"Come on, it'll be fun."

"There's that word again," she said, her face downturned as she stared at something on the ground.

He tugged on her hair again. "Don't knock it till you've tried it. Are you in or what, Lizzy?"

She thought about it for a moment. Then she lifted her face and met his eyes.

"Yes, I'm in."

"DUCK!" NATE YELLED.

Elizabeth clapped a hand onto the ridiculous floppy sun hat he'd insisted she wear and flattened herself against the trampoline as the boom swung over her head. Her safety vest shifted awkwardly, pressing underneath her armpits. She tugged it down again when she heard the hiss of ropes sliding through pulleys as Nate worked to tie the boom in its new position.

"You can come up now, Lizzy."

She knew without looking that he was laughing at her. He'd been laughing at her all morning. As a sailor, she apparently made a fantastic clown. The stupid hat and cumbersome life vest and pale pink zinc cream he'd spread over her nose didn't help much in that area, she suspected.

She couldn't help smiling in response, however. It was hard not to when they were racing across the water, Nate's elegant catamaran skating across the surface of the waves, its twin hulls slapping salt spray into the air. The deep aquamarine of the ocean beneath them, the almost-painful cornflower-blue of the sky overhead, the warmth of the sun, Nate's laughter—it was exhilarating, there was no other word for it.

The perfect antidote to the phone call from her father.

Instead of sitting upright again, Elizabeth rolled onto her side and edged toward the front of the boat. The black trampoline fabric was hot beneath her legs as she lay full length and peered over the front beam, staring down at the sea as it whipped past.

To say that her father had been unenthusiastic about her appearance in his life was putting it mildly. He'd actually sounded put out when he spoke to her, as though he'd been burdened with an unwanted responsibility at the worst possible time. She was an inconvenience, apparently. Not that he'd said as much. But she could read between the lines. She'd offered to fly to Sydney to meet him, but he'd claimed he was too busy drilling before the big race. She'd agreed to wait until he could fly back to Melbourne after the race finished, but she was in two minds now about whether she would wait for him or not.

He'd known about her. All along, he'd known he had a daughter, and yet he'd never tried to contact her. It was a body blow, there was no denying it. She'd fooled herself that she'd come without expectations, because the reality was that she'd hoped that there'd been some reason for his absence in her life. Some proof that her grandfather's judgment that her father was "not someone they wanted involved in her life" was wrong. But apparently her father wasn't even vaguely curious about his child born on the other side of the world.

She stretched her arm out and trailed it in the icy water, feeling the tug against her fingers as it resisted her invasion.

Maybe this whole trip had been a huge mistake. A gross miscalculation on her behalf. Maybe she should cut her losses and go home now, save herself from further rejection.

"Come back up this end, Lizzy. We're going to tack and head downwind and I need your weight back here."

"How flattering," she said.

She pushed herself up onto her hands and knees and made her way to the rear of the trampoline where Nathan sat at the helm, one hand on the tiller, the other on the line that controlled the boom.

She felt uniquely inelegant as she plopped down beside him in her borrowed board shorts and T-shirt. Fabric was bunched around her middle where she'd cinched his too-large shorts tight and the fluorescent orange safety vest made her feel ten times her normal size.

Nate reached across to tug her hat lower on her face.

"Careful with that complexion, Lizzy. And when we run downwind, we have to keep the bow up out of the water to avoid pitchpoling. That's why I need you back here with me."

"What's pitchpoling?"

"It's when the bow pushes down under the force of the wind so much that it dips under the water."

He made a tipping motion with his hand to illustrate.

"Are you saying that the whole boat could flip over?" she asked, alarmed.

"Relax. I haven't pitchpoled the *Rubber Ducky* for years."

"Dear God," she said under her breath, glancing around the small, sleek catamaran with new eyes. It had all seemed so innocuous up until now.

"Here," Nathan said, and she found herself holding the tiller as he scrambled forward to do something with the sail.

"Isn't this a little like asking a passenger to volunteer to fly the plane?" she asked nervously. The tiller vibrated beneath her hand with the force of their movement through the water.

"How are you going to learn to sail if you don't get some time at the helm?" Nate asked, his deft fingers threading rope through a cleat.

"Learn to sail?" she squeaked. "Are you kidding?"

She stared up at the mast towering overhead with its acres and acres of taut sail. Never in a million years would she feel confident enough to captain such a delicately balanced piece of engineering.

"What did you think this was? A leisure cruise?"

He sat beside her. "Okay, so we're heading downwind at the moment…"

He explained the theory of tacking to her, pointing out the tightly bound boom—close hauled, in sailor speak—and showing her how they were keeping the wind on one side of the *Ducky* or the other as they worked their way across the bay. Then he took her through a tack, talking her through each stage and forcibly pushing her head down when she became so absorbed she forgot to duck as the boom swept from one side of the boat to the other.

"I did it!" she whooped as the sail bellied out over her head and the *Ducky* started to move again.

"Yes, Captain, you did," Nate said, offering her a salute.

After a couple more tacks they sailed back to shore. Elizabeth watched, fascinated, as Nate lifted the rudders and glided the boat straight up onto the sand.

"And that doesn't hurt the thingies at all?" she asked.

"The hulls? Nope. They're made out of superstrong fiberglass. Of course, we probably don't want to beach on a chunk of rock."

She accepted his help to scramble off the trampoline and stood upright for the first time in hours, a big, goofy smile on her face, her board shorts dripping with seawater.

"That was wonderful. I can't understand why I've never done it before," she said.

"Maybe because you live on a little island where it rains most of the year?"

She wrinkled her zinc-covered nose at him. Nate stepped closer and for a moment she thought he was going to kiss her, but he reached for the clasp on her life vest and worked it loose.

"Oh. Thanks."

The vest loosened around her waist and she shrugged out of it.

"Thank heaven. It's like wearing a straitjacket," she said as she threw it on the trampoline.

Nate shrugged out of his own vest. She couldn't help admiring the way his wet T-shirt clung to his chest.

"Now, the not-so-fun part—packing up," he said.

She worked alongside him to bring the sail down, then carried it with him up to the clubhouse where they washed it down with freshwater to remove any salt spray. Once it was dry, they rolled it and stowed it in a long canvas bag. Then she helped him coil ropes, copying his expert moves in her own fumbling way.

"Sailing can be addictive, so you'd better be careful," Nate said as he tied off a coil of rope and dropped it onto the trampoline. "Sam's like that—not happy unless he's on the water."

It was the first time he'd ever mentioned her father and she shot him a look. His face was absolutely neutral as he checked to make sure the rudders were locked upright. As though they were discussing the weather or something equally banal.

"Sam'll do pretty much anything to get out there," he said. "A lot of small yacht deliveries for rich guys who need their boats sailed from one port to another, crewing with bigger yachts when the work comes up. He's more than happy to spend days out on the water on his own. Which probably explains why he's a taciturn bastard at the best of times."

It took her a moment to understand what he was doing: letting her know that her father's rejection wasn't personal, that he was an isolate by nature. She stroked her finger along the silky weave of the rope she was coiling, assessing the conversation she'd had with her father from this new perspective.

If her father was a shy man, a loner, socially awkward…it was possible that his first response to contact from a long-lost child might be retreat.

"Thanks," she said quietly.

Nate wiped his brow with the hem of his T-shirt, leaving a pink smear on the fabric from the zinc across his nose and cheeks. "Better go see if there's anyone in the clubhouse who can give us a lift back up to the racks. Unless you're hiding muscles I don't know about, Lizzy?"

"No, I'm afraid not."

"Didn't think so."

She watched as he made his way up the sand. He'd gone out of his way to be kind to her today, taking her out on the water to distract her from her disillusionment then offering her some insight into her father's character so she could better understand his behavior. Nathan was clearly uncomfortable with having that kindness acknowledged, however. She remembered how he'd told her he didn't want to get involved in any *This Is Your Life* situations that first time they'd met—then proceeded to follow her to her car and reassure her, as well as make contact with her father on her behalf.

She realized she was staring after him like a love-struck teenager and forced herself to turn away and concentrate on coiling the last rope. She needed to tread carefully. She'd already acknowledged that he was different from any other man she'd ever met. He'd introduced her to a world of sensual pleasure she'd only ever suspected existed, and he'd been very kind to her, in his own quiet, low-key way. Then there was the intense, intelligent, intriguing conversation they'd shared last night....

She was smart enough to know that all those things together were a pretty deadly combination, no matter how many times she assured herself she understood that he was a good-time guy and this was only a holiday fling.

The sound of masculine laughter heralded Nathan's return with three other men, all of whom were tanned and fit-looking, dressed casually in T-shirts and board shorts like Nathan.

"Lizzy, this is David, Gary and Steve," Nathan said.

"Hi," Elizabeth said, offering them all a wave of her hand.

She tugged on the hem of her soggy, oversize T-shirt, aware she probably looked like something the cat had dragged in.

As though he sensed her self-consciousness, Nate draped an arm around her shoulders and dropped a kiss onto her nose before ushering her to one side.

"Stand back and let us men do our thing," he said in a deliberately deep, gravelly voice.

"Should I cheer you on? Or maybe squeal a little?" she offered drily.

Nate stripped off his wet T-shirt, tossing it over to her.

"Save the squealing for later," he said with a wink.

The other men laughed, and Elizabeth rolled her eyes as they each grabbed a corner of the boat and hefted. Muscles rippled down Nate's arms and back, and she forgot what she'd been about to say in response.

She followed them as they carried the catamaran up the beach. She couldn't take her eyes off Nate. And it wasn't just because of his body.

Be very careful, Elizabeth.

But it was hard to listen to common sense when the sun was shining and she was walking on the wild side for the first time in her life.

7

NATE WOKE TO FIND Elizabeth curled into his side again. Even as his cock rejoiced, his shoulders tensed.

He shouldn't have invited her to stay for dinner last night. The sailing lesson was one thing, but he shouldn't have cooked her dinner, then pulled her into the studio afterward and peeled off her clothes and laid his body over hers. Definitely he shouldn't have wrapped his arms around her afterward and fallen asleep nuzzling her neck.

What he should have done was send her home and nipped this thing in the bud. She was a good person—a nice person. He didn't want to hurt her. But it was inevitable if they kept seeing each other like this.

The problem was, he really liked her. The sex was fantastic, and she was smart and funny and she didn't play games.

And he was a guy who could barely get through the night without nightmares. A guy who'd retreated to the far corner of his own life in an attempt to stop himself from going completely nuts—if it hadn't happened already.

He had no business starting something with her that he couldn't finish. He had nothing to offer beyond sex, and somehow, despite his best intentions, this thing between them was already moving past that.

So. It was time to pull the pin. She might hate him for it in the short term, but she'd thank him in the long run.

Having made his decision, he told himself to get out of bed and start putting distance between them. Instead, he smoothed his hand down her shoulder, savoring the cool silk of her hair against his fingers. Then he lowered his head and inhaled the warm smell of her skin—sweet, with just a hint of her citrusy perfume lingering.

There was no getting around it. He'd found more peace, more comfort in her arms the past few nights than he had for months. Ridiculous as it seemed after such a short time, he was going to miss her.

Get out of bed. Get out of bed. Get out of bed.

He knew the voice in his head was smart and rational, but he didn't move. Instead, he waited another half hour until she woke, her eyes fluttering, a slight frown on her face. She smiled when she saw he was awake already, the warmth in her eyes making him hard and uneasy at the same time.

"Hello," she said.

"Hi."

She glanced down and noticed his hard-on.

"And good morning to you, too," she said.

She smoothed a hand down his belly. He caught it just before she wrapped her fingers around his cock and forced himself to say what needed to be said.

"Listen. I have to leave the island for a few days," he said.

She stilled and he knew that she understood the unspoken message behind his casual words.

She withdrew her hand. "Are you, um, heading off today?" she asked, her tone carefully light.

"This afternoon, most likely," he lied.

She nodded. "Well. Have a good trip."

"Yeah. Thanks. I will."

It was a ludicrously stiff and formal conversation to be having while naked, lying side by side in bed. He threw off the sheet and stood. Elizabeth's dress and underwear were folded neatly on the chair in the corner and he passed them to her. She gave him a small smile of thanks that didn't reach her eyes.

He turned away and pulled on a pair of cargo shorts.

"Might go make some coffee," he said.

He left her to get dressed, crossing the dewy grass to the house, cursing himself every step of the way for being about as subtle as a sledgehammer.

But he only had to remember the flash of hurt he'd seen in her eyes to know he'd done the right thing.

He was pushing open the back door when someone spoke behind him.

"Nate."

He looked over his shoulder. Jarvie stood near the corner of the house, a wary expression on his face. His business partner looked tired, older than when Nate had last seen him. It took Nate a moment to find his voice.

"What are you doing here?"

Jarvie lifted his hand and Nate saw he was holding another one of those damned envelopes.

"I brought your mail."

Nate stepped back onto the lawn. "Last time I looked, there were a bunch of people they paid to do that."

"Last time I looked, people actually opened their mail."

"You've got my vote. Do what you like with the business."

"It's your company, too, Nate. I can't make all the decisions on my own."

Jesus. They'd been over all this a million times. He stared at the ground, his jaw tight, not saying anything. He didn't want to think about any of this. Couldn't. All of it—the company, his old life—belonged to a man who didn't exist anymore. And Jarvie knew that. Yet he kept sending mail and now he was here, asking for something Nate didn't have it in his power to give.

"We can't keep going on like this. The company works best when we're both there. We need you," Jarvie said.

"Believe me, you don't. I gave you power of attorney over my share of the business. Just do whatever you need to do."

"It's not that simple and you know it. You're the one who wrote the software. No one knows it better than you. We've had requests for new features, modifications…"

"Hire more programmers."

"They're not you. They don't know Smartsell like you do."

"They'll work it out. It's not rocket science."

Nate could feel himself getting angrier and angrier. Why couldn't Jarvie leave him the hell alone? He knew why Nate was here. He knew everything. So why did he keep pushing and pushing?

"Nate—"

"You think I want this? You think I like living like this? Do you have any idea—" He broke off, breathing hard. He clenched and unclenched his hands, hot pressure building at the back of his eyes.

"Listen, I know it's tough, man. But you can't just lock yourself away down here. You need to come back up to the city, start seeing that doctor again. She was helping, right? And maybe if you came into work a few days a week, things would start looking up again."

Looking up again.

Right.

Nate laughed. Jarvie had no idea. Standing there talking about Nate returning to the city and returning to work. As though there was nothing in the world stopping Nate from doing any of those things if he wanted to.

But, of course, as far as Jarvie was concerned, there wasn't. He didn't understand that after six months Nate still had to anesthetize himself with beer or vodka to get to sleep each night. Jarvie had no idea that all it took was the screech of tires or the wrong combination of noises or simply Nate letting his guard down and he was in the middle of a flashback to those long hours in the car, at the mercy of his own messed-up subconscious. Jarvie didn't have his little sister's voice in his head, pleading with him to do something, anything, to stop the pain.

He didn't have to live with the knowledge that he'd taken the life of the one person he loved more than any other in all the world.

Nate stared at his old friend, his body shaking with the force of his fury. For a moment he teetered on the brink of giving in to the urge to pound on something, anything, to release the anger and self-hate and fear inside himself. Then he reminded himself that this was Jarvie, his oldest friend, his business partner, and even if Jarvie didn't understand, he was here for the right reasons.

"You should get out of here," Nate said, turning away.

Jarvie stepped into his path. "You have to stop running from this, man."

"Get out of the way."

"Not until you listen to me."

"Move," Nate said between his teeth.

"No."

Nate's hand curled into a fist, his arm muscles bunching, his shoulders squaring. If Jarvie wanted a fight, he'd come to the right place.

"Nathan, don't!" Suddenly Elizabeth was between them,

her hand on his arm. She was barefoot, her hair a tangle around her head.

He had no idea how long she'd been watching, how much she'd heard. Jarvie released his grip and Nate took a step away from his old friend.

"Don't come again," Nate said.

Then he turned and fled the accusation in his old friend's eyes.

ELIZABETH WATCHED NATE walk around the corner of the house. She couldn't believe he'd been on the verge of a fight before she'd intervened.

"Shit," Nate's visitor said, the single word full of frustration and regret.

She glanced at him. He was about the same age as Nate, dressed casually but expensively in designer jeans and a Paul Smith shirt with striped cuffs.

He returned her regard, his gray gaze flicking up and down her body assessingly.

Since she didn't know what else to do she offered her hand.

"I'm Elizabeth Mason," she said.

When in doubt, be polite.

He stared at her hand as though he didn't quite know what to do with it before reaching out to shake it.

"Jarvie Roberts."

"I'm sure Nate will be back shortly," she said.

Because surely he would be. He couldn't leave his friend hanging like this.

Jarvie smiled cynically. "No, he won't. He won't come back until he knows I've cleared out."

"Oh."

Jarvie's gaze slid over her again, then he bent and collected the envelope from the ground. He handed it to her.

"Would you mind giving this to him?"

"Certainly."

"Thanks, I appreciate it," he said. He raised his hand in farewell as he strode up the driveway.

Elizabeth sighed and pushed her hair away from her forehead.

What in hell had all that been about?

She looked at the envelope in her hands. She hadn't heard much of the heated conversation, but she'd heard enough to gather that Nate was partners in some sort of business with the other man and that he'd recently walked away from it. She eyed the logo on the envelope. Smartsell. She'd never heard of it, but that didn't mean anything.

Nathan didn't strike her as a man who'd abandon a business on a whim. Even though her first impression had been that he was a lazy, feckless beach bum, she knew him a little better now.

She went into the kitchen and propped the envelope against the salt and pepper shakers on the kitchen table so he would see it as soon as he came in. As she was turning away, her gaze fell on a magazine rack in the far corner, overflowing with similar-looking envelopes. She stepped closer to examine them. Sure enough, they all bore the Smartsell logo.

Confused and worried, she walked to the beach in search of Nate.

She told herself she was being stupid, that Nate did not want her chasing him. He'd cut her loose this morning, in no uncertain terms. She might not be very experienced with men, but she recognized a kiss-off when she heard one.

Still, she walked to the waterline and shaded her eyes, looking up and down the beach for him.

His whole body had been trembling when she touched his arm to stop the fight. And the look in his eyes...

Her gut told her that something was very wrong, and she

was worried about him. Maybe that made her foolish, but so be it. She could be embarrassed about it later, when she'd assured herself he was all right.

She walked along the beach for fifteen minutes in both directions, then she went to the pub and checked both the beer garden and the public bar. There was no sign of Nate anywhere, and the barman, Trevor, said he hadn't seen him.

Which left her at a standstill. She didn't know Nate well enough to guess where else he might go. Which pretty much said everything, really.

Just leave it, Elizabeth. He's not your responsibility. You had some good sex, he cut you loose, that's it. Let it go.

Good advice, but it didn't stop her from descending the stairs to the main bar earlier than usual that night, hoping Nathan would be there. He wasn't and she was on edge all evening, waiting for him to appear. By eleven he hadn't and she figured he wasn't going to. She went upstairs to her room and told herself it was just as well.

Her island fling was well and truly over.

NATE SUCKED DOWN THE LAST of his beer and threw the empty bottle onto the grass beneath the hammock. It clinked against another empty bottle, which wasn't exactly a miracle since he'd been drinking heavily since he returned to the house in the late afternoon and the lawn was littered with bottles.

Despite all the beer, the agitated, unsettled feeling still gripped his chest and gut, as it had all day.

Bloody Jarvie. Coming down here, ruining Nate's peace. He'd given the guy carte blanche to do whatever he wanted with the business—why couldn't he just piss off and leave Nate to what was left of his life? Why did he have to keep inserting himself into things, reminding Nate of the way things used to be?

It had taken Nate months to develop a routine that got him

through the days and the nights. After too many hangovers to count he'd finally discovered the perfect amount of beer to consume to achieve an undisturbed night's sleep without making the next day a disaster. Between the beer and the surfing and the occasional hook-up with a warm and willing woman from town, he'd survived the past four months. Just.

Then Jarvie had barged in this morning with his demands, bringing Nate's old life with him.

He closed his eyes and pressed his fingers against his eyelids, thinking about the envelope Jarvie had left on his kitchen table and all that it represented.

Why can't he understand? I don't want it. I don't want any of it anymore.

The success he'd worked so hard to achieve. The big house and expensive car and invitations from people who knew people. None of it meant anything anymore.

It wasn't like he hadn't tried to pick up the pieces after the accident. He'd gone back to work. He'd even tried to drive once his concussion specialist had told him he was clear to do so.

Nausea burned the back of Nate's throat and he swallowed urgently. It was pathetic, but the memory of the afternoon he'd tried to get behind the wheel again still had the power to freak him out. Opening the car door. The smell of leather and expensive electronics. The steering wheel, the gearshift, the windshield. He'd slid into the driver's seat and been instantly transported to that night. The sound of screeching rubber, the smash of rending metal and shattering glass, the explosion of the airbags. The blood. The pain. The helplessness.

Nate gripped the edge of the hammock and swung his legs to the ground. He braced his legs wide and stared hard at the grass, his body tense, his breath coming fast as he battled with remembered panic and fear.

He closed his eyes, but nothing could block out the sound

of Olivia's screaming. She was always there, in the back of his mind. Dying over and over again. And there was nothing he could do to help her or stop the pain or soothe her.

Anger and despair welled up inside him. This was Jarvie's fault. If he hadn't come… Why couldn't he leave Nate alone?

It took five minutes to get the nausea under control. Nate pushed himself to his feet and crossed to the house, heading straight for the fridge. He needed more beer to drown Olivia out. He needed to drink until he was numb again.

He stared at the empty shelves in the fridge. It took him a few seconds to understand there was nothing left to drink. He swore under his breath and pulled the freezer door open, looking for the bottle of vodka he kept there. He dragged it out and swore again when he saw there was barely an inch left.

How had he let that happen? He always had beer and vodka on hand. Always. He slammed the freezer door shut and leaned his forehead against the cool white metal. He hadn't restocked because he'd been so busy thinking about Elizabeth, fantasizing about getting her naked again, that it hadn't seemed important.

Stupid. So stupid.

He'd have to go into town, buy some more beer. Enough to get him through the night. He headed for the door but the clock on the kitchen wall caught his eye. It was past twelve. Which meant the pub would be closed for the night.

He stood frozen in the middle of the kitchen, panic fluttering in his chest. He needed that beer. How was he going to get through the night without it?

He walked into the living room and sank onto the couch. Maybe if he tried to sleep now, before the beer buzz wore off, he'd be able to get past this shit that Jarvie had stirred up. Then tomorrow it would be business as usual, back to his routine.

He'd stock up on alcohol again, make sure he had backup this time. Batten down the hatches and wait for things to settle.

He lay down and rolled to face the back of the couch. His legs were too long and he bent his knees and drew them up. He had a sudden flash of how he must look—a grown man, huddled on the couch like a child.

Pathetic. So freaking weak.

He wrapped his arms around himself as the trembling began. He could hear Olivia screaming. He squeezed his eyes tightly closed and prayed to whoever might be listening to let him make it to dawn.

ELIZABETH WOKE FROM A DEEP sleep to the sound of someone pounding on her hotel-room door. She sat up with a start and reached for the robe she'd left lying across the end of her bed. The glowing bedside clock told her it was three o'clock as she crossed to the door.

She was pretty sure she knew who it was, but she stood on tiptoes and looked through the spy hole just in case. Nate stood on the other side, his face downturned as he leaned one arm against the door, his expression distorted by the fish-eye lens.

She twisted the lock and opened the door. Nate dropped his arm and straightened.

"Hey."

"What's going on?" she asked.

She could smell beer. He was glassy-eyed, with a fine sheen of sweat on his face. He smiled, but it didn't even come close to reaching his eyes.

"Can I come in?" he asked.

She stepped to one side silently, watching him carefully as he entered her room. Something was going on. He'd clearly been drinking—hardly new—but there was something else. Something wrong behind his eyes.

"How about I make us a coffee?" she said.

She turned toward the small counter in the corner but Nate came up behind her and slid his arm around her, his hand sliding unerringly onto her breast. He began massaging her through the silk of her robe, his hips pressing against her backside as he nuzzled the nape of her neck.

Impossible to stop herself from responding to his touch, but there was something so desperate about the way he held her, as though he was trying to merge his body with hers. He started to peel off her robe, his movements jerky and impatient.

"Nate. Has something happened?" she asked.

She twisted in his arms so that she could see his face but he immediately ducked his head and started kissing her, forcing her head back on her neck with his need.

His hands cupped her backside through her robe, lifting her against his hips as he rubbed himself against her over and over. His whole body was trembling, his muscles bunched as he held her tight.

Emotion closed her throat. He hadn't said a word, but she could feel the pain in him—he *vibrated* with it like a struck tuning fork. She wrapped her arms around him and smoothed her palms up and down his back, trying to reassure and calm him.

"It's okay, Nate," she murmured against his mouth. "Whatever it is, it's okay."

His breath seemed to get stuck in his throat then and he broke their kiss, pressing his face into the soft skin beneath her ear, his arms as hard as steel as he held her close. The trembling increased and he made a strangled noise in the back of his throat. She had no idea what to say or do, so she followed her instincts, soothing him with her hands, offering him what reassurance she could.

"It's okay, Nate," she said again. "You're safe here."

She rested one hand on top of his bowed head, the other

in the middle of his back, holding him to her as tightly as he was holding her. She wasn't going anywhere and she wanted him to know it.

Slowly the trembling faded. She felt Nate come back into himself and a new kind of tension took over his body. He started to push her away, no doubt feeling self-conscious now that the moment of crisis had passed. She didn't give him a chance to withdraw; instead, she encouraged him toward the bed.

"Sit down," she instructed.

He hesitated a moment. She knew he was trying to formulate an excuse so he could leave. She pushed him toward the bed.

"Go on," she said.

His face was shuttered when he looked at her. Then he took a step backward and sat on the bed. She knelt and pulled off his boots and socks, then she tugged at the waistband on his jeans and unzipped his fly. He leaned back as she peeled his jeans over his hips.

"Lie down," she said.

This time he obeyed as meekly as a child, shuffling over to make room for her. She lay down beside him and drew his head onto her chest, wrapping her arms around as much of him as she could hold. He lay there tensely for a beat, resisting the comfort she offered. Then his body relaxed and he turned his face into her breast, his breath coming in noisy gusts.

She felt dampness against her skin and knew he was crying. Tears stung her own eyes but she blinked them away and simply held him, her hands smoothing soothing circles on his back.

After a while Nate's grip softened. His breathing became deep and slow. She brushed the hair from his forehead and looked down into his face, still tight with anguish even though he was asleep.

Whatever was wrong, she was deeply touched that he'd come to her, even if he'd had to dress it up as sexual need to allow himself to do so. Which was crazy when she considered how long they'd known each other.

A warning bell sounded in her mind. She silenced it. Right now, Nate needed her. That was the only important consideration. Reality could wait until morning.

8

NATE WOKE TO DARKNESS and the soft rise and fall of Elizabeth's breast beneath his cheek. It took a moment for memory to fully return. Scorching heat rose up his chest and into his face as he remembered the way he'd pounded on her door and then jumped on her like a desperate madman. God only knew what she must think of him. It was a wonder she hadn't called security and had him thrown out.

He eased away from her until he was on his back, his head on a pillow instead of the cushioning warmth of her body. His face felt stiff from his tears. He ground his teeth together, furious and humiliated in equal measure.

He'd lost it last night. Big-time. Not since the early days after the accident had he been such a basket case.

He almost laughed as a thought occurred to him: if Jarvie could have seen him last night, there was no way he'd want him back in the business. Maybe next time the night terrors struck he should record it and send the disk to Jarvie for his edification. No doubt he'd never be bothered again once his old friend understood exactly how screwed up Nate really was.

"How are you feeling?"

The gentle inquiry came out of the darkness. He tensed.

He'd planned on being long gone by the time she woke. Save them both from the awkwardness of having to look each other in the eye after his meltdown.

"Do you want some water? Maybe some aspirin?"

"I'm fine. Thanks."

There was a short silence. Then he heard her inhale.

"Want to talk about it?"

He smiled grimly. Did he want to talk about it—the million dollar question. Everybody who claimed any friendship with him had been eager to talk in those early days. They'd all wanted to "be there" for him. And all he'd wanted to do was forget.

But he couldn't simply pull on his jeans and bugger off, not when he'd cried like a baby in Elizabeth's arms. He owed her something. Some explanation, at least.

"Sorry for barging in on you like that. It won't happen again," he said.

"I didn't ask for an apology, Nathan. But if you don't want to talk, I understand."

Her hand found his arm, then his hand. She slid her palm against his and wove their fingers together. She didn't say anything further, simply squeezed his hand comfortingly.

Hot emotion choked his throat for the second time. He swallowed, the sound audible in the quiet room.

Bloody hell. He really was losing it. Might as well hand his cojones over now.

"I noticed that some of the other catamarans had two sails up yesterday. Is that normal or are they different from the *Rubber Ducky?*" Elizabeth asked.

For a moment he was thrown by the abrupt change of subject. Then he understood what she was doing: giving him some breathing room. He squeezed her hand and she returned the gentle pressure.

"You're talking about a jib," he said. His voice caught and

he cleared his throat. "They make the cat more maneuverable and help with tacking. We had a good northerly the other day, though, so I didn't bother rigging it."

"Right. So when you're sailing alone, how do you manage it as well as the main sail?"

"You cleat the main sail first, then move forward to set the jib…"

They talked sailing for a few minutes. The faintest tinge of light was starting to creep beneath the blind. Gradually the tension in his chest eased. He turned his head and studied Elizabeth's profile, barely discernible in the dim light. Her small nose, the shape of her mouth and slope of her cheek.

He made a decision and returned his gaze to the ceiling.

"I had a car accident," he said. "Six months ago. I was driving to Melbourne from the island with my little sister, Olivia. There'd been another accident earlier. There was oil on the road. The car skidded…"

Elizabeth's hand tightened on his and he took a deep breath.

"We hit a tree, front left-hand side. The car…the car folded like a piece of freaking origami. I hit my head, passed out for a bit. Olivia—"

His throat closed as his sister's screams echoed in his head.

"You don't have to tell me. It's okay," Elizabeth said.

"I want to."

It took him a couple of shots at it. He held on to her hand for dear life as he told her how he'd woken and found Olivia pinned by twisted metal. How her face had been dark with blood, how icy her hand had been when he'd found it. How she'd whimpered and cried and begged. How he couldn't do anything, trapped beneath the steering wheel and the collapsed dash.

He stopped only when he got to the end. He couldn't make

himself say it. Couldn't explain how Olivia had pleaded with him to do something to stop the pain, right up until the moment she'd fallen silent and the desperate, labored rasp of her breathing had stopped, and how he'd held her hand until the rescue crew arrived and cut him free and forced him to relinquish his grip.

Elizabeth rolled onto her side and put her arms around him and held him tightly. Neither of them said anything for a long time. Then she lifted her face and pressed a kiss to his chin.

"I've sorry. Which is woefully inadequate, of course, and does nothing to change anything. But I'm sorry it happened, and I'm sorry your sister died. And I'm sorry you have to live with the memories. I can only imagine how hard that must be."

He hadn't told her because he wanted her pity or her sympathy or even her empathy. He'd told her because she deserved to understand why a grown man had hammered down her door and tried to lose himself in her arms last night.

And yet somehow, her calm, honest words soothed something inside him.

He pressed a kiss to her forehead, then her closed eyelids, then the end of her nose. She lifted her face and he found her mouth, returning the gentle pressure of her lips against his.

Slowly his offering of gratitude turned into something more needy and demanding. She shifted against him, her hips pressing against his thighs. His tongue slid into her mouth and stroked hers slowly, languorously. Her hand smoothed beneath his T-shirt to slide up onto his chest, her fingers shaping his pecs before skimming over his nipple.

He rolled toward her, pushing her silk robe out of the way. She arched her back as he lowered his head to pull a nipple into his mouth. Her hands found his shoulders and kneaded the muscles there as he suckled and teased and tasted her.

They pressed together, skin seeking skin, hardness seeking

softness. She tugged on the waistband of his boxer-briefs, releasing his hard-on. Then she lifted her leg over his hip and guided him into her wet heat. He gritted his teeth as his erection slid inside her.

She felt so good, so tight and good. He rocked his hips and she rocked with him. He cupped her breasts and teased her nipples and kissed her and kissed her. Her palms smoothed across his back, her fingers clenching into his skin with each slow, slippery thrust.

And then she was coming, throbbing around him as she gasped into his mouth and his own climax was washing through him like a tidal wave, relentless and all-conquering and undeniable.

He stayed inside her afterward, savoring the closeness. His eyes were very heavy and he closed them briefly.

She knew now. She knew everything. Pressing one last kiss to her cheek, he drifted into sleep.

ELIZABETH WAITED UNTIL HE was breathing steadily and slowly before pulling away from him. He frowned as she slipped free and she caressed his chest soothingly until he settled again.

She crossed to the bathroom and shut the door as quietly as possible. Then she sat on the closed toilet lid and pressed her face into her hands.

The horror of what he'd been through was almost impossible to comprehend. Being trapped with his sister yet unable to do anything as she died.…

It was more than any person should have to bear. It was cruel and unlucky and hard. The stuff of nightmares.

For a moment Elizabeth teetered on the brink of crying, overwhelmed by his pain and grief. She breathed through her mouth in big gulps, pressing her fingertips against her closed eyelids, willing the tears away.

Slowly she got a grip on herself. Her losing it wasn't going to change anything. Nate didn't need her to beat her chest with anguish over his sad story. He was living with the aftermath of major trauma. Grappling with grief and guilt and anger and loss on a daily, perhaps hourly basis. He needed comfort and support and patience, not tears.

She let her hands fall into her lap, then she stood and went to the basin and ran the taps. She washed her face and patted it dry. With a bit of luck, Nate would still be asleep and she could climb back into bed with him.

It took a few seconds for her eyes to adjust to the dimmer light of the bedroom when she exited the bathroom, but the moment they did she saw what her instincts had already told her—the bed was empty.

Nate was gone.

She was surprised, and yet she wasn't. He was a man, with more than his fair share of pride. She'd heard the shame and self-laceration in his voice when he'd told his story. She bet he gave himself a hard time for every moment of weakness or doubt.

She sat for a moment, thinking. Just as they had yesterday, her instincts told her to go after Nate. But there was something she needed to do first. For both of them.

She showered and dressed and walked up the hill to the backpacker's lodge where she'd noticed a sign advertising an Internet café. She paid her money, then settled into a worn-out office chair in front of a worn-out computer and rested her fingers on the worn-out keyboard.

She wasted a few minutes logging in to check her e-mail account. There was a note from Violet there, full of apologies for "blabbing to D.D." about Elizabeth's whereabouts. Elizabeth sent a quick response, assuring her friend that she'd done the right thing. She explained that she and Martin had agreed to part as friends and started writing a description of the island

and the weather before she caught herself and realized she was stalling.

She deleted the travelogue, assured Violet that she'd write more soon and sent the e-mail. Then she called up a search engine and typed in *post-traumatic stress*. She hit enter and waited to see what Google would offer her.

Lots, was the answer. More than she could ever take in in a lifetime. She read for over three hours about the various symptoms and treatment of post-traumatic stress disorder. By the time she pushed the chair away from the desk she had as many questions as she did answers. Nate's drinking, his reliance on distraction, his avoidance of his business partner and retreat from his former life...it seemed to her that he must be suffering from a broad range of classic PTSD symptoms: reexperiencing the event in the form of flashbacks; avoiding places and events that might trigger one; hyperarousal or being on edge; problems with sleep and angry outbursts. But it was impossible for her to know without talking to him.

She made note of a few book titles and went to the bookstore five doors up to see what they had to offer. There was one self-help title that didn't look very promising, but she had more luck at the local library. By the end of the day she felt reasonably well-informed.

Well-informed enough to understand what she was getting into if she tried to pursue this thing with Nate.

It was clear that recovery was going to be long and slow, if it occurred at all. Some people never fully healed from the trauma that tore their lives apart. Like Nate, they retreated into a corner and survived as best they could. Many of them turned to alcohol and drugs.

It was a lot to take on. Which meant she had a decision to make. A big one.

She'd known Nathan Jones for five days, give or take a few hours either way. She didn't know what school he'd gone to or his parents' names or what his favorite color was or the name of his first pet. She didn't know which way he leaned politically or whether he gave to charity or which five people, living or dead, he'd invite to dinner.

What she did know was that he needed her. She knew that when he touched her she felt beautiful and sexy and brave. She knew he was kind and generous, despite the fact that his own life was overshadowed by tragedy and trauma.

And she knew that when he'd pressed his head to her chest and sobbed out his pain she'd wanted to take his burden away from him with a fierce, bone-deep urgency that defied logic and common sense.

So, it really wasn't a decision at all, when it came down to it.

Maybe she was crazy to feel this way after only five days. But she was sure stranger things had happened in the world. And at the end of the day, it was what it was. And what it was was this: she was invested. Heavily.

So.

Armed with her new knowledge, self and otherwise, she went searching for Nate.

NATE AVOIDED MAIN STREET for the next few days. Every time he thought about what he'd done—running crying to Elizabeth like a little kid and dumping all his ugly, messed-up shit on her in one foul swoop—he got angry with himself and life and fate all over again.

Apparently it wasn't enough that he'd lost his sister and his business and everything that had once made him feel complete and successful and alive. Apparently he had to throw the last remnants of his pride and self-respect on the table, too, and barter them away for a few moments of comfort and succor.

It was freaking humiliating. And what scared him the most

was how much he wanted to do it all over again. Talking to Lizzy, having her hold him and listen and understand, had been the most difficult and yet comforting few hours he'd experienced in months. For a short time, the constant tension binding his chest and shoulders had eased.

Which was why he had to stay away from Main Street and the Isle of Wight Hotel and anywhere Lizzy might be. They'd had sex a handful of times. He'd helped her out with her father, given her a sailing lesson and her first experience of oral sex. None of those things gave him the right to impose on her the way he had. He'd stepped over the line, way over the line. She'd been incredibly generous, listening to him, soothing him, but he already knew she was a good person. No way was he going to impose on her goodwill again and take advantage of her good nature. No. Way.

It didn't stop him from thinking about her all the time, of course. About the crisp, cool sound of her voice and the warm light in her eyes and the way she frowned when she didn't quite understand if he was joking or not.

Amazing that you could miss someone who had barely arrived in your life, and yet that was the way he felt. Just as well he was never going to see her again.

He killed the days with beer and surfing and sailing, and when that still left the night hours to fill he walked the beach, following the sand around the island until the rising tide forced him to turn back.

On the third day of his self-imposed Elizabeth ban, he looked up from rigging the main sail on the *Ducky* to find her walking across the beach toward him. She was wearing a pair of bright pink board shorts and a long-sleeved aqua lycra rash vest. White zinc covered her nose and cheeks and a floppy hat shaded her face.

She should have looked ridiculous but she didn't. Lust and

need and want hit him in the solar plexus and he fixed his gaze on the shackle he was tightening and hoped he didn't look as goddamned desperate as he felt.

"You're a hard man to track down," she said when she came to a halt beside the catamaran.

"I've been busy."

He fed the headboard into the mast and began pulling on the halyard to hoist the sail.

"I see."

He concentrated on the sail, making sure it was locked in place before wrapping the halyard around the mast cleat.

Maybe if he simply ignored her, she would go away. Then he wouldn't have to look at her and want her and remind himself of all the good reasons why whatever had been happening between them was done and why it had never had a future in the first place.

It was such a childish notion that he immediately rejected it. At the very least he owed her an apology for the other night and for leaving the way he had.

He cleared his throat and forced himself to look at her. "Listen. About the other night. I'm sorry for barging in on you like I did. I was out of line and too pissed to make much sense and it shouldn't have happened."

He waited for her to respond, but she simply stared at him for a long moment before reaching for one of the coils of rope on the trampoline.

"This is the one we thread through the pulleys on the boom, right?" she asked.

He didn't understand why she was here. What she wanted. Then the penny dropped and he got it: she felt sorry for him. Poor old Nate, crying out his pain and fear. Boo freaking hoo.

He reached out and tugged the coil of rope from her hands.

"You should go," he said tersely.

"Should I?" She snatched the rope back.

He frowned. "I said I was sorry, okay? There's nothing more to say and I don't need a social worker."

"If I was your social worker, Nathan Jones, I would be up in front of an ethics committee in a flash. Now, where does this rope go?"

When he didn't do anything except continue to frown at her, she began uncoiling the rope.

"Fine. I'll do it my way and you can fix it later."

She moved to where one of the clam cleats was fixed on the starboard hull and started feeding the rope through it. A strand of hair slid out of her hat as she worked, grazing her cheek before coming to rest in a curl over her breast.

He told himself to tell her to go away again. He didn't want her pity. He wasn't sure what he did want from her, but it certainly wasn't that.

She glanced up then and he looked straight into the deep blue of her eyes.

"You owe me another sailing lesson," she said.

It wasn't as simple as that, and they both knew it. But he didn't have the resolve to push her away a third time, which probably made him a weak bastard. But then that was nothing new, was it?

NATE BARELY SPOKE A word as they prepared the *Ducky* for sailing. He gave her instructions and took care to avoid touching her and only made eye contact when necessary. She took her cue from him and worked in silence until they were ready to co-opt some of the other club members into helping them carry the *Ducky* to the water. This time she lent her might to the effort, even though it was mostly token might since there was a man at each corner. Still, it was symbolic. She was here to participate.

She moved to the opposite side of the cat as Nate once they were in the shallows, guiding the boat into deeper water.

"Up you get," Nate said, and she scrambled onto the trampoline, water streaming from her legs.

He joined her a few seconds later and they concentrated on getting the boat out. She ducked when he told her to and shuffled from side to side as he tacked first one way then another. She took the tiller when he raised the jib, then followed his instructions to reset it each time they tacked.

Slowly, over first one hour then two, the taut, distant expression left his face. Then and only then did she stretch out full length on the trampoline and rest her head on his thigh as he sat at the tiller, closing her eyes and crossing her ankles. She felt him look down at her but she didn't open her eyes. The tense thigh beneath her head slowly relaxed. After a few minutes, she turned her head and pressed a kiss against his skin.

"Lizzy..." he said. His voice was very low.

"Yes?"

"This isn't going to happen."

"Why not?"

He swore under his breath. "You know why not."

"No, Nathan, I don't." She sat up and turned to face him.

He was frowning again, and the taut look was back on his face.

"I don't want your pity, Elizabeth."

Amazing how unfriendly her own name sounded coming from him when she'd gotten so used to the way he called her Lizzy.

"Just as well, because you don't have my pity. You are the least pitiful person I know, as a matter of fact. I *empathize* with you. I feel for you. I regret your pain. But I don't pity you, Nathan. And if you don't understand the difference then maybe you should think about cutting back on all that beer you drink."

"I don't want your empathy, either." He sounded as sulky and out of sorts as a child but she understood that his weakness the other night struck at the heart of how he saw himself in the world.

"What do you want? My vagina? My breasts? My mouth? Am I leaving out any other useful body parts?"

He glared at her. "You came looking for me. Remember?"

"And you came looking for me the other night," she countered.

He looked away. "That was a mistake."

"Nathan…"

Because she didn't know what else to do, how to get through to him, she grabbed a fistful of his hair and pressed her mouth to his. He resisted her kiss at first, then his mouth opened beneath hers and his tongue slid into her mouth. She kissed him until they were both breathless. When they drew apart, he stared straight into her eyes and she saw so much desperation and need in him it made her chest ache.

"You don't understand," he said. "The other night—that's just the tip of the iceberg."

She nodded and raised her hand, counting off the points she'd researched. "Let me guess—flashbacks, night sweats, anxiety attacks, insomnia, quick to anger. How am I doing?"

A muscle tensed in his jaw. "I can't drive."

It was her turn to frown as she thought over all their time together. Sure enough, they'd walked everywhere.

"I take it you've tried?" she asked after a brief silence.

"Yes."

"Do you mind being in a car when someone else is driving?" she asked.

He brushed a hand over his hair and squinted toward the horizon. He clearly hated talking about this stuff, was about as comfortable as a cat having its fur stroked the wrong way.

"I tolerate it," he said. "It's not my favorite thing in the world, but I can do it. But I don't like driving at night."

She nodded. "Okay."

He glanced across at her. "That's it?"

She shrugged. "It's good to know these things."

"Lizzy."

"You keep saying that," she said. Then she leaned close and laid her cheek against his. "I like you, Nathan Jones. You make me laugh and you challenge me and you're very, very good in bed. I want to keep spending time with you. What's so hard about any of that?"

"I'm a basket case, Lizzy."

"I'm not exactly a bargain myself, you know. I've spent my entire adult life pleasing other people. I'm fresh out of an engagement I never should have agreed to in the first place. Before I met you I'd never had sex in any position other than missionary."

His gaze searched hers and she held his gaze unflinchingly.

"You should be running for the hills," he said.

"But I'm not."

He reached out and framed her face with his hands. "If I was a better person, I'd make you run."

"You could try. There's no guarantee you'd succeed, though. I've discovered a stubborn streak lately."

"Lizzy."

"There you go again with the Lizzy-ing." Then, because she could see how much this small moment of connection meant to him, how much he needed it, and she was very afraid that any minute the emotion welling up inside her was going to translate into waterworks, she leaned close and kissed him again.

THAT NIGHT, NATE TURNED away from rinsing the last of their dinner plates at the sink to find Elizabeth absorbed in the local paper at the kitchen table.

The overhead light shone in her pale blond hair and cast shadows beneath her cheekbones. He stood at the counter, folded the tea towel and resisted the urge to go to her and make love to her for the third time that day.

She was beautiful and funny and generous and prim—and he couldn't believe she was here. Couldn't believe that she hadn't backed off at a million miles an hour after his performance the other night or the revelation that he was still so haunted by the accident that he couldn't do something as simple and everyday as drive a car.

But she hadn't flinched, hadn't so much as looked away when he'd confessed his weakness. And when they'd come back to his place after sailing, she'd pushed him down onto the bed and left him in no doubt as to whether she still wanted him, despite everything.

Lying in bed with her in his arms, he'd caught a glimpse of a future that might not be simple, bare-bones, batten-down-the-hatches survival. A future that wasn't simply about endurance.

He walked around the counter and rested his hand on the back of her chair.

"Having a nice time there?" he said.

She glanced over her shoulder at him. "Did you know they delivered twin wombats at the local wildlife reserve? There's a picture here but they said they're not letting anyone in to see them until they're fully weaned. Look how cute they are."

He dutifully scanned the photograph accompanying the story. "Cute."

"We don't have wombats in England," she said. "The closest we have are the Wombles of Wimbledon Common."

She was being funny and he rewarded her with a kiss. "Want to toast marshmallows on what's left of the fire in the barbecue?" he asked.

"Why, sir, I thought you'd never ask."

They lay on the picnic blanket and made themselves sick and sticky with gooey marshmallows.

"I never know when to stop," Elizabeth said as she rubbed her stomach. "My mother used to call me a pelican—eyes too big for my belly-can."

"You miss her."

She pulled a face. "Stupid, huh? She's been gone for more than twenty years."

"Not stupid," he said. Impossible to stop his thoughts from going to Olivia. There were so many things he missed about her. The sound of her off-key singing when she danced to her iPod, her shoes cluttering the front hallway thanks to her habit of kicking them off the moment she entered the house, the way she'd send him little text messages through the day— their own personal Twitter—keeping him up-to-date on her world.

"You never mention your parents," Elizabeth said.

It took him a moment to change gears, push Olivia deep inside himself.

"They're both dead. Dad had a car accident when I was ten. Mum died a few years ago. Cancer."

"I'm so sorry."

"Yeah. We're not exactly the lucky Joneses, are we?" he said.

She shifted beside him, rolling onto her side and propping her head on her bent arm. "It must have made it harder. Losing

Olivia, I mean. Because you were her parent for the past few years."

For longer than that. His mother had battled for nearly two years before dying. Olivia had come to live with him when she was twelve. He'd had five years of being her everything before she died.

He'd been silent too long and Elizabeth reached out to touch his chest.

"You don't like to talk about it."

"Not much to say, is there?"

She leaned close and kissed him. "No, I guess there isn't."

She settled down beside him again, her head on his shoulder this time, her arm across his chest. She didn't say anything else, and neither did he.

He made love to her when they turned in for the night, swallowing her moans as he pushed himself deep inside her. She wrapped her legs around his waist and dug her fingers into his back as she came, her body strung as tight as a bow. He hung on to the pleasure for as long as he could before he succumbed. Then he tucked her body against his own and fell asleep.

9

NATE WOKE WITH AN idea fully formed in his mind the next morning. He wanted to give Elizabeth something back, something in return for her thoughtful silences and silken body and warm eyes. Something to make her smile.

He eased out of bed to find his phone and slipped outside to make a couple of calls.

Elizabeth was sitting up and blinking by the time he returned.

"No sailing today. I've got a surprise," he said.

"What have you been up to?" she asked suspiciously.

"Come on. Out of bed and into the shower. We've got places to go, people to see."

"Nathan. What's going on?"

"It's a surprise."

"What kind of a surprise?"

She looked so adorable, with her mussed hair and faintly imperious frown. He ducked his head to kiss her before responding.

"The kind of surprise that's a surprise."

She was even more curious when he walked into town with her to collect her car.

He could feel her looking at him as he buckled his seat belt, knew what she was thinking. It was the first time he'd driven with her, and she had to be wondering how he'd cope.

"I'll be fine, don't worry," he said.

It would have been true, too, if a car full of teenage surfers hadn't blown through an intersection on the way out of town. Elizabeth braked sharply and they both jerked forward in their seats. The strap bit into his chest and he lifted his hands instinctively to shield his face.

"God. I'm so sorry. He came out of nowhere," Elizabeth said.

She was pale from shock and Nate tried to find the words to reassure her but there was something in his throat and he couldn't seem to breathe around it.

Not now. Don't you do this to me. Don't you dare freaking do this to me.

But his stupid, messed-up subconscious was off and running, running a highlights reel from the night of the accident. Cold adrenaline swept through him as the car pulled over to the curb. He heard the sound of a car door opening and closing. Then Elizabeth was unbuckling his seat belt and pulling him out of the car.

"Sit. Put your head between your legs," she said, pushing him onto the grass at the side of the road.

He had no choice but to comply, sitting with his legs drawn up, his head hanging between his knees as he concentrated on slowing his breathing. In, out. In, out. After what felt like an age the shaking stopped. He opened his eyes and stared at the grass between his feet.

Shit.

Shit, shit, shit, shit.

He'd organized something fun for her, then screwed it up with his bullshit. A simple drive out of town, no big deal, and he'd turned it into a three-ring circus.

The futility of what they were doing—what he'd been

fooling himself they were doing—hit him. This was never going to work. He was a selfish prick for even trying to keep her by his side.

A warm hand landed in the center of his back.

"How are you doing?"

He was so frustrated, so freaking over it, he could barely stand to have her touch him. Especially when he knew how he must appear right now, hunched over on the side of the road like the basket case he was.

"I'm good," he said between gritted teeth.

"I wish I'd got their license plate number. Horrible little oiks. I'd love to send a note to their parents. I'm sure they'd be thrilled to know their children were driving around like maniacs."

Not quite what he'd expected her to say. But Elizabeth was always surprising him. He risked a glance at her. She was watching him, a question in her eyes.

There was no pity there. No contempt or regret or embarrassment.

It occurred to him that he was one lucky bastard to have opened the door to Elizabeth Mason just over a week ago. Possibly the luckiest bastard on the planet.

"Would this note be on monogrammed stationery?" he asked after a long silence. "I'm assuming you have some."

"Of course. But unfortunately I didn't bring it with me. So I'd have to make do with some from the Isle of Wight."

"Yes. That would definitely get their attention—a stern reprimand on letterhead from the local pub."

She smiled and gave a little shrug.

She was so damned gorgeous and sweet and funny....

She stood and dusted off the seat of her pants.

"It's not a bad idea, you know—writing a note to their parents. You'd be surprised how many big, bad boys are still afraid of their mothers."

He pushed himself to his feet.

"Come on. We'll go home and you can give me some sailing pointers," she said.

The thought of going home and disappearing inside his bubble of Elizabeth and beer and sun and silence seemed pretty good with the last of the adrenaline still making itself felt in his body.

But he'd been walking backward for so long. Retreating, retreating, retreating. No way was he going to cap the whole cowering-by-the-side-of-the-road thing by running home with his tail between his legs.

And he wanted to do this for Elizabeth.

"I'm not ready to go home yet," he said.

Elizabeth eyed him steadily. "You can surprise me another day, you know. If that's what it's about."

He gestured toward the car. "Let's go."

She hesitated a moment, then she walked around to the driver's side door. Nate stepped toward the open passenger door. He kept his gaze fixed on the seat in front of him, but it was impossible to stop the tension that banded his chest and choked his throat.

But he knew he could do this. He'd done it before, after the accident. He'd allowed people to drive him around, back and forth to doctors and consultants. To Olivia's funeral. To the office. He hadn't liked it, but he'd done it. And he'd finally gotten used to it, eventually.

So. It would be bad when he first got in. But it would get better. It would.

He took a couple of deep belly breaths, then slid into the car. His immediate impulse was to get the hell out. It was too small, too closed in. And once the car started moving, there'd be the speed to deal with, the world rushing up at him.…

He closed his hand around the seat belt clasp and pulled the belt across his chest. He clicked it in place, then gripped the fastener as tightly as he could. Just to know that he could release the belt any time he wanted.

Elizabeth put on her own belt and started the car. She signaled to pull onto the road, but didn't make any move to shift the car in gear or release the hand brake.

"We don't have to do this," she said.

"Yeah, we do."

She didn't say anything else, simply put the car in gear, released the handbrake and pulled out onto the road. A wash of anxiety rushed through Nate's body, the instinctive desire to escape something that terrified him. He kept breathing into his belly, the way his therapist had taught him, and slowly his heart rate slowed and the hectic, swirling chatter in his mind settled.

He loosened his grip on the seat belt, then deliberately relaxed the muscles in his shoulders. Finally he focused on the road ahead.

"We need to turn right up ahead," he said. "I'll tell you when."

"Okay." She glanced across at him. "Would it help if I sang?"

"Are you any good?"

"No."

He smiled. "Sure. Why not?"

She thought for a moment, then started singing "God Save the Queen." She hadn't been lying—she had a terrible singing voice. When she'd finished the British national anthem, she moved on to Abba.

By the time the turnoff came into view his hands were loose in his lap and most of the tension was gone.

"Right here," he said.

She nodded and turned and he gave her directions the rest of the way. Soon they were pulling into the parking lot of the Phillip Island Wildlife Park. She read the sign, then spun toward him with a hopeful smile.

"This is the place where they have the baby wombats."

He put on his best poker face. "Is it?"

"Nate…"

"Patience is a virtue. Surely your grandmother taught you that one?"

She poked her tongue out at him but followed him inside the administration building. The head ranger, Henry, came to the ticket booth when Nate gave his name to the cashier. They all shook hands and the older man led them into the park and along a dusty dirt track.

"This isn't the usual tour, is it?" Elizabeth asked after a few minutes.

"I'm not sure," Nate lied.

She nudged him with her elbow. "Is he taking us to see the baby wombats or not?"

"You're the kind of kid who used to snoop around under the Christmas tree, feeling up her presents, aren't you?"

"Yes."

She looked so hopeful that he couldn't help laughing. He slid his arm around her shoulder.

"Relax, Lizzy. All will be revealed."

It took them five minutes to reach the wombat enclosure. Henry paused before letting them inside.

"These joeys are six months old and they're still in the pouch. They won't leave permanently for another two to four months, but they come out regularly to look around. Be warned—their claws are long and strong, even though they're only babies."

Elizabeth nodded her understanding and followed him into the enclosure. Nate stood to one side and watched her face as Henry delivered a small, hairy bundle into her arms.

A slow, incredulous smile curled her mouth and her eyes

lit with pleasure. "Oh. He's beautiful! Nate, look at him, isn't he adorable? Or is it a she?"

"They're both boys," Henry said.

"He's so soft." She ran her hands over his fur, then she glanced across at Nate, inviting him to share her pleasure.

Their eyes met and held and for a few precious seconds there was nothing else in the world. Then Henry brought over the second wombat and the moment was gone.

They spent fifteen minutes in the enclosure and Elizabeth was able to nurse both the baby wombats as well as pat their mother.

She caught his hand once they had left the park, forcing him to stop.

"Thank you. I don't know how you arranged for that to happen, but it was wonderful. Just…wonderful."

He shrugged, embarrassed by her gratitude. "Smartsell donated some money to the park's on-site hospital building fund last year. I made a phone call or two. It was no big deal."

"It was to me." She stood on tiptoes and kissed him.

He smiled. Couldn't help himself. He'd wanted to give her something, a small moment of pleasure, and he had.

Later that night, he rolled her onto her knees and took her from behind, the way he knew she liked it. She rocked her hips and cried out when she came, then he grit his teeth and hung on and made it happen all over again before he let himself lose control. When they were both lying limp and breathless afterward, he ran his fingers through her hair and tried to remember what it was like before she came into his life.

He couldn't. Probably because he didn't want to. She made everything better. Her smile, her laughter—God, he loved to make her laugh. He also loved the way she shivered when he touched her, and the way she was simply there when his stuff got on top of him, how she looked at him so calmly, not judging, before saying something incredibly prosaic and everyday and grounding....

She was smart and practical and generous and bloody brave. And she was in his arms, right now. In his life. It was almost too good to be true.

"You should give up your room at the pub, move in here," he said, before he had a chance to second-guess himself.

He felt her body tense in his arms, then she lifted her head so she could look into his face. They stared into each other's eyes for a long moment, then she returned her head to his chest.

"Okay."

He waited for her to say more, but she didn't.

"We can move into the main house, if you'd prefer it," he said.

She lifted her head to look at him again. "What about my father? Wouldn't he want to have a say in that...?"

Nate shrugged. "There are two bedrooms. He offered to move into the studio when I first came down to the island, but I didn't much care where I was."

She frowned, then her brow cleared. "This is your place, isn't it? God, I'm so dense sometimes. All this time, I thought you were renting from my father, but it's the other way around, isn't it?"

"I bought this place to renovate it. Was going to do something big and modern like the place next door."

She wrinkled her nose and he laughed.

"Maybe you should take a look inside before you pass judgment. It's pretty nice over there. Imported stone floors. Teak woodwork. State-of-the-art everything."

"And absolutely no charm or character, I bet. No, thank you. I'll take these four walls and two windows and wooden floor over that perfect place every time. *Every time.*"

He was silent for a moment. "So I take it that's a no to moving into the main house?"

"Correct."

She returned her head to his chest and he resumed combing his fingers through her hair.

She was moving in. He knew it was only temporary, until Sam returned from the Sydney-to-Hobart race. Knew that she had no solid plans for what might happen after she met her father, and that her life was elsewhere, about as far from Nate's very circumscribed world here on the island as it was possible to be...

But for now, she was staying. That was more than enough for a guy who had turned taking it day-by-day into an art form.

IT TOOK ELIZABETH ALL OF twenty minutes to move out of the pub and into Nate's place the next day: she packed her bag, paid her bill then drove the rental to his house and parked in the drive.

There wasn't a single doubt in her mind that she was doing the right thing as she dragged her suitcase from the trunk of the car. Whatever it was that was happening between her and Nate, it felt right. This place, right now, was exactly where she wanted and needed to be.

When she entered the studio, Nate was shoving a huge old wardrobe into the corner.

"Where did that come from?" she asked.

"Spare room. Thought you'd want somewhere to put your things."

"Ah. Other than on the floor or the bed, you mean?"

Then she glanced around and realized he'd cleaned up. Even the bed was freshly made.

"Dear me. Don't you think it's dangerous to set standards

that may never be met again?" she asked, absurdly touched
that he'd gone to so much trouble for her.

"It's all downhill from here, baby," he said, but he was
smiling.

"I guess I'd better unpack, then."

He helped her, then they walked to the yacht club and
took the *Ducky* out for the afternoon, gliding across the deep
blue ocean, the salt spray on their faces and the wind in their
hair.

It became a routine of sorts over the next week—whatever
needed to be done was tackled in the morning, then they went
sailing or Nate surfed while she paddled in the shallows and
watched him defy Mother Nature and gravity all at once.

Twice the postman delivered fat envelopes from Smartsell.
Nate barely glanced at them before adding them to the pile in
the corner. She didn't say a word. One day, he'd want to pick
up the threads of his old life, but clearly he wasn't ready yet.
So be it.

After much deliberation, she made contact with her grandparents for the first time after arriving in Australia. She and
her grandfather exchanged a few very polite words about
the weather and her grandmother's health before Elizabeth
told him about Sam being interstate and that she most likely
wouldn't be home for Christmas because she was waiting for
him to return to the Island. There was a short pause and she
pictured her grandfather's face, knew that he was probably
aching to tell her what a mistake she was making, what a huge
mistake she'd already made by ending things with Martin.

"Well. We'll miss you, of course. But if this is something
you feel you have to do…"

"It is."

"Then we both wish you the best of luck, Elizabeth," her
grandfather said.

It was hard to stay angry when she could hear the sadness

in his voice. They talked for a few more minutes before ending the call and afterward she went for a long walk along the beach to clear her head.

When she returned to London, she was going to insist that they all sit down and talk honestly, adult to adult, for perhaps the first time in her life. Perhaps then they would all have a better understanding of one another.

A WEEK TO THE DAY after Elizabeth had moved in with Nate, they arrived home from an afternoon out on the *Ducky* to find a beaten-up four-wheel drive parked behind her car in the driveway.

"Looks like you've got a visitor," she said.

She glanced at Nate, but he was frowning.

"Who is it?" she asked.

He threw her an unreadable look. "That's Sam's car."

She stilled. Sam. As in Sam Blackwell. Her father.

"I thought he wasn't due back until after the New Year?"

It was only the fifteenth. She hadn't even begun to think about coming face-to-face with him yet. Hadn't even begun to think about what she wanted to say to him, what she wanted to ask.

"He wasn't."

Nate took her hand and gave it a squeeze. "You okay?"

She thought about it for a second, then nodded. "Yes. I mean, I have to meet him sometime, don't I?"

They walked down the driveway and past the house. The rear door was open, the bead curtain swinging in the breeze. The radio was on in the kitchen and she could see someone moving around inside. Her father.

Nate walked toward the back steps but she resisted his lead. He stopped and looked at her.

"You want a moment?"

She nodded, appreciating his understanding. He didn't say

anything else, simply squeezed her hand one last time before releasing it and climbing the steps to the house.

Elizabeth pressed her palm flat against her churning stomach as he disappeared inside.

Her father. She was about to meet her father. Unexpectedly, despite the fact that she'd been waiting for him for more than two weeks now. She wanted so much from this meeting. She wanted to have a father again. She wanted to belong to someone.

It was a hell of a lot of expectation to bring to a first meeting, but there wasn't much she could do about that.

She could hear conversation inside the house. She took a deep breath, let it out, then climbed the back steps.

The bead curtain announced her arrival and two heads turned toward her as she stopped just inside the door. A nervous smile curled her mouth as she stared at the very tanned, fit-looking man leaning against the kitchen counter. His hair was cropped short and mottled with gray, and he was dressed neatly in a pair of dark navy tracksuit pants and a polo shirt. His eyes seemed very blue against his dark skin as he looked at her, the lines around her eyes and mouth deeply scored. She tried to find some point of resemblance between them. The eye color, perhaps—although her mother had been blue-eyed, too. Maybe the shape of her chin? And perhaps her high forehead...?

She took a tentative step forward. "Hello. Um, I'm Elizabeth."

He nodded. "Sam."

He'd been studying her, too, and she waited for him to say something else, ready to take her cue from him. But he didn't say anything. Instead, he turned to Nathan and resumed their interrupted conversation.

"Anyway, they reckon it'll take weeks just for the swelling

to go down, let alone for them to work out if they can operate or not. Bloody doctors."

Elizabeth stared at his profile, utterly thrown. She hadn't expected her father to throw his arms around her and hold her to his bosom or anything as dramatic as that, but she'd expected *something*. Some recognition that she was more than a casual acquaintance.

Across the room, Nate was frowning, his gaze going from her to Sam and back again.

"Sam was just telling me that he's torn a ligament in his knee. Which is why he's home early," he said.

For the first time Elizabeth noticed the crutches propped in the corner and the bulge around her father's left knee beneath his tracksuit pants.

"That must have been very disappointing for you. I know you were looking forward to the race," she said.

Sam glanced at her briefly before looking away again. "*Disappointing* isn't the word. I'm going to miss all the majors this season now, on top of losing a major charter to the Caribbean. I'll be stuck on these bloody things for months." He thumped the crutches with a fist.

She tried to think of something else to say, but her mind was a complete blank. "Well. That's disappointing," she said again.

Her father shrugged impatiently and reached for his crutches.

"Better go unpack." His gaze took in the plates in the sink and the newspaper Nate had left folded on the kitchen table. "Looks like there's plenty of work to do around here, anyway."

He tucked the crutches under his arms and started down the hallway.

Elizabeth stared at his retreating back for a long beat. Then she swiveled on her heel and headed for the door. She barreled down the stairs and across the yard and didn't stop until she was in the studio. Then she simply stood, hands loose by her sides, and tried to understand what had happened.

She'd just met her father for the first time. They'd introduced themselves. And then he had proceeded to ignore her.

"You okay?" Nate's warm hands landed on her shoulders, his thumbs brushing the nape of her neck.

"I just— I thought—" She shook her head, unable to articulate the jumble of hurt, outrage, anger and disappointment churning inside her.

Nate slid an arm around her, his forearm beneath her breasts as he pulled her against him. He pressed a kiss into her hair and laid his cheek against her head. His silent support helped calm her thoughts and finally she faced the reluctant truth.

"This isn't going to be what I want it to be, is it?"

Nate pulled her tighter against his body. "Give it time."

"Nate. The man is not interested. Never has been."

"It's not about you, Lizzy. He doesn't even know you. Whatever is going on is Sam's problem. He's always been more happy on his own than with anyone else. That's why he looks after this place for me. In the off season, there are only about seven thousand people on the island, and he likes it that way."

She understood what he was saying but it felt like a cruel joke to have found a parent only to learn that he wanted nothing to do with her.

"Want to walk into town and buy some fresh fish for dinner?" Nate asked.

She nodded, unable to speak past the emotion choking her throat. He turned her around in his arms and tilted her chin so she was forced to meet his gaze.

"It's his loss, Lizzy. Believe me."

There was so much warmth in his eyes. It went a long way to assuaging her hurts. She reached out to touch his face. He was such a good person. It continually amazed her that in the midst of all the crap he was dealing with he found room to care for others.

For a long moment she battled with the urge to say the things that were in her heart. It was too soon, her gut told her. But one day she wouldn't bite her tongue. One day she would tell this wonderful, wounded, generous man how she felt about him.

She dropped her hand.

"Let's go."

NATE HELD HIS TONGUE ALL afternoon and well into the evening. He watched Sam sit silently through a meal of fish and grilled prawns and salad, never once asking Elizabeth about her life, her teaching, her dreams, her past, and told himself that it was Sam's problem and not Nate's place to interfere. He'd never been the kind of person who stuck his nose into other people's business. It simply wasn't his style. He dealt with his crap and he let other people deal with theirs, a mindset that had only become more entrenched since the accident. He didn't want people offering him unsolicited advice, getting in his face, and he extended the same courtesy to others.

But listening to Elizabeth make polite conversation with her father over dinner, watching her take Sam's indifference on the chin again and again as Sam offered monosyllables and shrugs and avoided eye contact made Nate want to hurt something. Preferably Sam.

Not surprisingly, Sam made an excuse about catching up on his sleep after dinner and disappeared to his room. There was a small silence, then Elizabeth turned to Nate with a bright smile.

"Want to toast marshmallows on the barbecue again?"

That brave, bright smile pretty much tore it for him.

"Sure. Why don't you get a head start and I'll be out in a tick?" he said easily.

"Okay. But remember, he who snoozes loses."

"Sure. I won't be long."

What he had in mind would take about sixty seconds—he figured that was about how long it would take for him to grab Sam by the scruff of the neck and shake some sense into him.

Nate waited until Elizabeth had gone outside before walking to Sam's bedroom. The door was slightly ajar and he knocked on the door frame and waited, temper simmering.

"Who is it?" Sam asked.

Nate pushed the door open. Sam was sitting on the edge of the bed, his bad leg extended in front of him. He'd stripped to his boxer shorts and polo shirt and for the first time in all the years Nate had known him he looked older than his fifty-two years.

"What the hell is wrong with you?" Nate demanded.

"Just leave it, mate."

"No, *mate,* I won't. She's your daughter. Have a conversation with her. Get to know her."

"It's not that simple."

"Yeah, it is. It's really simple."

"Look, I know you're only looking out for her, but it's best this way. I just spoke to a mate up in Melbourne, he's going to let me bunk down with him for a few weeks."

"So, what? You're just going to head off tomorrow? You're giving her *one night?* When she's flown halfway around the world to find you?"

Sam didn't say anything.

"You're an asshole, you know that?" Nate said. "A selfish asshole."

Sam's mouth tightened and he pushed himself awkwardly to his feet. "You finished? Had your say?"

He hobbled forward, trying to crowd Nate out of the room.

Nate jabbed a finger at him. "If you do this, if you take off tomorrow, you're the biggest pussy I know."

"That'd sting a whole lot more if it didn't come from a guy who's been hiding in the bottom of a beer bottle for the past four months."

Nate flinched.

"What's wrong? You can dish it out but you can't take it?" Sam said. "Don't come in here on your high moral horse, telling me what to do and how to behave when you don't even have the balls to open *your own bloody mail*."

The other man's face was red and a vein pulsed at his neck.

"If you go, don't bother coming back," Nate said.

He turned and walked away. The door slammed behind him, the sound echoing up the hallway. Nate strode into the kitchen and swore viciously. He really, really wanted to punch something. His hand curled into a fist and he tensed, ready to smack a hole in one of the overhead kitchen cabinets. Then he remembered Elizabeth was outside, waiting for him.

He didn't want her to know what had gone down. Didn't want her to know he'd had to threaten her father to try and make the guy stick around.

He let his breath hiss between his teeth and braced his hands on the counter, dropping his head and taking a few seconds to let the anger drain out of him. If Sam went ahead with his plan and bailed on Elizabeth tomorrow... Nate was going to be sorely pressed not to punch his lights out.

He lifted his head and released his grip on the counter. He would deal with whatever came tomorrow when it happened. Right now, Elizabeth was waiting for him.

He turned toward the door but his gaze snagged on the pile of envelopes overflowing from the magazine rack in the corner.

For a moment he stood frozen. Then he brushed a hand over his head.

Bloody Sam.

Annoyed all over again, he grabbed a couple of beers from the fridge and took them outside. Elizabeth looked up from toasting a stick full of marshmallows as he exited the house.

"Everything okay?" she asked.

"Yeah. Why wouldn't it be?" he said, even though he could hear the edge in his own voice.

"You're frowning, for starters."

She paused, waiting, and when he didn't say anything she cocked her head to one side. "Going to play it strong and silent on me, huh?"

"Silent, anyway."

He sat on the picnic blanket and she held the stick out to him.

"Have a marshmallow, then."

It was one of the things he loved about her the most, the calm way she had of simply accepting things the way they were. She never pushed. She never clung or offered advice he hadn't asked for or tried to tell him what to do or how to be.

He slid a marshmallow off the gooey stick and put it in his mouth. It tasted like burned sugar and she laughed when he pulled a face.

"Not my best batch."

He caught her hand and pulled her down onto the blanket.

"You okay?" he asked.

Her smile faded a little. "I'll survive."

He fought a battle with his conscience as he looked into

her eyes. Was it better to warn her or not? If Sam chose to go tomorrow, there was no way she could fail to take it as a kick in the teeth. But if he warned her in advance and Sam didn't wind up going, he would have upset her for nothing.

"You're frowning again."

She reached out and pressed her fingers against his forehead.

"Sam's talking about heading up to Melbourne tomorrow."

Her gaze dropped to the blanket. He reached for her hand and squeezed it. Still she didn't say anything and he used their joined hands to pull her into his lap. He wrapped his arms around her and she pressed her face into his neck.

They sat in the dark, the fire dying to embers, not saying a word for a long time.

10

ELIZABETH'S FATHER packed up his car and left the next morning. He had an excuse for his departure—a friend who wanted his advice on buying a boat. She listened to his thin explanation, then walked away without a word. A few weeks ago she would have smiled and waved and done her bit to smooth things over to keep the peace. For good or for ill, she wasn't that woman anymore. She wasn't going to deny herself or pretend anymore. Her father had made his decision, which was his right, just as it was her right to feel the way she felt in response. So be it.

She channeled her disappointment into cleaning the house, giving the kitchen and bathroom and living room a thorough going-over. Nate watched her wield the vacuum cleaner for a few minutes before wisely stepping away and leaving her to it. She cleaned out the fridge and wiped down the stove and scoured the sink and slowly, slowly let go of the tight, hurt feeling inside her.

Her father had rejected her. There. She'd admitted it. It wasn't a matter of simple disinterest. He didn't want to know her.

Stupid to pretend it didn't hurt—of course it did. But at least Nate had warned her last night and she'd had the chance to prepare herself. She'd lain awake in his arms, hoping against hope that Sam would choose to stay.

So much for hope.

She moved on to clearing the kitchen table, discarding yesterday's paper, culling a black banana from the fruit bowl, returning the salt and paper shakers to the cupboard. Her gaze fell on the pile of Nate's unopened mail and she drew the magazine rack toward herself and began to pile the envelopes together. Even if Nate was never going to open them there was no need for them to remain an eyesore.

He entered the kitchen as she finished stacking the envelopes into two neat piles.

"Hi. Where do you want these?" she asked, lifting her hair off the back of her neck. It was heading toward the hottest part of the day and the house was stuffy and warm.

Nate glanced at the envelopes. "They're fine where they are."

"I could help you go through them, if you like? Just in case there's anything you need to worry about."

"There isn't."

She hesitated a moment, then nodded. "All right."

She grabbed the first stack and knelt beside the magazine rack.

"Wait. Give them to me. I'll toss them," Nate said suddenly.

She looked up at him, surprised, but he was already scooping up the pile from the table. Wordlessly she handed over the remainder and watched as he walked out the back door.

She glanced at the empty magazine rack, feeling uneasy. Perhaps she should have left that particular sleeping dog lie. It was so hard to know what to do. She understood that Nate had worked out a strategy for himself over the past four months. He had his routines, his coping mechanisms. Who was she to push or pull him in another direction? Given what had happened to him, how it haunted him, it seemed to her that he was entitled to whatever peace he could find.

But she was also aware that it wasn't a long-term solution. She wanted more for him than this circumscribed life.

She sighed heavily and pushed herself to her feet. If he wanted to throw away his Smartsell paperwork, then it was up to him. She only hoped that one day, one of the letters would arrive and he'd feel an itch to open it.

NATE WALKED AROUND THE side of the house and dumped the armful of envelopes in the recycle bin. Something he should have been doing right from the start. Why the hell Jarvie felt the need to keep him in the loop he had no idea.

Okay. That was a lie. He knew why—Jarvie wanted him to come back. He hoped to entice Nate back to Melbourne and into the office with dispatches from the front line.

It wasn't going to work. Jarvie was going to have to live with things the way they were. Nate was now a silent partner. It was better for everyone that way.

Because he knew it had been a crappy day for Elizabeth, Nate rang her English friends, Lexie and Ross, and the four of them went out for dinner. He listened to her talk and laugh, watched the play of light over her face and the way she tilted her head when she was listening to something that engaged her.

Sam was a jerk for bailing on her.

It hit him during dessert that there was nothing holding Elizabeth in Australia anymore. With Sam gone, there was no reason for her to stay. Christmas was a few days away—it only made sense for her to return home to spend it with her grandparents and her friends.

He twisted his wineglass on the table.

He didn't want her to go.

He didn't want to contemplate what his life would be

without her. Couldn't even imagine trying to get through the night without her in his arms. But his need was not even close to being enough of a reason to ask Elizabeth to stay. He'd chosen to live this way—she had not. She had a life in London. A career as a teacher. Grandparents and friends.

Despite his best intentions, ways and means to bind her to his side raced through his mind. They could move into the main house. They could renovate, in whatever style or way Elizabeth dictated. Money wasn't an issue, after all. She wouldn't have to work if she didn't want to. He could give her anything—anything—that her heart desired.

He swallowed the last of his wine.

He wasn't going to do any of those things. No matter how much he wanted to.

He loved her too much to trap her.

He allowed the knowledge to wash over him. Of course he loved Lizzy. She was smart and kind and generous. She drove him wild in bed. She amused him endlessly. She made him wish he could turn back time. Six months ago, he would have pursued her and made her his. He would have done whatever it took to make her happy.

But he wasn't that man anymore. He couldn't drive. Until recently he couldn't get through the night without waking at least once, bathed in sweat, Olivia's screams in his head. He was no good to anyone. Fine for a holiday fling, but a liability in the long term.

The knowledge sat like a rock on his chest for the rest of the evening.

"You know, I don't think I even knew what summer was until I came here," Elizabeth said as they walked home along the beach. The wind blew her hair across her face and she caught the length of it in her hand and draped it over one shoulder. "It's hard to believe that it's probably snowing back home."

They turned onto the track to his street and he waited for her to toe on her sandals before they walked the short distance to his house.

Elizabeth flicked a glance at the steel-and-glass showpiece next door and shuddered theatrically.

"Promise me you won't ever build one of those," she said.

He looked at her, her hair silver, her eyes a very dark blue in the moonlight. "I promise."

"You want to lie on the blanket and watch the stars?"

"No."

A slow smile curled her mouth. "Really. What did you have in mind?"

He showed her, leading her to the studio and peeling her clothes off slowly. Kissing the tan lines on her shoulders and breasts. Pushing her back onto the bed and taking her nipple into his mouth. She moaned her pleasure and spread her legs languorously. He licked and sucked and nibbled his way down her belly, smiling when her breath caught as she understood where he was going.

He loved the way she responded to his touch. So openly, so unashamedly. Despite her very proper accent and her perfect manners and her very practical nature, in bed she was a willing, greedy wanton and he loved it.

He hooked his thumbs into the waistband of her panties and tugged them down. She drove her fingers into his hair and lifted her hips as he lowered his head and inhaled the good, clean scent of her.

He parted her with his fingers, then tasted her. She shivered, her thighs tightening against his shoulders. He explored her soft folds, teasing, flicking, stroking until she was panting and arching her back, on the verge of climax. He shed his T-shirt and shorts in record time and surged into her.

He closed his eyes, deliberately fixing this moment, this

sensation in his mind. If he had to have all the bad stuff, all the horror, he should be able to have this, too. And maybe some nights when she was gone he'd dream of her and of being with her instead of the other.

She pulled him down on top of her. They kissed as he stroked in and out of her. He knew she was close and he ran his hands over her breasts and belly and thighs. She called his name, her fingers clenching into his backside. And then she was coming, her head thrown back, her breasts lifting. He drove deep inside her and held her close as his own climax hit him.

He started to roll away from her but she held him still.

"Not yet."

"I'm too heavy."

"No, you're not."

She wrapped her arms around him and he lay on top of her, breathing to her rhythm, feeling her heart beat against his chest. After a while she pressed her face into his neck and inhaled deeply.

"Okay," she sighed.

He smiled faintly as he rolled to one side. "We can do it again if you give me twenty minutes to recover."

"Okay. But the clock is on, Mr. Jones."

She fell asleep after the second time and he lay beside her listening to the sound of her breathing for a long time before he fell asleep.

NATE WOKE IN THE EARLY hours and lay staring at the ceiling in the dark, trying to ignore the promptings of his conscience. After half an hour he eased away from Elizabeth and climbed out of bed. Dressed in only a pair of boxer-briefs, he padded outside to where the recycling bin was stored.

The envelopes were where he'd left them, piled on top of a stack of newspapers. He grabbed them and took them into the kitchen, then he grabbed a knife from the butcher's block and sat at the table.

By the time dawn was turning the sky apricot he'd opened four months' worth of financial reports, marketing strategies and client account summaries. He knew the business was doing okay. Not brilliantly, but okay. Something to be expected in these tough economic times, perhaps, but Smartsell had been on a huge growth curve six months ago and there was still plenty of juice left in the market. Their point of sale and stock keeping program had blown the existing players out of the water when they'd launched four years ago. Their competitors' systems were older, based on inflexible, outdated platforms. Smartsell was cheaper, faster, more efficient and more user-friendly. By rights, the company should still be converting retailers by the bucket load.

Looking over the marketing reports, Nate could see that Jarvie had pulled back on advertising and other promotional activity. Operations and development had always been Nate's responsibility, marketing and roll-out Jarvie's. But it was clear that with Nate's absence from the business, Jarvie was letting marketing flounder in order to keep operations ticking over.

It wasn't a dire picture, by any means. Smartsell was in no danger of folding. But it wasn't the way it should be. Not by a long shot.

He was jotting down notes when the bead curtain rattled and Elizabeth entered the kitchen.

"You're up early," she said. Her gaze took in the discarded envelopes and piles of paper.

"Couldn't sleep."

He sat back and rubbed the heels of his hands against his eyes. Then he looked at her.

"How do you feel about a trip to the city?"

ELIZABETH TRIED TO HIDE her excitement as she drove Nate into Melbourne later that morning. He'd opened the envelopes. He'd absorbed their contents, and now he wanted to reengage with his old life. She was no psychologist, but she figured this had to be a good sign. A great sign. He'd been drinking less lately, too. And although he had never specifically admitted it, she knew he was sleeping better—through the night, in most cases.

Maybe...

Maybe time was working its magic. Maybe his mind was slowly coming to terms with that horrible night and the loss of his sister.

He started giving her directions when they hit one of the main highways into the city, and soon she was pulling up out the front of a high-rise building on a wide, tree-lined boulevard that Nate told her was called St. Kilda Road.

She glanced up at the building, assuming it was Smartsell's headquarters. It was pretty damn impressive. Clearly, Nate and his business partner had done well for themselves.

"I'm probably going to be a while. There's good shopping in the city center, and two art galleries," Nate said as he gathered his papers and jacket.

"Don't worry. If there's a shoe shop, I'll be right for hours."

"There are lots of shoe shops."

He already had her phone number and they agreed he'd call her when he was ready to be collected. She put a hand on his arm when he was about to slide out of the car.

"Good luck."

He smiled tightly and exited the car. It was busy, nearly eleven o'clock, and there were lots of cars speeding past and a steady flow of people in and out of the building. She watched Nate glance around, clearly ill at ease. *She* was finding all the rush and noise and urgency a little overwhelming after only a few weeks on the island. She could only imagine what a culture shock it was for him to be in the thick of commerce again.

He glanced back at her and caught her watching. He forced a smile, then he turned and walked into the building. She stared after him, wishing she could go with him. But Nate would hardly want to have her playing shotgun while he reimmersed himself in his business.

She found parking under one of the big buildings in the city center and made her way into a large department store. Christmas decorations hung from the ceilings and display ends. She hadn't given much thought to Christmas—since meeting Nate the world had devolved to just the two of them.

She spent the next hour searching for suitable gifts for her family. She found a pair of leather gloves for her grandfather and a cashmere shawl in her grandmother's favorite periwinkle-blue. She spotted a set of frilly, silly pajamas that absolutely screamed Violet and added them to her haul.

What to buy Nate presented a bigger problem. The one thing she wished for him in all the world—peace of mind— was not hers to give. Everything else seemed incredibly frivolous by comparison. She settled for buying him a new wallet, since she'd noticed the corner was frayed on his, as well as a bottle of the aftershave she knew he liked.

She waited in line to have her presents wrapped, then she waited in line at the post office to put the bulk of them in the mail. With a bit of luck they'd make it home by Christmas.

She'd had enough of fighting her way through crowds of shoppers by then and she took herself on a tour of the city. She had wandered inside the stately Parliament House and was admiring the Victorian columns and high-arching ceilings when her eye fell on a sign advertising the government departments housed in the building. She paused as she saw that the Department of Education was located on the next level.

Twenty minutes later, she was reading over the sheaf of papers she'd been handed when she asked about applying to work as a teacher in Australia. It seemed a fairly straightforward process, especially since she could now claim an Australian as her parent. She smiled a little grimly to herself. Perhaps Sam Blackwell might be of some use to her, after all.

She was having a coffee in the State Library when Nate called.

"Hi. Are you ready to go?" she asked. She checked her watch and blinked when she saw that it was a quarter to four.

Which meant Nate had been at Smartsell for nearly five hours. That had to be good news.

She wanted to ask how he was doing, how he was feeling, but she knew better than to come right out with it.

"All done. Want to come pick me up?"

"I'm in the city," she said. "I'm not sure how long it will take me, but I'm leaving now."

She gathered the application forms she'd been going over and stuffed them into her handbag, then she walked to the car. Rush hour was starting and it took her nearly half an hour to make her way back to St. Kilda Road where she'd left Nate.

He was standing at the front, a folder of papers in hand, and he walked to the car and got in the moment she pulled over.

"I'm so sorry. I think maybe I came the worst possible way," she said.

"No worries. I figured it'd be pretty busy out there. How was the shopping?"

"Competitive. I nearly had to wrestle a woman to the ground over a cashmere shawl for my grandmother."

He seemed more relaxed than when they'd arrived and

she wondered if she should even raise the thought that had occurred to her on the drive over: the fact that with traffic the way it was, there was no way they'd be able to reach the island before nightfall.

"Nate, it's pretty late. If we head off now…"

His face tightened. "Yeah."

She waited in silence as he mulled the situation over.

"How do you feel about a night in town?" he finally asked.

He didn't look at her. He was embarrassed. Probably ashamed, too, knowing Nate. It wasn't enough that he had to deal with the repercussions of the accident, he had to give himself a hard time for being human, too.

"Great. Then we can drive back first thing in the morning," she said.

"We could do a hotel, or we can go to my place. Your choice."

Nate's place. Useless to pretend she didn't want to see where he lived. But she couldn't help but notice the flat tone in his voice, and the fact that he'd given her a choice.

"Which would you prefer?" she asked.

"I'm not a child, Lizzy. Pick whatever suits you. I don't need to be coddled every step of the goddamned way."

She flinched at the sharp tone in his voice. There was a taut moment of silence in the car, then he sighed heavily.

"Sorry."

He didn't say anything else but he reached across the console and took her hand. She looked at their joined hands, his skin still so much browner than hers.

"I picked up some forms from the education department today," she said in a rush. "The woman at the desk said I'd have no problem having my qualification recognized and registering for work if I wanted to teach in Australia."

She glanced across at him, trying to read his reaction. He was very still, his face expressionless.

"What about your grandparents? Your life back in London?"

"I'll miss them, of course. But London doesn't have you, Nate."

She held her breath, waiting for his response. It wasn't long in coming.

"Bloody hell, Lizzy," he said.

Suddenly she was in his arms, being held so tightly she could hardly breathe.

A slow smile crept across her face.

He wanted her to stay. He was glad she wasn't going home.

"I guess that answers my question, then," she said.

Nate's grip eased and he pulled back so he could look into her face. He lifted a hand and touched the angle of her jaw, then he smoothed a finger along one of her eyebrows.

"Lizzy."

He kissed her, an almost violent, needy, urgent kiss that left her gasping when he finally broke away.

"Hotel or my place?" he asked as they grudgingly let each other go.

She glanced at the hard ridge in his jeans. "Which is closer?"

"My place."

She started the car and looked at him expectantly.

"Take the first left," he said.

She didn't need to be told twice.

11

IT TOOK TEN MINUTES for Elizabeth to drive to Nate's Albert Park home. It had been four months since Nate had been back. It had been too hard, waking up in a space that held so many memories of Olivia.

But if he hadn't wanted to come here, he shouldn't have given Elizabeth a choice.

"Oh, this is like London, with all the grand, la-di-da houses facing the central garden square," Elizabeth said as she pulled up to the front of his house in St. Vincent Place.

"Mmm. Except our garden is public, not private," he said.

"You colonials. I don't know where you get your egalitarian values from."

She gave him a cheeky look as she got out of the car. When he joined her on the pavement she was staring up at his house.

"Very elegant," she said with an approving nod. "Did you choose the colors?"

He shook his head and knew she'd guessed that Olivia had.

"Well, she had excellent taste. I love the taupe facade with the glossy black lacework."

Nate concentrated on finding the right key on his key ring. "She was great at all that sort of stuff. Designing clothes, colors, music. She was always working on something."

Because he couldn't delay it any longer, he opened the front gate and walked up the short path to the elaborately tiled porch.

His key slid into the lock and the door opened. He inhaled the smell of beeswax and sunshine and the faintest, lightest hint of raspberry lip gloss. Olivia's favorite.

Elizabeth followed him inside, her footsteps echoing loudly on the wooden floor.

"This is lovely, too. Are you going to give me a tour?" she asked, glancing up the wide hallway.

There was no expectation in her tone. She was simply asking, giving him the opportunity to say yes or no as suited him. As usual, her cool, matter-of-fact approach gave him the breathing room he needed to adjust.

"It's not exactly a mansion, but I'll do my best to get us lost," he said.

He led her through the airy, light living room and listened as she admired the cream-and-taupe decor, then through to the country-style kitchen with its white cabinets and pine counters and old-fashioned butler's sink. She ran a hand over the smooth, worn surface of his French provincial dining table, one of Olivia's must-haves from a local antique dealer, then walked through to the more casual and modern family room with its modular furniture and huge flat-screen TV.

"Your sister had a good eye," she said. She wandered over to the French doors and looked out at the garden.

He moved to stand beside her. He'd paid the cleaner to come in once a week and air the place out, but the garden had been let go and the flower beds were bristling with weeds. The splash of bright red at the end of the garden drew his eye to the cheerful smiling grill of Olivia's Mini Cooper parked to one side of the double car port. He'd bought it for her for her seventeenth birthday so she could learn to drive. She'd never had a chance to take it out on her own.

He turned away in time to see Elizabeth pick up a photo frame from the bookshelf. He and Olivia at the beach. She was only fourteen and just showing the promise of the beauty she would one day become.

Elizabeth studied the photograph for a long moment, then she returned it to the bookshelf without saying anything and he led her into the hall and up the stairs.

"Spare bedroom, bathroom, study, my room," he said, pointing to each doorway as they walked past. He didn't mention the closed door at the other end of the hall.

Elizabeth stepped into his room and assessed the king-size bed and black-and-white photography on his walls with one sweeping glance. Then she reached for the buttons on her shirt and started to undress.

"Correct me if I'm wrong, but I believe there was an implied promise of sex upon arrival," she said when he simply stood and watched her.

She let her shirt fall down her arms and crossed the room to slide her arms around him. She hugged him tightly for a long beat, then she began undoing his belt and unzipping his jeans.

Despite the weight bearing down on him, he felt himself becoming aroused. He took charge, walking her back toward his bed and pushing her down onto the mattress.

She watched as he stepped out of his jeans. He pushed up her skirt and pulled her panties down, then he slid his fingers into her slick folds and teased her, watching her face all the while. Her eyes grew heavy-lidded and she bit her lip. Her muscles tightened around him when he slid a finger inside her. He kept it there as he used his thumb to stroke her. She lifted her hips and clenched her hands in the quilt cover and moaned low in her throat.

He knew her sounds by now and he gripped his cock in his hand and stroked the slick seam of her sex with it, up and down, up and down.

"Yes, Nate, please," she pleaded.

He slid inside her in small degrees, reveling in the way she sighed when he finally filled her.

Then there was just the slide of skin on skin and her hands gripping his shoulders and arms and backside as he pumped into her. They came together, shuddering out their pleasure in counterpoint. He rested his forehead on the bed beside her for a long moment afterward, then he turned his head and kissed her.

"Thank you," he said quietly.

She didn't say a word, but he knew she understood. She always did.

They ordered in for dinner—Thai takeout from the place around the corner. Elizabeth insisted on them sharing a bath afterward and her skin was still damp when they made love for the second time later that night.

She fell asleep afterward. Nate waited until she was breathing deeply before climbing out of bed and walking barefoot to Olivia's room.

The doorknob was cool in his hand and he hesitated a moment. Did he really want to do this? He closed his eyes for a long beat. Then he twisted the doorknob and pushed the door open. He flicked the light on and blinked in the sudden bright.

Everything was as she'd left it. If he didn't know any better, he'd think his sister had simply stepped out for the night. Her iPod lay abandoned on her bedside table, the wires for her earphones dangling to the floor. A pair of jeans were thrown over the end of the bed and her usual clutter covered her dressing table—makeup and books and notes to herself and jewelry. He fingered one of her rings, picked up a book and opened it to where she'd bent the page to mark her spot.

He returned to the bed and sat on it. He knew he should pack up her room, that it was morbid and maybe even unhealthy to leave it this way, but there was so much of her in here: the photos she'd taped to the walls, the quilt she'd made for the bed and the curtains for the window. He didn't want to pack it away. He wasn't ready to say goodbye yet.

Grief closed his throat and he reached for her iPod to distract himself. The battery was dead, so he opened the bedside drawer instead. Her diary was in there, along with a jumble of pens and the old slide phone she'd abandoned when the iPhone became the must-have accessory of the year. The dull shine of light on foil caught his eye and he shifted her diary to one side and picked up the small, square packet.

A condom.

He ran his thumb over the giveaway circle beneath the foil. Six months ago he would have been unthrilled in the extreme to find this in his sister's drawer. Like any big brother, he'd hated the idea of her being hurt or taken advantage of or vulnerable.

Now, he hoped like hell that she'd had the pleasure of being skin to skin with someone she cared about before she died. He hoped she'd experienced lust and joy and desire.

He hoped—

He closed his hand, crushing the foil packet within his fist. For a long moment he sat, his head bowed. Then he stood and flicked off the light and went back to bed.

NATE WAS QUIET IN THE morning and Elizabeth did her best to lighten his mood. She insisted that he take her to his favorite local breakfast place, then she suggested a walk through the nearby market. By the time they returned to the house and

Nate had grabbed some extra clothes from his wardrobe it was midafternoon and he was smiling more readily.

She couldn't help wondering if that was because she'd done such a great job distracting him or because they were leaving this beautiful, sad house and its ghosts behind.

She kept up a steady stream of chatter as she drove to the island, telling him what she'd bought for her grandparents for Christmas and challenging him to guess what she'd bought for him. She'd been hoping he might reciprocate by talking about his experience at Smartsell the previous day but he didn't and she reminded herself that Nate had been living in his self-created, hermetically sealed isolation for a long time. When he was ready to share, he would.

They drove over the San Remo bridge just after five. They stopped in town to get groceries, and it was nearly six by the time she turned into their street. A shiny black sports car was parked in the driveway at Nate's place and she slowed as she approached the house.

"That's Jarvie's car, isn't it?" she asked, recognizing it from Jarvie's last visit.

"Yeah."

The driver's door on the sports car opened as she parked at the curb, and Nate's business partner stood, pulling off his sunglasses and tossing them into the car. He stared through the windshield at Nate, his expression grim.

"What's going on, Nate?" she asked, but he was already opening his door and getting out.

She didn't understand why Jarvie was here and why he was looking so thunderous. He and Nate had spent almost the whole day together yesterday, and even though Nate hadn't spoken about it last night, he'd seemed happy enough with his day's work. So why was Jarvie looking as if he wanted to rip the head off something?

She scrambled to exit the car and was in time to see Jarvie

toss a folder at Nate. Nate was too slow to catch it and the folder hit his chest and bounced off, sending a sheaf of closely typed pages fanning across the front lawn.

"No. Never gonna happen. You got that?" Jarvie said.

Nate shrugged. "If you don't want it, I'll offer it to someone else."

"You can't do that," Jarvie said.

"According to my lawyer, I can. If I offer my half of the business to you and you don't want it, I'm free to sell it to someone who is mutually acceptable to both of us."

Elizabeth stood to one side, trying to catch up with what was going on. Nate was selling his half of the business? And why was he talking about his lawyers?

"No one is going to be acceptable to me. We started that business together, Nate. You and me."

"If you look over the offer, it's more than fair. I know you can raise the funds. In a couple of years, you'll be debt free and Smartsell will be all yours."

Nate's voice and demeanor were very calm and reasonable and she realized that he'd been expecting this. Which was why he hadn't seemed surprised to see Jarvie waiting for them when they pulled up.

"You didn't go to Smartsell yesterday," she guessed. "You went to your lawyer, didn't you?"

Nate glanced at her. She saw the answer in his eyes.

"What's wrong with the way things have been going?" Jarvie said. "I know I've been bugging you, and I'll back off if that's what you want. But selling out is a mistake, Nate. When you've had some more time, when you're ready to come back into the business—"

"That's never going to happen."

"Bullshit. I know the accident knocked you around. You're cut up about Olivia. But you'll get past it and you'll want back in and I'm more than happy to wait—"

"You need to listen to what I'm saying, okay? It's over. Smartsell isn't fine, it needs more focus. You need to move on, and I'm holding you back. Take the offer, Jarvie."

"No."

"Then I'll sell to someone else."

Jarvie's jaw bunched. He took a step toward Nate. Elizabeth tensed, worried things were going to get physical. Jarvie was so wound up and Nate so determined....

"Don't do this. You don't need to. Smartsell will wait. We'll wait as long as it takes."

"Trust me. In a few days' time, you'll realize this is the best option for everyone."

Nate turned to go but Jarvie grabbed the front of his shirt in both fists.

"You can't just walk away. Not this time. I won't let you. This was our dream, man. We freaking well clawed that business up out of nothing. You can't flush all that away." Jarvie's face was stark with anger and grief. "I don't want to do this without you, man," he said, his voice catching. "Please, think about what you're doing."

Elizabeth pressed her fingertips against her lips. The emotion on Jarvie's face was so raw, so intimate, she had to look away.

"Let me go," Nate said. He tried to pull free but Jarvie wouldn't release him.

"You can't throw everything away because of one bad thing, Nate. You've got a life, a good life. You can't trash it. You can't walk away from everything, change everything..."

Jarvie's voice broke and he lowered his head, his knuckles showing white as he clasped Nate's shirt. Nate didn't say anything, simply waited patiently as he stared over Jarvie's shoulder.

The expression on his face made Elizabeth's blood run cold. She'd thought he was getting better, slowly but surely.

She'd thought yesterday had been a huge step forward. But the bleakness she saw, the resignation…

After a long, tense moment, Jarvie unclenched his hands. Nate hovered for a beat as though some other force held him, then he turned and strode into the street and took the track to the beach.

12

ELIZABETH GLANCED AT JARVIE. The other man's face was twisted with grief and she immediately looked away again. She bent and began collecting the papers strewn across the lawn to give him a moment to compose himself. After a short beat, Jarvie joined her. They worked in silence, then she stood and handed her stack of papers over to him.

"Would you like to come in for a cup of coffee?"

He shook his head. "I need to get back. But thanks."

He walked to his car. She wanted to say more to him, to reassure him that Nate would change his mind, that this decision to opt out of the business once and for all was only a knee-jerk reaction. But she knew it hadn't been. Nate had stayed up half the night reviewing the accumulated Smartsell paperwork. Then he'd made a very cold, very considered decision and asked her to drive him to the city so he could act on it.

Jarvie's engine fired and she stepped to one side as the car shot out into the street. Gravel spurted under the wide tires as the car took off.

She walked up the driveway, and with each step her anger grew. Nate had made huge decisions—major, life-changing decisions—and hadn't said a word to her during the two-hour drive to the city. He hadn't said a word last night, either, or this afternoon when they drove home again. She'd told him about her plans to apply for a teaching job in Melbourne—to move *countries,* goddamn it—and he'd been sitting on this huge, monumental decision all along.

She unlocked the house, then stood in the kitchen frowning and fuming and feeling helpless. Nate selling his half of the business was a mistake—a huge one. The life he was living now—this small niche he'd carved out for himself of sun and surf and sex and beer—was a coping mechanism, a holding pattern. It wasn't forever. It certainly wasn't the measure of his world. She understood that perhaps he couldn't see that right now, that he was too busy surviving one day at a time and keeping his demons at bay, but she could and she knew that he would regret divesting himself of what was once obviously a huge part of his life.

So many times over the past few weeks she'd bitten her tongue and chosen not to push Nate. But maybe she should have. Maybe she should have urged him to find a therapist, or return to his therapist, if he'd ever had one. She'd been quietly encouraging him to drink less and open up more, but maybe she should have forced him to talk every time he clammed up instead of waiting for him to talk in his own stubborn time.

She sighed and pushed her fingers through her hair. She didn't know. She wasn't an expert. She'd simply been following her instincts where he was concerned, but maybe they'd been wrong.

She looked at the clock on the kitchen wall. He'd been gone for nearly half an hour. If he was acting true to form, he wouldn't be back for hours yet.

It was nearly full dark by now. She paced a little, then decided to have a quick shower to wash away the stress of the past few hours. Maybe by the time she was done Nate would be back and they could have the heart-to-heart they so sorely needed.

She headed into the bathroom and turned the shower on. Water sprayed out onto the bathroom floor and she tugged the shower door closed to stop the tiles from getting soaked while she undressed. The door slid two inches before jumping its tracks and wedging itself open. She ground her teeth. This was exactly what she didn't need. She gave the screen an experimental tug, but it didn't budge.

Is it too much to ask for this one thing to go right? This one little thing?

Setting her jaw, she got a grip on the jammed panel and tried to force it into moving. For some reason it seemed incredibly important that she solve this problem right now.

"Stupid blooming thing."

She and the door remained locked in mortal combat for a full twenty seconds as she grunted and pushed and pulled. She was about to give up when the door suddenly gave with a clattering rush. She staggered, off balance, and her feet slipped on the wet tiles.

Instinctively she flailed to try and regain her balance. Her hand smashed into the glass of the shower door and it splintered with an almighty crack. She felt a lancing pain as jagged glass slashed into her arm. She barely had time to register the sting before blood spurted from the wound.

It was so red and there seemed to be so much of it so quickly that for a moment she simply stood there, transfixed. There was blood dripping down her arm, blood on the glass, blood circling the shower drain, blood on the bathroom floor.

In the back of her mind, a calm voice told her that she needed to stop the flow—quickly. The towel was on the floor and she squatted to pick it up. The world went black around the edges at the movement and she dropped to her knees.

She blinked, fighting the dizziness. The last thing she

wanted to do right now was faint. Not while her arm was bleeding freely.

Warmth dripped from her fingers in an unending stream and she folded the towel with her left hand and wrapped it around her right forearm. She glanced down at the wound as she did so and immediately wished she hadn't. A long, gaping slit bisected her forearm and she could see the deep red of muscle.

The dizziness hit again and she pressed the towel tightly over the gash. She remembered that she'd read somewhere that she should raise it, too, to keep the wound above her heart. Or was that for a snake bite? She shook her head. It was hard to think straight.

Belatedly it occurred to her that she needed an ambulance.

Talk about being slow off the mark—an ambulance should have been the first thing she'd thought of. Her right arm pressed to her side and her left hand clamped over the towel, she leaned her shoulder against the bathroom wall and tried to stand so she could reach the phone in the kitchen. Her thighs quivered with the effort and her vision got dark around the edges again. She sank back onto the floor.

Fine. She'd crawl to the phone. Not a problem.

But even that was beyond her trembling limbs. She looked down and saw that the towel was soaked through and it occurred to her that she was in big trouble. Really big.

She closed her eyes, and all she could think of was Nate. If she didn't get to a phone, she'd never see him again. The past few weeks would be it. Short and sweet. She would never see him recover. She would never get a chance to tell him that she loved him. He would come home and find her and the blood... God, no, she couldn't do that to him. She had to move. Had to.

Somehow she rolled onto her knees. Her shoulder against

the wall, she made it to the hallway. She stared at the distant rectangle of the kitchen doorway. It seemed a very long way away. But she had to keep moving.

Move or die, Lizzy.

The voice in her head spoke with Nate's voice, in the exact tone he used when he was ordering her about on the *Ducky*. She tucked her head into her chest and shuffled forward another foot.

Come on, Lizzy. Pick it up. Snoozers are losers.

She grit her teeth and fought against the horrible weakness stealing over her. It was only fifteen feet away. She could crawl fifteen feet. Of course she could.

NATE SAT ON THE BEACH until it was almost full dark. He thought about going to the pub, but he knew Elizabeth was waiting for him at home. With questions, no doubt.

He'd done the right thing. For Smartsell, for Jarvie. For himself. He had. Absolutely.

And yet doubt still gnawed at him. He and Jarvie had spent countless hours sweating in his rental apartment while they perfected the code for Smartsell 1.0. They'd recruited a handful of retailers and offered the prototype software for free, then they'd risked everything they owned to get a business loan to finance their start-up. Nathan had been so determined to make it work. His mother had been sick by then and he'd known it would soon be just him and Olivia. He'd been terrified of letting her down, not providing for her, not giving her everything she would have had if their parents were alive. He'd worked around the clock, tirelessly. He'd given the business his blood, sweat and tears and he'd loved every minute of it. Been fiercely proud and more than a little bit cocky. For a while he'd even gone a little overboard—the expensive car, the big house, lots of splashy dinners. Then he and Jarvie had settled into their success and starting really digging in and building the business.

And then he'd had the accident, and the world had shifted on its axis and all the rules had changed.

Olivia was gone. All that effort, and she was gone and none of it meant a thing. The money, the house, the success—he'd swap it all in a heartbeat to have her back. But that was never going to happen.

The tide was starting to come in. He watched the waves chase each other up the sand for a few more minutes, then pushed himself to his feet. Shoes in hand, he trudged up the beach.

The kitchen light was on as he walked up the driveway. He tossed his shoes beside the back steps and entered the house.

He'd expected to find Elizabeth making dinner, but the kitchen was empty. He was about to go check the studio to see if she was out there when something caught the corner of his eye. He glanced toward the hallway and saw a figure huddled on the carpet. Dread thumped low in his belly and he lunged forward.

She was unconscious, her face gray, and there was blood everywhere—on her chest, down her jeans, smeared along the carpet. A towel was wrapped around her forearm, the fabric stained crimson.

"Lizzy. Jesus."

He threw himself to his knees and pressed his trembling fingers to her neck. A pulse throbbed faintly against his fingers. He let his breath out on a relieved hiss.

She was alive. Thank God.

He and Jarvie had insisted all their staff have first-aid training, and snatches of information flashed across his mind. He needed to stop the bleeding by binding it and elevating her arm. Then he needed to get her to help because she'd lost a lot of blood.

Memories from another night threatened to take over but he pushed them away and scrambled to his feet again. He flung open the hall cupboard, snatching up a handful of clean towels. Then he was at her side again, pulling the soaked towel off her arm. His stomach lurched when he saw the extent of her injury. Quickly he wrapped the towel around her arm, pulling it brutally tight. He held it in place while he dragged his belt off one-handed and used the leather strap to cinch the towel in place. Then he lifted Elizabeth's hand and held it upright while he dragged his cell phone from his back pocket.

He was starting to shake and his hands were so slick with her blood he fumbled the number for emergency services. He tried again, his gaze constantly flicking to Elizabeth's face. She was so pale. So goddamned pale. And her hand in his was so cold....

"Emergency services. Please state the nature of the emergency."

"I need an ambulance. She's cut herself, I don't know how. There's a lot of blood. She's unconscious."

"Sir, you're calling from a cell and I can't pinpoint your location. Do you have an address for me?"

"It's 14 Radcliffe Street, Cowes."

"Cowes on Phillip Island?"

"That's right. How soon can you get an ambulance here? She's lost a lot of blood."

"Is it a private residence, sir?"

"Yes. Tell me how long it's going to take?" He was yelling, but he didn't give a shit. Elizabeth needed help now.

"Sir, I'm checking the system and there has been a car accident near the bridge and all three ambulances on the island are in attendance. The wait time is thirty minutes."

"What? No!"

"Sir. I need you to remain calm. Are you able to get the victim to hospital yourself? The nearest emergency facility is Wonthaggi Hospital. I can give you directions."

Nate closed his eyes for a brief second.

"I know where it is."

Wonthaggi Hospital was where they'd taken him after the accident.

"Tell them I'm coming in," he said.

He ended the call and shoved the phone into his pocket. Then he slid his arms beneath Elizabeth and lifted her. He surged to his feet and headed for the door, not thinking about what he'd committed to doing.

She'd left the car keys on the kitchen counter and he leaned to one side to snatch them up. Then he was racing down the back steps and down the driveway to the car. Somehow he got the car door open, then he slid her into the front passenger seat, cranking it back as far as it would go before clicking her seat belt on. He slammed the door shut and ran around to the driver's side.

His subconscious was way ahead of him as he slid into the driver's seat. His whole body was already trembling, his breathing was shallow, his chest tight. Nausea burned the back of his throat as he pulled the driver's door shut and shoved the key into the ignition.

Don't think about it, just do it. Just do it.

His teeth started chattering as he slammed the car into reverse and planted his foot. The car swerved out into the street.

The feel of the wheel beneath his hand, the closeness of the roof, the dark pressing in from outside…

He pushed the car into Drive and took off, panting and shaking.

Don't think about it, don't think about it.

Olivia's screams filled his ears, begging him to help her.

He was clammy with sweat and his breathing was so loud he could hear himself gasping.

There was no traffic and he sped toward the intersection with Main Street. He signaled, checked the road and turned. Headlights flashed across the interior of the car and he swerved instinctively toward the curb. The other car drove past and he realized it was on the opposite side of the road and there had never been any danger of the two cars crossing paths.

I can't do this. I can't do this. I can't do this.

The knowledge gripped him with dread certainty. He couldn't make himself put his foot down. He was paralyzed, utterly powerless against the adrenaline and remembered trauma storming his mind. He closed his eyes and leaned forward, pressing his forehead into the hard plastic of the steering wheel.

She's going to die, you bastard. Lizzy is going to die if you don't get your freaking act together and drive.

He bared his teeth in an anguished grimace and banged his head once, twice, three times against the steering wheel. The small, sharp pain served to focus him, dragging him back from the edge.

Breathe. Breathe, you bastard. Put your foot down and save her.

He sucked in big belly breaths. Then he sat back in the driver's seat and checked the road and pulled away from the curb.

The car surged into the night. He kept breathing into his solar plexus. Fighting the fear with every muscle in his body. His hands gripped the wheel so tightly his knuckles ached.

Slowly the initial panic receded, leaving him shaky and so freaking grateful he'd survived that tears pricked his eyes.

"It's going to be okay, Lizzy. We're going to get through this," he said.

She didn't respond and he glanced at her. She was very still.

He released his death grip on the wheel to press his fingers into her neck again. Her pulse fluttered against his fingers, faint but detectable.

She was alive. She had a chance. Renewed determination flooded through him. He flattened his foot to the floor and watched as the speedometer rose past a hundred.

Time seemed to ebb and flow in strange, unpredictable surges as he sped through the night. Trees flashed by outside, but it took forever to reach the San Remo bridge, and then suddenly the signs for Dalyston were flashing by and he knew he only had about eight kilometres to go until he hit the outskirts of Wonthaggi.

He pulled his phone from his pocket and called to the hospital, letting them know he was minutes away.

A low moan tore his attention from the road as he passed the first outlying houses of Wonthaggi township, and he glanced over to see Elizabeth's eyes flickering open.

"Lizzy. It's all right. We're almost at the hospital. Stay still, sweetheart. We're nearly there."

He touched her shoulder reassuringly. Jesus, she was so cold and clammy.

"Nate." Her voice was barely a whisper.

"I'm here, sweetheart. We're all good."

She frowned as her wavering gaze focused on him. "You're driving."

"Hang in there, Lizzy."

She lifted her good hand and made a feeble attempt to touch him.

"So proud of you," she said weakly.

Her eyes fluttered closed again.

Nate took the final turn at full speed. The hospital's blue-and-white sign was a beacon at the end of the street. He slewed into the emergency drive and slammed his fist onto the horn as he braked sharply. Then he was out of the car and running around to the passenger door as the medical staff barreled outside with a stretcher.

"We'll take her, sir," a nurse said, pulling him out of the way.

"Do you know what blood type she is?" someone else demanded.

"No. But she's lost a lot. I tried to keep her arm elevated..."

The team transferred Elizabeth to the stretcher with practiced efficiency. Then she was being rushed through the double doors, the attending doctor yelling instructions.

Nate was left behind, hands hanging slack by his sides.

He'd made it.

He'd been convinced that he would never drive again, but he'd conquered his fear and he'd made it. He'd gotten Lizzy the help she needed.

When push had come to shove, he'd battled his demons and won.

He didn't feel a rush of triumph, however.

He didn't feel anything.

ELIZABETH WOKE TO THE SMELL of antiseptic and the sound of voices. She frowned and tried to roll onto her side but something was holding her back. She protested groggily and forced her eyes open, only to blink in surprise when she registered the overwhelming white of a hospital room.

What on earth...?

Then it all came rushing back—the trip to Melbourne, Jarvie and Nate's confrontation, the shower door, trying to get to the phone.

Nate driving her to the hospital.

She frowned. Was she remembering correctly? But the

picture in her head was indelible—Nate behind the wheel, telling her not to move, telling her everything was going to be all right.

She lifted her head, but the chair by her bed was empty.

Where was he? She was so proud of him. He'd driven her to safety. He'd saved her life. She wanted to see him and talk to him and thank him and tell him all the things she'd kept inside.

She reached for the buzzer pinned to her pillowcase, automatically using her right hand. Pain washed up her arm and she subsided with a groan.

She was so incredibly tired. Utterly washed out. She let her head drop on the pillow and realized there was an IV drip beside the bed, the tube attached to her other arm.

Weariness made her eyelids heavy. She let them fall closed. She'd rest for a minute, then she'd call someone and ask all the questions teeming in her mind....

When she woke again the hospital was quieter, the lights dimmer. Nighttime, then. But which nighttime? How many days had passed? She twisted her head to see if Nate was there but again the chair beside her bed was empty. She subsided onto her pillow. Where was he? She wanted to see him. She *needed* to see him.

She sniffed, aware that she was feeling very sorry for herself and not a little weepy. Then movement at the door caught her eye and she turned her head in time to catch a figure retreating away from the doorway.

"Nate?" she called.

No one answered.

"Nate? Is that you?"

Still no response. She shifted higher on her pillows, which was when it occurred to her that the figure had been too short to be Nate. He was much bigger and broader.

So where was he?

A young dark-haired nurse entered the room, a tray in hand. "You're awake. Excellent. I'm Jodie, I'll be looking after you tonight. How are you feeling? How's your pain level?"

She slid the tray onto the table at the foot of Elizabeth's bed.

"Um. I'm fine. A little uncomfortable but not overly so. Can you tell me, there was a man in the doorway just now…?"

Jodie shook her head. "Sorry. I didn't see anyone. Might have been one of the other patients' visitors. Although it's well past visiting hours. Do you feel up to eating?"

"I don't know."

"Maybe some soup and some juice? You've lost a lot of blood and even though you've had a transfusion food will definitely help to get you back on track."

"All right. I'll try some soup," Elizabeth said.

Jodie helped her sit up, propping an extra pillow behind her.

"Can I ask—has anyone been in to see me? A tall, dark man? Blue eyes?" *Really sexy, utterly gorgeous? Love of my life?*

"I'm sorry, no. Not that I know of. I can check at the nurses' station to see if there are any messages for you, though?"

"Thanks."

Jodie moved the table closer and removed the plastic cover from the bowl of soup on the tray.

"Chicken vegetable, and for a change it's actually quite edible," she said with a wry wink.

Elizabeth tried to smile but all she could manage was a weak twist of her lips. She didn't understand. Nathan had driven her to the hospital. Why wasn't he here?

She ate the soup and half a bowl of yogurt, then she had a visit from her doctor who explained that she'd cut her radial artery and that despite having received a blood transfusion she'd need to take it very easy while her body recovered.

"The stitches can come out in seven to ten days, and the nutritionist will be around to talk to you about your diet. You'll need to take in a lot of protein for the next six to eight weeks."

"When can I go home?" she asked.

"We need to do a few tests tomorrow, but there's no reason why you can't leave afterward as long as you're prepared to take it very easy. Lots of bed rest, no standing quickly, no heavy lifting."

She nodded dutifully and waited patiently while the doctor conferred with her nurse at the foot of her bed. Then they left and she was alone again. She sighed and rolled onto her left side, facing the window. She felt incredibly alone and the sudden, childish urge to call her grandparents overtook her. Just to hear the sound of their voices. She couldn't, of course. Not from hospital. No way would her grandmother's health cope with learning Elizabeth had had an accident on the other side of the world. And her grandfather would insist on flying out to see her, and he'd want her to come straight home the moment she was good to fly....

She could call Violet, however. She was reaching for the phone when she glanced up and saw a reflection in the window—a man hovering in her doorway, a pair of crutches propped beneath his armpits.

She shuffled around in bed but by the time she'd gotten herself turned around Sam Blackwell was gone.

"I know you're there, Sam," she called.

There was a brief silence, then Sam returned to the doorway. There was no mistaking the chagrin on his face—he looked like a kid caught with his hand in the cookie jar.

Despite everything—his dismissive attitude, his abrupt departure—her heart squeezed at the sight of him.

Stupid heart. She reminded herself that this man had already disappointed her more than once.

"Why are you here?" she asked coolly.

"Nate called me." He remained in the doorway, unprepared to make even the small commitment of entering her room.

"I see. And you rushed straight to my bedside, I take it?"

She was being sarcastic, but the fiery blush that swept up his neck and into his cheeks gave her pause.

Had he really come rushing to her side, then? Was that what that fierce blush was about?

"Why? Why bother when you didn't even want to give me the time of day back on the island?"

His gaze slid over her shoulder to focus on the water jug on her bedside table. "Wanted to make sure you were all right."

She pushed herself higher in the bed and eyed him across several feet of scuffed linoleum.

"If we're going to have this conversation, could you at least come into the room so I don't have to shout? I assume there might be some patients next door who'd like to get some sleep."

He entered the room with visible reluctance. If it wasn't so heartbreaking, it might almost be funny.

"I thought you weren't interested in me?" she asked.

"I never said that. Don't put words in my mouth."

"Well, someone has to, since you never say anything for yourself."

Bugger being polite. She'd tiptoed around him enough.

"I was doing what I thought was best. That's all you need to know."

Elizabeth slapped her good hand palm-down onto the bed. "No, damn you, that's not all I need to know! I'm your daughter, Sam. The very least you can do is look me in the eye and tell me why you don't want anything to do with me. I've had a bloody gutful of people deciding what's best for me—my grandparents, my fiancé. I'm the one who gets to decide what's best for me, not you."

Sam frowned. "Fiancé? I thought you and Nate were on with each other? Don't tell me he's proposed?"

Elizabeth shook her head. "No. I'm not telling you a thing until you explain why you left and why you're here now and why it's *for the best* that you ignore me."

She eyed him belligerently. She wasn't going to give an inch until he offered her something. Some sign that he cared.

He stared at the ground, his hands opening and closing on the hand rests of his crutches. The fierce frown on his forehead told her he was debating something internally. She held her breath, waiting. If he turned away now, she knew in her heart that she would never see him again. It would be over, for good.

His chin came up and at last he met her eyes.

"All right. You want to know, I'll tell you. Then you can tell me to go to hell and we'll be right back where we started from."

She didn't say anything, simply waited.

"I met your mother in Greece. She'd just finished school and was traveling with friends. She was good fun, beautiful, loved a party. We, um, hit it off right away. Then her friends went home and Elle decided to stay on, and even though I had a charter I was supposed to crew on, I stayed on, too, and we got a little place on one of the islands, down near the water."

Elizabeth frowned. It was strange to hear her mother's name shortened and to hear that the cool, slightly sad woman she'd known as her mother had once been a party girl, someone a young man could "hit it off" with.

"Did you love her?"

Her father shrugged, not meeting her eyes. "We were both nineteen years old. What did we know?"

Elizabeth decided to count that as a yes.

"She told me she was pregnant after the first month. I—" Sam brushed a hand over his face, momentarily hiding his expression from her. After a minute he started talking again. "I didn't take it well. I was angry. She was supposed to be on the pill. I thought she was trying to trap me. I took off. Took a charter to Turkey. Left her all on her own, with nothing."

Elizabeth frowned. "What does that mean, with nothing?"

"What does it sound like?" Sam said, his tone sharp. "No money, no food, no way of getting home or getting help. She was in trouble with her parents for staying on, so she couldn't turn to them. Her friends had gone. But I didn't think about any of that. I wanted to take off, so I did."

Elizabeth could hear the self-condemnation in his tone. She spared a thought for her nineteen-year-old mother, pregnant and abandoned by her lover in a foreign country.

"What happened then? I take it she went home to England?"

"I don't know. I wasn't around, was I? I always assumed she called your grandparents."

Elizabeth looked at her hands. It wasn't exactly a beautiful romance, but there was nothing particularly surprising in it, either. Her father had behaved like a selfish, immature young man, and her mother had paid the price for her youthful impulsiveness. It was a story as old as time.

"After a while, I got to thinking. I'd had a few good charters, I was offered a steward's job, regular work. I started thinking that maybe having a kid wouldn't be so bad, that I'd be able to look after the two of you without things changing that much. So I hitched a ride to England with a mate and went to find Elle.

"She'd had you by then. I tracked her down, went around to see her at your grandparents' place. They didn't want me to talk to her, but she said she wanted to see me. She brought you downstairs with her. You were—"

Sam cleared his throat.

"You were really small. Lots of blond hair. Big blue eyes, like my mom's. Elle told me that she'd met a new bloke, that they were getting married. That the new guy wanted to adopt you. Then he came in and I realized I'd left my run too late. I'd stuffed up and I'd missed out."

Sam lowered his head and wiped his mouth with the back of his hand.

She waited for him to say more, but he didn't.

She frowned. She didn't understand. If that was the extent of the story, what possible reason could he have had to keep her at arm's length? From what he was saying, he'd come looking for her. A little late in the day, perhaps, but he had still wanted to claim her. And yet he was standing here, unable to look her in the eye.

"There's something else, isn't there?" she guessed.

He glanced toward the door, his reluctance palpable. Then he sighed and lifted his head.

"I could dress it up, tell you how your new dad sweet-talked me and your grandfather leaned on me. But it doesn't change what happened. After Elle took you upstairs to put you down for your afternoon nap, your grandfather came in with his checkbook."

Elizabeth stared at him. "They offered you money to stay away from me?"

"And I took it." He held her eye as he said it, and she could see how deeply the shame ran in him.

"How much?"

"Ten thousand."

"What did you do with it?" Her throat was tight.

"Drank it, mostly. I kept telling myself I was going to put it toward a boat, or put it in a trust and send it to you when you were eighteen or something noble like that. But I drank it, bit by bit. Pissed it up against the wall."

There was a profound silence in the room. Elizabeth could hear the squeak of rubber soles in the corridor outside and the rattle of a curtain being pulled around a bed in the room across the way.

She didn't know what to think. What to say. At the ripe old age of twenty her father had taken ten thousand pounds to disappear from her life and pretend he'd never existed. He'd sold off his claim to her.

"So now you know." Sam's voice was gravelly with suppressed emotion. "You know what kind of man I am, and you know why I figured it was best to make myself scarce."

He turned toward the door. White-hot anger burned inside her as she watched her father prepare to walk away from her for the third time in her life.

"I get it. You don't deserve to know me and so you're taking yourself off. Am I getting this straight?" she said.

He stilled. His face was in profile to her but she knew she'd struck home.

"You're a real saint, aren't you? Sure, you walked away from me once for money, but this time it's because you're protecting me from yourself. How very damned noble of you."

He swung to face her.

"You telling me you want me hanging around? A man who'd sell his own kid?"

"As opposed to what? Having nothing? Knowing there's a man out there in the world who gave me life who I don't know anything about?"

"Some would say that's a better deal."

"Well, they're not me. They didn't grow up in a big house with two old people who didn't know what to do with a little girl who missed her parents so badly she cried herself to sleep every night for six months."

Her voice had risen and a nurse appeared in the doorway to her room.

"Is everything okay in here?"

"Yes," Elizabeth said at the same time that her father did.

They looked at each other. After a moment the nurse shrugged and walked away.

"I want to know where I come from," Elizabeth said. "I want to know my own father."

She could hear the emotion vibrating in her voice and she blinked furiously. Her father stared at her for a long moment. Then he made his way to the chair beside her bed. He slid his crutches from beneath his arms but didn't immediately sit. He looked at her, as though he was waiting for her to object. As though he still couldn't quite believe she was giving him this second chance.

She didn't say anything. He was her father. She wanted a relationship with him, even if he wasn't perfect.

After a few seconds he lowered himself into the chair.

13

THEY TALKED INTO THE small hours, until Elizabeth couldn't keep her eyes open any longer. She learned that her father had had an interesting life, full of adventure. A lonely life, too. He'd never settled down with another woman and she was his only child. Reading between the lines, she guessed that the events of thirty years ago still weighed heavily on him.

He was as interested in her life as she was in his. He listened quietly as she filled in the blanks for him, asking questions, occasionally passing comment. By the time he stood to take up his crutches again she had a solid sense that there was a relationship to be had—if they both wanted it. She hoped that the habit of isolation wasn't so ingrained in her father that he'd revert to his earlier distance. But only time would tell.

She asked about Nate before Sam left. He had no information for her. Nate had called him to let him know what had happened, told Sam where she was, and ended the call without saying anything else.

Despite being bone-weary, Elizabeth lay on her side staring out the darkened window for a long time after her father had gone.

Why hadn't Nate called or come by?

A nervous, fluttery anxiety tightened her belly as she tried to understand. Perhaps he had been unable to find someone to drive him to the hospital. Just because he'd conquered his fears to drive during an emergency did not mean he was cured, after all. Post-traumatic stress was an ongoing condition, not something that was healed with the flick of a switch.

But even if he'd been unable to catch a lift, he could have called. And he hadn't.

Something was wrong, and she was worried.

When she'd woken and remembered Nate driving, her first thought had been that he'd had a breakthrough. But maybe there was something she was missing here. Maybe being forced to confront his fear had pushed him backward, not forward.

Impossible to know without seeing him, and all this speculation was making her head ache. She closed her eyes and forced herself to think of something else, and after what felt like a long time she finally fell sleep.

The first thing she did when she woke the next morning was roll over and check the chair beside her bed. Again it was empty.

Disappointment descended on her, along with anxiety. She didn't understand what was going on. Then she pulled herself up in the bed and glanced toward the door and he was standing there.

"You're here," she said stupidly.

She waited for him to come to her side, to kiss her, but Nate didn't move.

"How's your arm?" he asked.

"It's fine. A little tender, but in the end I only needed a dozen or so stitches. Pretty amazing, huh?"

She smiled but he didn't smile back. All the doubts she'd

fought off in the small hours returned tenfold. She'd been telling herself there was an explanation, warning herself not to jump to conclusions, but now Nate was standing there looking cold and distant and she was afraid.

"Nate...? What's going on?"

Then her gaze moved beyond him and for the first time she saw her suitcase sitting just inside the door, her overnight bag set neatly beside it.

"I think I got everything. If there's anything else, I'll send it on," he said.

"I don't understand." Although she did. Of course she did.

"You should go home. Spend Christmas with your family."

"But...what about us?"

"You should go home," Nate repeated.

He was starting to really scare her. The flat, dead look in his eyes. The cool, resolved finality in his voice.

This was how he'd been with Jarvie. He'd cut Jarvie out of his life just as coldly. And now he was trying to do the same with her.

"What's going on, Nate? Talk to me. Whatever it is, we can work it out."

"There's nothing to work out. This should never have happened in the first place."

"Why not?"

"Because it was never going to work."

"That's not true, Nate—"

"I'm a mess. My life is screwed. I had no right dragging you into any of that."

"Your life is not a mess, Nate. You're recovering from major trauma, yes, but that doesn't mean your life is over. Every day you get better. The night sweats have stopped. And you drove,

Nate. You got in a car and drove. Doesn't that tell you that the way you're feeling has to shift?"

"Right. And then all the little bunny rabbits will skip down rainbow lane. It doesn't work like that, Elizabeth. Take it from someone who has lived with this shit for six months."

There was so much bitterness and anger in his voice. She set her jaw. He might not be able to see the light at the end of the tunnel, but she could. And she would continue to be the lamp holder for him on this if that was what it took to get him through.

"I know what you've gone through is hard. But you'll get there. I know you will. You'll get your old life back. I firmly believe it. We'll take it slowly, step by step. But it'll happen. We'll do it together. We'll do whatever it takes—"

"You don't know what you're talking about. You didn't hear her scream. You didn't watch them zip her into a body bag like a lump of meat. Nothing will ever be the same. *Nothing.*"

Elizabeth sat back against her pillows. She'd seen Nate's anxiety, his fear of driving, she'd seen him in the grip of night terrors. She'd watched him anesthetize himself with alcohol to take the edge off. She'd read about hypervigilance and depression and broken sleep. She'd seen the way he'd corralled himself into a corner, turning away from his old life and using his self-taught coping mechanisms to get through each day. She'd seen the pain and the shame and the fear.

But what she hadn't seen or understood until now was that underneath it all lay deep, soul-destroying guilt.

Nate blamed himself for his sister's death.

It was so simple, and yet she hadn't seen it until now.

He blamed himself. And he punished himself.

On some unconscious level, he welcomed the symptoms of his post-traumatic stress as due and just penance for his crime.

The anxiety, the inability to drive, the loss of his business—these were all fit punishments for a man who'd taken the life of the one person he loved above all others. The woman he'd raised almost as a daughter. The woman he'd strived so hard to provide for. The woman he would have died for.

Then Elizabeth had come along, and things had shifted, gotten better....

"You don't want to get better, do you?" she asked. "You think you deserve it. Don't you?"

"Spare me the pop psychology. What we had was a holiday fling. It's over. End of story. We both move on."

"No, Nate. What we *have* is a relationship, present tense, and I love you and you love me and the thought of having so much happiness within reach scares the hell out of you. The past few weeks, things have been changing for you, haven't they? You've been feeling better. Happier. More content. Which is why you sacrificed the business. God forbid you have Smartsell *and* me. One of those things had to go. And then you drove, breaking down another barrier and suddenly I'm on the chopping block, too.

"I thought you couldn't see the light at the end of the tunnel. But I was wrong, wasn't I? You *can* see it—you just don't think you deserve it. You won't let yourself have it. You want to keep paying penance for Olivia."

"This is bullshit. I'm selling the business because it's the right thing to do. And I'm ending things with you because there's no future in it."

"Answer me this, then, Nate. How did you get here today? Did you drive?"

It was a stab in the dark, but she knew Nate well enough to know that once he knew he could beat something, he wouldn't allow it to beat him. The expression on his face confirmed her guess and she smiled sadly.

"You're getting better. But it doesn't make you happy, does it?"

Nate's gaze fixed on a point over her shoulder. "I spoke to the travel agent on Main Street. There's a flight to London tomorrow night and there are plenty of seats."

"Were you speeding?"

He was taken off guard by her abrupt question and his gaze snapped back to her.

"What?"

"Were you speeding, the night of the accident?"

"No."

"Were you drunk? On drugs?"

He simply stared at her. She already knew the answer. Nate was too responsible to be so reckless.

"Did you try to steer out of the skid?"

Nate locked his jaw.

"Did you try to steer out of the skid?" she repeated.

"Yes."

"Tell me what else you could have done. Tell me what else you should have done to save her."

His jaw worked. There was so much guilt and anger in his eyes, so much grief.…

"It was an accident, Nate. A horrible, pointless, unlucky accident. Not your fault. No one's fault. And I understand that that's maybe hard for you to deal with when you've lost someone you love so much, but you turning away from life is not going to bring Olivia back."

He dropped his head and lifted a hand to his face. For a moment she thought she'd finally gotten through to him, but when he lifted his head again the cool, distant expression was back in place.

"I hope your arm recovers quickly." He turned to leave.

"Nate. Don't you dare walk away from this."

He kept walking.

She threw off the covers and swung her legs over the edge of the bed. Her drip line got caught on the bed frame and she wasted precious seconds untangling it. When she was finally free to slide to her feet the abrupt movement sent a wave of dizziness washing over her.

She couldn't believe this was happening. By some miracle they'd found each other when, by rights, they should never have even crossed paths. She'd fallen in love with him, baggage and all. And now he was throwing their love away without even fighting for it.

Was he really so broken? And if so, what hope did she have of convincing him he deserved to be happy?

"Would Olivia want you to live like this, Nate? Would she?" she called after him.

She had no idea if he heard her. All she knew was that she felt as though she had just lost the most important battle of her life.

NATE TOLD HIMSELF HE'D done the right thing. All the way back to the island he told himself not to think about what Elizabeth had said. That she was upset and disappointed and that soon she'd forget about him and their time together.

He told himself that she didn't understand. That she had no idea. That things were better this way. Before she'd come along, he'd had it all worked out. And once she was gone, things would settle again. Go back to the way they were.

But she'd guessed he'd driven in to see her.

There was no way she could have known that he'd borrowed Trevor's car for a couple of hours yesterday and again this morning, forcing himself to work through his anxiety and the flashes of memory that washed over him. Forcing himself past the sweating and the shallow breathing until he was able to get in the car and put his hands on the steering wheel without hearing his sister pleading with him.

But Elizabeth had guessed. She'd known that once he'd proven to himself that he could drive if he had to, he wouldn't be able to let the fear beat him again.

He parked Trevor's car in the parking lot behind the pub and dropped off the keys at the bar. Then he walked down to the beach and headed home along the sand.

He'd become a master at blocking out things he didn't want to think about or feel over the past six months, but it was impossible to stop himself from mulling over what Elizabeth had said to him in her hospital room.

That he wanted to punish himself.

That he blamed himself for Olivia's death.

That he believed he didn't deserve to be happy.

He wanted to deny it all as a bunch of gobbledygook from the self-help section of the bookstore, but deep inside her words had struck a chord.

It *was* his fault that Olivia was dead, after all. He'd been driving. Her care—her life—had been in his hands. And he'd failed her.

Elizabeth could talk about luck and accidents and blame all she wanted, but the truth was immutable. It was his responsibility, all of it. Because of him, Olivia would never take the trip to Paris she'd always dreamed about. She'd never know if she could have made it into the School of Fashion and Textiles at the Royal Melbourne Institute of Technology. She'd never fall in love and marry and have a family of her own.

She was gone. His little sister.

And he was still here, not a scratch on him. Not even a freaking scar to show for the accident once the bruising had faded and the swelling gone down. He still had his wealth, his health, his life. Everything.

So, yeah. Maybe he did think there was a certain justice in

the night terrors and the flashbacks and the whole can't-get-behind-the-wheel-of-a-car thing. A life for a life. What could be more simple? More fitting?

The sun was hot as he walked from the beach into his street. There was beer in the fridge, he knew, and vodka in the freezer. He could numb himself with alcohol. Just to get through the next few days before Elizabeth was gone. And then it would be back to the usual. The days. The bar. The nights.

He entered the house through the back door. He'd cleaned the blood that first night—mopped it out of the kitchen and bathroom, soaked it out of the carpet in the hallway. It hadn't come out completely, of course. If he looked to his right, he'd see the dark stain where Elizabeth had collapsed in the hall.

He didn't look. He went to the fridge and grabbed a beer. Then he sat at the kitchen table and drank it down, staring at the wall and willing himself not to think.

Would Olivia want you to live like this, Nate?

He should never have hooked up with Elizabeth. He should never have let himself get involved with her or her quest to find her father. He should never have sought comfort and solace in her arms.

Would Olivia want you to live like this?

He slammed the bottle down onto the table and beer frothed over the top. He swore, then stood and went to the fridge. Clearly, reinforcements were called for. Beer wasn't going to cut it today.

He opened the freezer and found himself staring at ice cream and frozen vegetables and meat. Only then did he remember that Lizzy had relegated his vodka bottle to the cupboard. She'd claimed it was because they needed the freezer space, but he'd known it was part of her quietly determined effort to encourage him to drink less.

He crossed the kitchen and pulled open the cabinet over the counter. He could see the vodka bottle, lying on its side along the back, but his gaze was drawn to the pink-and-white plastic bag of marshmallows sitting at the front of the shelf. A sticky note was attached to the bag, Lizzy's old-school cursive script curling across the small square of paper: *Don't even think about finishing these without me!!!*

Like a physical blow, clarity tensed his gut and made him take a step backward.

He would never see Elizabeth again. He'd ensured that with his words and actions today. There would be no more of her laughter and dry looks and calm certainty. He would never touch the silk of her skin or taste her kisses or see the warm, clear light in her eyes. He would never walk into a room and smell her perfume and know she was nearby. As far as he was concerned, it would be as though she had died that night in his bloodstained hallway. She would become nothing but a memory.

But she wouldn't really be dead. She would be in London, living her life. He imagined how it might be—Lizzy at school teaching her kids, finding her way again on the other side of the world. Her tan fading, along with her memories of him. And then, eventually, she would meet someone else and fall in love. She'd get married and have children. And some other lucky bastard would get to sleep with her each night and grow old with her and comfort her when she needed it and make her laugh when she was sad and infuriate and challenge and adore her.

He sucked in a ragged breath.

Jesus, he wanted to be that lucky bastard. He wanted the peace of waking in her arms. He wanted the joy of being inside her, her body warm against his. He wanted to watch her bloom as she discovered all the things about herself she'd been too scared and dutiful to acknowledge. He wanted the happiness she offered so easily, so openly.

He wanted a future full of hope and possibility, not this quarter-life of regret and fear and loneliness.

The moment he acknowledged his own desire, the old guilt rose inside him. How could he open himself to so much happiness when Olivia was gone? How could he allow himself to live fully without her? If he picked up the threads of his life, if he kept growing Smartsell and he allowed himself to have Elizabeth, if he could truly *live* again, it would be as though he was denying Olivia ever existed. As though her death meant nothing to him.

You turning away from life is not going to bring Olivia back.

Nate closed his eyes. He knew Lizzy was right. Olivia was dead. He missed her like crazy, would probably continue to miss her like crazy every day for the rest of his life, but all the guilt and pain and self-flagellating in the world was not going to bring her back.

The bottom line was that she was gone. And he was not.

And he didn't want to keep living like this. He didn't want to be a victim of his own memories. He didn't want to let fear control his world.

But most of all he didn't want to let Lizzy go. In a few short weeks she had turned his life upside down. He needed her. He wanted her. He loved her. And maybe it made him a bad brother and a weak, selfish bastard, but so be it.

He chose life. He chose Lizzy.

If she'd still have him.

He was on his feet in a split second, out the door a heartbeat after that. He broke into a run. He'd go back to the pub, ask Trevor for his car again. Lizzy would still be at the hospital. And if she wasn't, he'd track her down. Wherever she'd gone.

His step faltered as he registered the beaten-up four-wheel drive parked out the front of his house. A woman was sliding carefully out of the passenger seat, a man on crutches hovering protectively at her side.

"Lizzy," he said, stopping in his tracks.

Her head came up and the look she gave him was pure defiant challenge.

"Don't bother telling me to go away, Nathan, because I'm not going anywhere. It's taken me half my life to work out what I want and no way am I walking away from it now. So I don't care what you say, I'm staying, and I'm going to keep loving you, and there's nothing you can do about it."

He closed the distance between them in three strides. Then he pulled her into his arms, resting his cheek against the crown of her head, breathing in the smell of her.

Elizabeth was very still in his arms. He pressed a kiss to the top of her head. Slowly her body relaxed and she wrapped her good arm around him.

"This had better mean what I think it does," she said, her voice muffled by the front of his shirt.

He smiled slightly.

"That was your cue to say something reassuring. In case you missed it," she said.

He loosened his arms enough to look into her face. "I love you."

She bit her lip. He cupped her face and brushed his thumb along her cheekbone.

"Did I mess up my line?" he asked.

"No. It was perfect. I just thought I was going to have to wrestle you to the ground before I got you to admit it."

"I want this, Lizzy. I want you. I want to make it work. I know it's been tough. It's probably going to be tough again. I'll go back to my therapist, talk to my doctor about medication. I'll do what I can. But—"

She pressed her fingers to his lips. "My love doesn't come with *buts*. It just is. Whatever happens, we'll deal with it."

She looked into his eyes, her own very steady and certain.

"Lizzy," he said, but the rest of the things he wanted to say got caught in his throat.

She smiled and stood on her toes to press a kiss to his lips.

"I know."

Epilogue

Six months later

ELIZABETH CHECKED HER watch and stood on her toes again, trying to see around the people standing in front of them at the international arrivals gate.

Nate put his arm around her shoulders. "Relax, Lizzy. They'll walk through the doors, we'll see them. It's a pretty simple process."

This was their second trip to the airport for the week. Her grandparents had arrived on Monday, flying in easy stages from London for her grandmother's benefit. No one had been more surprised than Elizabeth when they announced they were coming to visit. She and Nate had already planned to fly to London for their wedding, but her grandparents' announcement had led to a hurried reorganizing of events, the upshot of which was that two weeks from now, she and Nate would walk down the aisle at a beautiful Gothic revival church in Albert Park with both her grandparents and her father in attendance.

She'd be lying if she said she wasn't worried about how her grandparents and Sam would cope with coming face-to-face after so many years and so many mistakes on both sides.

But Sam was a part of her life now whether her grandparents liked it or not so they were going to have to work things out between them.

"Remind me again how long we're going to have all these houseguests?" Nate said.

"Grandmama and Grandpa for three weeks. Violet for four."

He pulled a face. "That seems like a pretty long time."

She knew what he was thinking about—having her grandparents in residence definitely put a damper on their sex life.

"We could always sneak away for a weekend. Go down to the island."

His eyes lit up. "Keep talking."

"We could hole up in the studio and not come out all weekend," she said.

Nate lowered his head to whisper in her ear. "And then?"

She lowered her own voice and turned to face him, looping her arms loosely around his neck. "Then you could help me grade all the papers for Year Nine English."

"Hmm. Not quite what I had in mind."

He was smiling and she reached up to smooth his hair.

"Let me think about it. See if I can come up with a little something else," she said.

"You do that."

His phone rang and she let her arms drop so he could move away to take it. She could tell by the way his gaze grew distant that it was a business call. He'd started back at Smartsell four months ago, working part-time at first and gradually increasing his hours until he was fully back into the swing of things. To say that Jarvie was happy was an understatement. He was like an overly affectionate dog when he was around Nate, hugely grateful to have his old friend back on deck.

It hadn't all been smooth sailing. Nate had had trouble

sleeping again when he returned to his therapist, the therapy stirring up difficult memories. There had been bouts of withdrawal and bad temper, too, in the early days. He'd become so used to being on his own, to keeping his own counsel. But they had both persevered, and things had slowly shifted. He was still uncomfortable with night driving—he made himself do it, but she was always aware that it was an effort, a sort of trial-by-endurance that he made himself face. She knew he was still prone to the occasional anxiety attack, but they were getting better, too.

And last month, they'd cleaned out Olivia's room. It had been heartbreaking, packing away the remnants of a life that had barely started. It had been Nate's decision, reached in his own time. Elizabeth had kept aside a few things—some soft toys, some cushions Olivia had sewn, a handful of well-thumbed children's books. One day, when she and Nate had children, she wanted them to have a connection to their aunt.

"Lizzy."

Elizabeth started out of her introspection to glance at Nate.

"Is it just me, or is that what's-his-name?" he asked as he pocketed his phone.

She followed his sight line and blinked.

What on earth was Martin doing here? Then a familiar redhead appeared over his shoulder. Martin and Violet. *Together?*

It was such an absurd idea she laughed. It must be a coincidence.

Then Violet looked up and caught Elizabeth's eye, and the guilt and defiance and hope in her friend's face made Elizabeth press her fingers to her lips with shock.

"Let me guess—that's Violet?" Nate said close to her ear.

"Yes. But they hate each other, Nate. They used to fight

like cat and dog. She used to call him Droopy Drawers and he could barely say her name without sneering."

Nate shrugged. "Stranger things have happened, Lizzy."

She met his eyes. There was so much love and understanding there that she couldn't help but smile.

"Yes, they have, haven't they?" Their hands found each other, fingers weaving together.

Thank God he'd forgiven himself. Thank God he'd given them a chance.

"Come on," he said. "Let's go hear their story."

* * * * *

FROM FLING
TO FOREVER

BY
AVRIL TREMAYNE

Avril Tremayne read *Jane Eyre* as a teenager and has been hooked on tales of passion and romance ever since. An opportunistic insomniac, she has been a life-long crazy-mad reader, but she took the scenic route to becoming a writer—via gigs as diverse as shoe sales-girl, hot-cross-bun-packer, teacher, and public relations executive. She has spent a good chunk of her life travelling, and has more favourite destinations than should be strictly allowable.

Avril is happily settled in her hometown of Sydney, Australia, where her husband and daughter try to keep her out of trouble—not always successfully. When she's not writing or reading she can generally be found eating—although she does not cook!

Check out her website: www.avriltremayne.com or follow her on Twitter: @AvrilTremayne and Facebook: www.facebook.com/avril.tremayne.

Dedication

This book is dedicated to my fellow writer PTG Man and Dr John Sammut with many, many thanks for the generous medical advice. Thanks also to Dr John Lander and Dr Hynek Prochazka. Any errors that snuck in despite their best efforts are mine, all mine!

I would also like to acknowledge the amazing Angkor Hospital for Children (AHC)—a non-profit pediatric teaching hospital that provides free quality care to impoverished children in Siem Reap, Cambodia. All the characters, settings and situations in FROM FLING TO FOREVER are fictional—however, during the course of my research, I learned so much from AHC, which has provided over one million medical treatments, education to thousands of Cambodian health workers, and prevention training to thousands of families since it opened in 1999. You can find out more about the hospital at www.angkorhospital.org.

CHAPTER ONE

WEDDINGS.

Ella Reynolds had nothing against them, but she certainly didn't belong at one. Not even this one.

But her sister, Tina, had insisted she not only attend but trick herself out as maid of honour in this damned uncomfortable satin gown in which there was *no* stretch. Add in the ridiculous high heels and hair twisted into a silly bun that was pinned so tightly against her scalp she could practically feel the headache negotiating where to lunge first.

And then there was the stalker. Just to top everything off.

She'd first felt his stare boring into her as she'd glided up the aisle ahead of her sister. And then throughout the wedding service, when all eyes should have been on the bride and groom. And ever since she'd walked into the reception.

Disconcerting. And definitely unwanted.

Especially since he had a little boy with him. Gorgeous, sparkly, darling little boy. Asian. Three or four years old. Exactly the type of child to mess with her already messed-up head.

Ella looked into her empty champagne glass, debating whether to slide over the legal limit. Not that she was driving, but she was always so careful when she was with her family. Still… Tina, pregnant, glowing, deliriously happy, was on the dance floor with her new husband Brand—and not paying her any attention. Her parents were on the other side of the room, catching up with Brand's family on this rare visit to Sydney—and not paying her any attention. She was alone at the bridal table, with *no one* paying her any attention. Which was just fine with her. It was much easier to hold it all together when you were left to yourself. To not let anyone see the horrible, unworthy envy of Tina's pregnancy, Tina's *life*.

And—she swivelled around to look for a waiter—it made it much easier to snag that extra champagne.

But a sound put paid to the champagne quest. A cleared throat.

She twisted back in her chair. Looked up.

The stalker. *Uh-oh.*

'Hi,' he said.

'Hello.' Warily.

'So…you're Ella,' he said.

Oh, dear. *Inane* stalker. 'Yep. Sister of the bride.'

'Oh.' He looked surprised. And then, 'Sorry, the accent. I didn't realise…'

'I speak American, Tina speaks Australian. It does throw people. Comes of having a parent from each country and getting to choose where you live. I live in LA. Tina lives in Sydney. But it's still all English, you know.' Good Lord—*this* was conversation?

He laughed. 'I'm not sure the British see it that way.'

Okay—so now what? Ella wondered.

If he thought she was going to be charmed by him, he had another think coming. She *wasn't* going to be charmed. And she was *not* in the market for a pick-up tonight. Not that he wasn't attractive in a rough sort of way—the surfer-blond hair, golden tan and bursting muscles that looked completely out of place in a suit was a sexy combination. But she'd crossed the pick-up off her to-do list last night—and that had been a debacle, as usual. And even if she hadn't crossed it off the list, and it hadn't been a debacle, her sister's wedding was not the place for another attempt. Nowhere within a thousand *miles* of any of her relatives was the place.

'Do you mind if I sit and talk to you for a few minutes?' he asked, and smiled at her.

Yes, I do. 'Of course you can sit,' she said. Infinitesimal pause. 'And talk to me.'

'Great.' He pulled out a chair and sat. 'I think Brand warned you I wanted to pick your brains tonight.'

She frowned slightly. 'Brand?'

He smiled again. 'Um…your brother-in-law?'

'No-o-o, I don't think so.' Ella glanced over at Brand, who was carefully twirling her sister. 'I think he's had a few things on his mind. Marriage. Baby. Imminent move to London. New movie to make.'

Another smile. 'Right, let's start again and I'll introduce myself properly.'

Ella had to give the guy points for determination. Because he had to realise by now that if she really wanted to talk to him, she would have already tried to get his name out of him.

'I'm Aaron James,' he said.

Ella went blank for a moment, before the vague memory surfaced. 'Oh. Of course. The actor. Tina emailed me about a…a film?' She frowned slightly. 'Sorry, I remember now. About malaria.'

'Yes. A documentary. About the global struggle to eradicate the disease. Something I am very passionate about, because my son… Well, too much information, I guess. Not that documentaries are my usual line of work.' Smile, but looking a little frayed. 'Maybe you've heard of a television show called *Triage*? It's a medical drama. I'm in that.'

'So…' She frowned again. 'Is it the documentary or the TV show you want to talk to me about? If it's the TV show, I don't think I can help you—my experience in city hospital emergency rooms is limited. And I'm a nurse—

you don't look like you'd be playing a nurse. You're playing a doctor, right?'

'Yes, but—'

'I'm flying home tomorrow, but I know a few doctors here in Sydney and I'm sure they'd be happy to talk to you.'

'No, that's not—'

'The numbers are in my phone,' Ella said, reaching for her purse. 'Do you have a pen? Or can you—?'

Aaron reached out and put his hand over hers on the tiny bronze purse. 'Ella.'

Her fingers flexed, once, before she could stop them.

'It's not about the show,' he said, releasing her hand. 'It's the documentary. We're looking at treatments, mosquito control measures, drug resistance, and what's being done to develop a vaccine. We'll be shooting in Cambodia primarily—in some of the hospitals where I believe you've worked. We're not starting for a month, but I thought I should take the chance to talk to you while you're in Sydney. I'd love to get your impression of the place.'

She said nothing. Noted that he was starting to look impatient—and annoyed.

'Brand told me you worked for Frontline Medical Aid,' he prompted.

She controlled the hitch in her breath. 'Yes, I've worked for them, and other medical aid agencies, in various countries, including Cambodia. But I'm not working with any agency at the moment. And I'll be based in Los Angeles for the next year or so.'

'And what's it like? I mean, not Los Angeles—I know what— Um. I mean, the aid work.'

Ella shifted in her seat. He was just not getting it. 'It has its highs and lows. Like any job.'

He was trying that charming smile again. 'Stupid question?'

'Look, it's just a job,' she said shortly. 'I do what every

nurse does. Look after people when they're sick or hurt. Try to educate them about health. That's all there is to it.'

'Come on—you're doing a little more than that. The conditions. The diseases that we just don't see here. The refugee camps. The landmines. Kidnappings, even.'

Her heart slammed against her ribs. Bang-bang-bang. She looked down at her hands, saw the whitened knuckles and dropped them to her lap, out of Aaron's sight. She struggled for a moment, getting herself under control. Then forced herself to look straight back up and right at him.

'Yes, the conditions are not what most medical personnel are used to,' she said matter-of-factly. 'I've seen the damage landmines can do. Had children with AIDS, with malnutrition, die in my arms. There have been kidnappings involving my colleagues, murders even. This is rare, but...' She stopped, raised an eyebrow. 'Is that the sort of detail you're looking for?' She forced herself to keep looking directly into his eyes. 'But I imagine you'll be insulated from the worst of it. They won't let anything happen to you.'

'I'm not worried about that,' Aaron said, with a quick shake of his head. Then, suddenly, he relaxed back in his chair. 'And you don't want to talk about it.'

Eureka! 'It's fine, really,' she said, but her voice dripped with insincerity.

The little boy Ella had seen earlier exploded onto the scene, throwing himself against Aaron's leg, before the conversation could proceed.

'Dad, look what Tina gave me.'

Dad. So, did he have an Asian wife? Or was the little boy adopted?

Aaron bent close to smell the small rose being offered to him.

'It's from her bunch of flowers,' the little boy said, blinking adorably.

'Beautiful.' Aaron turned laughing eyes to Ella. 'Ella, let me introduce my son, Kiri. Kiri, this is Tina's sister, Ella.'

Kiri. He was Cambodian, then. And he'd had malaria—
that was Aaron's TMI moment. 'Nice to meet you Kiri,'
Ella said, with a broad smile, then picked up her purse.
'Speaking of Tina and flowers, it must be time to throw
the bouquet. I'd better go.'

She got to her feet. 'Goodbye Aaron. Good luck with
the documentary. Goodbye Kiri.'

Well, that had been uncomfortable, Ella thought as she left
the table, forcing herself to walk slowly. Calm, controlled,
measured—the way she'd trained herself to walk in moments of stress.

Clearly, she had to start reading her sister's emails more
carefully. She recalled, too late, that Tina's email had said
Aaron was divorced; that he had an adopted son—although
not that the boy was Cambodian, because *that* she would
have remembered. She'd made a reference to the documentary. And there probably had been a mention of talking
to him as a favour to Brand, although she really couldn't
swear to it.

She just hadn't put all the pieces together and equated
them with the wedding, or she would have been better
prepared for the confrontation.

Confrontation. Since when did a few innocent questions
constitute a confrontation?

Ella couldn't stop a little squirm of shame. Aaron wasn't
to know that the exact thing he wanted to talk about was
the exact thing she couldn't bring herself to discuss with
anyone. Nobody knew about Sann, the beautiful little Cambodian boy who'd died of malaria before she'd even been
able to start the adoption process. Nobody knew about
her relationship with Javier—her colleague and lover, kidnapped in Somalia and still missing. Nobody knew because
she hadn't *wanted* anyone to know, or to worry about her.
Hadn't wanted anyone to push her to talk about things, relive what she couldn't bear to relive.

So, no, Aaron wasn't to be blamed for asking what he thought were standard questions.

But he'd clearly sensed something was wrong with her. Because he'd gone from admiration—oh, yes, she could read admiration—to something akin to dislike, in almost record time. Something in those almost sleepy, silver-grey eyes had told her she just wasn't his kind of person.

Ella's head had started to throb. The damned pins.

Ah, well, one bouquet-toss and last group hug with her family and she could disappear. Back to her hotel. Throw down some aspirin. And raid the mini-bar, given she never had got that extra glass of champagne.

Yeah, like raiding the mini-bar has ever helped, her subconscious chimed in.

'Oh, shut up,' she muttered.

Well, that had been uncomfortable, Aaron thought as Ella Reynolds all but bolted from the table. Actually, she'd been walking slowly. Too slowly. Unnaturally slowly.

Or maybe he was just cross because of ego-dent. Because one woman in the room had no idea who he was. And didn't *care* who he was when she'd found out. Well, she was American—why *would* she know him? He wasn't a star over there.

Which wasn't the point anyway.

Because since when did he expect people to recognise him and drool?

Never!

But celebrity aside, to be looked at with such blank disinterest…it wasn't a look he was used to from women. Ella Reynolds hadn't been overwhelmed. Or deliberately *under*-whelmed, as sometimes happened. She was just…hmm, was 'whelmed' a word? Whelmed. Depressing.

Ego, Aaron—so not *like you.*

Aaron swallowed a sigh as the guests started positioning themselves for the great bouquet toss. Ella was in the thick of it, smiling. Not looking in his direction—on purpose, or he'd eat the roses.

She was as beautiful as Tina had said. More so. Staggeringly so. With her honey-gold hair that even the uptight bun couldn't take the gloss off. The luminous, gold-toned skin. Smooth, wide forehead. Finely arched dusky gold eyebrows and wide-spaced purple-blue eyes with ridiculously thick dark lashes. Lush, wide, pouty mouth. No visible freckles. No blemishes. The body beneath the figure-hugging bronze satin she'd been poured into for the wedding was a miracle of perfect curves. Fabulous breasts—and silicone-free, if he were any judge. Which he was, after so many years in the business.

And the icing on the cake—the scent of her. Dark and musky and delicious.

Yep. Stunner.

But Tina had said that as well as being gorgeous her sister was the best role model for women she could think of. Smart, dedicated to her work, committed to helping those less fortunate regardless of the personal danger she put herself in regularly.

Well, sorry, but on the basis of their conversation tonight he begged to differ. Ella Reynolds was no role model. There was something wrong with her. Something that seemed almost...dead. Her smile—that dazzling, white smile—didn't reach her eyes. Her eyes had been beautifully *empty*. It had been almost painful to sit near her.

Aaron felt a shiver snake down his spine.

On the bright side, he didn't feel that hot surge of desire—that bolt that had hit him square in the groin the moment she'd slid into the church—any more. Which was good. He didn't want to lust after her. He didn't have the time or energy or emotional availability to lust after anyone.

He turned to his beautiful son. 'Come on, Kiri—this

part is fun to watch. But leave the bouquet-catching to the girls, huh?'

We're not going down that road again, bouquet or not, he added silently to himself.

CHAPTER TWO

ELLA HAD BEEN determined to spend a full year in Los Angeles.

But within a few weeks of touching down at LAX she'd been back at the airport and heading for Cambodia. There had been an outbreak of dengue fever, and someone had asked her to think about helping out, and she'd thought, *Why not?*

Because she just hadn't been feeling it at home. Whatever 'it' was. She hadn't felt right since Tina's wedding. Sort of restless and on edge. So she figured she needed more distraction. More work. More…something.

And volunteering at a children's hospital in mosquito heaven is just the sort of masochism that's right up your alley, isn't it, Ella?

So, here she was, on her least favourite day of the year— her birthday—in northwest Cambodia—and because it *was* her birthday she was in the bar of one of the best hotels in town instead of her usual cheap dive.

Her parents had called this morning to wish her happy birthday. Their present was an airfare to London and an order to use it the moment her time in Cambodia was up. It was framed in part as a favour to Tina: stay with her pregnant sister in her new home city and look after her health while Brand concentrated on the movie. But she knew Tina would have been given her own set of orders: get Ella to rest and for goodness' sake fatten her up—because her mother always freaked when she saw how thin and bedraggled Ella was after a stint in the developing world.

Tina's present to Ella was a goat. Or rather a goat in Ella's name, to be given to an impoverished community in India. Not every just-turned-twenty-seven-year-old's cup of tea, but so totally perfect for this one.

And in with the goat certificate had been a parcel with a note: 'Humour me and wear this.' 'This' was sinfully expensive French lingerie in gorgeous mint-green silk, which Ella could never have afforded. It felt like a crime wearing it under her flea-market gypsy skirt and bargain-basement singlet top. But it did kind of cheer her up. Maybe she'd have to develop an underwear fetish—although somehow she didn't think she'd find this kind of stuff digging around in the discount bins the way she usually shopped.

A small group of doctors and nurses had dragged her out tonight. They'd knocked back a few drinks, told tales about their life experiences and then eventually—inevitably—drifted off, one by one, intent on getting some rest ahead of another busy day.

But Ella wasn't due at the hospital until the afternoon, so she could sleep in. Which meant she could stay out. And she had met someone—as she always seemed to do in bars. So she'd waved the last of her friends off with a cheerful guarantee that she could look after herself.

Yes, she had met someone. Someone who might help make her feel alive for an hour or two. Keep the nightmares at bay, if she could bring herself to get past the come-on stage for once and end up in bed with him.

She felt a hand on her backside as she leaned across the pool table and took her shot. She missed the ball completely but looked back and smiled. Tom. British. Expat. An…engineer, maybe? *Was* he an engineer? Well, who cared? Really, who cared?

He pulled her against him, her back against his chest. Arms circled her waist. Squeezed.

She laughed as he nipped at her earlobe, even though she couldn't quite stop a slight shudder of distaste. His breath was too hot, too…moist. He bit gently at her ear again.

Ella wasn't sure what made her look over at the entrance to the bar at that particular moment. But pool cue in one hand, caught against Tom's chest, with—she realised in one awful moment—one of the straps of her top hanging off her shoulder to reveal the beacon-green silk of her bra strap, she looked.

Aaron James.

He was standing still, looking immaculately clean in blue jeans and a tight white T-shirt, which suited him way more than the get-up he'd been wearing at the wedding. Very tough-guy gorgeous, with the impressive muscles and fallen-angel hair with those tousled, surfer-white streaks she remembered very well.

Actually, she was surprised she remembered so much!

He gave her one long, cool, head-to-toe inspection. One nod.

Ah, so he obviously remembered her too. She was pretty sure that was not a good thing.

Then he walked to the bar, ignoring her. *Hmm.* Definitely *not a good thing*.

Ella, who'd thought she'd given up blushing, blushed. Hastily she yanked the misbehaving strap back onto her shoulder.

With a wicked laugh, Tom the engineer nudged it back off.

'Don't,' she said, automatically reaching for it again.

Tom shrugged good-humouredly. 'Sorry. Didn't mean anything by it.'

For good measure, Ella pulled on the long-sleeved, light cotton cardigan she'd worn between her guesthouse accommodation and the hotel. She always dressed for modesty outside Western establishments, and that meant covering up.

And there were mosquitoes to ward off in any case.

And okay, yes, the sight of Aaron James had unnerved her. She admitted it! She was wearing a cardigan because Aaron James had looked at her in *that* way.

She tried to appear normal as the game progressed, but every now and then she would catch Aaron's gaze on her and she found it increasingly difficult to concentrate on the game or on Tom. Whenever she laughed, or when Tom let out a whoop of triumph at a well-played shot, she would feel Aaron looking at her. Just for a moment. His eyes on her, then off. When Tom went to the bar to buy a round. When she tripped over a chair, reaching for her drink. When Tom enveloped her from behind to give her help she didn't need with a shot.

It made her feel…dirty. Ashamed. Which was just not fair. She was single, adult, independent. So she wanted a few mindless hours of fun on her lonely birthday to take her mind off sickness and death—what was wrong with that?

But however she justified things to herself, she knew that tonight her plans had been derailed. All because of a pair of censorious silver eyes.

Censorious eyes that belonged to a friend of her sister. Very sobering, that—the last thing she needed was Aaron tattling to Tina about her.

It was probably just as well to abandon tonight's escapade. Her head was starting to ache and she felt overly hot. Maybe she was coming down with something? She would be better off in bed. Her bed. Alone. As usual.

She put down her cue and smiled at Tom the engineer. Her head was pounding now. 'It's been fun, Tom, but I'm going to have to call it a night.'

'But it's still early. I thought we could—'

'No, really. It's time I went home. I'm tired, and I'm not feeling well.'

'Just one more drink,' Tom slurred, reaching for her arm.

She stepped back, out of his reach. 'I don't think so.'

Tom lunged for her and managed to get his arms around her.

He was very drunk, but Ella wasn't concerned. She'd been in these situations before and had always managed to extricate herself. Gently but firmly she started to prise Tom's arms from around her. He took this as an invitation to kiss her and landed his very wet lips on one side of her mouth.

Yeuch.

Tom murmured something about how beautiful she was. Ella, still working at unhooking his arms, was in the middle of thanking him for the compliment when he suddenly wasn't there. One moment she'd been disengaging herself from his enthusiastic embrace, and the next—air.

And then an Australian accent. 'You don't want to do that, mate.'

She blinked, focused, and saw that Aaron James was holding Tom in an embrace of his own, standing behind him with one arm around Tom's chest. How had he got from the bar to the pool table in a nanosecond?

'I'm fine,' Ella said. 'You can let him go.'

Aaron ignored her.

'I said I'm fine,' Ella insisted. 'I was handling it.'

'Yes, I could see that,' Aaron said darkly.

'I was,' Ella insisted, and stepped forward to pull futilely at Aaron's steel-band arm clamped across Tom's writhing torso.

Tom lunged at the same time, and Ella felt a crack across her lip. She tasted blood, staggered backwards, fell against the table and ended up on the floor.

And then everything swirled. Black spots. Nothing.

The first thing Ella noticed as her consciousness returned was the scent. Delicious. Clean and wild, like the beach in winter. She inhaled. Nuzzled her nose into it. Inhaled again. She wanted to taste it. Did it taste as good as it smelled? She opened her mouth, moved her lips, tongue. One small lick. Mmm. Good. Different from the smell but…good.

Then a sound. A sharp intake of breath.

She opened her eyes. Saw skin. Tanned skin. White next to it. She shook her head to clear it. Oh, that hurt. Pulled back a little, looked up. Aaron James. 'Oh,' she said. 'What happened?'

'That moron knocked you out.'

It came back at once. Tom. 'Not on purpose.'

'No, not on purpose.'

'Where is he?'

'Gone. Don't worry about him.'

'I'm not worried. He's a big boy. He can take care of himself.' Ella moved again, and realised she was half lolling against Aaron's thighs.

She started to ease away from him but he kept her there, one arm around her back, one crossing her waist to hold onto her from the front.

'Take it easy,' Aaron said.

A crowd of people had gathered around them. Ella felt herself blush for the second time that night. Intolerable, but apparently uncontrollable. 'I don't feel well,' she said.

'I'm not surprised,' Aaron replied.

'I have to get home,' she said, but she stayed exactly where she was. She closed her eyes. The smell of him. It was him, that smell. That was…comforting. She didn't know why that was so. Didn't care why. It just was.

'All right, people, show's over,' Aaron said, and Ella realised he was telling their audience to get lost. He said something more specific to another man, who seemed to be in charge. She assumed he was pacifying the manager. She didn't care. She just wanted to close her eyes.

'Ella, your lip's bleeding. I'm staying here at the hotel.

Come to my room, let me make sure you're all right, then I'll get you home. Or to the hospital.'

She opened her eyes. 'Not the hospital.' She didn't want anyone at the hospital to see her like this.

'Okay—then my room.'

She wanted to say she would find her *own* way home *immediately*, but when she opened her mouth the words 'All right' were what came out. She ran her tongue experimentally over her lip. *Ouch*. Why hadn't she noticed it was hurting? 'My head hurts more than my lip. Did I hit it when I fell?'

'No, I caught you. Let me…' He didn't bother finishing the sentence, instead running his fingers over her scalp. 'No, nothing. Come on. I'll help you stand.'

Aaron carefully eased Ella up. 'Lean on me,' he said softly, and Ella didn't need to be told twice. She felt awful.

As they made their way out of the bar, she noted a few people looking and whispering, but nobody she knew. 'I'm sorry about this,' she said to Aaron. 'Do you think anyone knows you? I mean, from the television show?'

'I'm not well known outside Australia. But it doesn't matter either way.'

'I don't want to embarrass you.'

'I'm not easily embarrassed. I've got stories that would curl your hair. It's inevitable, with three semi-wild younger sisters.'

'I was all right, you know,' she said. 'I can look after myself.'

'Can you?'

'Yes. I've been doing it a long time. And he was harmless. Tom.'

'Was he?'

'Yes. I could have managed. I *was* managing.'

'Were you?'

'Yes. And stop questioning me. It's annoying. And it's hurting my head.'

They were outside the bar now and Aaron stopped. 'Just one more,' he said, and turned her to face him. 'What on earth were you thinking?'

Ella was so stunned at the leashed fury in his voice she *couldn't* think, let alone speak.

He didn't seem to need an answer, though, because he just rolled right on. 'Drinking like a fish. Letting that clown slobber all over you!'

'He's not a clown, he's an engineer,' Ella said. And then, with the ghost of a smile, 'And fish don't drink beer.'

He looked like thunder.

Ella waited, curious about what he was going to hurl at her. But with a snort of disgust he simply took her arm again, started walking.

He didn't speak again until they were almost across the hotel lobby. 'I'm sorry. I guess I feel a little responsible for you, given my relationship with Brand and Tina.'

'That is just ridiculous—I already have a father. And he happens to know I can look after myself. Anyway, why are you here?' Then, 'Oh, yeah, I remember. The documentary.' She grimaced. '*Should* I have known you'd be here now?'

'I have no idea. Anyway, you're supposed to be in LA.'

'I was in LA. But now— It was a sudden decision, to come here. So it looks like we've surprised each other.'

'Looks like it.'

Aaron guided Ella through a side door leading to the open air, and then along a tree-bordered path until they were in front of what looked like a miniature mansion. He *would* be in one of the presidential-style villas, of course. He didn't look very happy to have brought her there, though.

'How long will you be in town?' she asked, as he unlocked the door.

'Two weeks, give or take.'

'So, you'll be gone in two weeks. And I'll still be here, looking after myself. Like I've always done.' She was pleased with the matter-of-factness of her voice, because in reality she didn't feel matter-of-fact. She felt depressed. She blamed it on the birthday.

Birthdays: misery, with candles.

'Well, good for you, Ella,' he said, and there was a definite sneer in there. 'You're doing such a fine job of it my conscience will be crystal clear when I leave.'

Hello? Sarcasm? Really? Why?

Aaron drew her inside, through a tiled hallway and into a small living room. There was a light on but no sign of anyone.

'Is your son with you?' she asked. *Not that it's any of your business, Ella.*

'Yes, he's in bed.'

'So you've got a nanny? Or is your wife—?' *Um, not your business?*

'Ex-wife. Rebecca is in Sydney. And, yes, I have a nanny, whose name is Jenny. I don't make a habit of leaving my four-year-old son on his own in hotel rooms.'

Oh, dear, he really did *not* like her. And she was well on the way to actively disliking *him*. His attitude was a cross between grouchy father and irritated brother—without the familial affection that would only just make that bearable.

Aaron gestured for Ella to sit. 'Do you want something to drink?'

Ella sank onto the couch. 'Water, please.'

'Good choice,' Aaron said, making Ella wish she'd asked for whisky instead.

He went to the fridge, fished out a bottle of water, poured it into a glass and handed it to her. She didn't deign to thank him.

She rubbed her forehead as she drank.

He was watching her. 'Head still hurting?'

'Yes.'

'Had enough water?'

Ella nodded and Aaron took the glass out of her hand,

sat next to her. He turned her so she was facing away from him. 'Here,' he said tetchily, and started kneading the back of her neck.

'Ahhh...' she breathed out. 'That feels good.'

'Like most actors, I've had a chequered career—massage therapy was one of my shorter-lived occupations but I remember a little,' Aaron said, sounding not at all soothing like a massage therapist.

'Where's the dolphin music?' she joked.

He didn't bother answering and she decided she would *not* speak again. She didn't see why she should make an effort to talk to him, given his snotty attitude. She swayed a little, and he pulled her closer to his chest, one hand kneading while he reached his other arm around in front of her, bracing his forearm against her collarbone to balance her.

She could smell him again. He smelled exquisite. So clean and fresh and...yum. The rhythmic movement of his fingers was soothing, even if it did nothing to ease the ache at the front of her skull. She could have stayed like that for hours.

Slowly, he finished the massage and she had to bite back a protest. He turned her to face him and looked at her lip. 'It's only a small tear. I have a first-aid kit in the bathroom.'

'How very *Triage* of you, Aaron.' He looked suitably unimpressed at that dig.

'Just some ice,' she said. 'That's all I need. And I can look after it myself. I'm a nurse, remember?'

But Aaron was already up and away.

He came back with a bowl of ice and the first-aid kit.

Ella peered into the kit and removed a square of gauze, then wrapped it around an ice cube. 'It's not serious and will heal quickly. Mouth injuries do. It's all about the blood supply.'

Not that Aaron seemed interested in that piece of medical information, because he just took the wrapped ice from her impatiently.

'I promise you I can do it myself,' Ella said.

'Hold still,' he insisted. He held the ice on her bottom lip, kept it pressed there for a minute.

'Open,' he ordered, and Ella automatically opened her mouth for him to inspect inside. 'Looks like you bit the inside of your lip.' He grabbed another square of gauze, wrapped it around another cube of ice and pressed it on the small wound.

He was looking intently at her mouth and Ella started to feel uncomfortable. She could still smell that heavenly scent wafting up from his skin. Why couldn't he smell like stale sweat like everyone else in that bar? She blinked a few times, trying to clear her fuzzy head.

Her eyes fell on his T-shirt and she saw a smear of blood on the collar. Her blood. Her fingers reached out, touched it. His neck, too, had a tiny speck of her blood. Seemingly of their own volition her fingers travelled up, rubbing at the stain. And then she remembered how it had got there. Remembered in one clear flash how she had put her mouth there, on his skin. She felt a flare of arousal and sucked in a quick breath.

He had gone very still. He was watching her. Looking stunned.

CHAPTER THREE

'SORRY,' ELLA SAID. 'It's just… I—I bled on you.'

'Ella, I don't think it's a good idea for you to touch me.'

'Sorry,' Ella said again, jerking her fingers away.

Aaron promptly contradicted himself by taking the hand she'd pulled away and pressing it against his chest. He could actually *hear* his heart thudding. It was probably thumping against her palm like a drum. He didn't care. He wanted her hand on him. Wanted both her hands on him.

He could hear a clock ticking somewhere in the room, but except for that and his heart the silence was thick and heavy.

I don't even like her. He said that in his head, but something wasn't connecting his head to his groin, because just as the thought completed itself he tossed the gauze aside and reached for her other hand, brought it to his mouth, pressed his mouth there, kept it there.

Okay, so maybe you didn't have to like someone to want them.

He really, really hadn't expected to see her again. She was supposed to be in LA. Their 'relationship' should have begun and ended with one awkward conversation at a wedding.

And yet here he was. And here she was. And he had no idea what was going to happen next.

When he'd walked into that bar tonight and seen her

with that idiot, he'd wanted to explode, drag her away, beat the guy senseless.

And he *never* lost his temper!

He'd been so shocked at his reaction he'd contemplated leaving the bar, going somewhere else—a different bar, for a walk, to bed, anything, anywhere else. But he hadn't.

He'd only been planning on having one drink anyway, just a post-flight beer. But nope. He'd stayed, sensing there was going to be trouble. She'd laughed too much, drunk too much, Tom the idiot engineer had fondled her too much. Something was going to give.

And something definitely had.

And of course he'd been there smack bang in the middle of it, like he couldn't get there fast enough.

And then his arms had been around her. And she'd snuggled against him. Her tongue on his neck. And he'd wanted her. Wanted her like he'd never wanted anyone in his life.

And it had made him furious.

Was making him furious now.

So why was he moving the hand he'd been holding to his mouth down to his chest, instead of letting it go?

His hands were only lightly covering hers now. She could break away if she wanted to. Bring him back to sanity. *Please.*

But she didn't break away.

Her hands moved up, over his chest to his collarbones then shoulders. Confident hands. Direct and sure.

He stifled a groan.

'You don't want me.' She breathed the words. 'You don't like me.' But her hands moved again, down to his deltoids, stopping there. Her fingers slid under the short sleeves of his T-shirt, stroked.

This time the groan escaped as his pulse leapt.

Ella moved closer to him, sighed as she surrounded him with her arms, rested the side of her face against his chest then simply waited.

He battled himself for a long moment. His hand hovered over her hair. He could see the tremor in his fingers. He closed his eyes so the sight of her wouldn't push him over the edge. That only intensified the sexy smell of her. Ella Reynolds. Tina's *sister*. 'I can't,' he said. 'I can't do this.' Was that his voice? That croak?

He waited, every nerve tingling. Didn't trust himself to move. If he moved, even a fraction...

Then he heard her sigh again; this time it signalled resignation, not surrender.

'No, of course not,' she said, and slowly disentangled herself until she was sitting safely, separately, beside him. *Whew. Catastrophe averted.*

'A shame,' she said. Her voice was cool and so were her eyes as she reached out to skim her fingernail over his right arm, at the top of his biceps where the sleeve of his T-shirt had been pushed up just enough to reveal the lower edge of a black tattoo circlet. Her lips turned up in an approximation of a smile. 'Because I like tattoos. They're a real turn-on for me. Would have been fun.'

He stared at her, fighting the urge to drag her back against his chest, not quite believing the disdainful humour he could hear in her voice, see in her eyes. Wondering if he'd imagined the yielding softness only moments ago.

At Tina and Brand's wedding he'd sensed that there was something wrong with her. It had made him uncomfortable to be near her. Made him want to get away from her.

He had the same feeling now. Only this time he couldn't get away. He would be damned if he'd let Tina's sister stagger home drunk and disorderly, with a pounding head and a split lip. *Oh, yeah, that's the reason, is it? Tina?*

Ella shrugged—a dismissive, almost delicate gesture. 'But don't worry, I won't press you,' she said calmly. 'I've never had to beg for it in my life and I won't start now, tattoos or not.'

She stood suddenly and smiled—the dazzling smile that didn't reach her eyes. 'I'd better go,' she said.

'I'll take you home,' he said, ignoring the taunt of all those men she hadn't had to beg. None of his business.

'I'll walk.'

'I'll take you,' Aaron insisted.

Ella laughed. 'Okay, but I hope we're not going to drag some poor driver out of bed.'

'Where are you staying?'

'Close enough. I can walk there in under ten minutes.'

'Then we'll walk.'

'All right, then, lead on, Sir Galahad,' Ella said lightly, mockingly.

And that was *exactly* why he didn't like her.

Because she was just so unknowable. Contrary. Changeable. Ready to seduce him one moment and the next so cool. Poised. Amused. They made it to the street without him throttling her, which was one relief. Although he would have preferred a different relief—one for inside his jeans, because, heaven help him, it was painful down there. How the hell did she *do* that? Make him both want her and want to run a mile in the opposite direction?

Ella led off and Aaron fell into step beside her, conscious of her excruciatingly arousing perfume. The almost drugging combination of that scent, the damp heat, the sizzle and shout of the street stalls, the thumping music and wild shouts from the tourist bars, was so mesmerisingly exotic it felt almost like he was in another world. One where the normal rules, the checks and balances, didn't apply.

The minutes ticked by. A steady stream of motorbikes puttered past. A short line of tuk-tuks carrying chatty tourists. Jaunty music from a group of street musicians. Sounds fading as he and Ella walked further, further.

'Needless to say, tonight's escapade is not something Tina needs to hear about,' Ella said suddenly.

'Needless to say,' he agreed.

A tinkling laugh. 'Of course, you wouldn't want it getting back to your wife either. At least, not the latter part of the evening.'

'Ex-wife,' Aaron corrected her. He heard a dog barking in the distance. A mysterious rustle in the bushes near the road.

'Ah.' Ella's steps slowed, but only very briefly. 'But not really ex, I'm thinking, Sir Galahad.'

Aaron grabbed Ella's arm, pulling her to the side of a dirty puddle she was about to step into. 'It's complicated,' he said, when she looked at him.

She pulled free of the contact and started forward again.

'But definitely ex,' he added. And if she only knew the drug-fuelled hell Rebecca had put him through for the past three years, she would understand.

'Oh, dear, how inconvenient! An ex who's not really an ex. It must play havoc with your sex life.'

She laughed again, and his temper got the better of him. The temper that he *never* lost.

'What is wrong with you?' he demanded, whirling her to face him.

She looked up at him, opened her mouth to say—

Well, who knew? Because before he could stop himself he'd slapped his mouth on hers in a devouring kiss.

Just what he *didn't* want to do.

And she had the audacity to kiss him back. More than that—her arms were around him, her hands under his T-shirt.

Then he tasted blood, remembered her lip. Horrified, he pulled back. 'I'm sorry,' he said.

She ran her tongue across her lower lip, raised her eyebrows. '*Definitely* would have been fun,' she said.

'I'm not looking for a relationship,' he said bluntly. And where had that come from? It seemed to suggest he *was* after *something*. But what? What was he after? Nothing—nothing from her.

It seemed to startle her, at least. 'Did I ask for one?'

'No.'

'That's a relief! Because I'm really only interested in casual sex. And on that note, how fortunate that we're here. Where I live. So we can say our goodbyes, and both pretend tonight didn't happen. No relationship. And, alas, no casual sex, because you're married. Oh, no, that's right, you're not. But no sex anyway.'

'I should have left you with the engineer.'

'Well, I would have seen a lot more action,' she said. She started forward and then stopped, raised her hand to her eyes.

'What is it?' Aaron asked.

'Nothing. A headache,' she answered. 'I'll be fine.'

'Goodbye, then,' he said, and turned to walk back to the hotel.

A lot more action! Ha! Aaron was quite sure if he ever let himself put his hands on Ella Reynolds she wouldn't be able to think about another man for a long time. Or walk straight either.

But he was not going to touch her, of course. *Not.*

Ella made her way to her room, cursing silently.

Her head was throbbing and her joints were aching and she longed to lapse into a thought-free coma. She'd just realised she'd contracted either malaria or dengue fever. She wasn't sure which, but either way it sucked.

But when she'd taken two paracetamol tablets and clambered into bed, praying for a mild dose of whatever it was, it wasn't the pain that made the tears come. It was shame. And regret. And a strange sense of loss.

Aaron James had wanted her. Ordinarily, a man wanting her would not cause Ella consternation. Lots of men had wanted her and she'd had no trouble resisting them.

But Aaron was different. He'd kissed her like he was

pouring his strength, his soul into her. And yet he'd been able to fight whatever urge had been driving him.

Why? How?

She manhandled her pillow, trying to get it into a more head-cradling shape.

Not looking for a relationship—that's what he'd said. How galling! As though it were something she would be begging for on the basis of one kiss. All right, one *amazing* kiss, but—seriously! What a joke. A relationship? The one thing she *couldn't* have.

Ella sighed as her outrage morphed into something more distressing: self-loathing. Because she was a fraud and she knew it. A coward who used whatever was at her disposal to stop herself from confronting the wreck her life had become since Javier had been kidnapped in Somalia on her twenty-fifth birthday.

She'd been in limbo ever since. Feeling helpless, hopeless. Guilty that she was free and he was who-knew-where. In the year after his kidnapping she'd felt so lost and alone and powerless she'd thought a nervous breakdown had been on the cards.

And then she'd found Sann in a Cambodian orphanage, and life had beckoned to her again. Two years old, and hers. Or so she'd hoped. But he'd been taken too. He'd died, on her twenty-sixth birthday.

And now here she was on her twenty-*seventh* birthday. Still in limbo, with no idea of what had happened to Javier. Still grieving for Sann.

Panicking at the thought of seeing an Asian child with an adoptive parent.

Unable to entertain even the thought of a relationship with a man.

Pretending she was calm and in control when she was a basket case.

Her life had become a series of shambolic episodes. Too many drinks at the bar. Getting picked up by strange men, determined to see it through then backing out. *Always* backing out, like the worst kind of tease, because no matter how desperate she was to feel *something*, the guilt was always stronger. Coping, but only just, with endlessly sad thoughts during the day and debilitating dreams at night.

She knew that something in her was lost—but she just didn't know how to find it. She hid it from the people she cared about because she knew her grief would devastate them. She hid it from her colleagues because they didn't need the extra burden.

And she was just...stuck. Stuck on past heartbreaks. And it was starting to show.

No wonder Aaron James abhorred the idea of a 'relationship' with her.

Ella rubbed tiredly at her forehead. She closed her eyes, longing for sleep, but knowing the nightmares would come tonight.

Dr Seng slapped his hand on the desk and Aaron's wandering mind snapped back to him. 'So—we've talked about malaria. Now, a few facts about the hospital.'

Kiri had been whisked off to do some painting—one of his favourite pastimes—on arrival at the Children's Community Friendship Hospital, so Aaron could concentrate on this first meeting.

But he wasn't finding it easy.

He had a feeling... A picture of Ella here. Was this where she was working? He wasn't sure, but he kept expecting her to sashay past.

Dr Seng handed over an array of brochures. 'Pre-Pol Pot, there were more than five hundred doctors practising in Cambodia,' Dr Seng said. 'By the time the Khmer Rouge fled Cambodia in 1979 there were less than fifty. Can you imagine what it must have been like? Rebuilding an entire healthcare system from the ground up, with almost no money, no skills? Because that's what happened in Cambodia.'

Aaron knew the history—he'd made it his business to know, because of Kiri. But he could never come to terms with the brutal stupidity of the Khmer Rouge. 'No, I can't imagine it,' he said simply. 'And I'd say this hospital is something of a miracle.'

'Yes. We were started by philanthropists and we're kept going by donations—which is why we are so happy to be associated with your documentary: we need all the publicity we can get, to keep attracting money. It costs us less than twenty-five dollars to treat a child. Only fifty dollars to operate. Unheard of in your world. But, of course, we have so many to help.'

'But your patients pay nothing, right?'

'Correct. Our patients are from impoverished communities and are treated free, although they contribute if they can.'

'And your staff…?'

'In the early days the hospital relied on staff from overseas, but today we are almost exclusively Khmer. And we're a teaching hospital—we train healthcare workers from all over the country. That's a huge success story.'

'So you don't have any overseas staff here at the moment?'

'Actually, we do. Not paid staff—volunteers.'

'Doctors?'

'We have a group of doctors from Singapore coming in a few months' time to perform heart surgeries. And at the moment we have three nurses, all from America, helping out.'

'I was wondering if…' Aaron cleared his throat. 'If perhaps Ella Reynolds was working here?'

Dr Seng looked at him in surprise. 'Ella? Why, yes!'

Ahhhhh. Fate. It had a lot to answer for.

'I—I'm a friend. Of the family,' Aaron explained.

'Then I'm sorry to say you probably won't see her. She's not well. She won't be in for the whole week.'

Aaron knew he should be feeling relieved. He could have a nice easy week of filming, with no cutting comments, no tattoo come-ons, no amused eyebrow-raising.

But…what did 'not well' mean? Head cold? Sprained toe? Cancer? Liver failure? Amputation? 'Not well?'

'Dengue fever—we're in the middle of an outbreak, I'm afraid. Maybe a subject for your next documentary, given it's endemic in at least a hundred countries and infects up to a hundred million people a year.'

Alarm bells. 'But it doesn't kill you, right?'

'It certainly can,' the doctor said, too easily, clearly not understanding Aaron's need for reassurance.

Aaron swallowed. 'But…Ella…'

'Ella? No, no, no. She isn't going to die. The faster you're diagnosed and treated the better, and she diagnosed herself very quickly. It's more dangerous for children, which Ella is not. And much more dangerous if you've had it before, which Ella has not.'

Better. But not quite good enough. 'So is she in hospital?'

'Not necessary at this stage. There's no cure; you just have to nurse the symptoms— take painkillers, keep up the fluids, watch for signs of internal bleeding, which would mean it was dengue haemorrhagic fever—very serious! But Ella knows what she's doing, and she has a friend staying close by, one of the nurses. And I'll be monitoring her as well. A shame it hit her on her birthday.'

'Birthday?'

'Two days ago. Do you want me to get a message to her?'

'No, that's fine,' Aaron said hurriedly. 'Maybe I'll see her before I head home to Sydney.'

'Then let's collect Kiri and I'll have you both taken on a tour of our facilities.'

It quickly became clear that it was Kiri, not Aaron, who

was the celebrity in the hospital. He seemed to fascinate people with his Cambodian Australian-ness, and he was equally fascinated in return. He got the hang of the *satu*— the graceful greeting where you placed your palms together and bowed your head—and looked utterly natural doing it. It soothed Aaron's conscience, which had been uneasy about bringing him.

They were taken to observe the frenetic outpatient department, which Aaron was stunned to learn saw more than five hundred patients a day in a kind of triage arrangement.

The low acuity unit, where he saw his first malaria patients, a sardine can's worth of dengue sufferers, and children with assorted other conditions, including TB, pneumonia, malnutrition, HIV/AIDS and meningitis.

The emergency room, where premature babies and critically ill children were treated for sepsis, severe asthma, and on and on and on.

Then the air-conditioned intensive care unit, which offered mechanical ventilation, blood gas analysis and inotropes—not that Aaron had a clue what that meant. It looked like the Starship *Enterprise* in contrast to the mats laid out for the overflow of dengue sufferers in the fan-cooled hospital corridors.

The tour wrapped up with a walk through the basic but well-used teaching rooms, some of which had been turned into makeshift wards to cope with the dengue rush.

And then, to Aaron's intense annoyance, his focus snapped straight back to Ella.

Tina and Brand would expect him to check on her, right?

And, okay, *he* wanted to make sure for himself that she was going to recover as quickly and easily as Dr Seng seemed to think.

One visit to ease his conscience, and he would put Ella Reynolds into his mental lockbox of almost-mistakes and double-padlock the thing.

And so, forty minutes after leaving the hospital, with Kiri safely in Jenny's care at the hotel, he found himself outside Ella's guesthouse, coercing her room number from one of the other boarders, and treading up the stairs.

CHAPTER FOUR

AARON FELT SUDDENLY guilty as he knocked. Ella would have to drag herself out of bed to open the door.

Well, why not add another layer of guilt to go with his jumble of feelings about that night at the bar?

The boorish way he'd behaved—when he was *never* boorish.

The way he'd assumed her headache was the result of booze, when she'd actually been coming down with dengue fever.

The door opened abruptly. A pretty brunette, wearing a nurse's uniform, stood there.

'Sorry, I thought this was Ella Reynolds's room,' Aaron said.

'It is.' She gave him the appreciative look he was used to receiving from women—women who weren't Ella Reynolds, anyway. 'She's in bed. Ill.'

'Yes, I know. I'm Aaron James. A…a friend. Of the family.'

'I'm Helen. I'm in the room next door, so I'm keeping an eye on her.'

'Nice to meet you.'

She gave him a curious look and he smiled at her, hoping he looked harmless.

'Hang on, and I'll check if she's up to a visit,' Helen said.

The door closed in his face, and he was left wondering whether it would open again.

What on earth was he doing here?

Within a minute Helen was back. 'She's just giving herself a tourniquet test, but come in. I'm heading to the hospital, so she's all yours.'

It was gloomy in the room. And quiet—which was why he could hear his heart racing, even though his heart had no business racing.

His eyes went first to the bed—small, with a mosquito net hanging from a hook in the ceiling, which had been shoved aside. Ella was very focused, staring at her arm, ignoring him. So Aaron looked around the room. Bedside table with a lamp, a framed photo. White walls. Small wardrobe. Suitcase against a wall. A door that he guessed opened to a bathroom, probably the size of a shoebox.

He heard a sound at the bed. Like a magnet, it drew him.

She was taking a blood-pressure cuff off her arm.

'I heard you were ill,' he said, as he reached the bedside. 'I'm sorry. That you're sick, I mean.'

'I'm not too happy about it myself.' She sounded both grim and amused, and Aaron had to admire the way she achieved that.

'Who told you I was sick?' she asked.

'The hospital. I'm filming there for the next week.'

She looked appalled at that news. 'Just one week, right?'

'Looks like it.'

She nodded. He imagined she was calculating the odds of having to see him at work. Flattering—not.

He cleared his throat. 'So what's a tourniquet test?'

'You use the blood-pressure machine—'

'Sphygmomanometer.'

'Well, aren't you clever, Dr *Triage*! Yes. Take your BP, keep the cuff blown up to halfway between the diastolic and systolic—the minimum and maximum pressure—wait a few minutes and check for petechiae—blood points in the skin.'

'And do you have them? Um…it? Petechiae?'

'Not enough. Less than ten per square inch.'

'Is that…is that bad?'

'It's good, actually.'

'Why?'

Audible sigh. 'It means I have classic dengue—not haemorrhagic. As good as it gets when every bone and joint in your body is aching and your head feels like it might explode through your eyeballs.'

'Is that how it feels?'

'Yes.'

Silence.

Aaron racked his brain. 'I thought you might want me to get a message to Tina.'

Her lips tightened. Which he took as a no.

'That would be no,' she confirmed.

A sheet covered the lower half of her body. She was wearing a red T-shirt. Her hair was piled on top of her head, held in place by a rubber band. Her face was flushed, a light sheen of sweat covering it. And despite the distinct lack of glamour, despite the tightened lips and warning eyes, she was the most beautiful woman he'd ever seen.

'Shouldn't you keep the net closed?' he asked, standing rigid beside the bed. Yep—just the sort of thing a man asked a nurse who specialised in tropical illnesses.

'Happy to, if you want to talk to me through it. Or you can swat the mosquitoes before they get to me.'

'Okay—I'll swat.'

She regarded him suspiciously. 'Why are you really here? To warn me I'll be seeing you at the hospital?'

'No, because it looks like you won't be. I just wanted to make sure you were all right. See if you needed anything.'

'Well, I'm all right, and I don't need anything. So thank you for coming but…' Her strength seemed to desert her then and she rolled flat onto her back in the bed, staring at the ceiling, saying nothing.

'I heard it was your birthday. That night.'

An eye roll, but otherwise no answer.

He came a half-step closer. 'If I'd known…'

Aaron mentally winced as she rolled her eyes again.

'What would you have done?' she asked. 'Baked me a cake?'

'Point taken.'

Trawling for a new topic of conversation, he picked up the photo from her bedside table. 'Funny—you and Tina sound nothing alike, and you look nothing alike.'

Silence, and then, grudgingly, 'I take after my father's side of the family. Tina's a genetic throwback.' She smiled suddenly, and Aaron felt his breath jam in his throat. She really was gorgeous when she smiled like that, with her eyes as well as her mouth—even if it was aimed into space and not at him.

He gestured to the photo. 'I wouldn't have picked you for a Disneyland kind of girl.'

'Who doesn't like Disneyland? As long as you remember it's not real, it's a blast.'

Aaron looked at her, disturbed by the harshness in her voice. Did she have to practise that cynicism or did it come naturally?

Ella raised herself on her elbow again. 'Look, forget Disneyland, and my birthday. I *do* need something from you. Only one thing.' She fixed him with a gimlet eye. 'Silence. You can't talk about that night, or about me being sick. Don't tell Tina. Don't tell Brand. My life here has nothing to do with them. In fact, don't talk to anyone about me.'

'Someone should know you've got dengue fever.'

'*You* know. That will have to do. But don't worry, it won't affect you unless I don't make it. And my advice then would be to head for the hills and forget you were ever in Cambodia, because my mother will probably kill you.' That glorious smile again—and, again, not directed at him, just at the thought. 'She never did like a bearer of bad tidings—quite medieval.'

'All the more reason to tell them now.'

Back to the eye roll. 'Except she's not really going to kill you and I'm not going to drop dead. Look...' Ella seemed to be finding the right words. 'They'll worry, and I don't want them worrying about something that can't be changed.'

'You shouldn't be on your own when you're ill.'

'I'm not. I'm surrounded by experts. I feel like I'm in an episode of your TV show, there are so many medical personnel traipsing in and out of this room.'

Aaron looked down at her.

'Don't look at me like that,' Ella said.

'Like what?' Aaron asked. But he was wincing internally because he kind of knew how he must be looking at her. And it was really inappropriate, given her state of health.

With an effort, she pushed herself back into a sitting position. 'Let me make this easy for you, Aaron. I am not, ever, going to have sex with you.'

Yep, she'd pegged the look all right.

'You have a child,' she continued. 'And a wife, ex-wife, whatever. And it's very clear that your...encumbrances... are important to you. And that's the way it *should* be. I understand it. I respect it. I even admire it. So let's just leave it. I was interested for one night, and now I'm not. You were interested, but not enough. Moment officially over. You can take a nice clear conscience home to Sydney, along with the film.'

'Ella—'

'I don't want to hear any more. And I really, truly, do not want to see you again. I don't want— Look, I don't want to get mixed up with a friend of my sister's. Especially a man with a kid.'

Okay, sentiments Aaron agreed with wholeheartedly.

So he should just leave it at that. Run—don't walk—to the nearest exit. Good riddance. So he was kind of surprised to find his mouth opening and 'What's Kiri got to do with it?' coming out of it.

'It's just a…a thing with children. I get attached to them, and it can be painful when the inevitable goodbyes come around—there, something about me you didn't need to know.'

'But you're working at a children's hospital.'

'That's my business. But the bottom line is—I don't want to see Kiri. Ergo, I don't want to see you.' She stopped and her breath hitched painfully. 'Now, please…' Her voice had risen in tone and volume and she stopped. As he watched, she seemed to gather her emotions together. 'Please go,' she continued quietly. 'I'm sick and I'm tired and I— Just please go. All right?'

'All right. Message received loud and clear. Sex officially off the agenda. And have a nice life.'

'Thank you,' she said, and tugged the mosquito net closed.

Aaron left the room, closed the door and stood there.

Duty discharged. He was free to go. *Happy* to go.

But there was some weird dynamic at work, because he couldn't seem to make his feet move. His overgrown sense of responsibility, he told himself.

He'd taken two steps when he heard the sob. Just one, as though it had been cut off. He could picture her holding her hands against her mouth to stop herself from making any tell-tale sound. He hovered, waiting.

But there was only silence.

Aaron waited another long moment.

There was something about her. Something that made him wonder if she was really as prickly as she seemed…

He shook his head. No, he wasn't going to wonder about Ella Reynolds. He'd done the decent thing and checked on her.

He was not interested in her further than that. Not. Interested.

He forced himself to walk away.

Ella had only been away from the hospital for eight lousy days.

How did one mortal male cause such a disturbance in so short a time? she wondered as she batted away what felt like the millionth question about Aaron James. The doctors and nurses, male and female, Khmer and the small sprinkling of Westerners, were uniformly goggle-eyed over him.

Knock yourselves out, would have been Ella's attitude; except that while she'd been laid low by the dengue, Aaron had let it slip to Helen—and therefore everyone!—that he was a close friend of Ella's film director brother-in-law. Which part of 'Don't talk to anyone about me' didn't he understand?

As a result, the whole, intrigued hospital expected her to be breathless with anticipation to learn what Aaron said, what Aaron did, where Aaron went. They expected Ella to marvel at the way he dropped in, no airs or graces, to talk to the staff; how he spoke to patients and their families with real interest and compassion, even when the cameras weren't rolling; the way he was always laughing at himself for getting ahead of his long-suffering translator.

He'd taken someone's temperature. Whoop-de-doo!

And had volunteered as a guinea pig when they'd been demonstrating the use of the rapid diagnostic test for malaria—yeah, so one tiny pinprick on his finger made him a hero?

And had cooked alongside a Cambodian father in the specially built facility attached to the hospital. Yee-ha!

And, and, and, *and*—give her a break.

All Ella wanted to do was work, without hearing his name. They'd had their moment, and it had passed. Thankfully he'd got the message and left her in peace once she'd laid out the situation. She allowed herself a quick stretch before moving onto the next child—a two-year-old darling named Maly. *Heart rate. Respiration rate. Blood pressure. Urine output. Adjust the drip.*

The small hospital was crowded now that the dengue fever outbreak was peaking. They were admitting twenty additional children a day, and she was run off her still-wobbly legs. In the midst of everything she should have been too busy to sense she was being watched…and yet she knew.

She turned. And saw him. Aaron's son, Kiri, beside him.

Wasn't the hospital filming supposed to be over? Why was he here?

'Ella,' Aaron said. No surprise. Just acknowledgement.

She ignored the slight flush she could feel creeping up from her throat. With a swallowed sigh she fixed on a smile and walked over to him. She would be cool. Professional. Civilised. She held out her hand. 'Hello, Aaron.'

He took it, but released it quickly.

'And *sua s'day,* Kiri,' she said, crouching in front of him. 'Do you know what that means?'

Kiri shook his head. Blinked.

'It means hello in Khmer. Do you remember me?'

Kiri nodded. '*Sua s'day*, Ella. Can I go and see her?' he asked, looking over, wide-eyed, at the little girl Ella had been with.

'Yes, you can. But she's not feeling very well. Do you think you can be careful and quiet?'

Kiri nodded solemnly and Ella gave him a confirming nod before standing again. She watched him walk over to Maly's bed before turning to reassure Aaron. 'She's not contagious. It's dengue fever and there's never been a case of person-to-person transmission.'

'Dr Seng said it deserved its own documentary. The symptoms can be like malaria, right? But it's a virus, not a parasite, and the mosquitoes aren't the same.'

Ella nodded. 'The dengue mosquito—' She broke off. 'You're really interested?'

'Why wouldn't I be?'

'I just…' She shrugged. 'Nothing. People can get bored with the medical lingo.'

'I won't be bored. So—the mosquitoes?'

'They're called *Aedes aegypti*, and they bite during the day. Malaria mosquitoes—*Anopheles*, but I'm sure you know that—get you at night, and I'm sure you know that too. It kind of sucks that the people here don't get a break! Anyway, *Aedes aegypti* like urban areas, and they breed in stagnant water—vases, old tyres, buckets, that kind of thing. If a mosquito bites someone with dengue, the virus will replicate inside it, and then the mosquito can transmit the virus to other people when it bites them.' Her gaze sharpened. 'You're taking precautions for Kiri, aren't you?'

'Oh, yes. It's been beaten it into me. Long sleeves, long pants. Insect repellent with DEET. And so on and so forth.'

'You too—long sleeves, I mean. Enough already with the T-shirts.'

'Yes, I know. I'm tempting fate.'

Silence.

He was looking at her in that weird way.

'So, the filming,' she said, uncomfortable. 'Is it going well?'

'We're behind schedule, but I don't mind because it's given me a chance to take Kiri to see Angkor Wat. And the place with the riverbed carvings. You know, the carvings of the genitalia.' He stopped suddenly. 'I—I mean, the…um…Hindu gods…you know…and the—the…ah… Kal…? Kab…?'

Ella bit the inside of her cheek. It surprised her that she could think he was cute. But he sort of was, in his sudden embarrassment over the word genitalia. 'Yes, I know all about genitalia. And it's Kbal Spean, you're talking about, and the Hindu God is Shiva. It's also called The River of a

Thousand Lingas—which means a thousand stylised phal-
luses,' she said, and had to bite her cheek again as he ran
a harassed hand into his hair.

'So, the filming?' she reminded him.

'Oh. Yeah. A few more days here and then the final bit
involves visiting some of the villages near the Thai border
and seeing how the malaria outreach programme works,
with the volunteers screening, diagnosing and treating people in their communities.'

'I was out there a few years ago,' Ella said. 'Volunteers
were acting as human mosquito bait. The mosquitoes would
bite them, and the guys would scoop them into test tubes to
be sent down to the lab in Phnom Penh for testing.'

'But wasn't that dangerous? I mean...*trying* to get bitten?'

'Well, certainly drastic. But all the volunteers were
given a combination drug cocktail, which meant they didn't
actually develop malaria.'

'So what was the point?'

'To verify whether the rapid treatment malaria programme that had been established there was managing to
break the pathways of transmission between insects, parasites and humans. But you don't need to worry. That was
then, this is now. And they won't be asking you to roll up
your jeans and grab a test tube.'

'Would you have rolled up your jeans, Ella?'

'Yes.'

'And risked malaria?'

'I've had it. Twice, actually. Once in Somalia, once here.'

'Somalia?'

Uh-oh. She was not going there. 'Obviously, it didn't
kill me, either time. But I've *seen* it kill. It kills one child
every thirty seconds.' She could hear her voice tremble so
she paused for a moment. When she could trust herself,
she added, 'And I would do anything to help stop that.'

Aaron was frowning. Watching her. Making her feel uncomfortable. Again. 'But you're not— Sorry, it's none of my business, but Kiri isn't going with you up there, right?'

'No.' Aaron frowned. Opened his mouth. Closed it. Opened. Closed.

'Problem?' she prompted.

'No. But… Just…' Sigh.

'Just…?' she prompted again.

'Just—do you think I made a mistake, bringing him to Cambodia?' he asked. 'There were reasons I couldn't leave him at home. And I thought it would be good for him to stay connected to his birth country. But, like you, he's had malaria. Before the adoption.'

'Yes, I gathered that.'

'I'd never forgive myself if he got it again because I brought him with me.'

Ella blinked at him. She was surprised he would share that fear with her—they weren't exactly friends, after all— and felt a sudden emotional connection that was as unde-niable as it was unsettling.

She wanted to touch him. Just his hand. She folded her arms so she couldn't. 'I agree that children adopted from overseas should connect with their heritage,' she said, ul-tra-professional. And then she couldn't help herself. She unfolded her arms, touched his shoulder. Very briefly. 'But, yes, we're a long way from Sydney, and the health risks are real.'

'So I shouldn't have brought him?'

'You said there were reasons for not leaving him be-hind—so how can I answer that? But, you know, these are diseases of poverty we're talking about. That's a horrible thing to acknowledge, but at least it can be a comfort to you. Because you know your son would have immediate atten-tion, the *best* attention—and therefore the best outcome.'

He sighed. 'Yes, I see what you mean. It is horrible, and also comforting.'

'And it won't be long until you're back home. Meanwhile, keep taking those precautions, and if he exhibits any symptoms, at least you know what they are—just don't wait to get him to the hospital.'

She swayed slightly, and Aaron reached out to steady her.

'Sorry. Tired,' she said.

'You're still not fully recovered, are you?' he asked.

'I'm fine. And my shift has finished so I'm off home in a moment.'

Ella nodded in Kiri's direction. The little boy was gently stroking the back of Maly's hand. 'He's sweet.'

'Yes. He's an angel.'

'You're lucky,' Ella said. She heard the…thing in her voice. The wistfulness. She blinked hard. Cleared her throat. 'Excuse me, I need to— Excuse me.'

Ella felt Aaron's eyes on her as she left the ward.

Ella was doing that too-slow walk. Very controlled.

She'd lost her curves since the wedding. She'd been thin when he'd visited her a week ago, but after the dengue she was like a whippet.

But still almost painfully beautiful. Despite the messy ponytail. And the sexless pants and top combo that constituted her uniform.

And he still wanted her.

He'd been furious at how he'd strained for a sight of her every time he'd been at the hospital, even though he'd known she was out of action. Seriously, how pathetic could a man be?

He'd tried and tried to get her out of his head. No joy. There was just something…something under the prickly exterior.

Like the way she looked at Kiri when he'd repeated her Cambodian greeting. The expression on her face when she'd spoken about diseases of the poor. It was just so hard to reconcile all the pieces. To figure out that *something* about her.

He caught himself. Blocked the thought. Reminded himself that if there *was* something there, he didn't want it. One more week, and he would never have to see or think of her again. He could have his peace of mind back. His libido back under control.

He called Kiri over and they left the ward.

And she was there—up the corridor, crouching beside a little boy who was on one of the mattresses on the floor, her slender fingers on the pulse point of his wrist.

Arrrggghhh. This was *torture.* Why wasn't she on her way home like she was supposed to be, so he didn't have to see her smile into that little boy's eyes? Didn't have to see her sit back on her heels and close her eyes, exhausted?

And wonder just who she really was, this woman who was prickly and dismissive. Knowledgeable and professional. Who wouldn't think twice about letting mosquitoes bite her legs for research. Who looked at sick children with a tenderness that caused his chest to ache. Who made him feel gauche and insignificant.

Who made him suddenly and horribly aware of what it was like to crave something. Someone. It was so much more, so much *worse*, than purely physical need.

'Ow,' Kiri protested, and Aaron loosened his hold on Kiri's hand.

Ella looked up, saw them. Froze. Nodding briefly, she got to her feet and did that slow walk out.

This was not good, Aaron thought.

A few days and he would be out of her life.

Ella felt that if only she didn't have to converse with Aaron again, she would cope with those days.

But she hadn't banked on the *sight* of him being such a distraction. Sauntering around like a doctor on regular rounds, poking his nose in everywhere without even the excuse of a camera. Not really coming near her, but always *there*.

It was somehow worse that he was keeping his distance, because it meant there was no purpose to the way she was perpetually waiting for him to show up.

Him and the boy, who reminded her so much of Sann.

It was painful to see Kiri, even from a distance. So painful she shouldn't want to see him, shouldn't want the ache it caused. Except that alongside the pain was this drenching, drowning need. She didn't bother asking why, accepting that it was a connection she couldn't explain, the way it had been with Sann.

On her fourth day back at work, after broken sleep full of wrenching nightmares, the last thing she needed was Aaron James, trailed by his cameraman, coming into the outpatient department just as a comatose, convulsing two-year-old boy was rushed up to her by his mother.

The look in Ella's eyes as she reached for the child must have been terrible because Aaron actually ran at her. He plucked the boy from his mother's arms. 'Come,' he said, and hurried through the hospital as though he'd worked there all his life, Ella and the little boy's mother hurrying after him.

This was a child. Maybe with malaria. And Aaron was helping her.

How was she supposed to keep her distance now?

CHAPTER FIVE

AARON SIGNALLED FOR the cameraman to start filming as what looked like a swarm of medical people converged on the tiny little boy in the ICU.

Ella was rattling off details as he was positioned in the bed—name Bourey, two years old, brought in by his mother after suffering intermittent fever and chills for two days. Unable to eat. Seizure on the way to the hospital. Unable to be roused. Severe pallor. Second seizure followed.

Hands, stethoscopes were all over the boy—pulling open his eyelids, taking his temperature. Checking heart rate, pulse and blood pressure. *Rash? No.* Feeling his abdomen.

I want a blood glucose now.

Into Bourey's tiny arm went a canula.

Blood was taken, and whisked away.

Intravenous diazepam as a slow bolus to control the seizures.

The doctor was listening intently to Bourey's breathing, which was deep and slow. The next moment the boy was intubated and hooked up to a respirator.

Every instruction was rapid-fire.

'Intravenous paracetamol for the fever.'

'Intravenous artesunate, stat, we won't wait for the blood films—we'll treat for falciparum malaria. Don't think it's menigococcus but let's give IV benzylpenicillin. We'll hold off on the lumbar puncture. I want no evidence of focal neuro signs. What was his glucose?'

'Intravenous dextrose five per cent and normal saline point nine per cent for the dehydration—but monitor his urine output carefully; we don't want to overdo it and end up with pulmonary oedema, and we need to check renal function. And watch for haemoglobinuria. If the urine is dark we'll need to cross-match.'

Overhead an assortment of bags; tubes drip, drip, dripping.

How much stuff could the little guy's veins take?

A urinary catheter was added to Bourey's overloaded body. Empty plastic bag draped over the side of the bed.

A plastic tube was measured, from the boy's nose to his ear to his chest, lubricated, threaded up Bourey's nose, taped in place.

'Aspirate the stomach contents.'

'Monitor temp, respiratory rate, pulse, blood pressure, neuro obs every fifteen minutes.'

Hypoglycaemia, metabolic acidosis, pulmonary oedema, hypotensive shock. Watch the signs. Monitor. Check. Observe.

Aaron's head was spinning. His cameraman silent and focused as he filmed.

And Ella—so calm, except for her eyes.

Aaron was willing her to look at him. And every time she did, she seemed to relax. Just a slight breath, a softening in her face so subtle he could be imagining it, a lessening of tension in her shoulders. Then her focus was back to the boy.

The manic pace around Bourey finally eased and Aaron saw Ella slip out of the ICU. Aaron signalled to his cameraman to stop filming and left the room.

They had enough to tell the story but they needed a face on camera.

He went in search of Dr Seng, wanting to check the

sensitivity of the case and get suggestions for the best interviewee.

Dr Seng listened, nodded, contemplated. Undertook to talk to Bourey's family to ascertain their willingness to have the case featured. 'For the interview, I recommend Ella,' he said. 'She knows enough about malaria to write a textbook, and she is highly articulate.'

Aaron suspected the ultra-private Ella would rather eat a plate of tarantulas and was on the verge of suggesting perhaps a doctor when Ella walked past.

Dr Seng beckoned her over, asked for her participation and smiled genially at them before hurrying away.

Ella looked at Aaron coolly. 'Happy to help, of course,' she said.

They found a spot where they were out of the way of traffic but with a view through the ICU windows. The cameraman opted for handheld, to give a sense of intimacy.

Great—intimacy.

'Well?' she asked, clearly anxious to get it done.

'Don't you want to…?' He waved a hand at his hair. At his face.

'What's wrong with the way I look?'

'Nothing. It's just that most people—'

'What's more important, how my hair looks or that little boy?'

'Fine,' Aaron said. 'Tell me about the case.'

'This is a two-year-old child, suffering from cerebral falciparum malaria. Blood films showed parasitaemia—'

'Parasitaemia?'

'It means the number of parasites in his blood. His level is twenty-two per cent. That is high and very serious. Hence the IV artesunate—a particular drug we use for this strain—which we'll administer for twenty-four hours. After that, we'll switch to oral artemisinin-based combination therapy—ACT for short. It's the current drug regime for falciparum. We'll be monitoring his parasitaemia, and we'd expect to see the levels drop relatively quickly.'

She sounded smart and competent and in control.

'And if they don't drop?' Aaron asked.

Her forehead creased. 'Then we've got a problem. It will indicate drug resistance. This region is the first in the world to show signs of resistance to ACTs, which used to kill the parasites in forty-eight hours and now take up to ninety-six hours. It was the same for previous treatments like cloroquine, which is now practically useless—we're like the epicentre for drug resistance here.'

'How does it happen, the resistance?'

'People take just enough of the course to feel better. Or the medicines they buy over the counter are substandard, or counterfeit, with only a tiny fraction of the effective drug in it. Or they are sold only a fraction of the course. Often the writing on the packet is in a different language, so people don't know what they're selling, or buying. And here we have highly mobile workers crossing the borders— in and out of Thailand, for example. So resistant strains are carried in and out with them. The problem is there's no new miracle drug on the horizon, so if we don't address the resistance issue...' She held out her hands, shrugged. Perfection for the camera. 'Trouble. And if the resistance eventually gets exported to Africa—as history suggests it will—it will be catastrophic. Around three thousand children die of malaria every day in sub-Saharan Africa, which is why this is a critical issue.'

He waited. Letting the camera stay on her face, letting the statistic sink in. 'Back to this particular case. What happens now?'

'Continuous clinical observation and measuring what's happening with his blood, his electrolytes. I could give you a range of medical jargon but basically this is a critically ill child. We hope his organs won't fail. We hope he doesn't suffer any lifelong mental disabilities from the pressure on his brain. But, first, we hope he survives.'

A forlorn hope, as it turned out.

One minute they had been working to save Bourey's life, preparing for a whole-blood transfusion to lower the concentration of parasites in Bourey's blood and treat his anaemia. The next, Ella was unhooking him from the medical paraphernalia that had defined his last hours.

She left the ICU and her eyes started to sting. She stopped, wiped a finger under one eye, looked down at it. Wet. She was crying. And what was left of the numbness—one year's worth of carefully manufactured numbness—simply fell away.

She heard something and looked up. She saw Aaron, and tried to pull herself together. But her body had started to shake, and she simply had no reserves of strength left to pretend everything was all right.

A sobbing sort of gasp escaped her, a millisecond before she could put her hand over her mouth to stop it. Her brain and her heart and her body seemed to be out of synch. Her limbs couldn't seem to do what she was urging them to do. So the horrible gasp was followed by a stumble as she tried to turn away. She didn't want Aaron to see her like this. Didn't want anybody to see her, but especially not Aaron. He knew her sister. He might tell her sister. Her sister couldn't know that she was utterly, utterly desolate.

'I'm fine,' she said, as she felt his hand on her shoulder, steadying her.

Aaron withdrew his hand. 'You don't look fine,' he said.

Ella shook her head, unable to speak. She took one unsteady step. Two. Stopped. The unreleased sobs were aching in her chest. Crushing and awful. She had to get out of the hospital.

She felt Aaron's hand on her shoulder again and found

she couldn't move. Just couldn't force her feet in the direction she wanted to go.

Aaron put his arm around her, guiding her with quick, purposeful strides out of the hospital, into the suffocating heat, steering her towards and then behind a clump of thick foliage so they were out of sight.

Ella opened her mouth to tell him, again, that she was fine, but... 'I'm sorry,' she gasped instead. 'I can't— Like Sann. My Sann. Help me, help me.'

He pulled her into his arms and held on. 'I will. I will, Ella. Tell me how. Just tell me.'

'He died. He died. I c-c-couldn't stop it.'

Aaron hugged her close. Silence. He seemed to know there was nothing to say.

Ella didn't know how long she stood there, in Aaron James's arms, as the tears gradually slowed. It was comforting, to be held like this. No words. Just touch. She didn't move, even when the crying stopped.

Until he turned her face up to his. And there was something in his eyes, something serious and concerned.

A look that reminded her Aaron James could not be a shoulder to cry on. He was too...close, somehow. She didn't want anyone to be close to her. Couldn't risk it.

Ella wrenched herself out of his arms. Gave a small, self-conscious hunch of one shoulder. 'It shouldn't upset me any more, I know. But sometimes...' She shoved a lank lock of hair behind her ear. 'Usually you think if they had just got to us faster...they are so poor, you see, that they wait, and hope, and maybe try other things. Because it is expensive for them, the trip to the hospital, even though the treatment is free. But in this case I think...I think nothing would have made any difference... And I...I hate it when I can't make a difference.'

She rubbed her tired hands over her face. 'Usually when I feel like this I donate blood. It reminds me that things that cost me nothing can help someone. And because the hospital always needs so much blood. But I can't even do that now because it's too soon after the dengue. So I've got nothing. Useless.'

'I'll donate blood for you,' Aaron said immediately.

She tried to smile. 'You're doing something important already—the documentary. And I didn't mind doing that interview, you know. I'd do anything.'

She started to move away, but he put his hand on her arm, stopping her.

'So, Ella. Who's Sann?'

Ella felt her eyes start to fill again. Through sheer will power she stopped the tears from spilling out. He touched her, very gently, his hand on her hair, her cheek, and it melted something. 'He was the child I wanted to adopt,' she said. And somehow it was a relief to share this. 'Here in Cambodia. A patient, an orphan, two years old. I went home to find out what I had to do, and while I was gone he…he died. Malaria.'

'And you blame yourself,' he said softly. 'Because you weren't there. Because you couldn't save him. And I suppose you're working with children in Cambodia, which must torture you, as a kind of penance.'

'I don't know.' She covered her face in her hands for one long moment. Shuddered out a breath. 'Sorry—it's not something I talk about.' Her hands dropped and she looked at him, drained of all emotion. 'I'm asking you not to mention it to Tina. She never knew about Sann. And there's no point telling her. She doesn't need to know about this episode today either. Can I trust you not to say anything?'

'You can trust me. But, Ella, you're making a mistake. This is not the way to—'

'Thank you,' she said abruptly, not wanting to hear advice she couldn't bear to take. 'The rain…it's that time of the day. And I can feel it coming. Smell it.'

'So? What's new?'

'I'd better get back.'

'Wait,' he called.

But Ella was running for the hospital.

She reached the roof overhang as the heavens opened. Looked back at Aaron, who hadn't moved, hadn't taken even one step towards shelter. He didn't seem to care that the gushing water was plastering his clothes to his skin.

He was watching her with an intensity that scared her.

Ella shivered in the damp heat and then forced her eyes away.

The next day Helen told Ella that Aaron James had been in and donated blood.

For her. He'd done it for her.

But she looked at Helen as though she couldn't care less. The following day, when Helen reported that Aaron had left for his visit to the villages, same deal. But she was relieved.

She hoped Aaron would be so busy that any thought of her little breakdown would be wiped out of his mind.

Meanwhile, she would be trying to forget the way Aaron had looked at her—like he understood her, like he knew how broken she was. Trying to forget *him*.

There was only one problem with that: Kiri.

Because Kiri and Aaron came as a set.

And Ella couldn't stop thinking, worrying, about Kiri. Knowing that the cause was her distress over Bourey's death didn't change the fact that she had a sense of dread about Kiri's health that seemed tied to Aaron's absence.

Which just went to prove she was unhinged!

Kiri has a nanny to look after him. It's none of your business, Ella.

She repeated this mantra to herself over and over.

But the nagging fear kept tap-tapping at her nerves as she willed the time to pass quickly until Aaron could whisk his son home to safety.

When she heard Helen calling her name frantically two days after Aaron had left, her heart started jackhammering.

'What?' Ella asked, hurrying towards Helen. But she knew. *Knew.*

'It's Aaron James. Or rather his son. He's been taken to the Khmer International Hospital. Abdominal pains. Persistent fever. Retro-orbital pain. Vomiting. They suspect dengue fever.'

Ella felt the rush in her veins, the panic.

'They can't get hold of Aaron,' Helen said. 'So the nanny asked them to call us because she knows he's been filming here. I thought you should know straight away, because— Well, the family connection. Ella, what if something goes wrong and we can't reach Aaron?'

Ella didn't bother to answer. She simply ran.

Aaron had been unsettled during his time in the monsoonal rainforest.

Not that it hadn't been intriguing—the medical challenges the people faced.

And confronting—the history of the area, which had been a Khmer Rouge stronghold, with regular sightings of people with missing limbs, courtesy of landmines, to prove it.

And humbling—that people so poor, so constantly ill, should face life with such stoic grace.

And beautiful, even with the daily downpours—with the lush, virgin forest moist enough to suck at you, and vegetation so thick you had the feeling that if you stood still for half an hour, vines would start growing over you, anchoring you to the boggy earth.

But!

His mobile phone was bothering him. He'd never been out of contact with Kiri before, but since day two, when they'd headed for the most remote villages that were nothing more than smatterings of bamboo huts on rickety stilts, he'd had trouble with his phone.

He found himself wishing he'd told Jenny to contact

Ella if anything went wrong. But Jenny, not being psychic, would never guess that was what Aaron would want her to do—not when she'd never heard Ella's name come out of his mouth. Because he'd been so stupidly determined *not* to talk about Ella, in a misguided attempt to banish her from his head. And what an epic fail *that* had been, because she was still in his head. Worse than ever.

He'd hoped being away from the hospital would cure it.

Not looking likely, though.

Every time he saw someone with a blown-off limb, or watched a health worker touch a malnourished child or check an HIV patient, he remembered Ella's words at the wedding reception. *I've seen the damage landmines can do. Had children with AIDS, with malnutrition, die in my arms.* He hadn't understood how she could sound so prosaic but now, seeing the endless stream of injuries, illness, poverty, he did.

And anything to do with malaria—well, how could he not think of her, and that searing grief?

The malaria screening process in the villages was simple, effective. Each person was registered in a book. *Ella, in the outpatient department, recording patient details.*

They were checked for symptoms—simple things like temperature, spleen enlargement. *Ella's hands touching children on the ward.*

Symptomatic people went on to the rapid diagnostic test. Fingertip wiped, dried. Squeeze the finger gently, jab quickly with a lancet. Wipe the first drop, collect another drop with a pipette. Drop it into the tiny well on the test strip. Add buffer in the designated spot. Wait fifteen minutes for the stripes to appear. *Ella, soothing children as their blood was siphoned off at the hospital.*

Aaron helped distribute insecticide-impregnated mosquito nets—a wonderfully simple method of protecting against malaria and given out free. *Ella, blocking him out so easily just by tugging her bed net closed.*

Arrrgggghhh.

But relief was almost at hand. One last interview for the documentary and he would be heading back to Kiri. Jenny would have already packed for the trip home to Sydney. Ella would be out of his sight, out of his reach, out of his life once they left Cambodia.

Just one interview to go.

He listened closely as the village volunteer's comments were translated into English. There were three thousand volunteers throughout Cambodia, covering every village more than five kilometres from a health centre, with people's homes doubling as pop-up clinics. Medication was given free, and would be swallowed in front of the volunteers to make sure the entire course was taken. People diagnosed with malaria would not only have blood tested on day one but also on day three to assess the effectiveness of the drug treatment. *Ella, explaining drug resistance. Mentioning so casually that she'd had malaria twice.*

Half an hour later, with the filming wrapped up, they were in the jeep.

Twenty minutes after that his phone beeped. Beeped, beeped, beeped. Beeped.

He listened with the phone tight to one ear, fingers jammed in the other to block other sounds.

Felt the cold sweat of terror.

If he hadn't been sitting, his legs would have collapsed beneath him.

Kiri. Dengue haemorrhagic fever. His small, gentle, loving son was in pain and he wasn't there to look after him.

His fault. All his. He'd brought Kiri to Cambodia in the middle of an outbreak. Left him while he'd traipsed off to film in the boondocks, thinking that was the safer option.

He listened to the messages again. One after the other. Progress reports from the hospital—calm, matter-of-fact, professional, reassuring. Jenny—at first panicked, tearful. And then calmer each time, reassured by one of the nurses.

Rebecca frantic but then, somehow, also calmer, mentioning an excellent nurse.

Three times he'd started to call the Children's Community Friendship Hospital to talk to Ella, wanting her advice, her reassurance, her skills to be focused on Kiri. Three times he'd stopped himself—he *had* expert advice, from Kiri's doctor and a tropical diseases specialist in Sydney he'd called.

And Ella had made it clear she wanted nothing to do with him.

And his son wasn't Ella's problem. Couldn't be her problem.

He wouldn't, couldn't let her mean that much.

The hospital where Kiri had been taken was like a five-star hotel compared with where Ella worked, and Kiri had his own room.

Ella knew the hospital had an excellent reputation; once she'd satisfied herself that Kiri was getting the care and attention he needed, she intended to slide into the background and leave everyone to it.

There was no reason for her to be the one palpating Kiri's abdomen to see if his liver was enlarged, while waiting to see if Kiri's blood test results supported the dengue diagnosis. Hmm, it was a little tender. But that wasn't a crisis and she didn't need to do anything *else* herself.

The blood tests came back, with the dengue virus detected. Plus a low white cell count, low platelets and high haematocrit—the measurement of the percentage of red blood cells to the total blood volume—which could indicate potential plasma leakage. Serious, but, as long as you knew what you were dealing with, treatable. He was still drinking, there were no signs of respiratory distress. So far, so good.

Hands off, Ella, leave it to the staff.

But... There was no problem in asking for a truckle to

be set up for her in Kiri's room, was there? At her hospital, the kids' families always stayed with them for the duration.

So all right, she wasn't family, but his family wasn't here. And kids liked to have people they knew with them. And Ella knew Kiri. Plus, she was making it easier for his nanny to take a break.

She'd got Aaron's cell number from Jenny, and was constantly on the verge of calling him. Only the thought of how many panicked messages he already had waiting for him stopped her. And the tiny suspicion that Aaron would tell her she wasn't needed, which she didn't want to hear—and she hoped that didn't mean she was becoming obsessive about his son.

By the time she'd started haranguing the doctors for updated blood test results, double-checking the nurses' perfect records of Kiri's urine output, heart and respiratory rates, and blood pressure, taking over the task of sponging Kiri down to lower his fever and cajoling him into drinking water and juice to ensure he didn't get dehydrated, she realised she was a step *beyond* obsessive.

It wasn't like she didn't have enough to do at her own place of work, but she couldn't seem to stop herself standing watch over Kiri James like some kind of sentinel—even though dashing between two hospitals was running her ragged.

Kiri's fever subsided on his third day in hospital—but Ella knew better than to assume that meant he was better because often that heralded a critical period. The blood tests with the dropping platelet levels, sharply rising white cells and decreasing haematocrit certainly weren't indicating recovery.

And, suddenly, everything started to go wrong.

Kiri grew increasingly restless and stopped drinking, and Ella went into hyper-vigilant mode.

His breathing became too rapid. His pulse too fast. Even

more worryingly, his urine output dropped down to practically nothing.

Ella checked his capillary refill time, pressing on the underside of Kiri's heel and timing how long it took to go from blanched to normal: more than six seconds, when it should only take three.

His abdomen was distended, which indicated ascites—an accumulation of fluid in the abdominal cavity. 'I'm just going to feel your tummy, Kiri,' she said, and pressed as gently as she could.

He cried out. 'Hurts, Ella.'

'I'm so sorry, darling,' she said, knowing they needed to quickly determine the severity of plasma leakage. 'You need some tests, I'm afraid, so I'm going to call your nurse.'

Ella spoke to the nurse, who raced for the doctor, who ordered an abdominal ultrasound to confirm the degree of ascites and a chest X-ray to determine pleural effusion, which would lead to respiratory distress.

'As you know, Ella,' the doctor explained, drawing her outside, 'a critical amount of plasma leakage will indicate he's going into shock, so we're moving Kiri to the ICU, where we can monitor him. We'll be starting him on intravenous rehydration. We'd expect a fairly rapid improvement, in which case we'll progressively reduce the IV fluids, or they could make the situation worse. No improvement and a significant decrease in haematocrit could suggest internal bleeding, and at that stage we'd look at a blood transfusion. But we're nowhere near that stage so no need to worry. I'll call his father now.'

'Aaron's phone's not working,' Ella said mechanically.

'It is now. He called to tell us he's on his way. I know you're a close friend of the family, so...'

But Ella had stopped listening. She nodded. Murmured a word here and there. Took nothing in.

The doctor patted her arm and left. The orderly would be arriving to take Kiri to ICU. This was it. Over. She wasn't needed any more. And she knew, really, that she had never been needed—the hospital had always had everything under control.

Ella braced herself and went to Kiri's bedside. 'Well, young man,' she said cheerfully, 'you're going somewhere special—ICU.'

'I see you too.'

Ella felt such a rush of love, it almost choked her. 'Hmm. In a way that's exactly what it is. It's where the doctors can see you every minute, until nobody has to poke you in the tummy any more. Okay?'

'Are you coming?'

'No, darling. Someone better is coming. The best surprise. Can you guess who?'

Kiri's eyes lit up. 'Dad?'

'Yep,' she said, and leaned over to kiss him.

The door opened. The orderly. 'And they'll be putting a special tube into you here,' she said, touching his wrist. 'It's superhero juice, so you're going to look like Superman soon. Lucky you!'

A moment later Ella was alone, gathering her few possessions.

Back to reality, she told herself. Devoting her time to where it was really needed, rather than wasting it playing out some mother fantasy.

Ella felt the tears on her cheeks. Wiped them away. Pulled herself together.

Walked super-slowly out of the room.

Ella was the first person he saw.

Aaron was sweaty, frantic. Racing into the hospital. And there she was, exiting. Cool. Remote.

He stopped.

If Ella is here, Kiri will be all right. The thought darted into his head without permission. The relief was immediate, almost overwhelming.

A split second later it all fell into place: Ella was the nurse who had spoken to Rebecca. His two worlds colliding. Ex-wife and mother of his child connecting with the woman he wanted to sleep with.

No-go zone.

He reached Ella in three, unthinking strides. 'It was you, wasn't it?'

His sudden appearance before her startled her. But she looked at him steadily enough, with her wedding face on. 'What was me?'

'You spoke to Rebecca.'

'Yes. Jenny handed me the phone. I wasn't going to hang up on a worried parent. I had no *reason* to hang up on her.'

'What did you tell her?'

She raised an eyebrow at him. 'That you and I were having a torrid affair.'

She looked at him, waiting for something.

He looked back—blank.

'Seriously?' she demanded. '*Seriously?*' She shook her head in disgust. 'I told her what I knew about dengue fever, you idiot. That it was a complex illness, and things did go wrong—but that it was relatively simple to treat. I shared my own experience so that she understood. I said that early detection followed by admission to a good hospital almost guaranteed a positive outcome. I explained that, more than anything else, it was a matter of getting the fluid intake right and treating complications as they arose.'

'Oh. I—I don't—'

'I told her Kiri was handling everything bravely enough to break your heart, and that Jenny and I were taking shifts to make sure he had someone familiar with him at all times. I didn't ask her why she wasn't hotfooting it out here, despite the fact that her son was in a lot of pain, with his joints aching and his muscles screaming, and asking for her, for you, constantly.'

'I—'

'Not interested, Aaron.'

'But just—he's all right, isn't he? In ICU, right?'

A look. Dismissive. And then she did that slow walk away.

'Wait a minute!' he exploded.

But Ella only waved an imperious hand—not even bothering to turn around to do it—and kept to her path.

CHAPTER SIX

WELL...IT BOTHERED Aaron.

Ella's saunter off as though he wasn't even worth talking to.

Followed by Jenny's report of Ella's tireless care: that Ella had begged and badgered the staff and hadn't cared about anyone but his son; the fact that she of all people had been the only one capable of reassuring Rebecca.

He had to keep things simple.

But how simple could it be, when he *knew* Ella would be visiting Kiri—and that when she did, he would have to tell her that, all things considered, she would have to stay away from his son.

Two days. The day Kiri got out of ICU. That's how long it took her.

Aaron had left Kiri for fifteen minutes to grab something to eat, and she was there when he got back to Kiri's room, as though she'd timed it to coincide with his absence.

It wrenched him to see the look on Ella's face as she smoothed Kiri's spiky black hair back from his forehead. To experience again that strange combination of joy and terror that had hit him when he'd seen her coming out of the hospital.

He would *not* want her. He had enough on his plate. And if Ella thought she got to pick and choose when their lives could intersect and when they couldn't—well, no! That was all. No.

She looked up. Defensive. Defiant. *Anxious?*

And he felt like he was being unfair.

And he was *never* unfair.

No wonder she made him so mad. She was changing his entire personality, and not for the better.

After a long, staring moment Ella turned back to Kiri. 'I'll see you a little later, Kiri. Okay?' And then she walked slowly away.

Kiri blinked at his father sleepily, then smiled. 'Where's Ella gone?'

'Back to her hospital. They need her there now. And you've got me.'

Kiri nodded.

He was out of danger, but he looked so tired. 'Are you okay, Kiri? What do you need?'

'Nothing. My head was hurting. And my tummy. And my legs. But Ella fixed me.'

'That's good. But I'm here now.'

'And I was hot. Ella cooled me down.'

'How did she do that?'

'With water and a towel.'

'I can do that for you, sport.'

'I'm not hot any more.' Kiri closed his eyes for a long moment, then blinked them open again and held out his skinny forearm, showing off the small sticking plaster. 'Look,' he said.

'You were on a drip, I know.'

'Superhero juice, Ella said.'

'To get you better.'

A few minutes more passed. 'Dad?'

'What is it, sport?'

'Where's Ella?'

Aaron bit back a sigh. 'She has a lot of people to look after. I'm back now. And Mum will be coming soon.'

'Mum's coming?'

'Yes, she'll be here soon.'

Kiri's eyes drifted shut.

The elation at knowing Kiri was out of danger was still with him. Even the prospect of calling Rebecca again to reinforce his demand that she get her butt on a plane didn't daunt him—although he hoped that, this time, Rebecca wouldn't be off her face.

Of course, breaking the other news to her—that he and Kiri would be heading to LA for his audition after Kiri's convalescence, and then straight on to London—might set off a whole new word of pain. He knew Rebecca was going to hate the confirmation that Aaron had landed both the audition and a plum role in Brand's film, because she resented every bit of career success that came his way.

He suspected she would try to guilt him into leaving Kiri in Sydney with her, just to punish him—for Kiri's illness and for the role in Brand's film—but that wasn't going to happen. Until Rebecca got herself clean, where he went, Kiri went.

So he would call Rebecca, get her travel arrangements under way so she could spend time with Kiri while he got his strength back, and tell her that London was all systems go.

Then he would have only two things to worry about: Kiri's convalescence; and figuring out how to forget Ella Reynolds and the way she had looked at his son.

Rebecca wasn't coming.

It was a shock that she would forego spending time with Kiri, knowing she wouldn't see him for months.

Aaron was trying to find the right words to say to Kiri and had been tiptoeing around the subject for a while.

The last thing he needed was Ella breezing in—triggering that aggravating, inexplicable and entirely inappropriate sense of relief.

Not that she spared Aaron as much as a look.

'You don't need to tell me how you are today,' she said to Kiri, leaning down to kiss his forehead. 'Because you look like a superhero. I guess you ate your dinner last night! And are you weeing? Oops—am I allowed to say that in front of Dad?'

Kiri giggled, and said, 'Yes,' and Ella gave his son that blinding smile that was so gut-churningly amazing.

She looked beautiful. Wearing a plain, white cotton dress and flat leather tie-up sandals, toting an oversized canvas bag—nothing special about any of it. But she was so…lovely.

She presented Kiri with a delicately carved wooden dragonfly she'd bought for him at the local market and showed him how to balance it on a fingertip.

Then Kiri asked her about the chicken game she'd told him about on a previous visit.

'Ah—you mean Chab Kon Kleng. Okay. Well they start by picking the strongest one—that would be you, Kiri—to be the hen.'

'But I'm a boy.'

'The rooster, then. And you're like your dad—you're going to defend your kids. And all your little chickens are hiding behind you, and the person who is the crow has to try and catch them, while everyone sings a special song. And, no, I'm not singing it. I'm a terrible singer, and my Khmer is not so good.'

'You asked me something about *ch'heu*. That's Khmer.'

'Yes—I was asking if you were in pain and forgot you were a little Aussie boy.'

'I'm Cambodian too.'

'Yes, you are. Lucky you,' Ella said softly.

Aaron was intrigued at this side of Ella. Sweet, animated, fun.

She glanced at him—finally—and he was surprised to see a faint blush creep into her cheeks.

She grabbed the chart from the end of Kiri's bed, scanning quickly. 'You will be out of here in no time if you keep this up.' Another one of those smiles. 'Anyway, I just wanted to call in and say hello today, but I'll stay longer next time.'

'Next time,' Kiri piped up, 'you'll see Mum. She's coming.'

'Hey—that's great,' she replied.

Aaron sucked in a quick, silent breath. Okay, this was the moment to tell Kiri that Rebecca wasn't coming, and to tell Ella that she wasn't welcome. 'Er...' *Brilliant start.*

Two pairs of eyes focused on him. Curious. Waiting.

Aaron perched on the side of Kiri's bed. 'Mate,' he said, 'I'm afraid Mum still can't leave home, so we're going to have to do without her.'

Kiri stared at him, taking in the news in his calm way.

'But she knows you're almost better, and so you'll forgive her,' Aaron continued. 'And I have to give you a kiss and hug from her—yuckerama.'

Kiri giggled then. 'You always kiss and hug me.'

'Then I guess I can squeeze in an extra when nobody's looking.'

'Okay.'

'Right,' Ella said cheerily. 'You'd better get yourself out of here, young man, so you can get home to Mom. You know what that means—eat, drink, do what the doctor tells you. Now, I'm sure you and Dad have lots to plan so I'll see you later.'

That smile at Kiri.

The usual smile—the one minus the eye glow—for him.

And she was gone before Aaron could gather his thoughts.

See you later? No, she would *not*.

With a quick 'Back soon' to Kiri, Aaron ran after her.

'Ella, wait.'

Ella stopped, stiffened, turned.

'Can we grab a coffee?'

Ella thought about saying no. She didn't want to feel that uncomfortable mix of guilt and attraction he seemed to bring out in her. But a 'no' would be an admission that he had some kind of power over her, and that would never do. So she nodded and walked beside him to the hospital café, and sat in silence until their coffee was on the table in front of them.

'I wanted to explain. About Rebecca.' He was stirring one sugar into his coffee about ten times longer than he needed to.

'No need,' she said.

'It's just she had an audition, and because Kiri was out of danger...'

She nodded. 'And he'd probably be ready to go home by the time she arrived anyway...'

Aaron looked morosely at the contents in his cup, and Ella felt an unwelcome stab of sympathy.

'Actually, the audition wasn't the main issue,' he said. 'I know the director. He would have held off for her.'

Ella waited while he gave his coffee another unnecessary stir.

'Has Tina told you about Rebecca?' he asked, looking across at her.

'Told me what?'

'About her drug problem?'

'Ah. No. I didn't know. I'm sorry.' That explained the not-really-divorced divorce; Sir Galahad wasn't the type to cut and run in an untenable situation.

'Things are...complicated,' he said. 'Very.'

'I'm sure.'

'It doesn't mean Rebecca isn't anxious about Kiri. I mean, she's his mother, and she loves him.'

'I understand. But he should recover quickly now. At this stage—the recovery phase—all those fluids that leaked out of his capillaries are simply being reabsorbed by his body. Like a wave—flooding, receding, balancing. But he'll be tired for a while. And there may be a rash. Red and itchy, with white centres. Don't freak out about it. Okay?'

Silence. Another stir of the coffee.

'Are you going to drink that, or are you just going to stir it to death?' Ella asked, and then it hit her: this was not really about Rebecca. 'Or…do you want to just tell me what this all has to do with me?'

Aaron looked at her. Kind of determined and apologetic at the same time. 'It's just…he's very attached to you. *Too* attached to you. I don't know how, in such a short time, but he is.'

'It's an occupational hazard for doctors and nurses.'

'No, Ella. It's you. And that makes things more complicated, given he won't be seeing you again once we leave the hospital. I—I don't want him to miss you.'

'Ahhh,' she said, and pushed her cup away. 'I see. Things are complicated, and he already has a mother, so stay away, Ella.'

'It's just the flip side of what you said to me—that you don't like saying goodbye to a child when a relationship goes south.'

'We don't have a relationship. And the fact you're a father didn't seem to bother you when you were kissing me, as long as we weren't *in* a "relationship".'

'Don't be naïve, Ella. It's one thing for us to have sex. It's another when there are two of us sitting together at my son's bedside.'

The hurt took her by surprise. 'So let me get this straight—you're happy to sleep with me, but you don't want me anywhere near your son?'

'We haven't slept together.'

'That's right—we haven't. And calm yourself, we won't. But the principle is still there: it would be *okay* for you to have sex with me, but because you *want* to have sex with me, it's *not* okay for me to be anywhere near your son. And don't throw back at me what I said about not wanting to get mixed up with a man with a kid—which would be my problem to deal with, not yours. Or tell me it's to protect him from the pain of missing me either. Because this is about *you*. This is because *you're* not comfortable around me. I'd go so far as to say you disapprove of me.'

'I don't know what to think of you.' He dragged a hand through his hair. 'One minute you're letting a drunk guy in a bar paw you and the next you're hovering like a guardian angel over sick kids. One minute you're a sarcastic pain in the butt, and the next you're crying like your heart's breaking. Do I approve of you? I don't even know. It's too hard to know you, Ella. Too hard.'

'And you're a saint by comparison, are you? No little flaws or contradictions in your character? So how do you explain your attraction to someone like me?'

'I don't explain it. I can't. That's the problem.' He stopped, closed his eyes for a fraught moment. 'Look, I've got Rebecca to worry about. And Kiri to shield from all that's going on with her. That's why I told you I couldn't develop a relationship with you. To make it cl—'

'I told *you* I didn't want one. Or are you too arrogant to believe that?'

'Wake up, Ella. If Kiri has developed an affection for you, that means we're *in* a relationship. Which would be fine if I didn't—'

'Oh, shut up and stir your coffee! This is no grand passion we're having.' Ella was almost throbbing with rage, made worse by having to keep her voice low. A nice yelling match would have suited her right now but you didn't yell at people in Cambodia.

She leaned across the table. 'Understand this: I'm not interested in you. I'm not here, after having worked a very long day, to see you. I'm here to see Kiri, who was in this hospital parentless. No father. No mother. Just a nanny. And me. Holding his hand while they drew his blood for tests. Coaxing him to drink. Trying to calm him when he vomited, when his stomach was hurting and there was no relief for the pain. Knowing his head was splitting and that paracetamol couldn't help enough. So scared he'd start bleeding that I was beside myself because what the hell were we going to do if he needed a transfusion and you weren't here? How dare you tell me after that to stay away from him, like I'm out to seduce you and spoil your peace and wreck your family?'

She could feel the tears ready to burst, and dashed a hand across her eyes.

He opened his mouth.

'Just shut *up*,' she said furiously. 'You know, I'm not overly modest about my assets, but I somehow think a fine upstanding man like you could resist making mad passionate love to a bottom feeder like me in front of Kiri, so I suggest you just get over yourself and stop projecting.'

'Projecting?'

'Yes—your guilty feelings on me! I have enough guilt of my own to contend with without you adding a chunky piece of antique furniture to the bonfire. It's not my fault your wife is a drug addict. It's not my fault you got a divorce. It's not my fault your son got dengue fever. It's not my fault you find me attractive, or a distraction, or whatever. I am not the cause or the catalyst or the star of your documentary, and I didn't ask you to lurk around hospital corners, watching me.'

She stood, pushing her chair back violently. 'I'm no saint, but I'm not a monster either.'

She headed for the door at a cracking pace, Aaron scrambling to catch up with her.

He didn't reach her until she was outside, around the corner from the hospital entrance.

'Wait just a minute,' he said, and spun her to face him.

'This conversation is over. Leave me *alone*,' she said, and jerked free, turned to walk off.

His hand shot out, grabbed her arm, spun her back. 'Oh, no, you don't,' he said, and looked as furious as she felt. 'You are not running off and pretending I'm the only one with a problem. Go on, lie to me—tell me you don't want me to touch you.'

He wrenched her up onto her toes and smacked her into his chest. Looked at her for one fierce, burning moment, and then kissed her as though he couldn't help himself.

In a desperate kind of scramble, her back ended up against the wall and he was plastered against her. He took her face between his hands, kissed her, long and hard. 'Ella,' he whispered against her lips. 'Ella. I know it's insane but when you're near me I can't help myself. Can't.'

Ella was tugging his shirt from his jeans, her hands sliding up his chest. 'Just touch me. Touch me!'

His thighs nudged hers apart and he was there, hard against her. She strained against him, ready, so ready, so—

Phone. Ringing. His.

They pulled apart, breathing hard. Looked at each other.

Aaron wrenched the phone from his pocket. Rebecca.

The phone rang. Rang. Rang. Rang. Stopped.

And still Ella and Aaron stared at each other.

Ella swallowed. 'No matter what you think of me—or what I think of myself right now, which isn't much—I don't want to make things difficult. For you, for Kiri. Or for me.' She smoothed her hands down her dress, making sure everything was in order. 'So you win. I'll stay away.'

'Maybe there's another way to—'

Ella cut him off. 'No. We've both got enough drama in our lives without making a fleeting attraction into a Shakespearean tragedy. I just…' Pause. Another swallow.

'I don't want him to think I don't care about him. Because he might think that, when I don't come back.'

Aaron pushed a lock of her hair behind her ear. It was a gentle gesture that had her ducking away. 'That's not helping,' she said.

'Don't think I don't know how lucky I am to have had you watching over Kiri. He knows and I know that you care about him. And I know how much, after Sann—'

'Don't you dare,' she hissed. 'I should never have told you. I regret it more than I can say. So we'll make a deal, shall we? I'll stay away and you don't ever, *ever* mention Sann again, not to anyone. I don't need or want you to feel sorry for me. I don't need or want *you*. So let's focus on a win-win. You go home. I'll go…wherever. And we'll forget we ever met.'

Ella walked away, but it was harder than it had ever been to slow her steps.

The sooner Aaron James was back in Sydney the better.

She was putting Sydney at number three thousand and one on her list of holiday destinations—right after Afghanistan.

CHAPTER SEVEN

'ELLA!'

Tina was staring at her. Surprised, delighted. 'Oh, come in. Come in! I'm so glad you're here. I was wondering when you'd use that ticket. Brand,' she called over her shoulder.

Ella cast appreciative eyes over the grand tiled entrance hall of her sister's Georgian townhouse. 'Nice one, Mrs. McIntyre,' she said.

Tina laughed. 'Yes, "nice".'

'So I'm thinking space isn't a problem.'

'We have *oodles* of it. In fact, we have other g—. Oh, here's Brand. Brand, Ella's here.'

'Yes, so I see. Welcome,' Brand said, pulling Tina backwards against his chest and circling her with his arms.

Ella looked at Brand's possessive hands on Tina's swollen belly. In about a month she would be an aunt. She was happy for her sister, happy she'd found such profound love. But looking at this burgeoning family made her heart ache with the memory of what she'd lost, what she might never have.

Not that Ella remembered the love between her and Javier being the deep, absorbing glow that Tina and Brand shared. It had been giddier. A rush of feeling captured in a handful of memories. That first dazzling sight of him outside a makeshift hospital tent in Somalia. Their first tentative kiss. The sticky clumsiness of the first and only time they'd made love—the night before the malaria had hit her; two nights before he was taken.

Would it have grown into the special bond Tina and Brand had? Or burned itself out?

Standing in this hallway, she had never felt so unsure, so…empty. And so envious she was ashamed of herself. Maybe it had been a mistake to come. 'If you'll show me where to dump my stuff, I'll get out of your hair for a couple of hours.'

Tina looked dismayed. 'But I *want* you in my hair.'

'I'm catching up with someone.'

'Who? And where?'

Ella raised her eyebrows.

Tina made an exasperated sound. 'Oh, don't get all frosty.'

Ella rolled her eyes. 'She's a nurse, living in Hammersmith. We're meeting at a pub called the Hare and something. Harp? Carp? Does it matter? Can I go? Please, please, pretty please?'

Tina disentangled herself from her laughing husband's arms. 'All right, you two, give it a rest,' she said. 'Brand— show Ella her room. Then, Ella, go ahead and run away. But I don't expect to have to ambush you every time I want to talk to you.'

Ella kissed Tina's cheek. 'I promise to bore you rigid with tales of saline drips and bandage supplies and oxygen masks. By the time I get to the bedpan stories, you'll be begging me to go out.'

London in summer, what was there not to like? Aaron thought as he bounded up the stairs to Brand's house with Kiri on his back.

He went in search of Brand and Tina and found them in the kitchen, sitting at the table they used for informal family dining.

'Good news! We've found an apartment to rent,' he announced, swinging Kiri down to the floor.

Tina swooped on Kiri to kiss and tickle him, then settled him on the chair beside her with a glass of milk and a cookie. She bent an unhappy look on her husband. 'Why do all our house guests want to run away the minute they step foot in the place?'

'We've been underfoot for two weeks!' Aaron protested. 'And we're only moving down the street.'

'It's her sister,' Brand explained. 'Ella arrived today, stayed just long enough to drop her bag and ran off to some ill-named pub. Princess Tina is *not* amused.'

Aaron's heart stopped—at least that's what it felt like—and then jump-started violently. He imagined himself pale with shock, his eyes bugging out. He felt his hair follicles tingle. What had they said while he'd been sitting there stunned? What had he missed? He forced himself to take a breath, clear his mind, concentrate. Because the only coalescing thought in his head was that she was here. In London. In this house.

He'd thought he would never see her again. Hadn't wanted to see her again.

But she was here.

'...when we weren't really expecting her,' Tina said.

Huh? What? What had he missed while his brain had turned to mush?

'You know what she's like,' Brand said.

What? What's she like? Aaron demanded silently.

'What do you mean, what she's like?' Tina asked, sounding affronted.

Bless you, Tina.

'Independent. Very,' Brand supplied. 'She's used to looking after herself. And she's been in scarier places. Somehow I think she'll make it home tonight just fine.'

'Yes, but what time? And she hasn't even told me how long she's staying. Mum and Dad are going to want a report. How can I get the goss if she runs away when she should be talking to me?'

Brand gave her a warning look. 'If you fuss, she *will* go.' He turned to Aaron, changing the subject. 'So, Aaron, when do you move in?'

'A week,' Aaron said, racking his brain for a way to get the conversation casually back to Ella. 'Is that all right? I mean, if your sister is here...' he looked back at Tina '...maybe Kiri and I should leave earlier.' He'd lost it, obviously, because as the words left his mouth he wanted to recall them. 'We can easily move to a hotel.' Nope. That wasn't working for him either.

He caught himself rubbing his chest, over his heart. Realised it wasn't the first time he'd thought of Ella and done that.

'No way—you're not going any earlier than you have to,' Tina said immediately, and Aaron did the mental equivalent of swooning with relief.

And that really hit home.

The problem wasn't that he didn't want to see Ella—it was that he did.

On his third trip downstairs that night, Aaron faced the fact that he was hovering. He hadn't really come down for a glass of water. Or a book. Or a midnight snack.

Barefoot, rumpled, and edgy, he had come down looking for Ella.

On his fourth trip he gave up any pretence and took a seat in the room that opened off the dimly lit hall—a library-cum-family room. From there he could hear the front door open and yet be hidden. He turned on only one lamp; she wouldn't even know he was there, if he chose the sensible option and stayed hidden when the moment came.

He was, quite simply, beside himself.

Aaron helped himself to a Scotch, neat, while he waited.

His blood pressure must have been skyrocketing, because his heart had been thumping away at double speed all day.

And he had *excellent* blood pressure that *never* skyrocketed.

He knew precisely how long he'd been waiting—an hour and thirteen minutes—when he heard it.

Key hitting the lock. Lock clicking. Door opening.

A step on the tiled floor. He took a deep breath. Tried—failed—to steady his nerves. Heard the door close. Then nothing. No footsteps. A long moment passed. And then another sound. Something slumping against the wall or the door or the floor.

Was she hurt? Had she fallen?

Another sound. A sort of hiccup that wasn't a hiccup. A hitched breath.

He got to his feet and walked slowly to the door. Pushed it open silently. How had he ever thought he might sit in here and *not* go to her? And then he saw her and almost gasped! He was so monumentally unprepared for the punch of lust that hit him as he peered out like a thief.

She was sitting on the floor. Back against the door, knees up with elbows on them, hands jammed against her mouth. He could have sworn she was crying but there were no tears.

He saw the complete stillness that came into her as she realised someone was there.

And then she looked up.

CHAPTER EIGHT

AARON WALKED SLOWLY towards Ella. She was wearing a dark green skirt that had fallen up her thighs. A crumpled white top with a drawstring neckline. Leather slide-on sandals. Her hair was in loose waves, long, hanging over her shoulders—he'd never seen it loose before.

He felt a tense throb of some emotion he couldn't name, didn't want to name, as he reached her. He stood looking down at her, dry-mouthed. 'Where have you been?' he asked.

'Why are you here?' she countered, the remembered huskiness of her voice scattering his thoughts for a moment.

The way her skirt was draping at the top of her thighs was driving him insane. *Concentrate.* 'Here? I've been staying here. I'm working here. In London, I mean. Brand's film.' He couldn't even swallow. 'Didn't they tell you?'

'No,' Ella said, sighing, and easily, gracefully, got to her feet. 'Well, that's just great. I guess you're going to expect me to move out now, so I don't corrupt Kiri—or you.'

'No. I don't want you to move out. We'll be leaving in a week, anyway.'

'Oh, that makes me feel *so* much better. I'm sure I can avoid doing anything too immoral for one lousy week.'

Her silky skirt had settled back where it was supposed to be. It was short, so he could still see too much of her thighs. He jerked his gaze upwards and it collided with her breasts. He could make out the lace of her bra, some indistinguishable pale colour, under the white cotton of her top.

His skin had started to tighten and tingle, so he forced his eyes upwards again. Jammed his hands in his pockets as he caught the amused patience in her purple eyes.

'Why are you waiting up for me?' she asked.

He had no answer.

She sighed again—an exaggerated, world-weary sigh. 'What do you want, Aaron?'

'I want you,' he said. He couldn't quite believe he'd said it after everything that had gone on between them, but once it was out it seemed so easy. So clear. As though he hadn't spent agonising weeks telling himself she was the *last* thing he needed in his life and he'd been right to put the brakes on in Cambodia. 'I haven't stopped wanting you. Not for a second.'

Her eyebrows arched upwards. Even her eyebrows were sexy.

'I think we've been through this already, haven't we?' she asked softly, and started to move past him. 'One week— I'm sure you can resist me for that long, Sir Galahad.'

His hand shot out. He saw it move, faster than his brain was working. Watched his fingers grip her upper arm.

She turned to face him.

He didn't know what he intended to do next—but at least she wasn't looking amused any more.

She looked hard at him for a moment. And then she took his face between her hands and kissed him, fusing her mouth to his with forceful passion. She finished the kiss with one long lick against his mouth. Pulled back a tiny fraction, then seemed to change her mind and kissed him again. Pulled back. Stepped back. Looked him in the eye.

'Now what?' she asked, her breathing unsteady but her voice controlled. 'This is where you run away, isn't it? Because of Rebecca. Or Kiri. Or just because it's me.'

That strange other being still had control of him. It

was the only explanation for the way he jerked her close, crushed his arms around her and kissed her. He broke the contact only for a second at a time. To breathe. He wished he didn't even have to stop for that. His hands were everywhere, couldn't settle. In her hair, on her back, gripping her bottom, running up her sides. And through it all he couldn't seem to stop kissing her.

He could hear her breathing labouring, like his. When his hands reached her breasts, felt the nipples jutting into his palms through two layers of clothing, he shuddered. He finally stopped kissing her, but kept his mouth on hers, still, reaching for control. 'Now what?' He repeated her question without moving his mouth from hers, after a brief struggle to remember what she'd asked. Kissed her again.

Ella wrapped her arms around his waist and he groaned. He looked down into her face. 'There doesn't seem to be much point in running away, because you're always there. So now, Ella, I get to have you.'

One long, fraught moment of limbo.

He didn't know what he'd do if she said no, he was so on fire for her.

But she didn't say no. She said, 'Okay. Let's be stupid, then, and get it done.'

Not exactly a passionate acquiescence, but he'd take it. Take her, any way he could get her.

He kissed her again, pulling her close, letting her feel how hard he was for her, wanting her to know. Both of his hands slipped into her hair. It was heavy, silky. Another time he would like to stroke his fingers through it, but not now. Now he was too desperate. He dragged fistfuls of it, using it to tilt her head back, anchoring her so he could kiss her harder still. 'Come upstairs,' he breathed against her mouth. 'Come with me.'

'All yours,' Ella said in that mocking way she had— but Aaron didn't care. He grabbed her hand and walked quickly to the staircase, pulling her up it at a furious pace.

'Which way to your room?' he asked.

Silently, she guided him to it.

The room next to his.

Fate.

The moment they were inside he was yanking her top up and over her head, fumbling with her skirt until it lay pool-like at her feet. The bedside lamp was on and he said a silent prayer of thanks because it meant he could see her. She stood before him in pale pink underwear so worn it was almost transparent, tossing her hair back over her shoulders. He swallowed. He wanted to rip her underwear to shreds to get to her. It was like a madness. Blood pounding through his veins, he stripped off his T-shirt and shoved his jeans and underwear off roughly.

She was watching him, following what he was doing as she kicked off her sandals. Aaron forced himself to stand still and let her see him. He hoped she liked what she saw.

Ella came towards him and circled his biceps with her hands—at least, partly; his biceps were too big for her to reach even halfway around. Aaron remembered that she liked tattoos. His tattooed armbands were broad and dark and intricately patterned—and, yes, she clearly did like what she saw. The tattoos had taken painful hours to complete and, watching her eyes light up as she touched them, he'd never been happier to have them. He hoped during the night she would see the more impressive tattoo on his back, but he couldn't imagine taking his eyes off her long enough to turn around.

He couldn't wait any longer to see her naked. He reached for her hips, and she obligingly released his arms and stepped closer. She let him push her panties down, stepped free of them when they hit the floor. Then she let him work the back fastening of her bra as she rested against him, compliant. As he wrestled with the bra, he could feel her against him, thigh to thigh, hip to hip. The tangle of soft hair against his erection had his heart bashing so hard and fast in his chest he thought he might have a coronary. Oh, he liked the feel of it. She was perfect. Natural and perfect. His hands were shaking so badly as he tried to undo her bra he thought he was going to have to tear it off, but it gave at last. Her breasts, the areoles swollen, nipples sharply erect, pressed into his chest as he wrenched the bra off. He was scared to look at her in case he couldn't stop himself falling on her like a ravening beast...but at the same time he was desperate to see her.

'Ella,' he said, his voice rough as he stepped back just enough to look. With one hand he touched her face. The other moved lower to the dark blonde hair at the apex of her thighs. He combed through it with trembling fingers. Lush and beautiful. He could feel the moisture seeping into it. Longed to taste it. Taste her. He dropped to his knees, kissed her there.

Aaron loved the hitch in her voice as his fingers and tongue continued to explore. 'I do want you, Aaron. Just so you know. Tonight, I do want you,' Ella said, and it was like a flare went off in his head. He got to his feet, dragged her into his arms, holding her close while his mouth dived on hers. He moved the few steps that would enable him to tumble her backwards onto the bed and come down on her.

The moment they hit the bed he had his hands on her thighs and was pushing her legs apart.

'Wait,' she said in his ear. 'Condoms. Bedside table. In the drawer.'

Somehow, Aaron managed to keep kissing her as he fumbled with the drawer, pulled it open and reached inside. His fingers mercifully closed on one quickly—thankfully they were loose in there.

He kissed her once more, long and luscious, before breaking to free the condom from its packaging. Kneeling between her thighs, he smoothed it on, and Ella raised herself on her elbows to watch. She looked irresistibly wicked, and as he finished the job he leaned forward to take one of her nipples in his mouth. She arched forward and gasped and he decided penetration could wait. She tasted divine. Exquisite. The texture of her was maddeningly good, the feel of her breasts as he held them in his hands heavy and firm. He could keep his mouth on her for hours, he thought, just to hear the sounds coming from her as his tongue circled, licked.

But Ella was shifting urgently beneath him, trying to position him with hands and thighs and the rest of her shuddering body. 'Inside,' she said, gasping. 'Come inside me. Now.'

With one thrust he buried himself in her, and then he couldn't seem to help himself. He pulled back and thrust deeply into her again. And again and again. He was kissing her mouth, her eyes, her neck as he drove into her over and over. The sound of her gasping cries urged him on until he felt her clench around him. She sucked in a breath, whooshed it out. Again. Once more. She was coming, tense and beautiful around him, and he'd never been so turned on in his life. He slid his arms under her on the bed, dragged her up against him and thrust his tongue inside her mouth. And with one last, hard push of his hips he came, hard and strong.

As the last waves of his climax receded, the fog of pure lust cleared from Aaron's head and he was suddenly and completely appalled.

Had he hurt her? Something primal had overtaken him, and he hadn't felt in control of himself. And he was *never, ever* out of control.

He kissed her, trying for gentleness but seemingly unable to achieve it even now, because the moment his mouth touched hers he was out of control again.

Aaron couldn't seem to steady his breathing. It was somehow beautiful to Ella to know that.

He sure liked kissing. Even now, after he'd exhausted

both of them and could reasonably be expected to roll over and go to sleep, he was kissing her. In between those unsteady breaths of his. He seemed to have an obsession with her mouth. Nobody had ever kissed her quite like this before. It was sweet, and sexy as hell, to be kissed like he couldn't stop. It was getting her aroused again. She'd sneered at herself as she'd put those condoms in the drawer, but now all she could think was: did she have enough?

He shifted at last, rolling onto his back beside her. 'Sorry, I know I'm heavy. And you're so slender,' he said.

'It's just the—' She stopped. How did you describe quickly the way long hours, fatigue and illness sapped the calories out of you at breakneck speed? 'Nothing, really. I'm already gaining weight. It happens fast when I'm not working.'

'So you can lose it all over again the next time,' Aaron said, and Ella realised she didn't have to explain after all.

His eyes closed as he reached for her hand.

Okay, so now he'll go to sleep, Ella thought, and was annoyed with herself for bringing him to her room. If they'd gone to his room she could have left whenever she wanted; but what did a woman say, do, to get a man to leave?

But Aaron, far from showing any signs of sleep, brought her hand to his mouth and rolled onto his side, facing her. He released her hand but then pulled her close so that her side was fitted against his front, and nuzzled his nose into the side of her neck. He slid one of his hands down over her belly and between her legs. 'Did I hurt you, Ella?'

Huh? 'Hurt me?'

'Yes. I was rough. I'm sorry.'

As he spoke his fingers were slipping gently against the delicate folds of her sex. It was like he was trying to soothe her. Her heart stumbled, just a little, as she realised what he was doing. And he was looking at her so seriously while he did it. He had the most remarkably beautiful eyes. And, of course, he was ridiculously well endowed, but she'd been so hot and ready for him it hadn't hurt. It had been more erotic than anything she could have dreamed.

How did she tell him that his fingers, now, weren't soothing? That what he was doing to her was gloriously *good*, but not soothing?

'No, Aaron, you— Ah…' She had to pause for a moment as the touch of his fingers became almost unbearable. 'I mean, no. I mean, you didn't hurt me.' She paused again. 'Aaron,' she said, almost breathless with desire, 'I suggest you go and get rid of that condom. And then hurry back and get another one.'

He frowned, understanding but wary. 'You're sure? I mean— Oh,' as her hands found him. 'I guess you're sure.' He swung his legs off the side of the bed and was about to stand but Ella, on her knees in an instant, embraced him from behind. Her mouth touched between his shoulder blades then he felt her tongue trace the pattern of the dragon inked across his back.

'I don't want to leave you,' he said huskily. 'Come with me.'

Ella, needing no second invitation, was out of the bed and heading for the en suite bathroom half a step behind him.

Ella trailed the fingers of one hand along his spine and snapped on the light with the fingers of her other. 'Oh, my, it's even better in the full light.'

Aaron discarded the condom and started to turn around. She imagined he thought he was going to take her in his arms.

'No, you don't. It's my turn,' Ella said.

She turned on the shower, drew Aaron in beside her, and as he reached for her again she shook her head, laughing, and dodged out of the way. 'I'm glad this is such a small shower cubicle,' she said throatily. 'Close. Tight.' She spun Aaron roughly to face the tiled wall, slammed him up against it and grabbed the cake of soap from its holder.

Lathering her hands, his skin, she plastered herself against his back, moving her breasts sensually against his beautiful tattoo as she reached around to fondle him. 'I love the size of you,' she said, as his already impressive erection grew in her hands. 'I want to take you like this, from behind.'

'I think I'd take you any way I could get you,' Aaron said, groaning as she moved her hands between his legs. He was almost panting and Ella had never felt so beautiful, so powerful.

At last.

She could have this, at last.

As her hands slid, slipped, squeezed, Aaron rested his forehead against the shower wall and submitted.

Aaron watched as Ella slept. She'd fallen into sleep like a stone into the ocean.

No wonder. Aaron had been all over her from the moment they'd left the shower. Inexhaustible. He didn't think he'd understood the word lust until tonight. If he could have breathed her into his lungs, he would have.

He didn't know why he wanted her so badly. But even having had her three times, he couldn't get her close enough. She was in his blood. What a pathetic cliché. But true.

The bedside light was still on, so he could see her face. She looked serious in her sleep. Fretful. Aaron pulled her closer, kissed one of her wickedly arched eyebrows. He breathed in the scent of her hair. Looking at her was almost painful. The outrageous loveliness of her.

Sighing, he turned off the bedside light. It was past five in the morning and he should go back to his room, but he wanted to hold her.

He thought about their last meeting, in Cambodia. The horrible things they'd said to each other. They'd made a pact to forget they'd ever met. How had they gone from that to being here in bed now?

What had he been thinking when he'd left the library, when he'd seen her slumped against the front door with her fists jammed against her mouth?

On a mundane level, he'd thought she must have been drinking. Or maybe he'd hoped that, so he could pigeon-hole her back where he'd wanted to.

Oh, he had no doubt she regularly drank to excess—it fitted with the general wildness he sensed in her. But to-night she'd smelled only like that tantalising perfume. And her mouth had tasted like lime, not booze. It was obvious, really, when he pieced together what he knew about her, what he'd seen of her: she wouldn't let Tina see her out of control. She would be sober and serene and together in this house. The way her family expected her to be. The way she'd been described to him before he'd ever met her.

He thought about the day he'd held her as she'd cried over Bourey's death. And the other boy, Sann, whose death had been infinitely painful for her. Things she didn't want anyone to know.

She was so alone. She chose to be, so her fears and sorrows wouldn't hurt anyone else.

Aaron pulled her closer. She roused, smiled sleepily at him. 'You should go,' she said, but then she settled her-self against him and closed her eyes, so he stayed exactly where he was.

Wondering how he could both have her and keep things simple.

CHAPTER NINE

ELLA ROLLED RESTLESSLY, absent-mindedly pulling Aaron's pillow close and breathing in the scent of him, wondering what time he'd left.

She didn't know what had come over her. She'd finally managed to get past second base—way past it, with a blistering home run. And it had been with her brother-in-law's friend under her sister's roof. Not that there had seemed to be much choice about it. It had felt like…well, like fate.

And Aaron wouldn't tell, she reassured herself.

She got out of bed, reached for her robe, and then just sat on the edge of the bed with the robe in her lap. She didn't want to go downstairs. Because downstairs meant reality. It meant Tina and Brand. And Aaron—not Lover Aaron but Friend-of-her-sister Aaron. Daddy Aaron.

She stood slowly and winced a little. It had been a very active night. A fabulous night. But she would have been relieved even if it had been the worst sex of her life instead of the best. Because she had needed it.

Yesterday she'd forced herself to think about Sann. Tina's pregnancy was an immutable fact, and Ella knew she had to come to terms with it; she couldn't run away every time a pang of envy hit her. So she had deliberately taken the memories out of mothballs and examined them one by one. A kind of desensitisation therapy.

But forcing the memories had been difficult. So when

she'd come home to find Aaron there, sex with him had offered an escape. A talisman to keep her sad thoughts at bay, hopefully ward off the bad dreams.

She had been prepared to make a bargain with herself—sex and a nightmare-free night, in exchange for guilt and shame today.

And she did feel the guilt.

Just not the shame.

What did that mean?

Get it together, Ella. It was just a one-night stand. People do it all the time. Simple.

Except it was *not* simple. Because she hadn't managed it before. And she recalled—too vividly—Aaron walking towards her in the hallway, and how much she'd wanted him as their eyes had met. She was deluding herself if she thought she'd only been interested in a nightmare-free night. Oh, he had certainly materialised at a point when she'd been at her lowest ebb and open to temptation, but she had wanted him, wanted the spark, the flash of almost unbearable attraction that had been there in Cambodia.

But now what?

Nothing had really changed. All the reasons not to be together in Cambodia were still there. Kiri. Rebecca. Javier.

Definitely time to return to reality.

Ella tossed the robe aside and strode into the bathroom.

She looked at herself in the mirror. Her mouth looked swollen. Nothing she could do to hide that, except maybe dab a bit of foundation on it to minimise the rawness. She could see small bruises on her upper arms—easily covered. There were more bruises on her hips, but nobody would be seeing those. She sucked in a breath as more memories of the night filled her head. Aaron had been insatiable—and she had loved it. She had more than a few sore spots. And, no doubt, so did he. Like the teeth marks she'd left on his inner thigh.

Ella caught herself smiling. Aaron had called her a vampire, but he hadn't minded. He hadn't minded at all, if the passionate lovemaking that had followed had been any indication.

The smile slipped.

He would have come to his senses by now. Remembered that he didn't like her. Didn't want her near his son.

Time to store the memory and move on.

Tina checked the clock on the kitchen wall as Ella walked in. 'So lunch, not breakfast.'

'Oh, dear, am I going to have to punch a time clock whenever I come and go?'

'Oh, for heaven's sake!'

'Well, sorry, Tina, but really you're as bad as Mom. Just sit down and tell me stories about Brand as a doting father while I make us both something to eat.'

Ella forced herself to look at Tina's stomach as she edged past her sister. Bearable. She could do this.

Tina groaned as she levered herself onto a stool at the kitchen counter. 'I am so over the doting father thing. We've done the practice drive to the hospital seven times. And he's having food cravings. It's not funny, Ella!'

But Ella laughed anyway as she laid a variety of salad vegetables on a chopping board. 'Where is he now?'

'On the set, thank goodness. Which reminds me—I didn't tell you we have other guests.'

Ah. Control time. Ella busied herself pulling out drawers.

'What are you looking for?' Tina asked.

Ella kept her head down and pulled open another drawer. 'Knife.'

'Behind you, knife block on the counter,' Tina said, and Ella turned her back on her sister and took her time selecting a knife.

'Where was I?' Tina asked. 'Oh yes, Aaron. Aaron James and his son. You know them, of course.'

Indistinct mumble.

'Aaron is in Brand's movie,' Tina continued. 'That's why he's in London. They've been staying with us, but they're only here for another week.'

'Why's that?' Ella asked, desperately nonchalant, and started chopping as though her life depended on the precision of her knife action.

'Aaron was always intending to find a place of his own, and yesterday he did.'

'So...would it be easier if I moved out for the week? Because I have friends I was going to see and I—'

'What is wrong with you people? Everyone wants to move out. We've got enough room to house a baseball team! And, anyway, I need you to help me look after Kiri.'

Uh-oh. 'What? Why?'

'Kiri's nanny had some crisis and can't get here until next week. Aaron's due on set tomorrow so I volunteered. I told him it would be good practice. And Kiri is adorable.'

Ella's hand was a little unsteady so she put down the knife. Kiri. She would be looking after Kiri. Aaron wouldn't want that. 'But what about—? I mean, shouldn't he have stayed in Sydney? With his mother?' *Drugs, Ella, drugs.* 'Or—or...someone?'

Tina looked like she was weighing something up. 'The thing is—oh, I don't know if... Okay, look, this is completely confidential, Ella.'

Tina put up her hands at the look on Ella's face. 'Yes, I know you're a glued-shut clam. Aaron is just sensitive about it. Or Rebecca is, and he's respecting that. Rebecca is in rehab. Drugs. Apparently, she auditioned for a role in a new TV show while Aaron was in Cambodia, but didn't get it. The director told her if she didn't get things under control, she'd never work again.'

'That's...tough. How—how's Kiri coping with the separation?'

'Aaron does all the parenting, so it's not as big a deal as you'd think. He has sole custody. But that's not to say

Rebecca doesn't see Kiri whenever she wants. It's just that the drugs have been a problem for some time.'

'Oh. *Sole* custody. Huh.' Ella scooped the chopped salad vegetables into a large bowl. 'But should he...Aaron... should he be here while she's there?'

'Well, they *are* divorced, although sometimes I wonder if Rebecca really believes that. But in any case, it's not a case of him shirking responsibility. Aaron found the clinic—in California, while he was over there auditioning for a new crime show—because Rebecca wanted to do it away from her home city where it might have leaked to the press. And he got her settled in over there, which pushed back filming here so it's all over the place, but what can you do? And of course he's paying, despite having settled a fortune on her during the divorce. He'll be back and forth with Kiri, who thinks it's a spa! But there are strict rules about visiting. Anyway, I hope it works, because Aaron needs to move on, and he won't until Rebecca gets her act together.' She slanted an uncomfortably speculative look at Ella.

'Don't even!' Ella said, interpreting without difficulty.

'Come on, Ella. He's totally, completely hot.'

Ella concentrated on drizzling dressing over the salad.

'Hot as Hades,' Tina said, tightening the thumbscrews. 'But also sweet as heaven. He is amazingly gentle with Kiri. And with me, too. He took me for an ultrasound last week. I had a fall down the stairs and I was petrified.'

Ella hurried to her sister's side, hugged her. 'But everything's all right. You're fine, the baby's fine, right?'

'Yes, but Brand was filming, and I couldn't bring myself to call him. Because I'd already had one fall on the stairs, and he was furious because I was hurrying.'

'Well *stop* hurrying, Tina.' Tentatively, Ella reached and placed a hand on Tina's stomach. The baby kicked suddenly and Ella's hand jerked away—or would have, if Tina hadn't stopped it, flattened it where it was, kept it there.

Tina looked at her sister, wonder and joy in her eyes, and Ella felt her painful envy do a quantum shift.

'So anyway, Aaron,' Tina said. 'He was home. Actually, he saw it happen. I don't know which of us was more upset. He must have cajoled and threatened and who knows what else to get the ultrasound arranged so quickly. He knew it was the only way I'd believe everything was all right. And he let me talk him into not calling Brand until we got the all clear and I was back home.' Tina smiled broadly. 'Unbelievably brave! Brand exploded about being kept in the dark, as Aaron knew he would, but Aaron took it all in his stride. He just let Brand wear himself out, and then took him out for a beer.'

Ella tried not to be charmed, but there was something lovely about the story. 'Well I'm here now to take care of you,' she said, navigating the lump in her throat.

'And I'm very glad.' Tina took Ella's left hand and placed it alongside the right one that was already pressed to her stomach. 'It really scared me, Ella. But I'm not telling you all this to worry you—and don't, whatever you do, tell Mum and Dad.'

'I wouldn't dream of it.'

'I just wanted you to know. I mean, you're my sister! And a nurse. And...well, you're my sister. And I wanted to explain about Aaron. Don't disapprove of him because of Rebecca. He takes his responsibilities very seriously. He practically raised his three young sisters, you know, after his parents died, and he was only eighteen. They idolise him. So does Kiri. And so do I, now. He'll do the right thing by Rebecca, divorced or not, and—more importantly—the right thing by Kiri.'

Ella moved her hands as Tina reached past her to dig into the salad bowl and extract a sliver of carrot.

'You're going to need more than salad, Ella,' Tina said. 'You're like a twig.'

'Yes, yes, yes, I know.' Ella moved back into the food preparation area. 'I'll make some sandwiches.'

'Better make enough for Aaron and Kiri—they should be back any minute.'

For the barest moment Ella paused. Then she opened the fridge and rummaged inside it. 'Where are they?'

'The park. Aaron's teaching Kiri how to play cricket.'

'Ah,' Ella said meaninglessly, and started slapping various things between slices of bread like she was in a trance.

'Yeah, I think that's enough for the entire Australian and English cricket teams,' Tina said eventually.

'Oh. Sorry. Got carried away.'

Breathe, Ella ordered herself when she heard Aaron calling out to Tina from somewhere in the house as she was positioning the platter of sandwiches on the table.

'In the kitchen,' Tina called back.

Tina turned to Ella. 'And I guess you'll tell me later about last night. Probably not fit for children's ears, anyway.'

Ella froze, appalled. Tina *knew*?

'I mean, come on, your mouth,' Tina teased. 'Or are you going to tell me you got stung by a bee?'

'Who got stung by a bee?' Aaron asked, walking in.

CHAPTER TEN

'OH, NOBODY,' TINA said airily.

But Aaron wasn't looking at Tina. He was looking at Ella.

And from the heat in his eyes Ella figured he was remembering last night in Technicolor detail. Ella felt her pulse kick in response. *Insane.*

'Nice to see you again, Ella,' he said.

Could Tina hear that caress in his voice? Ella frowned fiercely at him.

He winked at her. Winked!

'Kiri can't wait to see you,' he continued. 'He's got a present for you—he's just getting it.'

'Oh, that's— Oh.' She gave up the effort of conversation. She was out of her depth. Shouldn't Aaron be keeping Kiri *away* from her? Ella wondered if Aaron had taken a cricket ball to the head. They were deadly, cricket balls.

Ella was aware a phone was ringing. She noted, dimly, Tina speaking. Sensed Tina leaving the room.

And then Aaron was beside her, taking her hand, lifting it to his mouth, kissing it. The back, the palm. His tongue on her fingers.

'Stop,' she whispered, but the air seemed to have been sucked out of the room and she wasn't really sure the word had left her mouth.

Aaron touched one finger to her swollen bottom lip.
'I'm sorry. Is it sore?'

Ella knocked his hand away. 'What's gotten into you?'

The next moment she found herself pulled into Aaron's
arms. 'I've got a solution,' he said, as though she would
have *any* idea what he was talking about! Yep, cricket ball
to the head.

'A solution for what?'

'You and me. It's based on the KISS principle.'

'The what?'

'KISS: keep it simple, stupid.'

'*Simple* would be to forget last night happened.'

Ella started to pull away, but he tightened his arms.

He rested his forehead on hers. 'Let me. Just for a moment.'

Somehow she found her arms around his waist, and she
was just standing there, letting him hold her as though it
were any everyday occurrence. *Uh-oh. Dangerous.*

'There's no solution needed for a one-night stand,' she
said.

He released her, stepped back. 'I don't want a one-night
stand.'

'Um—I think you're a little late to that party.'

'Why?'

'Because we've already had one.'

'So tonight will make it a two-night stand. And tomorrow night a three-night stand, and so on.'

'We agreed, in Cambodia—'

'Cambodia-shmodia.'

'Huh?'

'That was then. This is now.'

'Did you get hit in the head with a cricket ball?'

'What?'

'You're talking like you've got a head injury.'

'It's relief. It's making me light-headed. Because for the

first time since Tina and Brand's wedding I know what I'm doing.'

'Well, I don't know what you're doing. I don't think I want to know. I mean, the *KISS* principle?'

'I want you. You want me. We get to have each other. Simple.'

'Um, *not* simple. Kiri? Rebecca? The fact you don't like me? That you don't even know me?'

'Kiri and Rebecca—they're for me to worry about, not you.'

'You're wrong. Tina wants me to help her look after Kiri. Surely you don't want that? Aren't you scared I'll corrupt him or something?'

'Ella, if I know one thing, it's that you would never do anything to hurt Kiri. I've always known it. What I said, in Cambodia…' He shrugged. 'I was being a moron. Projecting, you called it, and you were right. There. I'm denouncing myself.'

'I don't want to play happy families.'

'Neither do I. That's why your relationship with Kiri is separate from my relationship with Kiri, which is separate from my relationship with you. And before you throw Rebecca at me—it's the same deal. You don't even have a relationship with her, so that's purely my issue, not yours.'

'You said the R word. I don't want a relationship—and neither do you.'

Aaron took her hand and lifted it so that it rested on his chest, over his heart. 'Our relationship is going to be purely sexual. Casual sex, that's what you said you wanted. All you were interested in. Well, I can do casual sex.'

'You're not a casual kind of guy, Aaron,' she said.

He smiled, shrugged. 'I'll *make* myself that kind of guy. I said last night I would take you any way I could get you. We're two adults seeking mutual satisfaction and nothing more. An emotion-free zone, which means we can keep it strictly between us—Tina and Brand don't need to know, it's none of Rebecca's business, and Kiri is…well, protected, because your relationship with him is nothing to do with your relationship with me. Simple. Agreed?'

Ella hesitated—not saying yes, but not the automatic 'no' she should be rapping out either. Before she could get her brain into gear, the kitchen door opened.

As Ella pulled her hand free from where, she'd just realised, it was still being held against Aaron's heart, Kiri ran in, saw her, stopped, ran again. Straight at her.

'Kiri, my darling,' she said, and picked him up.

She kissed his forehead. He hugged her, his arms tight around her neck, and didn't seem to want to let go. So she simply moved backwards, with him in her arms, until she felt a chair behind her legs and sat with him on her lap.

Kiri kissed her cheek and Ella's chest tightened dangerously. Kiri removed one arm from around Ella's neck and held out his hand to her. His fist was closed around something.

'What's this?' Ella asked.

Kiri opened his fingers to reveal an unremarkable rock. 'From the beach where you live,' he said. 'Monica.'

Ella smiled at him. 'You remembered?'

Kiri nodded and Ella hugged him close. Santa Monica. He'd been to Santa Monica, and remembered it was where she lived.

She felt a hand on her shoulder and looked up. Aaron was beside her, looking down at her, and she couldn't breathe.

The door opened and Tina breezed in. She paused—an infinitesimal pause—as she took in Aaron's hand on Ella's shoulder, Kiri on her lap.

Aaron slowly removed his hand, but stayed where he was.

'So,' Tina said brightly, 'let's eat.'

* * *

Lunch was dreadful.

Kiri was at least normal, chattering away about Cambodia, about Disneyland, about Sydney, completely at ease.

But Tina was giving off enough gobsmacked vibes to freak Ella out completely.

And Aaron was high-beaming Ella across the table as though he could get her on board with the force of his eyes alone—and if they were really going to carry on a secret affair, he'd have to find his poker face pretty damned fast.

If? Was she really going the 'if' route? Not the 'no way' route?

Casual sex.

Could she do it? She'd liked having someone close to her last night. She'd felt alive in a way she hadn't for such a long time. And she hadn't had the dreaded nightmares with Aaron beside her. So. A chance to feel alive again. With no strings attached. No emotions, which she couldn't offer him anyway.

But, ironic though it was, Aaron James seemed to have the ability to make her want to clean up her act. Maybe it was the way he was with Kiri, or that he cared so much about an ex-wife who clearly made his life a misery, or his general tendency to turn into Sir Galahad at regular intervals and save damsels in distress—his sisters, ex-wife, Tina, her.

Whatever the reason, if she wanted to rehabilitate her self-image, was an affair the way to start? Every time she'd let a guy pick her up, determined to do it, just do it and move on, she'd hated herself. Now that she'd gone the whole nine yards, wouldn't she end up hating herself even more? Especially if it became a regular arrangement?

'I'll clear up,' Tina said, when lunch couldn't be stretched out any more.

'Ella and I can manage,' Aaron said quickly.

'No, *Ella and I* can manage,' Tina insisted. She stood and arched her back, grimaced.

Ella got to her feet. 'You should rest,' she told her sister. 'And you…' with an almost fierce look at Aaron '…should get Kiri into bed for a nap. He's sleepy.' She started gathering empty plates.

Aaron looked like he was about to argue so Ella simply turned her back on him and took an armload of plates to the sink. She stayed there, clattering away, refusing to look up, willing him to leave.

And then, at last, Tina spoke. 'The coast is clear. You can come up for air.'

Ella raised her head cautiously and waited for the inevitable.

'What's going on?' Tina asked simply.

'If you mean between me and Aaron, nothing.'

'Of course I mean you and Aaron. He's gaga. It's so obvious.'

'He's not *gaga*.'

'Oh, I beg to differ.'

'We just… We just got to know each other in Cambodia. I called in to check on Kiri a few times when he was ill with dengue fever and Aaron was out in the field, so he's…grateful. I guess.'

Tina snorted out a laugh. 'If that's gratitude, I'd like to get me a piece of it. I'm going to remind Brand tonight just how grateful he is that he met me.'

Ella had stayed out as long as public transport allowed but Aaron was nevertheless waiting for her when she got back, leaning against the library door.

No reprieve.

She'd three-quarters expected this, though, so she had a plan.

She would be *that* Ella—the cool, calm, untouchable one—so he knew exactly what he'd get if he pursued this insanity that she couldn't quite bring herself to reject. With luck, he would run a mile away from her, the way he'd run in Cambodia, and spare them both the heartache she feared would be inevitable if they went down this path.

If not...well, they'd see.

'Are you going to wait up for me every night?' she asked, in the amused tone that had infuriated him in the past.

'I can wait in your bed if you prefer.'

The wind having effectively been taken out of her sails, Ella headed slowly up the stairs without another word. Aaron followed her into her room, reached for her.

'Wait,' she said, stepping back. 'You really want to do this?'

'Yes.'

'One hundred per cent sure?'

'Yes.'

She sighed. 'It's going to end in tears, you know.'

'I'll take my chances.'

Another sigh. 'Okay, then—but, first, ground rules.'

He nodded, deadly serious.

'No PDAs,' she said. 'If this is casual sex, it stays in my bedroom—or your bedroom. No touchy-feely stuff beyond bed. And *absolutely* nothing in front of Tina or Brand or Kiri.'

'Agreed.'

'When one or the other of us decides the arrangement is over there will be no questions, no comments, no recriminations, no clinging. I will let you go as easily as that...' she clicked her fingers '...if you're the one ending things. And I expect you to do the same.'

He narrowed his eyes. 'Agreed.'

'No prying into my private life.'

He looked at her.

'Agreed?' she asked impatiently.

'I don't know what "prying" means to you—you're su-persensitive about things other people consider normal conversation, and I don't want you taking a machete to my head if I ask what any reasonable person would think is an innocuous question.'

'If you think I'm unreasonable, why do you want to go down this path?'

He smiled, a smile that held the promise of hot, steamy sex. 'Oh, I think you know why, Ella.'

She was blushing again.

'What about if I agree that you are under no obligation to tell me anything that makes you uncomfortable?' he asked.

She digested that. 'Fair enough. Agreed. And ditto for you.'

'No need. You can ask me anything you want, and I'll answer you.'

That threw her, but she nodded. 'But I won't ask. Any conditions from your side?'

'One. Monogamy. Nobody else, while you're sleeping with me.'

'Agreed,' she said, but she tinkled out a little laugh to suggest she thought that was quaint. 'Anything else?'

'No. So take off your clothes.'

CHAPTER ELEVEN

'I DO LIKE a masterful man,' Ella said. And then she reached for the hem of her dress.

But Aaron stopped her. 'I've changed my mind,' he said. 'Come here.'

Ella stepped towards him, her eyebrows raised in that practised, disdainful way that seemed to aggravate him.

When she reached him, he took the neckline of her cotton dress in his hands, and ripped the dress down the front.

A surprised 'Oh…' whooshed out of her. There went the practised disdain.

She looked up at him. His face was stark as he dragged her bra down her arms, imprisoning her with the straps, and bent his head to her breasts. He sucked one nipple, hard, into his mouth, and she gasped. Moved to the other. He eased back to look into her eyes as he pushed her tattered dress almost casually over her hips until it dropped to the floor. 'I'll buy you another,' he said.

She couldn't speak, couldn't raise her defensive shield of indifference. Could only wait and watch. Her arms were still trapped, and he made no move to free them. Instead, he brought his hands up to cup her breasts, thumbs smoothing across her nipples, and then lowered his mouth again.

How much time had passed—a minute? Ten? Longer? He wouldn't let her move, just kept up that steady pressure, hands and lips, until she was almost weeping with pleasure. Ella was desperate to touch him, but every time she tried to reach around to unhook her bra and free herself, he stymied her.

At last he stepped back, examined her with one long, lascivious look from her head to her toes. Then his hands went to the front of her panties and she felt, heard, the fine cotton tear. 'I'll replace those too,' he said softly, and then her breath shuddered out, rough and choppy, as one of his hands reached between her legs. Within moments she was shuddering as the pleasure tore through her like a monsoon. Hot, wet, wild.

He spun her, unhooking her bra with a swift efficiency that seemed to scorn his earlier languorous attention to her body. With the same speed, he stripped off his own clothes. Then his hands were on her again, arousing her, preparing her, as he backed the two of them towards the bed.

He fell onto the bed, on his back, and dragged her on top of him. 'Here, let me.' His voice was hoarse and urgent as he positioned her over him, moving her legs so that they fell on either side of his and thrusting blindly towards her centre.

'Wait,' she said.

It took only moments for her to raise herself, straddling him with her knees on each side of his straining body. She reached over him, grabbed a condom from the drawer. She ripped the package open with her teeth, slid the sheath onto him with slow, steady movements. Smoothing it as he jumped against her hand. And then she took him inside her with one undulating swirl of her hips. Stilled, keeping him there, not letting him move, deep inside her.

'No,' she said, as he started to buck upwards against her. 'Let me.' And, rising and falling in smooth, steady waves, she tightened herself around him until he gasped her name. Clutching her hips, he jammed her down on top of him and exploded.

Ella, following him into ecstasy, collapsed on top of him.

She stayed there, spent, as his hands threaded through her hair, stroking and sliding.

She wanted to stay like that all night, with Aaron inside her, his hands in her hair, his mouth close enough to kiss.

Except that he hadn't kissed her. Not once.

For some reason, she didn't like that.

It's just casual sex, she reminded herself.

On that thought, she disengaged herself from his body and got off the bed. Pulling her hair back over her shoulders, she smiled serenely down at him. 'Excellent, thank you,' she said. 'But there's no need for you to stay. I'll see you tomorrow night.'

Tina had assorted chores to do the next day, so she left Kiri in Ella's sole company.

Ella had taken him to the park to practise catching the cricket ball. Was that the hardest, unkindest ball in international sport? Ella thought so, as she looked at her bruised shin.

So for the afternoon she'd chosen a more intellectual pursuit—painting. It was a challenge to keep Kiri's paint set in the vicinity of the special child-sized activity table Tina had moved into the library for him, but they'd accomplished it.

As assorted paintings, laid out across every available surface, were drying, she and Kiri curled up together in one of the massive leather chairs, where she entertained him by letting him play with her cellphone.

She was laughing at Kiri's attempt at an emoticon-only text message when Aaron walked in.

'Shouldn't you be on set?' she asked, sitting up straighter.

'I'm on a break so thought I'd come back to the house. What happened to your leg?'

'Cricket-ball injury. That's a sport I am never going to figure out.' She gestured around the room. 'Check out Kiri's paintings while you're here. Which one's for Dad, Kiri?'

Kiri scrambled out of the chair. 'Two of them. Here's Mum…' He was pointing out a painting of a black-haired woman in an orange dress. 'And here's Ella.' In her nursing uniform.

Ella felt her stomach drop with a heavy thud. Just what the man needed; his ex-wife and his current lover, as depicted by his son, who knew nothing of the tension in either relationship.

But Aaron was smiling like it was the most wonderful gift in the world. 'Fabbo. One day, when you're famous, these are going to be worth a fortune.'

Kiri giggled, and then went to perch back with Ella. 'Ella's teaching me the phone,' he confided. 'I called Tina.'

'You're not international roaming, are you?' Aaron asked. 'That will cost you a fortune.'

Ella shrugged, not having the heart to deny Kiri. 'They're only short calls.' She smiled at Kiri as she scrolled through her contact list.

'See, Kiri, there's Dad's number. If you hit this, it will call him. Yes, perfect.'

Aaron's phone rang, and he dutifully answered it and had a moment's conversation with Kiri.

And then Aaron tossed metaphorical hands in the air. He asked Ella for her phone number, punched it into his contact list, then handed his phone to Kiri, showed him the entry and let him call her.

She and Kiri chatted for a while, as though they were on opposite sides of the world instead of sitting together.

Then Kiri looked pleadingly at his father. 'Dad, can I have a phone?'

Aaron laughed. 'Who do you need to call, mate?' he asked.

'You. Mum. Tina. Jenny. And Ella.'

'Well, calling Ella might be tricky,' Aaron explained,

and lifted Kiri into his arms. 'Because we'll never know where in the world she is. And we don't want to wake her up at midnight!'

An excellent reminder, Ella thought, of the transience of their current arrangement—because at some point in the near future she would indeed be somewhere else in the world, far away from Aaron and Kiri.

When Aaron took his leave a short while later, she felt ill at ease.

It had been a strange interlude. Why had he even come? Maybe he didn't trust her with Kiri after all, and was checking up on her.

But it hadn't felt like that. In fact, he'd seemed delighted at her obviously close relationship with Kiri. And not at all freaked out at having a painting of her presented to him as a gift, which must have been awkward.

Knowing how much Aaron adored Kiri, and how keen he'd been to keep the two parts of this London life separate, well, it didn't make sense.

And Ella didn't like it.

Ella spent the next three days in a kind of hellish heaven.

Taking care of Kiri during the day and spending her nights with Aaron.

She adored her time with Kiri. She took him to Madame Tussaud's and to see the changing of the guard at Buckingham Palace, toy shopping for the baby, and for him. In the process, falling a little more in love with him every day.

She longed for her nights with Aaron. The pleasure that made her want to sigh and scream, the roughness and gentleness, the speed and languor, and everything in between.

But the arrangement was playing havoc with her emotions. Kiri's innocent stories about his father were making her feel altogether too soppy about a casual sex partner. And there were moments during the steamy nights when she and Aaron seemed to forget their agreed roles, becoming almost like real parents having the whole family chat.

Minus the kissing.

An omission that should have reassured her that this was just sex...but didn't.

And then, after five consecutive nights of lovemaking, Ella opened the morning paper and the sordidness of her current situation was thrown into sudden, sharp relief.

Only one half-column of words, not even a photo. But, still, the wreck of her life came crashing back.

It was an article about Javier, full of platitudes from various authorities with no actual news of his fate. But it felt like an omen, and it savaged Ella's conscience. Because she realised that since being with Aaron, not only had she been free of nightmares but she hadn't had any thoughts about Javier either.

So when Aaron came to her room that night, carrying a bag, she pleaded a migraine, knowing she looked ill enough for him to believe her.

'Can I get you anything?' he asked, concern creasing his forehead as he dumped the bag carelessly on her bed.

She forced a strained smile. 'Hey, I'm a nurse, remember?'

He nodded, and then completely disarmed her by drawing her against him and just holding her. 'Sleep well, angel,' he said, and left her.

Angel?

That was going to have to be nipped in the bud.

She approached the bag with some trepidation. Pulled out a raspberry-coloured dress that even she could see was something special, and a bra and panties set in a matching shade that was really too beautiful to wear. The replacements for the things Aaron had ripped off her, obviously—although, strictly speaking, he didn't owe her a bra.

She stared at them, spread on the bed, and tried to shrug off the sense of doom that gripped her.

* * *

Aaron was dragged out of a deep slumber by a kind of screeching wail, abruptly cut off.

He sat up, perfectly still, perfectly silent, and listened. Nothing.

He shook his head to clear it.

Nothing. Imagination.

So—back to sleep. He gave his pillow a thump and lay back down.

Sat back up. Nope—something was wrong. He could feel it.

He got out of bed, padded out of the room, shirtless and in his shorts.

He opened the door to Kiri's room opposite and peered in. He was sleeping soundly.

So…Ella? He opened the door to her room quietly.

She was lying perfectly still, her eyes wide and staring, her hands jammed against her mouth.

He didn't think. Just slid into bed beside her, took her in his arms and arranged her limbs for maximum sleeping comfort.

She said nothing, but she didn't kick him away, which had to be a good sign.

'Just to be clear,' he said, 'I'm not asking questions. So don't even think of telling me to leave.'

She looked at him for one heartbeat, two, three. Then she closed her eyes, and eventually he felt her ease into sleep.

It wasn't going to be easy to not ask at some point. He'd better wear his thermal underwear to ward off the frostbite during that moment. Hmm. Oddly enough, it didn't daunt him. He snuggled her a little closer, kissed the top of her head. *One day, Ella, I'll know it all.*

Damn Aaron James.

It was his fault she was in a dingy hotel room that wasn't big enough to swing a rodent in, let alone a cat.

Not that she hadn't slept in an array of substandard places over the years, though none had ever cost her a staggering hundred and twenty pounds per night.

He'd had to come into her room last night when she'd been at her most vulnerable. And sneaked out this morning without waking her, without having the decency to talk about it so she could slap him down.

So here she was. Hiding out. Staying away until she could find the best way to end things with him. Because things were just not quite casual enough to make this arrangement work.

Aaron was moving house tomorrow. That should signal the end of their liaison. She shouldn't have let Aaron persuade her in the first place. Because look where it had landed her. She was confused about Aaron, guilt-stricken about Javier, miserable about everything—and in a shoe-box-sized room that was costing her a bomb.

Ella sighed heavily, and sat dispiritedly on the bed. It was kind of slippery, as if the mattress protector was plastic. She popped into the bathroom to splash some water on her face and the *eau de* public toilet aroma jammed into her nostrils.

Well, that settled one thing: she might have to sleep here, but she wasn't going to breathe in that smell until she had to. She was going out for the evening.

In fact, for this one night she was going to rediscover the excesses she'd left behind in Cambodia. And when she was sozzled enough, she would return to face the room.

She would *not* run headlong to Tina's and one last night with Aaron.

Which was how Ella found herself playing pool with Harry, Neal and Jerome; three gorgeous, safely gay guys.

She was hot. Sweaty. Dishevelled. A little bit drunk.

Just how you wanted to look for a surprise visit from your lover.

Because that was definitely Aaron James, entering the

pub just as she hit the white ball so awkwardly it jumped off the table.

Aaron James, who was standing there, glaring at her. Fate. It really wasn't working for her.

CHAPTER TWELVE

HE'D BEEN WORKING his way through the pubs in the vicinity
of Tina and Brand's because he'd known Ella wasn't staying with friends, as she'd told Tina, and he suspected she
wouldn't stray too far, given Tina's advanced pregnancy.
So it wasn't exactly fate that he'd found her, because this
was the seventh pub he'd tried. But it sure felt like it.

He should go, leave her to it. She didn't *have* to see him
every night. Didn't have to get his permission to stay out
all night. Didn't have to explain why she was laughing over
a pool table with three handsome men.

Except that she kind of *did* have to.

And it would have been stupid to search through the
pubs of Mayfair for her and then turn tail the moment he
found her.

She was wearing a skin-tight black skirt that would give
a corpse a wet dream. A clingy silver singlet top just covering those perfect breasts. Black high heels—that was a
first, and a very sexy one. Her hair was piled on her head,
who knew how it was staying up there? In fact, not all of it
was. Her messy hair made him think of having her in bed.

Aaron watched as she bounced the white ball off the
table. As all four of them chortled. He seethed as the blond
guy kissed her. Felt murderous as the other two hugged
her, one each side.

She knew he was here. He'd seen the flare in her eyes,

the infinitesimal toss of her head as she'd directed her
eyes away.

Oh no you don't, Ella. Oh, no. You. Don't.

Ella decided the best thing to do was carry on with her
evening as though she hadn't seen Aaron standing on the
other side of the pub with his hands fisted at his sides like
he was trying not to punch something. She was not going
to be made to feel guilty about this.

The guys started hunting in their pockets for beer
money. Ella dug into her handbag. 'Don't think so,' she
said mournfully, as she scrabbled around inside. And then
her eyes widened. 'Hang on,' she said, and triumphantly
drew a ten-pound note from the depths, along with one old
mint and a paper clip.

'Hooray!' Jerome exclaimed with great enthusiasm. 'Off
you go, my girl—to the bar.'

'Or maybe not.'

The voice came from behind Ella but she knew to whom
it belonged. That accent.

She'd known he would come to her. Had expected it.
Was she happy about it? Yes, unbelievably, given she'd intended to avoid him tonight, she was happy. *A bad sign.*

She looked over her shoulder at him. 'Hello, Aaron.'

'You and pool tables, what's up with that?' Aaron asked
mildly. He tucked a strand of loose hair behind one of Ella's
ears. 'Run out of money, sweetheart?'

'Yes,' she said, looking at him carefully as she turned
fully towards him. He wasn't giving off *sweetheart* vibes.
Aaron dug into his jeans pocket, pulled out a fifty-pound
note and handed it to her.

'Are you going to introduce me to your friends?' he
asked, as she stared at the cash as though she couldn't
believe she was holding it.

'Huh?' she said eloquently.

'Your friends?' he prompted.

Ella looked around as though she'd forgotten their existence. Pulled herself together as she noted her three new drinking buddies gazing at her with avid interest.

'Oh. Yes,' she said, and hastily performed the introductions.

'And do you really want another drink, or shall we hand that money over to the guys and head off?'

Ella was torn.

'Ella? Are we staying or going?' Aaron asked, steel in his voice.

She *should* tell him to go to hell. But she found she didn't want to fight with Aaron. Not here. Didn't want to fight with him, period.

'I guess we're going,' she said. 'So here you go, boys, thanks for buying my drinks all night and I hope this covers it.' She smiled at them. 'I had a brilliant time. And remember what I said about LA. If you're ever there…'

Assorted hugs and kisses later, Ella did her slow walk out of the pub.

'You're not fooling me with the slow walk, Ella,' Aaron said as they reached the footpath.

She stopped. Turned to him. 'I don't know what you m—'

He pulled her into his arms sharply, shocking that sentence right out of her head.

He moved to kiss her but Ella put her hands up, pushing against his chest. 'You don't kiss me any more.'

'Is that so?' Aaron asked. Purely rhetorical—she had no time to answer as he planted his mouth on hers like a heat-seeking missile hitting its target. His hands went to her bottom and he pulled her against him, pelvis to pelvis.

Ella gasped as he released her, and her fingers came up to touch her mouth. 'Why are you so angry with me?'

Aaron looked down at her, unapologetic. 'Because you left me.'

Ella couldn't help herself—she touched his cheek.

She went to pull her hand away but Aaron caught it, held it against his face. 'And because I'm jealous,' he said.

'Jealous?'

Aaron nodded towards the pub.

Ella was stunned. 'But they're gay.'

He didn't miss a beat. 'I don't care if they're eunuchs. Because it's not sex I'm talking about. We're monogamous, you and I, and I trust you with that.'

That certainty shook her. She swallowed hard. 'Then what?'

'It's the whole deal. Being with you. In the moment. In public. *That* smile. That's what I'm talking about.'

That smile? Huh? 'We're in the moment in public now,' she said. 'Which I hope you don't regret.' She tilted her head towards a small group of women as she tugged her hand free. They were staring at Aaron as they walked past. 'I think they know you. I keep forgetting you're a celebrity.'

'I don't care.'

'You're *supposed* to care. Just sex, on the quiet—no scandal. Look, let's be honest. It's not working out, this casual sex thing.'

'No, it's not.'

She couldn't think straight for a moment. Because he'd agreed with her. Which meant it was over. Just what she'd wanted.

'Right,' she said. And then, because she still couldn't think straight, 'Right.'

'We're going to have to renegotiate.'

'There doesn't seem to be much point to that, or much to negotiate *with*,' Ella said, as her brain finally engaged. 'Given you're moving out tomorrow, let's just call it quits.'

Aaron pursed his lips. 'Um—no.'

'No?'

'No.'

'Remember our agreement? No questions, no—'

'I don't give a toss about our agreement. We are not

going to go our separate ways because you decided to click
your fingers on a public street.'

'See? I told you it's not working. The casual sex deal
meant no messy endings. And you're making it messy.'

'But it's not casual, is it, Ella? And I don't want to let
you go.'

Her heart did that stuttering thing. She forced herself
to ignore it. 'You knew there couldn't be anything except
sex. And it will be too hard to keep even that going once
we're living in different places.' Swallow. 'And I—I have
an extra complication.'

'Which is?' he asked flatly.

'I have—I have...someone.'

'Look at me, Ella.'

She faced him squarely, threw back her head, eyes glit-
tering with defiance.

'No, you don't,' Aaron said.

'Oh, for goodness' sake, I do! I do, I do!'

'If you had someone, you couldn't be with me the way
you have been.'

She gasped. He couldn't have hurt her more if he'd
stabbed her.

Because he was right.

How could she love Javier if she could pour herself into
sex with Aaron in the no-holds-barred way that had become their signature? It had never happened before—only
drunken fumbling that she'd run away from every single
time. The antithesis of what she did with Aaron.

Aaron was looking at her with almost savage intensity.
'We need to settle this, and not here. Come with me.'

'Where are we going?'

'I don't know—a hotel.'

She laughed, but there was no softness in it. 'I have a
hotel room. It stinks like a public toilet and has a plastic
mattress protector. That sounds about right. Let's go there.
And don't flinch like that.'

'I think we can do better than that, Ella.'

Ella wanted to scream. But she also wanted to cry. And instead of doing either, she was goading him, making everything ugly and tawdry, turning it into the one-night stand it should have always been. 'All right, then. Let's "settle" this,' she said. 'One last time. I'm up for it. You can use my body any way you want, and I will show you there is nothing romantic about an orgasm—it's just technique.'

'Is that so?'

'Let's find out. But if I'm going to play the mistress, I warn you now that I'm going to want access to the mini-bar.'

'Any way I can get you, Ella,' he said, unperturbed. 'You can devour everything in the mini-bar, order everything off the room-service menu, steal the fluffy robe, take the towels—anything you want.'

'I've always wanted to steal the fluffy robe,' Ella said, and took his arm.

CHAPTER THIRTEEN

AARON HAILED A cab and asked to be taken to the closest five-star hotel. On the way, he called to check on Kiri and let Jenny, who'd arrived in the early evening, know he wouldn't be home that night.

Ella waited through the call, clearly still furious with him. Well, too damned bad.

Aaron hastily secured them a room for the night and as they headed for the hotel elevator, he drew Ella close to him, holding her rigid hand. He breathed in the slightly stale pub scent of her. But he couldn't have cared less whether she came to him straight from the shower or after running a marathon through the city sewers.

The elevator doors opened and then they were inside. Alone. The second the doors closed, he was kissing her, sliding his hands under her top. One hand moved up to cover her breast, moulding it to his palm, teasing the nipple to maddening hardness with unsteady fingers. He'd thought she might push him away but, no, she kissed him back, straining against him. He broke the kiss, his breath coming fast and hard now, and bent his mouth to her shoulder, biting her there.

The elevator stopped and they broke apart, staring at each other. Without a word, Aaron grabbed her hand and pulled her quickly out and along the corridor. His hands were shaking so much he almost couldn't work the door mechanism to their suite. And then they were inside and Aaron reached for her again. Wordless. Driven. Desperate.

But so was Ella.

She yanked his T-shirt up his chest and over his head. 'Ah,' she breathed, as her hands went to his hips and she pulled him toward her. She put her mouth on one of his nipples and held tight to his hips as he bucked against her.

'Ella,' he groaned, hands moving restlessly to try to hold onto her as her tongue flicked out. 'Let me touch you.'

'Not yet,' she said, and moved her mouth to his other nipple. As she did so, she started to undo the button fly of his jeans.

He groaned again but couldn't speak as her hands slid inside his underwear.

'Do you like me to touch you like this?' she asked.

'You know I— Ahh, Ella, you're killing me.'

Laughing throatily, Ella stepped back, started to undress.

'Hurry up,' she said, as he stood watching as she wriggled out of her skirt.

It was all the encouragement Aaron needed. In record time, he'd stripped.

Ella, naked except for her high heels, turned to drape her clothes over the back of a handily positioned chair. Aaron came up behind her and caught her against his chest. His arms circled her, hands reaching for her breasts.

She dropped her clothes and leaned back against him, thrusting her breasts into his hands. She moaned as he kissed the side of her neck, gasped as one questing hand dived between her thighs.

'Oh, you're good at this,' Ella said, as she felt her orgasm start to build.

'You can still talk,' Aaron said against her ear. 'So not good enough.'

With that, he bent her forward at the waist until she was clinging to the chair, and thrust inside her. His hands were on her hips as he continued to move inside her, pulling all the way out after each thrust before slamming into her again.

The feel of her bottom against him, the intoxicating sounds of her pleasure as she orgasmed, clenching around him until he thought he'd faint from desire, the exquisite friction of his movements in and out of her built together until the blood was roaring in his head and demanding he take her harder, harder, harder.

Ella. This was Ella.

His.

Ella slumped against Aaron. After that explosive orgasm, he'd turned her around to face him, kissed her for the longest time, and now he was holding her with every bit of gentleness his lovemaking had lacked.

What she'd meant to do was give him a clinical experience. Instead, she'd drenched herself in soul-deep, emotionally fraught lust. Her anger was gone. And the bitterness. She felt purged, almost. Which wasn't the way it was supposed to be.

Nothing had changed. Nothing that could open the way for her to have what she wanted with a clear conscience. Sex couldn't cure things. Even phenomenal sex. Life couldn't be that simple.

Javier was still out there, the uncertainty of his fate tying her to him. Aaron still had a problematic ex-wife and a little boy whose inevitable loss, when they went their separate ways, would devastate her.

'Did I hurt you?' he asked, kissing the top of her head.

'This really is a regular post-coital question of yours, isn't it?'

'No. It's just that I've only ever lost control with you.'

There was a lump in her throat. 'Well, stop asking,' she said, when she trusted herself to speak. 'You didn't hurt me.' *Not in that way.*

'I didn't even think about a condom,' Aaron said.

Ella shrugged restlessly, eased out of his arms. 'I know. I wasn't thinking straight either. And me a nurse.'

'I'm sorry.'

'Me too, but it's done. Not that it's really the point, but I'm on the Pill. So if that worries you, at least—'

'No. No—I'm not worried about that. At least, not for myself. I wish I *could* have a child with you, Ella. Not to replace Sann but for you.'

That lump was in her throat again. She turned away. 'Complicating as all hell, though, pregnancy, for casual sex partners,' she said, trying for light and airy and not quite making it. She remembered ordering him to never say Sann's name again. But it didn't hurt to hear the name now. Not from him.

Aaron—what an unlikely confidant. The only one who knew her pain.

She cleared her throat, 'But now, do you think we could actually move out of this hallway? And where are those fluffy robes?'

Aaron obligingly guided Ella into the lounge area of the suite. He fetched a robe for each of them, and watched as Ella belted hers on, then sat on the sofa to remove her shoes.

He came to sit beside her, slipped an arm around her shoulders and drew her back against him so that her head was against his shoulder.

'You know, don't you, that I'm not a nice person?' she said.

'No, I don't know that. I've watched you work. Seen how much you care. The way you are with Kiri. I know how protective you are of your family. I know you wanted to adopt an orphan from Cambodia, and I've seen what the grief of that did to you. These things don't add up to "not nice".'

'I've been jealous of my sister, of the baby. That's not nice.'

'It doesn't look to me like Tina's had her eyes scratched out,' Aaron said calmly.

'Well, I'm over it now,' she admitted. 'But it took some soul searching.'

'I'm thinking soul searching is a bit of a hobby of yours.'

'And I— Over the past year I've done things. Things I'm not proud of.'

'You've had a lot to deal with. Cut yourself some slack, Ella.'

'You stopped kissing me.'

'And you think that was some kind of judgement?' He broke off, laughed softly. 'That was a defence mechanism. That's all.'

'What?'

'Casual sex? Just sex—no kissing, because kissing is not casual.'

'Oh.'

They stayed sitting in silence, his arm around her, for a long moment.

Now what? Ella wondered.

But then Aaron broke the silence. 'So tell me, Ella, about the "someone". The someone I know you don't have. The someone I think you once *had*. Past tense. Right?'

'Had *and* have.'

'Hmm, I'm going to need a little more.'

'His name is Javier. He's a doctor. Spanish. He was kidnapped in Somalia.' *Whew.* 'There was an article in the paper this morning.' She looked up at him briefly. 'Hence my need to go a little off the rails tonight.'

Aaron nodded, saying nothing. And somehow it was easy to relax against him and continue. Aaron, her confidant. 'We were in love. Very newly in love, so new that nobody else knew about it, which was a blessing the way things turned out, because I couldn't have borne the questions, the sympathy.' Pause. 'I should have been with him that day. It was my twenty-fifth birthday, two years ago. I was supposed to be in the jeep with him.'

Long pause. She could almost hear her own pulse. 'You've got no idea how awful it was. The conditions. The soul-sapping struggle to provide healthcare to people who desperately needed it. Because even before you think about treating illnesses like malaria and TB and pneumonia and HIV, you know that the drought, the violence, the poverty, the poor harvests have made malnutrition a force that simply can't be reckoned with. The kids are starving. Sometimes walking hundreds of kilometres just to drop dead in front of you. And ten thousand people a day are dying.

'And your colleagues are being kidnapped or even murdered, and armed opposition groups make it almost impossible to reach people in need, even though everyone *knows* the suffering, and even hiring a vehicle to get to people is a tense negotiation with clans in constant conflict, and the very people who are providing the tiny bit of security you can get are okay with the deaths and the kidnappings.'

She stopped again. 'Sorry I'm so emotional.' She shook her head. 'No, I'm not sorry. It needs emotion. When you're resuscitating a one-year-old girl, and there is a tiny boy next to her so frail that only a stethoscope over his heart tells you he's alive, and two more critically ill children are waiting behind you, why *not* get emotional?'

His hand was in her hair, stroking, soothing. 'Go on, Ella. I'm here.'

'Anyway. Javier and I were heading to one of the refugee camps in Kenya. But I got malaria and I couldn't go. So I'm here and he's somewhere. Alive, dead, injured, safe? I don't know.' Ella drew in a shuddering breath. 'And I feel guilty, about having a normal life while he's lost. And guilty that I can be with you like this when I should be waiting for him. And just plain guilty. I'm a wreck.'

'Ah, Ella.' He eased her out from under his arm and turned her to face him. 'I'd tell you it's not your fault, that you have a right to go on with your life, that anyone who loved you would want that for you, that you wouldn't want Javier to be trapped in the past if your situations were reversed; but that's not going to set you free, is it?' He ran his fingers down her cheek. 'You have to be ready to let it go.'

'The thing is I don't know what he'd want me to do, or what he'd do in my place.'

'That says something, doesn't it? You were only twenty-five, and in a very new relationship. If you're really going to keep a candle burning in the window for the rest of your life, I'm going to have to find the guy and make sure he's worth it, and I don't really want to do that. Somalia is scary!'

Ella smiled. 'You really do have that heroic thing going on, don't you? I think you *would* go there if you thought it would help me.'

'Nah. It's not heroic, it's self-interest. Memories can bring on rose-tinted-glasses syndrome. Which, in this case, makes it really hard for a mere actor to measure up to a Spanish doctor kidnapped while saving lives in Africa. Even with the malaria documentary under my belt, I'm coming in a poor second.' He kissed her forehead. 'But it's just possible, in a real flesh-and-blood contest, I could edge past him. Unless he happens to be devastatingly attractive as well.'

'As a matter of fact…' Ella trailed off with a laugh.

'Well, that sucks. Maybe I *won't* go and find him after all.'

'Yeah, well, Somalia really *is* scary, so I wouldn't let you go. I wouldn't like to lose you too.' Ella resettled her head on his shoulder. 'Okay—now you know all the salient bits about my past. So, let's talk about you. You said I could ask you anything, and you'd answer.'

'Ask away.'

'I'll start with something easy. Tina told me you raised your sisters after your parents died.'

'Easy? Ha! It was like a brother-sister version of *The Taming of the Shrew*, but in triplicate.'

Ella smiled. 'And you love them very much.'

'Oh, yes. Lucinda, Gabriella and Nicola. My parents were killed in a boating accident when I was eighteen. The girls were fifteen, twelve and ten. I was old enough to look after them, so I did. End of story, really. Two of them are married with kids now, one is married to her job—she's an actuary but she looks like a fashion designer—and all of them are happy.'

'It can't have been easy.'

'We had some nail-biting moments over the years, no doubt about it. But I won't go into the scary boyfriend stories or the fights over schoolwork and curfews. We just belonged together. Simple.'

Pause. And then, 'Is it okay to ask about Rebecca? Like, how you met?'

'Sure. I met her through Brand. The way I meet all my women.'

Ella pinched his thigh.

'All right, not *all* of them,' he amended, laughing. 'Let me give you the abridged version. We met at one of Brand's parties. He was living in Los Angeles back then and I was over there, trying to make the big time— unsuccessfully. Rebecca was doing the same, equally unsuccessfully.'

'So you drowned your sorrows together?'

'Something like that. We were an item in pretty short order. Happily ever after. For a while at least.'

'What went wrong?'

'Nothing. That's what I thought, anyway.' He sighed. 'But looking back, it was all about work. When we returned to Australia I started getting steady jobs. We adopted Kiri and everything seemed fine. But I got more work. Better work. And more work. Making a fortune, no worries. But Rebecca's career stalled. She wasn't happy, and I was too busy to notice. Until it was too late. She started doing a few outrageous things to get publicity in the mistaken belief it would help things along. And before I knew it, it was party, party, party. Drugs. Booze. More drugs. I know Tina told you about the rehab. Well, Rebecca's been to rehab before. Twice.' He shrugged. 'I'm praying this time it will work. This place, it's called Trust, it really seems good.'

'Oh, Trust—I know it, and it is good. She's in safe hands there.'

'Thanks, Ella.'

Ella brought his hand to her lips and kissed it. 'So I guess you've been trying to make up for being too busy to notice when things started to go wrong.'

'That's about the sum of it.'

'Am I going to do the "not your fault" routine?'

Aaron touched her hair. 'No. I'm as bad as you are when it comes to guilt, I think.'

'And Kiri? Why adopt? And why do you have full custody?'

'The adoption? We'd always planned to adopt a child in need and that just happened to come before trying for our own. The custody thing? Well, no matter what's between Rebecca and me, she wants only the best for Kiri, and she recognised that that was living with me, because although she likes to pretend she's in control, she knows she's not.'

She touched his hand. 'You love her. Rebecca.'

'Yes, I do,' Aaron said. 'But it's no longer *that* love. I care about her, as a friend and as the mother of my son.'

'It sounds very mature.'

'Hmm, well, don't be thinking it's all sugar plums and fairy cakes, far from it. She likes to get what she wants.' He laughed. 'I suppose we all do, if it comes to that. But when she needs something, she tends to forget we're divorced and she's not above a bit of manipulation. That can make it hard for us to move on.'

'She wouldn't like it? The fact that I'm here with you.'

'Probably not,' he admitted. 'Unless she had someone first.'

'So you won't tell her.'

'That depends, Ella. On whether we're sticking to our initial arrangement.'

Silence.

Ella wasn't ready to face that.

She got to her feet, headed for the mini-bar and started looking through the contents. 'So,' she said, moving various bottles around without any real interest, 'getting back to the important stuff. Condoms. Or the lack of them. Pregnancy we've covered. But I can also reassure you that I was checked before I left Cambodia and am disease-free. It's something I do regularly, because of my work with AIDS patients.'

'Me too, disease-free, I mean. I've been an avid fan of the condom for a long, long time.'

She turned. 'But weren't you and Rebecca starting to try for…?'

'Trying for a baby? No. For the last year we weren't trying *anything*. You see, along with the drugs came other problems—new experiences Rebecca wanted, such as sex with a variety of men. Including two of my friends. *Ex*-friends,' he clarified. 'I could forgive her for that. I *did* forgive her, knowing what was going on with her. But I couldn't…well, I just couldn't after that.'

'I don't know what to say to that.'

'Not much *to* say. I did try to keep my marriage together, because commitments are important to me. But some things just…change.'

Ella thought about that. What a lovely thing to accept. *Some things just change.*

'Anyway, enough gloom.' He walked over to her, gave her a quick, hard kiss. 'Come and have a bath with me.'

Aaron grabbed the scented crystals beside the deep bath and threw them in as the tub filled. Then he lifted her in his arms and kissed her as he stepped into the water, settled. Kept kissing her until the bath was full. He took the soap from her and washed her, kissing, touching, until she was gasping for air. But he wouldn't take her. Not this time. 'Condoms, so you don't have to wonder,' he said, by way of explanation.

'I have some in my bag,' she said, shivering with desire.

'Monogamy, remember?' Aaron said. 'I don't think roaming around London with a bag full of condoms fits the principle.'

'Just handbag history—like the expired bus tickets in there. I wasn't going to use them.'

'It's okay, Ella. I know that. Somehow, I really do know that.' He got to his feet, streaming water, but before he could leave the tub Ella got to her knees. 'Not yet,' she said, and looked up at him as she took him in her mouth.

The next morning Aaron ordered a veritable banquet for breakfast.

He was whistling as he opened the door, as the food was laid out in the living room. The robe he'd purchased for Ella was in its neat drawstring bag, positioned on one of the chairs.

He'd left Ella in bed with the television remote control, and was halfway to the bedroom to fetch her for their lovers' feast, mid-whistle, when he heard it. A sound between a choke and a gasp.

'Ella, what is it?' he asked, hurrying into the room.

She was pale. Deathly so. Like the life had drained out of her. She looked up at him, and then, like she couldn't help herself, back at the television.

There was a man being interviewed. A gaunt man. Beautiful—not handsome, beautiful.

'It's him,' Ella said.

CHAPTER FOURTEEN

'HIM?' AARON ASKED. But he knew.

The news moved onto the next item and it was like a signal had been transmitted directly to Ella's brain.

She got out of bed. 'I have to go,' she said. But then she simply stood there, shivering.

'Go where?'

'Africa.'

'You can't go anywhere in that state, and certainly not Africa.'

'Don't tell me what to do,' she said, and started dressing. It took her less than a minute.

'Ella, you have to talk to me.'

'I did enough talking last night.'

'For God's sake Ella, I—'

'No,' she cried, and then raced to her bag. She looked up, wild-eyed. 'Money. I don't have money for a cab.'

'Calm down, Ella. I'll take you where you need to go.'

'I don't want you to take me anywhere. I want—I want—' She stopped, looked at him, then burst into tears.

Aaron tried to take her in his arms but she wrenched away from him, turned aside to hide her face and walked to the window. She cried as she looked out at the world. Cried as though her soul was shattering.

And just watching her, helpless, Aaron felt his life start to disintegrate.

Gradually, her sobs subsided. She stood leaning her forehead against the window.

Aaron came up behind her, touched her gently on the shoulder. She stiffened but didn't pull away.

'You're going to him,' he said.

'Of course.'

'You're still in love with him, then.'

Pause. And then, 'I have to be. And I have to go.' She turned to face him. 'I know I already owe you money but will you lend me enough for a cab?'

'You don't owe me anything, Ella.'

Aaron grabbed her by her upper arms and drew her forward. 'I'll wait for you to sort this out, Ella. I'll be here, waiting.'

'I don't deserve for anyone to wait for me,' she said, and her voice was colourless. 'Because *I* didn't wait. I *should* have been waiting for him. I *intended* to wait for him. But I didn't. Instead I—I was…' A breath shuddered in. Out. 'I can't stand it. I have to go. Now. I have to go.'

'All right.' Aaron grabbed his jeans and pulled out a handful of notes. 'Take this. And here…' He grabbed the hotel notepad and pen from beside the phone and scribbled a few lines. 'It's my address in London. We'll be there from today. And this…' he dashed another line on the paper '…is the phone number for the house. You've already got my mobile number. Whatever you need, Ella, whenever.'

'Thank you,' Ella said, and raced from the room without another word or glance.

Aaron looked at the sumptuous breakfast, at the robe he'd bought for Ella just because she'd joked about wanting to steal one. She hadn't seen it, wouldn't have taken it if she had.

Javier was back. And that was that.

And then, two days later, Rebecca disappeared from rehab in the company of a fellow addict, a film producer, and he knew he was going to have to fly to LA at some point to bail her out of some heinous situation.

Yep. That really was that.

Ella felt weird, being with Javier, even after a week together.

He was the same and yet not the same.

Every time she broached the subject of the past two years he closed the discussion down. He simply thought they would pick up exactly where they'd left off, as though those two years had never happened, but Ella couldn't get her head into the same space.

She couldn't bear to sleep with him, for one thing.

She told *him* it was to give them a chance to get to know each other again. She told *herself* it was because she'd been stupid enough to forget the condom with Aaron—that meant she had to wait and see, because things *did* go wrong with the Pill.

But, really, she just didn't want to.

She tried, desperately, to remember what it had been like, that one time with Javier, but the only images that formed were of Aaron.

So it would have been disloyal somehow. To Javier, who didn't deserve for her to be thinking about another man. And, bizarrely, to Aaron, who was now effectively out of her life.

Ella sighed and got out of bed in her tiny hotel room. Padded into the bathroom and looked in the cabinet mirror. What did Aaron see that made him fall on her like he was starving for the taste of her? She was beautiful, she'd been told that often enough to believe it, but had never thought it important. Until now. Because maybe Aaron wouldn't have wanted her so much if she'd looked different.

Was it shallow to be glad that something as insignificant as the shape of her mouth made Aaron kiss her as though it was the only thing in the world he needed?

Ella gave herself a mental shake. She had to stop thinking about Aaron. Javier was her future. Javier, who'd been
returned to her, like a miracle.

Today, they would fly to London so she could introduce
Javier to Tina, who'd had the Javier story thrown at her like
a dart as Ella had packed her bags. He would be there with
her for the baby's birth. Even her parents would be coming
in a month, to meet their grandchild...and the strange man
who'd been kept a secret from them. And wouldn't *that* be
interesting, after her mother's blistering phone soliloquy
on the subject of Ella keeping her in the dark?

Out of control, the whole thing. A runaway train, speeding her into an alien future.

Ella closed her eyes.

Did I hurt you? Aaron's voice whispered through her
memory.

Yes, she answered silently. *Yes, you did.*

Heathrow was bedlam, but Ella almost dreaded exiting
the airport.

She was so nervous.

About introducing Javier to Tina and Brand.

And about the inevitable meeting between Javier and
Aaron.

Javier, she'd discovered, was the jealous type. Not the
cute, huggable kind of jealous Aaron had been that night
outside the pub in Mayfair. Sort of *scary* jealous. The prospect of him and Aaron in the same room was enough to
make her break into a cold sweat.

She welcomed the flash of cameras as they emerged
from Customs. Javier was whisked away for a quick photo
op, and she was glad. It meant she would have a moment
to herself.

Or not.

Because, groan-inducingly, Aaron was there, waiting for her. In his T-shirt and jeans. Looking desperately unhappy.

He strode forward. 'Tina sent me instead of a limo. Sorry. I tried to get out of it, but nobody's allowed to say no to her at the moment, she's been so worried about you.'

'Everyone must hate me.'

'Nobody hates you, Ella. Everyone just wants things to work out.'

Ella could feel one of those awful blushes racing up her neck. 'I'm sorry. For running out like that, I mean. I should have explained, I should have—'

'Ella, don't. I know you. I know what you went through. I know why you had to go. I should have just stood aside. Please don't cry.'

Ella blinked hard, managed to gain her composure. 'You always seem to know. I wish… Oh, he's coming.'

Javier, unsmiling, put his arm around Ella the moment he reached them.

Aaron held out his hand, just as unsmiling.

It was like an old cowboy movie, trigger fingers at the ready, Ella thought, a little hysterically.

'Javier,' Aaron said. His hand was still out, ignored.

Ella took Javier's elbow. 'Javier, this is a friend of Tina and Brand's. And mine. Aaron James. He's very kindly giving us a ride.' Ugh, was that a *wheedle* in her voice? Disgusting.

'I'm pleased to meet you,' Javier said solemnly, at last taking Aaron's proffered hand for a single jerking shake.

Aaron gave him a narrow-eyed look. There was a small uncomfortable pause and then, taking their baggage cart, Aaron said, 'Follow me.'

Javier held Ella back for a moment. 'I don't like the way he looks at you,' he said.

Ella gritted her teeth. This was the fifth time in a week Javier had taken exception to the way a man had looked at her. She would have loved to tell him to get over it, but this particular time he had a right to be suspicious.

Aaron looked over his shoulder, no doubt wondering what was keeping them.

Looking straight ahead, Ella took Javier's arm and followed Aaron.

It was always going to be an uncomfortable drive, but this was ridiculous.

Aaron was fuming, relegated to the role of chauffer.

Javier spoke only to Ella, and only in Spanish.

Charming!

Ella answered him in English, but the agonised looks he was catching in the rear-view mirror told Aaron she knew her Spaniard was behaving like a jackass.

Okay—so maybe jackass was his word, not Ella's, but he stood by it. *Nice choice, Ella.*

It was a relief to pull up at the house. After he helped hoist their luggage out of the boot, Aaron drew Ella a little aside. 'Ella, so you know, Tina's insisting I come to dinner tonight,' he said softly.

'That…that's fine,' Ella said, glancing nervously at Javier, who was giving her a very dark look as he picked up their bags. With a poor attempt at a smile Ella hurried back to Javier, took his arm and ushered him quickly into the house.

Aaron sighed, wondered why he'd even bothered warning her about him being at dinner. However prepared any of them were, when you parcelled it all up—Ella's uncharacteristically submissive demeanour, Javier's haughty unfriendliness, the prospect of witnessing the reunited lovebirds cooing at each other all evening, and his own desire to do some kind of violence to Javier that would ruin at least one perfect cheekbone—dinner was going to be a fiasco of epic proportions.

* * *

Aaron had been braced ever since he'd got to Tina's, but he still couldn't help the way his eyes darted to the door of the living room when it opened for the final two guests.

Ella looked like a deer caught in the headlights. She was wearing a dress. Dark grey. Silky. Simple. Classy. She was wearing her black high heels. He wanted to run his hands up her legs. He could drool at any moment.

Their eyes met for one sharp, tense moment and she blushed.

Javier said something and Aaron shifted his gaze.

Javier was everything Aaron wasn't. It was more pronounced tonight than it had been at the airport. Javier was elegant and sophisticated. Stylish in that way Europeans seemed to manage so effortlessly. Javier's hair was jet black, lying against his perfect skull in well-behaved waves. His eyes were equally black—dramatically moody. He was dressed in black pants and a pale pinkish-purple shirt that not many men could carry off.

And since when had Aaron ever noticed, let alone cared about, what other men were wearing?

He tore his eyes away, took a bracing sip of his Scotch.

Hellos were said. A drink pressed into Javier's hand, another into Ella's. Tina kissed Javier on the cheek. Javier touched Tina's ringlets as though entranced.

Tina laughed. 'A curse, this hair. Only Brand likes it.'

Javier smiled. 'Not only Brand. I like it too. Lively hair.'

Tina laughed again, shaking her head until her curls danced a little.

Great, Aaron thought. Javier was going to be adored by Ella's sister. Just great.

Brand, who was standing beside him, made a disgusted sound and rolled his eyes. He'd always known Brand was an excellent judge of character.

Tina was saying something about the need to fatten Ella up.

'It's her work,' Javier said, pulling Ella very close. 'She worked too hard in Cambodia.'

'Getting any information out of Ella about her work is like pulling teeth, but Aaron told us a little about the conditions there.'

Javier looked straight at Aaron. Hostile.

Not that he could work out the whole backstory of Aaron's obsession with Ella from one glancing look.

Could he?

'And what were *you* doing, Aaron? In Cambodia?' Javier's voice was perfectly polite, and chilling.

'I was filming a documentary on malaria.' *And fantasising about your girlfriend.*

Tina was starting to take on a little of Ella's deer-in-the-headlights look. Sensing the undercurrents, no doubt. 'So, Javier,' Tina said, 'are you able to share with us a little about…about…your experience?'

Javier smiled at her, but to Aaron it looked almost dismissive.

'I was not badly treated,' Javier said. 'Just not free. But not, perhaps, a subject for tonight. Tonight is a celebration, you see. Ella and I…' He stopped, smiled again, drew Ella nearer.

How much closer could he *get* her, anyway? Aaron wondered furiously as he watched Ella. But she wouldn't meet his eyes. Wouldn't meet anyone's eyes.

'Ella and I would like to share our news,' Javier said, and raised Ella's hand to kiss the palm. 'Ella has done me the honour of accepting my proposal of marriage.'

Aaron caught the sparkle on Ella's finger, and turning away, swallowed the rest of his Scotch in one swig.

Aaron hadn't come looking for Ella.

Didn't want to be alone with her. Not now. When he felt so raw.

And yet there she was, in the kitchen, straightening up after putting something in the fridge.

And there he was. In the kitchen. Forgetting why.

He must have made some sound because she straightened. Turned. The fridge door swung closed behind her.

For a moment Aaron couldn't breathe.

'How are you, Aaron?' she asked quietly.

'Fine.' The word sounded as though it had been bounced into an airless room.

'And Kiri?'

'Fine. He misses you.'

He saw her swallow. She said nothing. Well, what did he expect her to say?

Aaron took a step closer to her. 'There were no consequences? I mean as a…a result of—'

'I know what you mean. I told you I was on the Pill. But just in case, I'm waiting…' Stop. Another swallow. 'I mean, I'm not doing anything… I'm not…with…' She drew an audible breath. 'Until I know.'

'That's good,' Aaron said, miraculously understanding. 'I mean, is it good? Yes, I guess it's good. I guess it's…' Nope. He couldn't finish that.

Silence.

Ella was turning the engagement ring round and round on her finger. 'How's Rebecca? Rehab? How's it going?'

'It's not. She left early; with a drug-addicted film producer. Never anything mundane for Rebecca.'

'Oh, I'm so sorry.'

He rubbed a hand behind his neck. 'Just one thing. I told her about you, about us. In case…'

Ella was fidgeting—which he'd never seen her do. Playing with the damned ring. 'Does that mean…? Does everyone know about us?' she asked.

'No. Nobody else. And Rebecca isn't talking—except to her publicist, who's working out how to go public with the film producer.'

'It's just…Javier's the jealous type. I don't want him to… You know what I mean.'

'I'll fix it so nothing rebounds on you, I promise. And I guess there's nothing to say, anyway. You're engaged.'

Another awful silence.

Aaron took one step closer. 'Have you picked a date? For the wedding?'

'No. Not yet.'

'Why are you doing it, Ella?'

She held out her hands. Imploring. 'How could I say no? How could I refuse him anything after what he's been through?'

He had a few pithy answers for that—but found he couldn't voice them, not when she looked so tormented. 'I'm glad you're not sleeping with him,' he said instead.

He took one more step, close enough now to take her hands, hold them. 'And I know that's unworthy, Ella, but I've discovered I'm not good at giving in gracefully.'

'This is not doing us any good, Aaron.' Ella tried to pull her hands free, but Aaron held on. 'Let me go. If you don't, I don't know how I'll bear it.'

He pulled her hands against his chest, held them there. 'Ella, we need to talk.'

'We are talking.'

'Not here, not like this.'

'I can't. I need to get back in there.' She pulled her hands free. '*Please*, Aaron. It's very difficult just now. Please.'

'*Porque estas tardano tanto?*'

Both Aaron and Ella turned towards the doorway, where a frowning Javier was standing.

'I'm coming now,' she said in English, and walked out of the room, pausing just outside the kitchen door to wait for Javier to join her.

'*Andante, te seguire pronto,*' he said.

Ella looked at Aaron quickly, nervously, then as quickly away. 'All right,' she said.

Javier moved further into the kitchen. He looked Aaron over and seemed to find nothing there to worry about if his slight sneer was anything to go by.

'You know Ella well.' Statement, not question.

'Yes. I do.'

'You watch her.'

The comment surprised Aaron; he'd been conscious of *not* looking at her all night. 'Do I?'

'I can understand. She is beautiful.'

Aaron was silent.

Javier smiled, but it wasn't a friendly smile. 'She is beautiful, and she is mine.'

'If she's yours, what's your problem?'

'I just want it to be clear. So, I think you were bringing the cheese? I'm here to help.'

Cheese. Of course. He had offered to go to the kitchen and get the cheese.

When the two men returned to the dining room, Ella smiled blindingly at her fiancé—the mouth-only version, ha!—put her hand over Javier's when he paused by her chair and touched her shoulder, then moved her chair a smidgeon closer to his when he sat beside her.

Ella's hand kept disappearing under the table and Aaron guessed she was giving Javier's thigh an intermittent pat. Probably reassuring him that she was not remotely attracted to the brooding thug at the other end of the table who now, perversely, couldn't seem to keep his eyes off her.

Which word was stronger—disaster or catastrophe?

Because he was designating this dinner party a catastrophic disaster or a disastrous catastrophe—whichever was worse.

CHAPTER FIFTEEN

WHEN ELLA'S CELLPHONE trilled the next morning and Aaron's name flashed, she felt a wash of emotion that was a weird hybrid of joy and anxiety.

'Hello? Ella?'

Ella gasped. *Not* Aaron. 'Kiri! Is everything all right?'

'Where are you, Ella?'

'I'm at Tina's darling, why?'

'We're going to see Mum, and I want to say goodbye. But Dad says you're too busy.'

'Where's Dad?'

'Filming.' Giggle. 'He forgot his phone.'

Her heart swelled with longing. 'When do you leave, Kiri?'

'Soon.'

Which was kid-speak for any time. Tomorrow. Next week. An hour.

Ella bit her lip, thinking. Aaron was on set so the coast was clear. Javier was out, and he didn't have to know. The apartment was within walking distance. Could she do this? See Kiri once more? 'What about if I come over now?' Ella found herself asking.

'Yes!' Kiri said, excited. 'I painted you a picture. Of you and me.'

'Well, I have to see that!' she exclaimed. 'I'll be there soon.'

* * *

It didn't take long for Aaron to realise he'd left his phone at home. He felt guilty that he'd be late to the set, because Brand had to head to York in the afternoon to check out locations for an evening shoot, and the schedule was already tight, but he just had to turn back for it. After Kiri's dengue fever episode Aaron liked to be instantly contactable at all times.

Aaron raced into the apartment. 'Jenny?' He called out, and hurried into the living room. 'I forgot my phone, so—' He broke off, and his heart leapt so savagely he couldn't catch his breath.

Ella. Here.

She was sitting with Jenny and Kiri, one of Kiri's paintings in her hands, but she seemed to be holding her breath as her beautiful violet eyes rose to his and stuck there.

Jenny, looking from one to the other of them, murmured something about Kiri needing something. She took Kiri by the hand, led him from the room.

Ella shrugged awkwardly. 'Sorry,' she said, putting down the painting and getting to her feet. 'But he called and I... He said you were leaving?'

'We are—in a few days. Rebecca overdosed. I've got to make sure she's okay.'

'Oh, Aaron.'

'But there's a bright side. It scared her. She's heading back to Trust.'

'That's good. Great.'

'And I'm going to meet Scott too.'

'Scott?'

'The film producer. He's with her. Thank heavens he seems to be on track. She says it's serious between them, and I need to think about what that means for Kiri.'

He could smell her. His heart was aching. He couldn't seem to stop his hand moving up to rub his chest, not that it ever made a difference to the pain.

'We're going to move to LA once the film is done,' he said. 'To support her. I had an audition there a while back, and I've got a callback, so hopefully...'

'That's great.' Ella smiled—that infuriating smile that didn't reach her eyes. She picked up her bag, preparing to leave. 'I'll be moving, too. Spain.'

'Not LA?'

She shook her head vehemently. 'Not LA. So maybe this time fate will do the right thing and keep us out of each other's way, huh?'

She laughed, but Aaron had never felt less like laughing, and her own dwindled away until she was staring at him, equally silent.

Aaron watched her closely. 'So, we're going to stand here, are we, Ella, and smile and laugh and pretend we don't mean anything to each other? Because I don't think I can do it.'

Her eyes widened. 'Don't,' she said. 'You and Rebecca and Kiri have a long path ahead of you. You need to concentrate on that.'

'And you have to concentrate on martyring yourself, is that it?'

'Stop it, Aaron. Loyalty is not martyrdom. I *owe* Javier this.'

'Two years apart, and then suddenly you get engaged? What do we even know about him?'

'*We* don't need to know anything. Only I do.'

'I told you I'd be waiting for you. And then—'

'Waiting for what? Don't throw Rebecca's new man in my teeth as though that's supposed to make a difference. You've just told me you're following her to America. Where does that leave me? Where?'

He crossed the floor to her. 'I *hoped* in LA. Close to me. Where we could work it out.'

'Oh, spare me. I'd just be carrying two loads of guilt—leaving Javier when he needs me, and being your bit on the side. Well, I'm not doing it.' She paced. One step. Two. Three. Back. 'I knew this would happen. Keep it simple, you said. Casual. And then you proceeded to make it anything but. I tried to make you leave me alone. Sydney, Cambodia, London—every time. Why couldn't you? Why?'

'Because.' *Oh, great answer. Who wouldn't buy that?*

She looked, rightly, incredulous. 'That's an answer?' She turned away, tearing her hands through her hair as though her head was aching.

'All right, I'll tell you why. Because I'm in love with you.'

She spun back to face him. Her mouth formed a silent 'O'. She seemed incapable of speech.

'It's true,' Aaron said, and felt a sense of wonder himself. 'I couldn't leave you alone, because I loved you. I *love* you.'

'I don't want you to.'

'You don't get to dictate to me on this, Ella. If I could have dictated *myself* out of it, I would have. Because, I can assure you, it's not something I wanted either.'

She backed away a step. 'It's just proximity. Because I'm here. And I threw myself at you.'

He laughed harshly. 'Except that I've been lugging it around since Cambodia.' It was true. True! Since *Cambodia*. Why hadn't he realised it before? 'And I'm the one who was doing the throwing,' he continued. 'Always, always me. You were the one running. And I'll tell you this: it's a pain in the butt. *You're* a pain in the butt most of the time, with your bad-girl routine and your secrets. But...' he shook his head '...I love you.'

'Well, stop it. This is a mess. We're a mess. Just as predicted.' Her breath hitched. 'And I—' She broke off, rubbed her hands over her face again. 'This is so frustrating. Why do we do this to each other? Why can't we ever have a normal discussion?'

'I think it's because I love you, Ella.'

'Stop saying that.'

'And I think it's because you don't want to hear it, so you prefer to fight.'

She did that thing where she got herself together, visibly changing from distraught to pale and blank and cool. 'Remember what I said about Disneyland? That it's a blast as long as you remember it isn't real? Let's just say we've had too many turns on the teacups. Your head will stop spinning soon.'

'No, it won't, Ella. My head will still be spinning. My heart will still be aching. And I will still be in love with you.'

She looked at him coldly. 'Then just be happy I'm refusing to help you mess up your life.'

CHAPTER SIXTEEN

ELLA HAD AN uncomfortable night.

Aaron loved her. *Loved* her.

But it didn't change anything. Because with Brand stuck in York and Tina needing a distraction from her constant back pains, it was *Javier* who took her and her sister out for dinner. It was *Javier* stopping outside Ella's bedroom door when they got home, kissing her, urging her with that sharp, impatient edge to his voice, '*Let me in, Ella. It's time, Ella. Why not, Ella?*'

Why not, Ella? Because Aaron loved her. How was she supposed to sleep with anyone else, knowing that?

It was a relief when Javier left the house after breakfast the next morning, so she didn't have to feel the heavy weight of his dark eyes on her, silently accusing her, questioning her, beseeching her.

Tina was restless, and irritable, and uncomfortable. Demanding a cappuccino from a particular café, which Ella took herself off to buy and bring back so Tina didn't have to get out of her nightgown. Ella hoped Brand's train was on time. She had a nervous feeling Tina's persistent backache meant the baby was preparing to introduce itself to its parents, and Tina would make Brand's life hell if he missed even a second of her labour.

The thought made her laugh as she walked into the house, takeaway coffee in hand. It always amused her to think of Brand—for whom the term alpha male could have been coined—as putty in her sister's hands. Because that's what—

The coffee cup slipped through Ella's fingers. 'Tina!' she cried, and ran towards her sister's crumpled form at the foot of the stairs.

Tina groaned.

Ella closed her eyes, silently thanking every deity she could think of. And then she crouched beside her sister. 'How many times do you have to fall down the stairs before you learn that you do *not* hurry when you're about to give birth?' Ella demanded. 'Brand is going to maim everyone in sight if anything happens to you.'

'It was only the last couple of stairs. I was feeling so awful, and I'm having those horrible Braxton-Hicks things, and I thought I'd go back to bed. So shut up, Ella, and just help me up.'

'Let me check you out first,' Ella said, but Tina was already struggling to her feet—only to slump back down again with a sharp cry.

'I can't get up, Ella. I think I sprained my ankle. And I...' She stopped, and her eyes widened as she looked down at herself, at the floor beneath her. 'Ella!'

She sounded scared. And Ella, seeing the puddle pooling around her sister, understood. Tina's waters had broken.

'But Brand's not here,' Tina wailed, and then she gasped and grabbed Ella's hand. A long, keening moan slipped out between her clenched teeth. 'Oh, no, oh, no,' she whimpered, as her hand loosened after a long moment. 'Ella, I can't do this without Brand. I promised him I wouldn't. He's going to kill me.'

Ella gave a shaky laugh. 'Tina, my darling, the only way he's going to kill you is by kissing you to death. Now, there will be ages to go, but if you're okay to stay there for a moment, I'll go and call the hospital and tell them we're coming in. And I'll call Aaron—he's on standby to drive you to the hospital, right?'

'Okay. Good. No!' Tina grabbed Ella's hand again and held on so tightly Ella wondered if her phalanges were about to snapped in two. Instinctively, she timed the hold. Counting down, counting, counting.

Seventy seconds. The contractions were coming close together. *Uh-oh.*

Tina let go, took a shaky breath.

'Right,' Ella said again, super-calm despite a finger of unease trailing a line down her spine. 'I have to let you go, okay? Just for a moment, to call the hospital.'

Tina, white-faced, nodded. 'And Brand. You have to call Brand. Oh, what's the time? He told me this morning he was trying for an earlier train.'

'I'll try. Just wait, okay?'

Ella raced for the phone and let the private hospital where Ella and Brand had chosen to deliver their baby know they were on their way in. She tried to call Brand but got his voicemail. Assuming he was out of range, she opted not to leave a message; if he got a message about Tina going into labour the moment he switched on his phone, he'd likely hijack the train and make the driver go faster!

She came haring back to Tina, who was in the throes of another contraction—*way* too soon. She allowed both her hands to be grabbed, the knuckles crunched, for the duration, but said, 'Try not to hold your breath, Tina. Just breathe, nice and deep and slow.'

Tina gave her a look that promised her a slow death, but she gave it a gasping try. At the end of the contraction Tina looked up at her. 'Did you get Brand?'

'He must be out of range, Tina. But I'm sure he'll be here soon.'

Tina started to cry, and Ella hugged her. 'Shh,' she said, kissing the top of Tina's head. 'Everything's going to be fine. But we need to get you off these hard tiles and clean you up, and I still need to call Aaron— Oh, hang on, someone's at the door.'

Praying it would be someone useful, Ella raced to the door, tugged it open. Aaron—in the process of knocking again—almost fell inside, and slipped on the spilled coffee. 'Whoa,' he said.

'Thank goodness!' Ella said, and dragged him further into the hall.

'Before you say anything, Ella, I'm not stalking you. I promised Brand I'd look in on Tina, so—' He broke off. 'What's happening?'

'It's Tina, she's in full-on labour!' Ella whispered.

At the same time Tina threw out a wobbly, wailing, 'I know, it *suuuucks*,' from the floor at the base of the stairs.

Ella gave Aaron a warning look. 'It does not suck,' she said, all brisk and professional. 'Because the hospital is expecting us and Aaron is going to get the car and Brand is going to arrive, and everything is going to go according to plan.' She smiled brightly at Tina as she hurried back to her—just in time to take her sister's hands as a scream, followed by a string of graphic curses, tore from Tina's throat.

When the contraction finally stopped, Tina was incoherent, so Ella quickly pulled Aaron aside. 'We're not going to make it to the hospital,' she told him.

'What's wrong?' he asked, sharp and serious.

'Her contractions are too close together, they're too intense, and they're lasting too long. I'm thinking precipitous labour.'

'That sounds bad! *Is* that bad?'

'Well, it's fast, and it's going to be very painful.'

'But if we get her into the car straight away?'

Ella was shaking her head before he'd finished. 'No, the way things are heading, we'll be delivering the baby by the side of the road, and that's *not* happening with this baby. I'm calling an ambulance, but childbirth isn't the highest condition on the triage list. So I'm going to get ready here, just in case. And I'm going to need you to help me.'

Aaron looked completely appalled, but he nodded. 'Just tell me what to do.'

'She's twisted her ankle so—'

A scream from Tina interrupted her. Another contraction.

Ella hurried back to her sister, Aaron beside her. Ella gripped her sister's hand, uttering useless, placating nothings, until the contraction passed. Then she brushed Tina's sweat-damp hair off her face. 'Right, darling, we're not taking any chances with an Aussie driving in London. I'm calling an ambulance instead, and then we're going to make you comfortable while we wait for it to get here, okay?'

Tina nodded, white with stress and pain and terror.

'Aaron's going to stay with you while I'm gone—just for a minute, okay?'

'Okay,' Tina said, sounding pitiful.

Ella drew Aaron aside again. 'Just keep her calm. Encourage her to breathe, deep and slow, deep and slow, but get ready for some screaming.'

'I can take it,' he said.

Tina, eyes glazed, wasted no time in grabbing Aaron's hand as he dropped beside her, squeezing tightly through another fierce contraction. Ella waited, roughly timing through a scream, scream, scream, to the whimper and slump. Ninety seconds.

'Hello, Hercules!' Aaron said admiringly. 'I need to get me some of whatever it is you're eating, bruiser.'

As Ella raced for the phone, she heard Tina give a strangled laugh. She gave another silent prayer of thanks, for Aaron's arrival. Aaron would look after her sister in every way possible—her health, her spirits, her dignity. What more could you ask for at a time like this?

Three calls later, the ambulance, Tina's private obstetrician and another fruitless try for Brand, and she raced up the stairs as another agonising contraction ripped through her sister, with Aaron encouraging her to scream her lungs out if that's what she felt like doing. Not exactly keeping her calm, but Ella had the felling Aaron had the right of it. If Tina wanted to scream her way through, let her!

Ella grabbed an armload of sheets, towels and blankets. She added a fresh nightgown. She then picked up several pairs of sterile surgical gloves from her ever-ready supply, a bandage for Tina's ankle, scissors, rubbing alcohol and an assortment of cotton wool and gauze pads. She winced as she heard Tina's wailing cry as another contraction hit her.

She juggled the goods into a semi-manageable pile in her arms and descended the stairs again. Halfway down, when Tina was silent again, she heard Aaron say, 'You know, Tina, women have been giving birth for thousands of years—and *you're* the one who gets to have Ella personally presiding over the action. How cool is that?'

'Very cool,' Tina gasped out, and met Ella's eyes as she arrived at the bottom of the stairs. 'Very, very cool.' She mouthed, 'I love you,' at Ella, and Ella almost cried.

'Love you too,' she mouthed back. And then she took a deep breath and hurried into the library. She shifted the couch so she had room to stand at the end of it, then quickly put down a thick layer of towels, covered them with a sheet, spread more towels where Tina's hips and thighs would go. She propped cushions, stacking more towels close by, and prepared blankets for when they'd be needed. Over the sounds of her sister screaming, she quickly used the rubbing alcohol to clean the surface of Kiri's activity table, then laid out on it everything else she'd brought from upstairs.

By the time she was back at the stairs, Tina was lying on her side, half on Aaron, abusing him for not massaging her in the right spot.

Aaron, accepting the abuse with equanimity, merely looked up at Ella and asked, 'Ready?'

'Ready,' Ella said.

'Tina,' he said, 'I'm going to lift you now, okay?'

Tina, distressed and almost incoherent, shook her head. 'I'm too messy. Look! I can walk. Or hop. Arm. Just your arm.'

'Tina, when did you start being such a girl?' he asked. 'Get over it and put your arms around my neck.' And then he effortlessly gathered Tina close and lifted her. He carried her into the library, oblivious to the amniotic fluid soaking his T-shirt and jeans.

'Can you balance her while I get her changed?' Ella asked.

'Sure, if you promise not to tell Brand I saw her naked,' Aaron said, and that gave Tina a much-needed laugh— quickly choked off as another contraction hit her.

Somehow, Ella and Aaron managed to get her stripped, freshly nightgowned and settled on the couch.

Ella stroked Tina's sodden hair off her face again. 'Shall I tie your hair back?' she asked,

'Yes, it's really annoying me.'

Ella whipped the elastic from her own hair and bundled Tina's heavy mass of ringlets into a ponytail high on her head. 'And now,' she said, 'I'm going to go and wash my hands, while Aaron waits with you.'

Five minutes later she was back. 'Tina, I need to check how dilated you are, okay?'

Tina cast a look in Aaron's direction.

Ella smiled, understanding. 'While I do that, Aaron is going to go and get me an ice pack for your ankle.' She looked quickly at Aaron. 'And I need some string or twine—I think I saw some in the kitchen drawer. And I need bowls and a plastic bag. Oh, and warm water, but you can get that next trip.'

'On it,' he said, and bolted from the room as Tina went mindless with another contraction, her painful, guttural cries making Ella wish she could take the pain for her.

'Ella. Ambulance. Not…going…to get…here,' Tina gasped as the contraction eased.

'I don't think so, darling,' Ella said 'My niece or nephew seems particularly impatient. Like you, always in a damned hurry.'

'Okay, so let's get onto the important question,' Tina panted out. 'Do you…th-think Brand…is going to be upset…when he finds out I'm in love…with Aaron?'

Ella forced a laugh as she snapped on her sterile gloves, marvelling that her sister could crack a joke at such a time—her precious, amazing sister! 'I think Brand is going to be in love with Aaron himself once all this is over,' Ella said, and searched her head for a distraction. 'So, names. I'm thinking Boadicea, Thorberta and Nathene for a girl. Burford, Lindberg and Ogelsby for a boy. Nice, huh?'

But Tina's strained chuckle was cut off by another moaning scream. 'Ella, Ella, I need to push.'

'Just hang on, hang on, darling. Try to breathe through it.'

'Breathe? Don't be so stupid, Ella. I need to push!'

Tina was sprawled, spread-eagled, with one leg off the couch. Ella positioned herself between her sister's thighs as Tina pushed, pushed hard. She lifted the sheet she'd draped over her sister's legs and, as soon as the contraction eased, inserted her fingers to find—

Oh, no. 'Tina, darling, I can feel the baby's head,' she said.

'What? What?' Tina panted.

'The baby's well and truly on the way. I think we can assume all those back pains you had yesterday weren't back pains, they were labour pains, so…'

But Tina was having another contraction, so Ella shut up, caught her sister as she surged up off the couch, held her and let her yell.

'You were saying?' Tina asked weakly, as she sagged back limply. But almost immediately another contraction hit her, and Ella held onto her again and simply breathed, hoping to calm her.

'I'm going to kill Brand. Kill him!' Tina screamed.

Aaron, coming back into the room loaded up with everything Ella had asked for, said, 'Let me do it for you.'

Tina's laugh turned into another screech, and then it was roller-coaster time.

The contractions had Tina in their vicious grip and wouldn't let her go. She was sweating gallons, and Aaron stayed by her side, hanging onto her hand when she needed it, wiping her brow, occasionally leaning over to wipe Ella's too.

Ella had gloved up again, and this time when Tina said she had to push she told Tina to go ahead, because nothing was going to slow this baby down.

All modesty had fled. Tina just wanted the baby out, even if Aaron had to reach in and yank it through the birth canal—which Aaron pronounced himself ready to do, only to be punched and to be told not to be such an idiot.

Ella was staring between her sister's legs. 'The head is crowning,' she said, very calmly. 'Not long now.'

The house phone was ringing. Then Ella's. Then Aaron's. All were ignored.

More contractions. 'Now push, Tina, push now.'

Phones ringing again. One after the other. Once again ignored.

Another contraction. Pushing, pushing, panting, pushing. Tina was shaking. 'Here comes the baby's head,' Ella said. 'Try to stop pushing now, Tina. Stop, the head is here. It's here, Tina.' Ella checked quickly to ensure there was no cord wrapped around the baby's neck. Breathed a sigh of relief. 'Beautiful. Oh, Tina, so beautiful.'

Aaron was holding a weeping Tina's hand, whispering encouragement, kissing her forehead, tears in his eyes, while Ella was supporting the baby's head.

Phones. Ignored.

'One more push and it will all be over,' Ella said, as the baby's head rotated to one side as though it knew what it was doing. And then one shoulder emerged, and the other, and the baby shot into Ella's hands like a bullet. Ella was crying, Tina was crying, Aaron was crying.

'It's a girl,' Ella announced, and, supporting the tiny baby's head and neck carefully, she tilted her to enable any fluids to drain from her nose and mouth.

The baby, eyes wide open like she was completely out-raged, gave a strong, angry cry, and Ella quickly checked that she was pink right down to her extremities, her limbs were strong and flexed and that basically she was alert and perfect and gorgeous. Tina held out her arms, and Ella laid the baby on her mother's chest.

Ella checked the wall clock as she took off her gloves. Forty-five minutes from the time she'd spilled that coffee in the hall to the birth of her niece. Incredible! 'Aaron, just pull Tina's nightgown down a little, off her shoulders. Tina, that will let you be skin to skin with the baby. It will help release oxytocin in your body, which will make the placenta slip out faster.'

Judging by the delirious look on Tina's face, Aaron could have done anything just then and she wouldn't have known it. As Aaron adjusted Tina's nightdress, Ella drew a blanket up over the baby's back, making sure Tina, who was shivering, was covered too.

'What can I do next?' Aaron asked, looking at the blood soaking the towels underneath Tina.

'The blood's nothing to worry about, Aaron.'

He passed a shaking hand over his eyes. 'Thank goodness.'

'There is just the placenta to go, if you can pass me that bowl,' she said.

'And then do we get to cut the cord?' Aaron asked.

We. Such a little word, but it made Ella want to kiss him. 'When it's stopped pulsing, if the ambulance isn't here.'

She ran a tired hand across her forehead. 'But first—the phones, Aaron. I'll bet it was Brand. Can you—?'

But Aaron didn't have to do anything, because Brand erupted into the room, wild-eyed, followed by two paramedics. 'What the hell—?' he started, and then came to a dead stop. His mouth dropped open as he stared at Tina. Then he rushed forward, fell to his knees on the floor beside the couch. 'Tina?' He sounded awed and shaken. 'How did this happen?'

Teary, exhausted, but smiling, Tina reached out a hand, and touched his cheek. Ella and Aaron shared a look as Brand grabbed Tina's hand, pressed a kiss to the palm—just a simple kiss and yet it was so intimate.

One of the paramedics came over to confer with Ella, who quickly provided details of the morning's drama.

And then Ella realised she and Aaron were *de trop*.

The baby was being checked; the placenta would be delivered and bagged; Tina would be taken care of. Brand was cooing at his wife and daughter.

With a smile at Aaron Ella inclined her head towards the door, and the two of them left the library. The stood in the hall, looking at each other. And then Aaron said, 'I never did get the warm water.'

Ella started to laugh.

'And where the hell did I put the ice pack?' he asked.

And then they were both laughing. They laughed, laughed, laughed, as Aaron—covered in dried amniotic fluid—pulled Ella—covered in blood—into his arms. He buried his face in her loose hair. They clung together for a long moment, before drawing apart slowly.

Euphoric, shaken, exhausted, they stared at each other. Ella's heart was aching, her breath jammed in her throat with a lurching, desperate need to touch him. To huddle against him and weep and sigh and just *have*.

Brand broke the spell, exploding out of the library with

the same energy with which he'd entered it. 'I cut the cord,' he announced proudly.

Next moment, he was grabbing Ella, hugging her. Ella could feel him shaking. 'I love you,' he whispered in her ear.

'I love you too, Brand,' Ella whispered back, and kissed his cheek. 'And your beautiful wife, and your adorable baby girl.'

'Audrey Ella McIntyre—that's her name,' he said. And then he freed one arm and reached for Aaron, dragged him in. 'Mate,' he said. Just one word, but it said everything, because in it was joy and love and excitement and gratitude.

'Do we get to smoke a cigar now?' Aaron joked, and was dragged closer still.

'You're an uncle now—no smoking,' Brand said, in a suspiciously husky voice.

Then Tina and the baby were being wheeled out of the library, and Brand, laughing maniacally, was off like an arrow as he followed his wife and daughter out of the house.

Aaron cocked an eyebrow at Ella. 'So, can I clean up that spilled coffee over there and make you a new one?' he asked.

He was very conscious of the butterflies swooping in his gut, now he was alone with her.

Butterflies? Did a grown man even *get* butterflies?

He *never* got butterflies.

Ella looked at him, biting her bottom lip. Was she going to say no?

'It wasn't my coffee. It was Tina's.'

'So I *can't* make you one?'

'Yes, yes, of course you can,' she said, but she looked nervous. 'I'll clean the spill later, though.' She took a deep breath. 'Right now, I really, really do need coffee. Just as soon as I wash myself up.'

Aaron did what he could to clean himself up, then made

his way to the kitchen. He wondered what kind of conversation they could have after delivering a baby together. And after yesterday's conversation, when he'd told her he loved her.

So, Ella, how's it going? Decided you love me yet?

His smile twisted. Maybe not.

Aaron realised he was standing there in a trance, looking at her while he rubbed his hand over his heart. He hated it that he did that when he looked at her, whenever he even *thought* of her. His T-shirts were all going to start showing wear and tear in that one spot.

He busied himself with boiling water, setting out cups, spooning instant coffee. Ella came in and took a seat at the kitchen counter.

Aaron handed her a mug. 'So, Ella, do you need…do you need…anything? From me? Now? Do you need…' *Me? Me, me, me? Do you need me, Ella?* 'Um…anything?'

'No. It's just…'

Just her voice. Her husky Yankee voice was enough to make him melt. 'Just?'

'I can't believe I was jealous—of my own sister, of this baby. Because now…' She stopped, shook her head. 'It's just so perfect. Isn't it? Perfect!'

'Yes it's perfect, so take off the hair shirt for a while, Ella, hmm?' He reached over, touched her hair, just once. 'Funny, isn't it? Brand had every specialist in Europe on speed dial, and all it took was you.'

'I was so scared,' she said, and he heard the steadying breath she dragged in. 'I don't know what I would have done if you weren't here.'

'Nobody would have known you were scared. You're just amazing, Ella. But, hey, if you want to fall apart now it's all over, here I am,' he said. 'You can cry all over me.'

Ella looked at him and smiled—that glorious smile, with her mouth and her eyes and her heart and her soul.

That smile.

It told him that, regardless of what they wanted or didn't want, they were connected.

It was fate.

'Oh, Aaron,' she said.

He thought she would say more, but then, outside the room, there was a quick burst of Spanish.

'I'd better go,' Ella said, and leaving her coffee, untouched, on the counter, she rushed from the kitchen.

Hmm. Fate had a lousy sense of timing, all things considered.

When Aaron and Kiri walked into Tina's hospital room that night, Ella was there, holding the sleeping baby.

Her eyes lit up when she saw him and his heart felt like it was doing a triple back somersault with a full twist. He caught himself doing that hand-rubbing thing over it again and had a bad feeling it wasn't a habit he was going to kick any time soon.

'Hello, Kiri,' she said. 'Aaron.' She looked kind of shy. It was entrancing. 'Recovered from today's high drama, then?'

'Yes,' he said. Not exactly a scintillating conversationalist tonight, but after the intimacy they'd shared at Audrey's birth—even though they'd been so focused on Tina they'd barely spoken to each other through the experience—he found himself tongue-tied. He was just so in love with her. He wondered how he hadn't seen his obsession with her for what it was sooner.

Love. If he'd admitted it to himself in Cambodia, they'd be married and she'd be pregnant by now; although, after today, how he'd actually *live* through Ella in labour he didn't know, and nobody would have the power to keep her from him—not even her.

'Ah, Kiri, my favourite boy,' Tina said. 'Did you come to see me or Audrey?'

'You *and* Audrey,' Kiri said, approaching the bed. His eyes were huge, staring at the baby.

'Smooth talker,' Tina said, laughing. 'Ella, let Kiri see her properly.'

Ella settled herself in the chair next to Tina's bed and beckoned Kiri closer.

When Kiri was beside her he asked, 'Can I touch her?'

'Yes,' Ella said. 'In fact…' She shot Tina a questioning look and waited for Tina to nod. 'You can hold her. But you'll have to sit very still in this chair. Can you do that?'

'Give Tina the picture first, mate,' Aaron told him, and Kiri handed it to his father without taking his eyes off the baby.

Aaron laughed as he presented it to Tina. 'I think we know where his priorities lie, Tina, and they're not with you or me—or even Ella, who used to be his favourite up until two minutes ago.'

Ella settled Audrey on Kiri's lap and positioned his arm so that it was firmly under her head. 'She doesn't have a strong neck yet, so you need to be careful that you hold her head like this. All right?'

Kiri nodded. Audrey didn't fret, just accepted this little boy who was holding her as though it was the biggest adventure of his life. Then Kiri leaned his face down to the baby and softly kissed her forehead.

Ella looked at Aaron. Aaron looked at Ella. Aaron reckoned an outsider could have mistaken them for the parents of both children.

Tina cleared her throat. 'Ella,' Tina said, 'why don't you take those flowers from Aaron?'

'Sure,' Ella said, and there was relief in her voice. 'I'll go and cajole another vase out of the nursing staff.'

Aaron perched on the edge of Tina's bed, watching Kiri with the baby.

'I'm so grateful, Aaron, for what you did today,' Tina said.

'I didn't do anything.'

'You kept me calm, you rubbed my aching back, you let me squeeze your fingers, you took more verbal abuse than any man should have to.' Slight pause. 'And you gave my sister strength, just by being there.'

Aaron shook his head. 'Ella didn't need me, Tina.'

Tina looked at him, like he was a puzzle. 'Men really are stupid, aren't they?' she asked. 'Look, Aaron, now that you've seen my lady bits being stretched to oblivion, I feel I know you well enough to be blunt with you. So I'm just going to come right out and ask you: what are you going to do about Ella?'

Aaron jerked so suddenly his leg slipped off the bed. 'I—I— She—'

'Yes, you're as articulate on the subject as she is. Look— you're divorced. Can you make like you really, really mean that, Aaron? And then get my sister away from that man.'

'I thought you liked him?'

'And that's what's stopping you, is it? The way you think I feel?'

'Ella doesn't feel that way about me.'

She fixed him with an incredulous stare. 'Don't be an imbecile. She won't *admit* to feeling that way about you while you've got a wounded animal to look after. Apologies to Rebecca, but you get the picture.'

'She won't leave Javier.'

Tina gave an exaggerated sigh. 'Stupid and so damned *aggravating*. All right, then, forget Ella. Stay in your rut, juggling all your balls and making sure none of them accidentally hits another while they're in the air, and let Javier have her. Because she will marry him, you know. She has a greater capacity for pity than Mother Teresa ever did. Oh, well, at least they'll have good-looking kids.' She turned to Kiri. 'Kiri, sweetheart, I think Daddy wants a turn. You come and tell me about this lovely painting.'

Aaron took that to mean she couldn't bear to speak to him.

He lifted Audrey out of Kiri's arms and stood there, staring down at the newborn and rocking her in his arms. And wondering...

Ella smiled at him as she came back into the room. 'Got a vase,' she announced, and positioned it, flowers already arranged, on the window ledge.

'I think Audrey's smiling at me,' Aaron said.

'If she is, Brand will beat you to a pulp,' Tina said, sounding like she was relishing the thought.

Ouch. 'All right, maybe she's not smiling,' he said. Her tiny mouth opened and closed a few times. 'Is that what you'd call gurgling, maybe?'

Ella laughed. 'No,' she said.

'Hmm. Man, she smells good,' he said after a moment.

'Yes. Babies always smell delicious.' She made a last adjustment to the flowers and then held out her arms for Audrey. 'Time for her to go back to bed,' she said. Aaron gently laid the baby in her arms so she could place her in her bassinette.

Oh, Lord, he thought as that mesmerising scent of Ella's hit his nostrils. She smelled more delicious than a thousand babies.

'Where's Javier tonight?' Tina asked, all innocence.

'He's out with some of his friends. There's a new medical mission in Ethiopia and...' She shrugged.

Tina raised her eyebrows. The picture of disapproval. 'So he's going back to Africa. Would that be before or after you're married, Ella?'

'I don't know, Tina. I guess he'll tell me when he tells me.'

A snort from the bed. 'Very wifely of you, waiting to be told. But not very Ella.'

'It's not like that.'

Another snort.

Aaron judged it time to step into the breach. 'I have

something to talk to Ella about.' he said to Tina. 'Can we leave Kiri with you for a few minutes?'

Tina gave him a beaming smile. 'Go. Please. Go.'

'I guess we'll go, then,' Ella said dryly.

Ella and Aaron paused outside the room. And then Ella burst out laughing. 'Is it hormones, or did I miss something?'

'You missed something. I don't know how to break this to you, but I don't think she's crazy about your fiancé.'

'Oh, I know that. Subtle, she isn't.'

'What happened?'

'Just a vibe, I think.' She looked hesitant. 'Do you think we can grab that coffee, without launching World War Three across the table?'

'I'm game if you are. I'll try to keep it at skirmish level rather than a heavy mortar attack.'

'Then I'll keep my grenade pins just half-pulled. Cafeteria, then? The coffee will be awful, but—'

'Cafeteria,' he agreed.

Ella wondered what the hell she was doing.

In a cafeteria, with Aaron, on purpose. Aaron, whose last attempt at drinking a cup of coffee with her had ended with her running to Javier. Aaron, whom she'd basically ordered not to love her.

'So what's the vibe?' Aaron asked, sliding a cup of coffee across the table to her.

Her mind went momentarily blank.

'Javier, Tina?' Aaron prompted. 'The vibe?'

'Oh. Well.' She stalled, taking a sip of coffee. 'She says he's too controlling.'

'Is she right?'

'He…' Another sip of coffee.

'What's wrong, Ella?'

'Huh?'

'If you can take two sips of that coffee and not make an

icky face, then you're not tasting it. Which means you're distracted. So, what's wrong?'

What was *wrong* was having this conversation with Aaron. But somehow, bizarrely, it was *right* too.

'Javier is…different,' she started, hesitantly. 'From what I remember, I mean.'

Aaron leaned back in his chair. 'And we're not talking good different.'

It wasn't a question, but Ella answered anyway. 'I think, no. But I don't really know yet. He won't talk about what happened. It makes it…hard.'

She watched as he absorbed that. His fists had clenched. And there was something in his eyes that urged caution.

'Go on,' he said.

She shook her head. 'This is a bad idea, talking to you about this. After…well, after—'

'After I declared my undying love and you threw it back in my face?'

'Yes, definitely a mistake.' She started to get to her feet.

He reached across the table, gripped her wrist. 'Sorry, Ella. If I promise to not let my skyrocketing testosterone get in the way, will you tell me?'

She relaxed into her seat. Nodded. Then she licked her lips, nervous. 'I told you he's the jealous type. Well, he *really* is.'

'You mean, of me?'

'Oh, yes. Even the thought of you helping me today with the baby? Well, let's just say it didn't go down well.'

'But that's insane.'

'And it's not just that. Not just you. He's jealous of everyone. Every man I talk to. Every man who looks at me.'

'Frankly, he's an insecure dirtbag.'

That surprised a laugh out of her. 'That's your testosterone not getting in the way, is it?'

'But he really *is* a dirtbag. Jealous of me? I get it. Because I want you. You know it. I know it. Tina and Brand know it. Tinkerbelle the neighbour's Chihuahua knows it. But, Ella, he does realise you're Hollywood-gorgeous, doesn't he? Every heterosexual man on the planet would take a second look at you. Come on! He's going to be living in hell if he can't cope with that—or he's going to make *you* live in hell because you won't be able to stop it. If he knew you, he'd trust you. So you're basically telling me he doesn't know you.'

Coffee. Sip. Ghastly. Okay, tasting the coffee was a good sign. 'You're so sure you know me that well?'

'I know that much about you. In fact, I'm wishing you were a little *less* faithful the way things are panning out. So, we're back to him being a dirtbag.'

'I haven't exactly been the poster girl for virtue, though, have I?'

'People do all kinds of things to get through tough times. They drink. They play pool with strange men.' Smile. 'They have sex with hunky Australian television stars.' Bigger smile. 'So what? Last time I looked, it wasn't the twelfth century. Nobody expects a twenty-seven-year-old woman to be a virgin, or to enter a convent to wait until her man rises from the dead.' He took her hand. 'Here's the sales pitch for me, just in case you ever end up interested: I wouldn't care if you'd had sex with a thousand men before me, Ella.'

She wanted to both smile and cry, but did neither. 'It wasn't like that, ever. In fact—'

He cut her off with a sharp, 'Hey, stop.'

'Stop?'

'Yes, stop. Don't tell me. And it's not because I'm squeamish either. Or *jealous*. It's just none of my business. As long as it was *before*. Now, after? Well, that's another story.'

'But it wasn't before, was it?' she said. 'It was after. I had the option of waiting for him and I didn't. I was with you.'

'You are *not* serious, Ella! He was missing for two years; maybe dead. And in my book you *were* waiting. You certainly weren't living.' He squeezed her hand. 'You're not really going all hair shirt on me, are you?'

'I don't think you're the right person to be lecturing me on excessive conscience, Mr Married-Not-Married.' Her shoulders slumped. 'I wish he was more like...' She cleared her throat. 'Nothing.'

'It's "not married". *Not* married. Just to be clear, in case that's what's stopping you from leaving him and throwing yourself at me.' Pause. 'And it's not nothing, I think.'

She smiled. 'It's just...well, you're very different from Javier. And I think he *would* care that I'd been with you. And I think...' Pause, swallow. 'I think I have to tell him. Don't you?'

He let go of her hand, sat back abruptly. 'How did we end up here? One minute we're talking about your sister's excellent intuition when it comes to fiancés and the next you're getting ready to throw yourself on your sword and confess something that's *none of his business*. Shall I say that again? *None of his business.*'

'But what if he finds out? *After* we're married?'

'Who's going to tell him?' Then Aaron seemed to catch himself. He shook his head, bemused. 'I can't believe I'm saying this! If it sounds like I'm talking you into marrying him, don't listen to me.'

'It just seems dishonest. Knowing how he feels about other men even looking at me, telling him is the honourable thing to do.' She looked Aaron straight in the eye. 'It's what you would do, isn't it?'

'I'd break up with him. That's what I'd do.'

'Be serious.'

'I am. Serious as a sudden home birth.'

'You told Rebecca about us.'

'Rebecca and I are divorced, remember?'

'And when you found out about Rebecca being unfaithful, you forgave her.'

He sighed. 'It's not the same, Ella. It's not as simple as

admitting you've been unfaithful—although in your case I'll dispute that to my dying day—and getting a blessing in return for being honest.'

'*You'd* forgive me.'

'As far as I'm concerned, there's nothing to forgive. But that's me. If he's the jealous type, and controlling…' He paused, seemed to be weighing his words. 'Who knows how he'll react?'

She looked at her watch. 'Anyway, we'd better get back to Tina. It's late and you need to get Kiri home.'

They left the cafeteria and walked in silence back to Tina's room.

'Thank you for listening,' she said, stopping him just outside. 'You know, don't you, that I've never been able to talk to anyone the way I talk to you? I *don't* talk to anyone like this. Only you. Do you know how much it means to me to have this?'

She reached up, cupped his cheek, and he pressed his hand over hers.

'You don't need to do this, Ella,' he said.

She removed her hand. 'I do,' she insisted. 'And I have to believe he'll forgive me.'

He blew out a breath. 'He will, if he's not a complete idiot. And, for the record, I'd forgive you anything shy of genocide.' He pursed his lips. 'Nah—I'd forgive you that as well.' He frowned down at her. 'And if he *is* a complete idiot, you've got my number. I told you I loved you and I meant it. And I told you I'd wait for you. I will, Ella.'

His hand was over his heart, rubbing. Ella, noticing it, frowned. 'Are you all right?'

'What?' He looked down, stopped the movement straight away. She was surprised to see a slight flush stain his cheekbones. 'Oh, yes,' he said.

Long pause. 'It's hopeless for us, you know that, Aaron.'

'No, I don't,' he answered. 'And I hope you realise I'm

in deep trouble with your sister. She thinks I'm out here convincing you to run away with me.'

'You don't want that, Aaron. Not really. Rebecca needs you. Kiri needs Rebecca. And Javier needs me. That's our lives.'

'You left out who you need, Ella. And who I need. I don't accept that our lives are about what everyone *except* us needs. If you could be a little less martyr-like about it—'

'I am not a martyr.'

'Maybe not all the time, but you're in training. Inconveniently, right after meeting me.' He took her hands in his, forestalling any more protestations. 'Anyway, just don't get married too soon. Make sure you get to know the man a little better first.'

'Ella?'

They broke apart and Ella whirled in the direction of Javier's voice.

Ella hurried towards Javier. 'I'm glad you made it.'

He made no move to touch her. 'Are you?' he asked, keeping his flashing black eyes trained on Aaron, who nodded at him and stayed exactly where he was.

Like he was on sentry duty.

Ella was torn between wanting to thump Aaron and wanting to kiss him. Here he was, protecting her from her fiancé in case Javier didn't like what he'd seen—when, really, what was there to like about it? Seeing your future wife holding another man's hands and gazing at him.

There was going to be an argument. And it wasn't going to be pleasant. But not here.

'Yes, I am,' Ella said, determinedly cheerful. 'Visiting hours are over but they're not too strict. Let's go and see Audrey. She looks just like Tina.' She looked at Aaron. 'Doesn't she?'

'Yes,' Aaron agreed. 'It was good to see you, Ella. I'll just pop in for a moment to say goodbye and collect Kiri, then leave you to it.' With what Ella could only describe as a warning look at Javier, Aaron walked into Tina's room, saying, 'Kiri, time to make tracks.'

Ella started to follow Aaron in but Javier stopped her with a hard grip on her arm. 'First, I think you had better tell me what is going on with you and him,' he said.

'Not in a hospital corridor.' Ella eased her arm free. 'Now, come in and see my sister. See the baby. Then we'll go home. And we'll talk.'

Javier didn't touch her on the way home. Didn't speak to her. Didn't look at her.

Ella dreaded the impending argument. But she longed for it too. Because they had to deal with everything—their pasts, their fears, their insecurities, their hopes—before they took another step towards marriage.

Having Aaron to talk to had made her realise she should never have kept her grief locked in for so long. Being able to talk to someone, confide in someone would have eased two long years of heartache.

So now she was going to talk to *this* man. She was preparing to share her life with him, and she couldn't do that without sharing how the past two years had changed her. And if Javier wouldn't confide in her in return, tell her how he'd stayed sane during two years of captivity...well, she didn't know what she'd do. Because she needed that knowledge. The insight. The trust.

They entered the house, went to Javier's room.

'So talk,' he said, and closed the door.

'I—I guess I should start with—'

'Start with what is going on with Aaron James. Why was he holding your hands?'

Ella stayed calm. 'He was comforting me. That's all.'

'Comforting you *why*?'

Still calm. But she licked her lips. 'Because I had just made a difficult decision.'

'What decision? And why were you with him when you made it? Why not me?'

Okay, not so calm. 'I was with him because the decision concerns you.'

His eyes narrowed. He said nothing. Just waited.

'To explain, I need to go back. To when you were kidnapped, and I tried so hard to find out what happened to you, and nobody could—or would—tell me anything. I wasn't a wife, I wasn't a sister. Nobody knew I was even a girlfriend. I'm not sure anyone would have helped me anyway. Because nobody knew anything. All I could do was wait. And wait. And…wait.'

He hadn't moved a muscle.

'It does something to you, the waiting,' she said, drowning. 'And I know you must know what I mean, because you were waiting too.'

'This is about you, Ella, not me.'

'But you never talk about it. You never—'

'You. Not me,' he rapped out.

She jumped. 'Right. Yes. Well…I—I—'

'Waited for me,' he finished for her, and it was more of a taunt than a statement.

'Yes, I did.'

'And you kept waiting, and waiting, and waiting.'

'Y-yes.'

'Until Aaron James came along.'

She sucked in a breath. Sudden. 'No. At least, yes but… no.'

He looked at her. Utterly, utterly cold. 'Yes but no?'

The snap in his voice had her stomach rioting.

'You slept with Aaron James. Just say it.'

She jumped, jolted. 'I thought you were dead.'

He had started pacing the room. 'You wished I was.'

'No!' she cried. 'Never, ever, ever.' She felt like she was running at a brick wall. It wouldn't yield; only she could.

Or try, at least. 'It's over between me and Aaron. He is no threat to you.'

Javier stopped, looked at her, incredulous. 'No threat to me? No *threat*?'

'I will be living in Barcelona, with you. He will be on the other side of the world.'

He shoved her against the wall. 'He is your sister's friend. He will be there, always.' He punched his fist into the wall beside her head. 'You have been denying me what you gave *him*. You introduced him to me. You made a fool of me.'

Ella stayed ultra-still, scared to move. 'I wanted to tell you. I am telling you. Now.'

'Now!' He looked into her face. He was only just holding his fury in check. 'Two years I survived, to come back and learn that you have slept around.'

'Don't say that,' Ella said.

'How do I know that you weren't sleeping with who knows how many men from the moment I was gone? We'd only known each other a few weeks when you slept with me. A woman like you would sleep with anyone. That's what I think you have spent the last two years doing. Now, just admit it, Ella.'

Ella thought of all the things she had planned to tell him tonight. The confession about Aaron, yes, but also about Sann, about her life in despairing limbo. And this is what it had come down to. 'No,' she said quietly. 'I will not admit to that.'

He raised his hand as if to hit her.

Her eyes blazed. 'If you touch me, I will make you sorry you're not still in Somalia,' she said.

'No, I won't hit you,' he said. 'You're not worth it, Ella.'

It took all of Ella's courage to turn from Javier. To walk slowly out of the room, not run, as his curses continued to rain on her.

She sat in her bedroom, shaking. She could hear drawers and cupboard doors slamming. Curses. Wheels on the floor—his bag. There was a pause outside her door. She imagined him coming in...

She held her breath, realised she was trembling like a leaf.

Then another inarticulate curse. Footsteps going down the stairs.

Out of her life.

Even three floors up she heard the front door slam.

'Some things just change,' she whispered to herself, and remembered Aaron saying exactly that to her.

She'd thought it would be comforting to accept that.

Instead, it made her cry.

CHAPTER SEVENTEEN

ELLA? ELLA PICK up. It's me.

Hellooo? Ella? Why didn't you return my call?

Ella, pick up! Come on, pick up!

Yeah, three messages were probably enough, Aaron decided, catching himself before he could leave a fourth.

He contemplated calling Brand to do some back-door sleuthing—but pictured his lifeless body sporting a variety of blunt and sharp force injuries should Ella get wind of that, and opted to spend the night tossing and turning instead as he wondered how the confession had gone. Whether Javier and Ella were in bed, burying the infidelity hatchet in a lusty bout of lovemaking.

No!

He would *not* imagine that.

He would, instead, plan what he would say, how he would act, tomorrow, when he made a last-ditch effort to woo Ella, regardless of what had happened between her sheets tonight.

And screw the best-buddy routine the two of them had enacted at the hospital; he should have whisked her off into the night instead of letting her saunter off with the darkly brooding doctor.

Anyway, enough dwelling on what he should have done. More important was the future.

So, back to what he was going to say to Ella.

And it was suddenly so clear! Why did it have to be three o'clock in the morning when he realised that keeping things simple was not about compartmentalising things to death? Ella in one corner, Rebecca in another, Kiri in a third. Him in the fourth, sashaying back and forth between them. Tina had put it best—he was juggling balls to make sure they didn't ever connect.

Dumb, dumb, dumb.

Because who wanted to juggle for eternity? It was exhausting. You had to stop some time and hold all the balls together in your hands, if you didn't want your arms to fall off.

Yep, it was crystal clear at three o'clock.

He was getting quite poetic.

And perhaps a little maudlin. Because he couldn't help revisiting every stupid argument he and Ella had ever had, wishing he could go back and fix every single one of them to get the right ending.

How arrogant he'd been, to insist they couldn't have a relationship because of his complicated life. Who *didn't* have a complicated life? Ella's was worthy of its own miniseries! All he'd managed to do was give Ella every argument she'd ever need to keep him at arm's length for the rest of their natural lives.

And she knew how to use them.

One. What was good for Rebecca. Well, if Rebecca knew she was the main obstacle to his relationship with Ella, she'd laugh herself sick.

Two. What was good for Kiri. As if being around Ella could ever be bad for him!

Three. His own initial disapproval of her. Short-lived it may have been, but Ella had turned out to be an expert at hurling that at his head.

He wanted to slap himself in the head when he thought back to how he'd made Ella feel like she wasn't good enough to be near his son. Except that he couldn't hit himself hard enough; he'd need some kind of mediaeval mace with all the spiky protuberances to do his self-disgust justice.

Just how was he going to fix the situation?

He could do better. He *would* do better. He would be sane, articulate, charming, passionate, clever. He would convince her that she belonged with him.

Tomorrow he would prove that love was really simple. Just being in it and grabbing it when it hits you and making your life fit around it, not it fit around your life. *Very* simple.

What time was a decent time to arrive at Brand's, given Tina and Audrey were coming home from the hospital? Just after lunch? That seemed good timing. For a sane, reasonable man who was insanely, unreasonably in love with a woman who held all the cards.

He found that he was rubbing his chest over his heart again.

Man, he hated that.

One look in the mirror the next day had Ella raiding Tina's store of make-up.

She couldn't look like one of the undead for Tina's return from the hospital.

And she would have to handle the news of her break-up with Javier carefully, with no mention of last night's awful showdown, if she didn't want Tina packing the electrical wires and blowtorch in a backpack and going off to hunt Javier down.

But she would, at last, tell her sister everything about the past two years, including what had happened with Sann. She would let her into her pain and grief the way she should have done all along.

And then she would go back to Los Angeles. And she would tell her parents.

And then it would be time for her to move on, and make new memories.

No guilt, no shame.

'She's not here, Aaron.'

Aaron heard the words come out of Brand's mouth but couldn't quite compute.

'Not here?' His eyes widened. 'Then where is she? *How* is she?'

'If it's the break-up with Javier you're talking about, she's fine. I'd go so far as to say she's relieved.'

Aaron felt a wave of intense happiness, until the look on Brand's face registered. 'So when will she be back?' he asked.

And then Brand put his arm around Aaron's shoulder, steered him into the library.

Not promising.

Brand poured Scotch into a glass, held it out for Aaron. 'Her flight home took off about half an hour ago,' he said.

Aaron took the glass, almost mechanically sipped.

Brand walked over to his desk, plucked a small envelope off it, handed it to Aaron.

Aaron.
I think we've all had enough upheavals for a while so let's not add any more drama. Good luck with Rebecca. And hug Kiri for me.
Ella

He looked up and caught Brand's eye.

'That's it?' he demanded.

'That's it.'

He reread the note.

'Yeah, screw that,' he said. 'When do we wrap up filming?'

'Four weeks.'

'Then that's how long she's got before I go after her.'

'Princess Tina will be pleased,' Brand said, and slapped him on the shoulder.

CHAPTER EIGHTEEN

ELLA WASN'T HOME.

Aaron almost laughed as he recalled the way he'd played this scene out in his head. He would knock on the door of her apartment. She would open the door, stare at him, smile that dazzling smile—the one that had her heart and soul in it—and then she would leap into his arms and kiss him. She would tell him she loved him, that she couldn't live without him. That she'd been waiting for him.

Very satisfactory.

Except that she wasn't home.

The only romance he'd had so far had involved charming Ella's young gay doorman into letting him into the building.

Well, he'd told Ella more than once he would wait for her. And here he was, waiting.

It had been four weeks. Enough time for Ella to miss him desperately. Enough time for him to get all the elements in place to counteract Ella's martyrish inclinations: Rebecca was doing brilliantly at Trust; her new love affair was steaming ahead and Aaron liked the guy; custody arrangements had been sorted; and Aaron had even managed to nab that lead role in the LA-based detective series he'd auditioned for.

Fate was lining up for him at last.

Now he just had to pray that Ella wasn't about to head

off to the Congo or float herself down the Amazon, and life would be perfect.

If he could just get her to say three little words.

He didn't really know if she could say those words. Or feel them.

He heard the elevator, and scrambled to his feet. He'd done this four times already—all false alarms—but, hey, he wasn't about to be found by the love of his life sitting on the floor.

Then he saw her. She was wearing the dress he'd bought her in London. That *had* to be a sign.

He felt those blasted butterflies again. Actually, forget butterflies; these were more like bats. Humongous bats.

He knew the moment she saw him. The hitch in her stride. Then the slow, gliding tread towards him.

'Well,' Ella said inadequately, with the smile that didn't reach her eyes.

All Aaron's optimism dropped through his gut to the floor. 'Don't,' he said. 'Don't smile like that. Not like that. Not now.'

'I don't—'

'And don't say you don't know what I mean. Because you do. Aren't you happy to see me, Ella?'

He heard her suck in a breath. And then she said, 'Is everything...? Is everything okay? Rebecca...'

'In rehab. Taking control. Doing great. But even if her life were off the rails, I'd still be here, Ella. What I would have told you, if you hadn't left London when you did, was that I was going to make things work for us come hell or high water. No matter what was happening with anyone else. Rebecca, Kiri, your family, even Javier—I'd still want you with me. All right, to be honest, I still want to damage one of Javier's cheekbones, so having him in our lives might take a little work.'

'Javier just couldn't forgive. Couldn't even accept. And I realised either he'd changed or I never really knew him.

But if you'd seen him, so heroic and caring and brilliant in Somalia, you—'

'Yeah, yeah, don't expect me to get all misty-eyed over his good doctor deeds, Ella. And he had nothing to forgive. I don't want to talk about him. I don't care about him. I only care about you.'

He stepped closer to her. 'I don't know what I'll do if I can't have you. You and I, we're supposed to be together. Can't you feel it? We've learned, both of us, that life isn't about hanging on the sidelines, waiting for things to get better. Or worse. Waiting for fate to come and toss a grenade or a bouquet or a wet fish. I'll catch every grenade, Ella, and I'll still love you. I'll navigate any difficulty to have you.'

She blinked hard. Again. 'Oh.'

'I'll follow you to Sierra Leone or Chad or Somalia or Laos.'

She shook her head. 'It's good old America for a long time to come, so you'll have to think of something else.'

'Hmm. So, what about…?' He held up his hands. They were shaking. 'What about this? Nobody else has ever made me shake just because they were near me, Ella.'

'Are you sure? Are you really sure, Aaron?'

He waved his hands at her. 'Look at them! Like a leaf in a gale.'

'I don't mean— I mean I don't want you to regret me. I don't want to become one more responsibility to bear. And you know, better than most, I've hardly been a saint, so I'd understand—'

'Stop talking like that!' He started undoing his shirt.

'What about Kiri? How will Rebecca take it?'

'Kiri loves you, and as for Rebecca—was I just talking about not caring? But if it will get you over the line, I swear I'll get her blessing in writing. My sisters—they've posted an embarrassing video on YouTube begging you to take me—wait until you see it. And I've already gone and—'

'What are you doing?' she asked, seeming to notice at last that he was removing his shirt. 'I'm not— I don't— I— Oh!'

'Do you like it?'

Ella came forward, put her hands on his chest. He'd had her name tattooed across his chest. Her name. Bold and beautiful.

And something else.

Dropping from the A over his left pectoral muscle was a gold ring that looked like it was entering his skin where his heart was, anchoring her name there. Her fingers traced it. 'Oh, Aaron. Yes, I like it.'

'I'll ink my whole body for you Ella, if you want.'

'No, just this,' she said. 'It looks…permanent.' She put her head on one side, querying him. 'Is it?'

'The things I'll do to get a green card,' Aaron quipped, and then gathered her in, held her against his chest, tilted her face up to his. 'Yes, it's permanent. And so are you. Are you ready, Ella, my darling? You know I want you. You know I'm obsessed, besotted, madly and wildly in love with you. Tell me you feel the same. Tell me you're ready. Come on, Ella. Say it. Say it.'

'I love you. And, yes,' she breathed. And then she smiled and her face lit up like the sun. Bright and gold and glowing. His smile. Just for him. 'I'm ready.'

He closed his eyes. Breathed in. Out. Opened his eyes. 'Then let's get inside. I want to have my way with you— No, wait! I want you to have your way with me. Hang on, I want— Oh, Ella, just open the door.'

* * * * *

MILLS & BOON®
By Request

RELIVE THE ROMANCE WITH THE BEST OF THE BEST

A sneak peek at next month's titles...

In stores from 16th November 2017:

- **His Best Acquisition** – Dani Collins, Rachael Thomas *and* Tara Pammi

- **Her Ex, Her Future?** – Lucy King, Louisa Heaton *and* Louisa George

In stores from 30th November 2017:

- **The Montoros Dynasty** – Janice Maynard, Katherine Garbera *and* Andrea Laurence

- **Baby's on the Way!** – Ellie Darkins, Rebecca Winters *and* Lisa Childs

---

Just can't wait?
Buy our books online before they hit the shops!
www.millsandboon.co.uk

Also available as eBooks.

MILLS & BOON®

Why shop at millsandboon.co.uk?

Each year, thousands of romance readers
find their perfect read at millsandboon.co.uk.
That's because we're passionate about
bringing you the very best romantic fiction.
Here are some of the advantages of
shopping at www.millsandboon.co.uk:

* **Get new books first**—you'll be able to buy
  your favourite books one month before they
  hit the shops

* **Get exclusive discounts**—you'll also be
  able to buy our specially created monthly
  collections, with up to 50% off the RRP

* **Find your favourite authors**—latest news,
  interviews and new releases for all your
  favourite authors and series on our website,
  plus ideas for what to try next

* **Join in**—once you've bought your favourite
  books, don't forget to register with us to rate,
  review and join in the discussions

Visit **www.millsandboon.co.uk**
for all this and more today!